FROM STARDUST TO STARDUST

SAMANTHA GARMAN

Tabula Rasa Publishing

Words call to me, arriving on the wind of sleep.

For now, I sit alone in candlelight.

I hated leaving our bed, leaving you—but my hand aches for a pen. It aches to tell our epic story.

I wish I could paint our legend in the sky, a constellation to be remembered forever—but I am no painter. I am a writer, a weaver of words, and I will inscribe our saga in the book of our lives.

One day, when we are old and gnarled, we will read it—our hearts still young. I will look at you, and see our journey in the smile lines of your eyes. Tears of joy will spill down my cheeks, and you will catch them with your lips like fallen stars.

Let me tell you the tale of our love.

Part I

Chapter 1

Kai

I unscrewed the flask and chugged. Liquor was water in a desert of pain.

"Easy there, son," Keith said, putting a large steadying hand on my shoulder.

I wiped my mouth with my fist. "I'm *not* your son." My tone was harsh, wanting to remind Reece's father that I was the one that lived.

As if the cowboy needed the reminder.

"You've always been a real son of a bitch. You know that, right?"

"I do," I stated. "Are we going to get on with this?"

Keith's clear blue eyes were resolute, clear of bourbon, and drowning in grief. He nodded once.

I had all but grown up on Keith's ranch. When we were kids, Tristan, Reece and I had helped muck out the stables countless times, along with other odd jobs. We had learned to ride, worked with heavy, weathered saddles and camped many nights on the

3

open trail. Memories of sweating horses frothy at the saddle and the smell of hot leather beat at my senses. It was the stench of guilt.

I hoped the bourbon would kick in soon.

A few days ago, Keith had dragged me out of some local dive, where I'd holed up and taken refuge. After sleeping off the worst hangover of my life in the guest room of the ranch house, I'd woken up only to have Reece's mother, Alice, slap me across the face. Her handprint left an angry red stain on my cheek.

"That's for your stupidity," she'd said, her tone mild. "And this," she handed me a cup of coffee, "is for your head."

Alice had balls the size of tractors. She always called us on our shit—and boy, did we get in the shit sometimes.

The sound of the cattle iron raking across hot coals dragged my attention back to the matter at hand. I removed my shirt, took a seat on the stool, and placed Tristan's University of Tennessee cap back on my head. I swiped hair out of my eyes, watching Keith approach with the brand, three inches in length.

Keith's hired hand moved behind me to grip my shoulders, and I shoved my t-shirt into my mouth and waited.

When the iron touched my left pectoral I screamed, the muffled sound of a man drowning in shame. Skin sizzled and burned. My head swam, and my vision blurred. I reared like a bucking stallion into the solid legs of the ranch hand. Just as I thought I couldn't stand the pain any longer, Keith flung the offensive rod away in disgust.

Pulling the shirt out of my mouth, I turned my head and vomited. I wiped my lips with faded green cotton, looked at Keith, and grinned.

My smile was ugly. "I'm glad it was the cheap bourbon."

————

My brand throbbed under its dressing, a reminder that I wasn't hollow. The black tie around my neck felt like a noose. I wanted to strip off my suit and run naked into the woods where I grew up; I was a Southern boy weaned on the land, a mountain child wild and free at heart.

My lungs burned and a small cloud of breath condensed in the winter air. The generic words of the minister were apathetic and uninspiring. Tristan and Reece deserved more than a rudimentary burial. It was a pathetic excuse for a eulogy. I should have been the one to give it, but I had refused.

I wished I was in the mountains and it was summertime.

The woman's hand clutched my arm, and I turned my head, just enough to see the top of her burnished red hair. I couldn't bear to look into her eyes, knowing if I did I would see they were as lost as my own. They were eyes worthy of a love sonnet, Tristan used to say.

The coffins hit the ground with the soft sound of finality.

The minister spoke of a better place. Heaven, he called it. Fuck Heaven. Tristan and Reece were forever wandering in the mountains—there's no place they would rather be.

But this? This was my Hell.

———

I sat alone on a comfortable black leather couch in the library of my parents' house and took a sip of my drink. My older brother attempted to keep me company, offering silent support. It pissed me off, so I yelled at Wyatt to leave me the hell alone.

He listened, but as he left the room I didn't know if I was grateful or not.

The funeral had been over for hours.

I took another long swallow of bourbon, but there wasn't enough liquor to make me forget the tears trailing down Alice's cheeks, Tristan's father looking somber and haunted. And Lucy... God, Lucy...Lucy's shoulders shaking as she buckled under the weight of her own sobs, the drape of red hair unable to hide her pain.

The door opened, and my father stared at me. "Mind if I join you?"

I shrugged.

Accepting it as an invitation, Dad went to the liquor cart and poured himself a double bourbon. *Like father, like son,* I mused. The resemblance stopped there. Wyatt took after Dad with his light hair coloring, golden eyes, and strong work ethic. But I had dark hair, blue-gray eyes, and a dreamless future.

Loosening his tie, Dad sighed and sat across from me.

"How's Lucy?" I asked.

Dad shook his head. "Laying down. She couldn't be out there anymore."

I understood, wishing I was far away. The winter sun had long since set, and a fire blazed in the hearth. The library would've been almost cheerful if I hadn't just buried my two best friends.

One Year later

Chapter 2

Sage

I took a sip of tea and reread the final sentence. I closed the novel, my finger tracing the spine. Late Saturday afternoon sunlight shone through the windows, bathing the book in warm light, like a heavenly beacon.

I sat on an old, cream colored couch, aged and familiar. I had cried many nights on that couch, when the hormones and trials of being a teenager had been too much for me to handle. My mother would put an arm around me, tell me high school girls were bitches, give me a mug of tea, and we'd watch black and white *I Love Lucy* episodes, laughing until we cried.

The Brooklyn apartment in Park Slope had been my home since I was born, and I had no desire to prove anything by moving out. I loved it there.

I heard the key in the lock just before Mom came through the door, setting grocery bags down on the kitchen table. We had the same gray eyes, but she knew more, saw more than me.

"You finished it," Mom said, "didn't you?"

I nodded. "I know I've read it in handwritten pieces, but it doesn't pack the same punch as holding it in my hands and turning the pages." I smiled. "You should be really proud of this one."

"What about the others?" Mom asked with a grin.

I peered at the dark wood shelves lined with Penny Harper's milestone achievements. She was a prolific writer, cranking out stories like a machine. But when she stalled, it took a seasoned mechanic to grease the wheels of her mind. That job fell to me. "Those are good. This—," I held it up, "no words, Mom. It's... indefinable, unlike anything you have ever written."

She smiled, pleased with my testimonial. "Thank you."

"Make you a cup of tea?" I asked, getting up off the couch.

"Sure, thanks." As I moved around the kitchen and steeped a cup of Earl Grey, Mom said, "You don't have any desire to see your words in print, do you?"

"Not this again..."

She took her mug and sat down in the living room. "Make me understand. Please?"

I wondered what I could say that would make sense to her. "I have a job Mom, what more do you want?"

She snorted in obvious mockery. "How can you enjoy going to that office every day? Working for someone else instead of yourself, surrounded by other people and pickled in fluorescent light? It's unnatural."

"What's it like, seeing your name on a book?" I asked instead, not bothering to defend my job.

"It's one of my greatest accomplishments. Are you going to tell me why you don't want to pursue writing?"

"I don't need to see my words in print. I don't need people to read my stories."

"You mean you don't want *me* to read your stories? Are you afraid you're better than I am?"

"No, that's not it," I lied.

I clenched my jaw shut so that hurtful words wouldn't pour out of me. It was one thing to live in another person's shadow; quite another to eclipse it. I was a writer in raw form; words came to me. I didn't need to coax stories; I often dreamed them.

But my mother worried that she'd already committed her best ideas to paper.

If I entered the same pool as Mom, the tidal wave of my success would wash over hers, and I wouldn't—couldn't—do that to her.

Mom laughed and shook her head. "God, I write characters for a living, yet I'm an idiot when it comes to understanding my own daughter. You *are* better than I am, and I couldn't be prouder of that fact. I'm a good writer, Sage, but you—you're a great one."

She said that now, but it would break her, some day in the future. We would stop being mother and daughter and become something else. Something that would make her choke on the bile of jealousy.

Mom got up and went to her bag, pulling out a manuscript and tossing it onto the table almost cavalierly.

I stared at a stack of my neatly typed words. "What did you do?"

"I read it. I want to show it to my agent."

I loved my mother, but sometimes she pushed me into a violent river of anger.

"You won't do anything with it otherwise," Mom said. "You can publish under a pen name. Do whatever you have to do. You're too good *not* to, Sage."

"I don't want to talk about this anymore. Put the manuscript back under the mattress. It's where it belongs. You should never have gone searching for it to begin with."

"And yet, I knew there was something to search for." Mom sighed in defeat. "Sometimes, I wonder if you're really my daughter."

I went to the coffee table, picked up her book, and flipped through the pages. "Sometimes, I wonder that myself."

———

"Is this good?" a male voice asked.

I continued scanning the paperbacks on the New Fiction table in the Union Square Barnes & Noble as I said, "I don't know."

The store was busy; the escalators were jammed with people, a reading was going on upstairs, and the line to check out was long. It was a good day to be in the book business.

"You have to actually look before you answer."

I sighed in frustration. My day had been shit and I wanted to be at home, curled up on the couch, sharing a bottle of wine with my best friend, who was visiting from upstate. But, it was rush hour, the trains were packed, and I didn't have the energy to stand and bump into other people, fighting for a seat. I'd wait half an hour and then begin the long trek.

This guy was adamant about yanking me out of my own little world—and I wasn't having it. In pure irritation, I glanced up and found myself staring into blue eyes as clear as a Caribbean lagoon. Despite my surliness, I felt my anger melt a little. He held the book in question close to his face. I smiled. "Yes, it's good. I've read it. Many times."

He frowned and lowered the novel. "It just came out."

"My mother wrote it," I explained.

The man with golden blond hair and a tall, slender physique gazed at me in surprise. "Really? What are the odds? I'm Connor Lancaster." He held out his hand, and I shook it.

"Sage. Sage Harper."

"And, your mother is Penny Harper, and she wrote a book."

"She wrote a book," I agreed, the day no longer annoying me.

"Do you want to get a cup of coffee?"

I tilted my head to one side. "Will you excuse me a second? I'll be right back." Not waiting for an answer, I went to the counter and a moment later returned with a pen.

I grabbed the book out of his hands, flipped it open to the first blank page, and wrote down my number before handing it back to him. "I can't right now, but I will go out to dinner with you—when you finish the book. Have to have something to talk about."

Connor smiled. "How's tomorrow night?"

"You'll be done with it in a day?"

"What can I say? You've motivated me."

I laughed. "As it turns out, I'm free tomorrow night. Bring note-cards." With a jaunty grin, I hoisted my bag higher on my shoulder and left the bookstore.

———

The door to the apartment burst open and Jules, my best friend since high school, stood in the doorway. Black curls framed large blue eyes in an expressive pixie face that flickered from thought to thought like pictures on an old film reel.

"About time you got here," Jules said as I stepped inside and stripped off my coat.

I headed to the bathroom and turned on the shower faucet. "Sorry, you know I hate riding the train at rush hour."

"I still can't believe you buy real books." Jules lurked in the doorway while I sat on the edge of the tub and ran hot water on my feet.

"E-readers make books look cheap, and they hurt my eyes. Besides, real men read real books, and I met one today at the store."

Jules raised an eyebrow. "Go on..."

I chuckled. "We're having dinner tomorrow night."

"Let me guess: tall, blond, blue eyes."

"Oh damn, I've become predictable."

"Great, I have to go to a boring seminar, and you get to have dinner with a hot guy who can actually read."

I laughed. "You've been talking about this seminar for six months, and you've never once said it would be boring."

Jules taught theater to middle schoolers in upstate New York. The small town didn't have a lot of culture—not like the city, which was culture on steroids. Jules came down every chance she could get and always stayed with us; she even had a key.

"You talk to Penny today?"

Sighing, I collapsed onto the couch and looked at my friend. Picking up a full wine glass, I downed a healthy swallow. "Briefly."

"How's the book tour going?"

"Fast and furious, as always."

"Was your conversation still riddled with things unsaid?"

"Oh, believe me. Things have been said. Nothing '*un*' about it." My tone was drier than the wine in my glass. "She found my manuscript and wants to show it to her agent."

"What? What manuscript? You've been writing again?"

I sighed heavily. "Yeah, but I wasn't going to show it to anyone."

"You want to tell me about it? Or let me read it?"

"No." I closed my eyes, thinking back to the dialogue with my mother a week ago. We'd existed in uncomfortable silence until she'd left for her book tour. It wasn't the first time we'd had that kind of conversation. In fact, they'd been increasing over the last year, but this one felt different—it was painted with new shades of my mother's disappointment.

Jules turned on the TV, but I didn't see the screen. I thought about my mother and the manuscript under the mattress. So much for thinking I had any secrets.

———

Connor took me to a candlelit wine bar on the Upper East Side, where we talked about Mom's new book and other things. Connor asked if I was a writer like my mother. I didn't know what to tell him.

Mom had been telling me I was a writer for as long as I could remember. It was hard to accept my fate when someone else was forcing it down my throat. I wrote my thoughts down in notebooks with no intention of letting anyone read them.

I let Connor hold my hand as we walked the streets of Manhattan. Bars were full of people laughing, the thought of finding a distraction for one night clouding their judgment.

We stopped by a bodega. Connor slipped inside and came back with a bouquet of flowers. The blooms were three days old and had lost their fragrance, but I smiled and thanked him for his thoughtfulness.

"So you'll remember me tomorrow," he said.

I laughed.

"When can I see you again?" Connor asked, as we stopped at the subway station that would take me home. Chivalry was a rarity in New York men; most were in too much of a hurry to open doors or hail us cabs. A lot of New York women didn't want it anyway, or so we pretended. It was odd what we'd grown to accept. Maybe Connor was a change from the norm.

"How about a late Sunday afternoon walk through Central Park?" Jules was leaving early that morning.

He smiled and leaned in to kiss me. It was nice, nothing magical, but nice nonetheless.

I didn't need magic; I lived in reality. And the reality was I didn't want to be a writer, I didn't want to dream.

Chapter 3

Sage

When I'd been dating Connor for six months, I introduced him to my mother. We ordered Chinese takeout and sat at the kitchen table of the Park Slope apartment. Connor was urbane, sophisticated, and polite. He had a job where he wore suits. His haircuts cost two hundred dollars, and his shoes were Italian leather. He was out of place among the eclectic, eccentric furniture and decor. His polish made me uncomfortable, but I couldn't say why.

Watching my mother and boyfriend interact was strange. I was the only commonality. They were two people who peered down the kaleidoscope of life and saw different things, wanted different things.

Which way would I lean? Would I be pulled in one direction over the other? Was there even a chance I could find my own way?

After Connor kissed me goodbye, I closed the door after him and turned to look at Mom, who watched me with steady gray eyes. "Just tell me."

"He's very nice." It was her version of saying nothing.

"Why am I not surprised? Can't you say something substantial?"

"What does Jules think of him?" she asked. Answer a question with a question—it was the way of Harpers.

Jules met Connor a while ago, and now that I recalled their encounter, she hadn't said a lot either. Oh, she listed off his *on paper* qualities like they were something to be admired, but I hadn't been able to tell what Jules thought. And Jules was full of thoughts.

Both of them seemed to be thought-*less* when it came to Connor.

I was missing something, I was sure of it.

"He's very driven—very wrapped up in his work."

"So are you," I pointed out.

"It's different."

"I don't want to debate the difference between an artist and an investment banker."

"He's not who I would've picked for you."

I rolled my eyes. "Who would you have picked for me?"

"I don't know. Someone else. Someone who understands you."

"Connor understands me," I protested.

"He understands who he thinks you are."

"What the hell does that mean?"

"It means that life is long, and you're six months in. Soon he'll know the real you, and he won't get it—he won't get you."

"You're the one that doesn't get it." I kept waiting for the wash of my anger, but it never came. Her words infiltrated the walls of my mind, moved in, put up curtains, and did a little dance that wasn't subtle in its mockery. Like illegal squatters, I couldn't evict them.

———

Connor never asked if my mother liked him. He didn't seem to care if he received her mark of approval or not. I admired him for it; he was secure in who he was and what he wanted. He wasn't a boy. He was a man who knew what he had to offer.

Later that week, I slept at his place, which wasn't unusual. We were spending most of our nights together. I had a few outfits hanging in his closet, and my commute to work was easier from his Midtown apartment. It was convenient.

I woke up, and took a moment to study his sleeping face. He was handsome in that all-American boy-next-door kind of way. He was familiar, comfortable. I wished our relationship didn't feel like sitting in an old lumpy chair that needed to be reupholstered.

That wasn't my thought, I reasoned, but my mother's.

Climbing out of bed, I went into the bathroom to shower. It was large and luxurious, the size of many people's entire apartments. Still, we had never showered together, even though there was plenty of space for two. I'd tried to convince him once, but he'd refused, claiming to like the time to himself. I didn't ask again.

By the time I finished, Connor was awake and drinking coffee at the custom designed kitchen table. I gave him a perfunctory kiss before getting my own cup.

"Do you want to meet for lunch?" I asked, wishing for spontaneity. Maybe I could convince him to have a quick tryst before going back to the banal routines of our day. It was easy to get stuck in a self-made rut.

He shook his head. "I can't. Working through it," he explained. "It will probably be a late night, too."

I nodded, wondering why I wasn't disappointed. Shoving my thoughts aside, I went to the bedroom and got dressed. I grabbed my shoulder bag by the front door and kissed Connor one more time before departing.

I left early, knowing I had some time before work. After getting off the subway, my feet carried me into a bookstore. I wandered the aisles, reaching out to touch the leather bound notebooks. Their beauty taunted me, and my desire for them crescendoed the more I tried to ignore them. I bought one of each.

It was one of those rare, perfect days in New York, sunny but not too hot, and not a cloud in the sky. The idea of being cooped up in a small cubicle in a gigantic building grated on me. Pulling out my cell phone, I called my office, saying I was sick.

Maybe I was sick—I was doing things and having thoughts I'd

never had before: Connor might not be the one for me, and I had a need to hold a pen in my hand and write until the ink ran dry.

This was my mother's fault.

———

I opened the door to the restaurant where I was meeting Connor for dinner. He chose his favorite spot to celebrate our one-year anniversary. It was dimly lit, and complete with white tablecloths and tiny portions. I didn't have the heart to tell him I thought it was pretentious. I would've been happier ordering Thai takeout.

But Connor hated Thai.

I wore my favorite dress, a small black slip that showed my back and hit above the knee. It made me feel elegant and luxurious.

"If you'll follow me, Miss Harper. Mr. Lancaster is already at the table," the maître d' said. I followed him through the restaurant. Connor stood, looking nervous as he leaned over and kissed me.

"Bottle of champagne, please. The best," Connor said after the maître d' pulled out my chair.

"Champagne?"

Connor smiled.

The waiter brought a vintage bottle of Dom Pérignon and opened it, pouring half a flute for each of us before putting it in an ice bucket and leaving us alone.

"A toast," Connor said, raising his flute. I did the same. "To milestones."

"What sort of milestones?"

"To anniversaries, for one. To promotions, for another."

"You got the promotion? I'm so proud of you." My words felt generic, like some actor's line in a mediocre play.

He reached across the table, grabbed my hand, and held it. "Your support means the world to me. I'm so excited about what life will bring."

I had stopped listening. Sometimes Connor would talk and talk, and I had no idea where he was going. But then he pulled out a black velvet jewelry box, and my vision narrowed on it.

His hand tightened on mine. "Sage? Will you marry me?" When he opened it, my breath wedged in my throat. The two-carat solitaire caught the candlelight, reflecting its brilliant perfection. I looked up into Connor's expectant face.

He was everything a woman could hope for. Smart, driven, handsome, and wealthy enough that I'd never have to worry about my future or our life together. But Connor felt like a consolation prize. Had he even spoken of love during his proposal?

I opened my mouth, unsure of what to say, yet what came out made him ecstatic. "Yes, Connor, I'll marry you."

———

"I'm engaged."

My mother took her time to look up from her computer.

"Say something."

"Does he make you happy?"

"Yes," I stated, though I couldn't be sure.

"Does he make you laugh?"

"Sometimes."

Mom sighed, removed her glasses, and pinched the bridge of her nose as if a headache was coming on.

"Say you're happy for me."

"Okay, I'm happy for you."

"Say it like you mean it," I demanded.

"I won't."

"You don't like Connor."

"I like him fine."

"You're a terrible liar."

"I never claimed to be a good one. Why do you care what I think anyway?"

"You're my mother."

"So what? You're going to do what you want, so what does it matter what I think?"

"Why can't you be happy for me? Why can't you be like other mothers and squeal for joy and start talking about wedding plans?"

"Because that's not who I am. It's not who you are, either. Life with Connor will be like forcing your feet into shoes that are too small. Do you think marriage to an investment banker is going to fulfill you? You'll be jogging down the road toward divorce before you know it."

I wished there was some sort of accusation in my mother's voice, but there was only truth—unyielding, remarkable truth. I didn't want to hear it.

I picked up my bag. "Thanks for the congratulations."

I stormed out of the Park Slope apartment where I'd grown up, wondering if I'd grown up at all.

———

"Make a wish," I said. "The clock turned 11:11."

"I don't have time." Connor's eyes remained on the legal pad as he scribbled down notes. It was the weekend. We should've been out celebrating our engagement, but instead we were stuck inside because he had to work.

"You don't have time to make a wish?" I demanded. Connor could be such a bore sometimes—no fun at all. He planned every-thing meticulously. At first I liked that about him. When did it start to annoy me? He had an organized sock drawer. I didn't need a shrink to tell me what that symbolized. Our sex had become stale and rudimentary long ago.

Nothing about him excited me.

"Do you think I'm beautiful?" I wondered why I had asked such a frivolous question. Shouldn't I have asked if he thought I was intelligent or wise? I didn't feel wise. Not lately, maybe never.

Connor glanced up. "Of course, I think you're beautiful. Do you still want me to make a wish?"

I looked at the clock—it was 11:12. "It's too late now."

———

"My Aunt Mimi and Uncle Richard make the guest list…two-hundred and eighty-five. What do you think?" Connor asked.

I took a deep breath. "I think I'm getting overwhelmed."

"I told you we should hire a wedding planner."

We had set the date; it was to be June of the following year on Long Island. Connor worked in finance, and it was important to him to have a large wedding; most of our guests would be business associates.

"I don't want—"

"Don't worry about the money. I told you I could afford to give you the wedding of your dreams."

Connor clearly didn't know that this wasn't how I had envisioned my wedding. A small ceremony in Vermont maybe, or on a remote beach—just family and friends. Not a wedding for show.

Mom had been acting strange, quiet and pensive with somber looks. I assumed it was because she was wrapped up in some new book she was writing, but every time I went to visit, her laptop was closed. Mom was going through something, but she wouldn't share until she was ready. She often withdrew from reality, spending time in make-believe because characters forced her there.

"A wedding planner sounds like a good idea," I conceded.

My mother wasn't convinced Connor was right for me, but she'd still be there to watch me say my vows.

Chapter 4

Sage

"Mom?" I called, letting myself into the Park Slope apartment. I'd moved in with Connor months ago, but I dropped by often. We steered clear of the subject of my fiancé and the wedding. Our relationship was strained, but we'd get past it—we always did. It would just take some time. I set a box of baked goods on the kitchen table and called again, "Mom?"

She made an appearance, coming out of her bedroom, wearing a gray sweater and a turtleneck. It was eighty-five degrees out.

"It's Indian summer. Are you getting a cold or something?" I demanded, heading into the kitchen and filling the teakettle with water.

"Or something," Mom murmured, taking a seat at the table.

I glanced at her as I turned on the burner. "What's wrong?"

"Come here, Sage." My mother's tone was battle weary, exhausted—I didn't like it one bit.

"No."

"Sage," Mom pleaded, "please."

Dropping into another chair, I waited, wondering what she would tell me. She didn't look tired; she looked beaten.

"I have stage four ovarian cancer." Mom had always been blunt; it's what defined her. There was no poetry for real life.

"Say it again."

She did.

"What are your options?"

She stared at me, her eyes stating more than words ever could. We didn't move for a very long time, not even when the teapot began to whistle on the stove, steam angrily escaping from the spout.

As the last of the water evaporated, the kettle sputtered to silence.

———

The idea that my mother was going to die had never entered my mind. But she would die; that was the brutal truth, a fact that could not be changed.

Her gaunt face peered at me from the bed, a pile of blankets smothering her. The thermostat was up to eighty, but still she shivered.

I caught a glimpse of her meager arm, her body wasting away from disease, and I went to put on a long sleeved shirt, not caring that I would sweat. I wouldn't parade my health.

But Mom never became envious or irate about fate's choice—she was accepting. Too accepting of something she couldn't change.

I was angry enough for both of us.

She deteriorated rapidly in the days following our conversation; cancer was a voracious animal with an insatiable appetite for death.

Though she had round-the-clock care, I temporarily stayed at the Park Slope apartment. I never asked Connor how he felt about it—I went ahead and did it. Nor did I wonder how her sickness affected him or our relationship. My conversations with Connor grew shorter, stilted, as if we'd already spent a lifetime together and there was nothing left to say.

"You shouldn't..." Mom's weak protests went silent on her

chapped lips; she didn't have the strength to go on, and she fell asleep as a new dose of morphine journeyed through her veins.

I hoped it gave her comfort—it didn't give me any.

Mom always had the power to make me reevaluate. I fought it most of my life, but now I was aware that soon she wouldn't be there to answer questions with questions. Who would ask me about the things I didn't want to face?

"Shouldn't *what?*" I queried her slumbering form. She slept twenty hours a day now.

She didn't reply.

———

I stared at my hands fisted in my lap, my eyes vacant and unseeing. It had been hours, but I hadn't been able to bring myself to leave the church, and had missed my mother's burial. The pew was solid beneath me, the quiet room an illusionary comfort.

I had told Connor I needed space, and like a fool, he'd left me.

After pushing him away for weeks, was I surprised he hadn't stayed?

Yes—he was my fiancé. He was supposed to console me, but he was uncomfortable with grief. He didn't contend with emotion; he didn't understand the abstract—and didn't want to.

He was a coward.

"Sage?"

I didn't turn at the sound of his voice.

"Are you ready to go home?"

Home. What a funny word. I hadn't slept beside him in weeks—I found I didn't care.

"I'm not coming home," I heard myself say in a cold, clear voice, like a bell ringing from afar.

"*What?* We're getting married—"

"No, we aren't. I'm sorry." But I wasn't sorry.

He reached out to put a hand on my shoulder and then thought better of it. He looked shocked and a little lost.

Not nearly as lost as me.

24

I twisted off the beautiful, two-carat prison and held it out to him. He regarded it a long moment before taking it. His quiet footsteps echoed as he walked away.

If only I felt relief. If only I felt sadness. If only I felt something.

———

"France? You can't move to France!" Jules' eyes widened in shock.

"Like hell I can't." I shoved clothes into my suitcases, not bothering to fold anything; I just wanted to get out of New York as quickly as possible.

"What about Connor?"

"What about him? We broke up."

"When?"

"Right after the funeral."

"Jesus—why?"

I shrugged.

"That's not an answer!"

"What am I supposed to say, Jules?" I demanded. "There's nothing left for me here."

"Come live with me in New Paltz."

"And do what? I don't need a babysitter."

"Don't do this. Don't move across an ocean; this is drastic."

"Yep."

"Who are these people?"

"My mother's oldest friends. I need to start over. I can't do that in New York, and I can't do that with you watching me with those eyes."

"What eyes?"

"You know, those Jules-judgmental eyes. You're worried I've gone off the rails."

"Haven't you? You broke up with your fiancé, and you're leaving the only city you've ever lived in."

"I quit my job, too."

"Obviously."

"Connor was a symptom," I murmured.

"I don't understand."

"When I found out my mother was going to die, I cried in the shower for hours. He pretended he didn't hear me, but I knew he was home."

Jules looked at me, words lost on her tongue.

I closed my eyes. "I just can't do it anymore—I'm tired."

"You'll be so far from—"

"Home? This isn't my home. Not anymore."

Chapter 5

Kai

"What is this?" the blonde asked in stilted English as she stroked a finger across the brand on my chest. It was puckered now, a callused souvenir of all that I'd lost. Sometimes I felt it burning, a phantom pain that was as real as any I'd ever known.

I winced at the memory; two years felt like yesterday. Time hadn't dulled my grief.

"A brand," I evaded, my mind sluggish. I was in Spain, or maybe Portugal. Most of the time I was too drunk to notice where I was, or where I slept—or the women. So many women, and the guilt—it's why I kept moving. Stay still and I'd sink like an old battleship.

"What's it for?" She pouted her sultry lips.

I found her irritating, and there were only two things to do at this point; get up and leave, or bury myself in her and lose my thoughts all together.

"You want to waste our time talking?" I asked, bringing her face close to mine for a kiss.

She purred in the back of her throat. Thankful for the brief respite, I grasped her hips and hauled her on top of me.

My memories disappeared like a wisp of smoke.

———

I left the blonde and headed to London without purpose.

It was raining. There was nothing unusual about the weather—it always rained in England; it didn't matter what time of year it was or what season.

The pub was dark, and I pushed back my University of Tennessee baseball cap in an attempt to see. I perched on a stool and grinned at an attractive woman that approached the wooden, scarred slab of a bar.

"Buy you a drink?" I drawled.

The brunette smiled, dimpling. A flush stole up her cheeks as I perused her with bold eyes. It was almost too easy—they never put up a fight, but I was glad because I didn't want the challenge. I wanted to forget.

"Sure."

"What will it be?"

"Surprise me," she said, her posh London accent rolling over me. She attempted to tease, yet I didn't get the tingling rush of the hunt.

It had been a long time since I'd felt much of anything—I doubted I'd recognize it when I did.

Dipping my hat, I ordered a bourbon and ginger ale and squeezed the lime into the glass. "There ya go. It's a good old fashioned Southern drink."

She raised an eyebrow, took a sip, and then smiled. "This is good!"

I chuckled. "Don't sound so surprised. What's your name?"

"Erin."

I didn't care; I wouldn't remember it in the morning. It was always the same. Every night, wherever I was I'd go to a bar, single out a pretty girl and go home with her, hoping it would be enough to see me through the next day.

Some nights I didn't even bother; it was too much effort, the guilt of being alive too much. Whenever that feeling stewed near the surface, I knew it was time to move on. Sometimes I had a few weeks in a place before that happened; sometimes it wasn't even a day.

I never knew peace.

Two years ago with only Tristan's baseball cap and my grandfather's mandolin, I picked up, headed for Asia, and hadn't talked to my family since. I walked dirt roads, ate unusual foods, and wondered why old men with craggy, brown faces and very few teeth were so happy—content even.

"Want to sit with me a minute?" I asked.

Erin looked over her shoulder at her three friends, who were seated at a battered table.

I leaned my five-ten frame toward her, appearing taller than most men over six feet. It was the confidence, Tristan used to say.

"Just a minute?" I coerced.

"Okay," she said, sliding onto the stool next to me. "What's your name?"

"Kai."

"Where are you from, Kai?"

"Wherever." Out of the corner of my eye, I glimpsed two blurry shadows. I swiveled my head, expecting my best friends to be sitting at the other end of the bar. Instead, I saw two middle-aged men, who looked nothing like Reece and Tristan, and they peered back at me in curiosity. I sighed. "Wanna get out of here?"

"Let me tell my friends—in case you're a crazy person." She smiled.

Already, I felt the drive to move on. After I said goodbye to what's-her-name in the morning, I'd hop a train or a plane bound for somewhere else.

Maybe Amsterdam. Tristan always wanted to visit the Red Light District. I'd go there.

What else did I have to do?

———

"I bet chicks are digging that brand of yours," Tristan says, pointing at my shirt-less chest.

I grin and shrug. We're both dressed in ratty jeans rolled up to the ankles and wading into the silvery water. I can almost feel the sun beating down on me, almost remember the smell of Monteagle in summer.

"What country are you in now?" Reece asks from the bank.

"Not sure."

"Have you become an alcoholic?" Tristan teases.

"I can still remember my name, so what do you think?" I quip.

"I think you're boozing hard," Reece says with concern.

"You always were the mother hen, weren't you?" Tristan laughs, but Reece doesn't smile.

"It's going to catch up to you, you know," Reece says, as if Tristan hadn't spoken.

"Don't listen to him, Kai. If you need to drink to get through this, then do it."

"It's been two years," Reece says, his anger evident. He rarely gets irate, so when he does, it means I have to listen. "You going to drink yourself to death? Is that what you want?"

"I want you guys back."

"We're dead. No amount of drinking will change that fact. Don't these dreams make you crazy?" Reece wonders aloud.

"These dreams feel more real than the life I've been living."

"You call this a life? Traveling from place to place, but not actually doing anything. Losing yourself in the arms of women you can't recall?"

"You guys are so melancholy. You're worse than a Nirvana album. Here." Tristan tosses me a fishing pole. "Morning's coming, and then Kai will have to leave. Might as well get in some good fishing. What do you say?"

I grip the rod, cast it into the lake, and get an immediate bite.

"How the hell do you do that?" Tristan asks.

"I'm a regular Huck Finn."

"Kai was always a better fisherman than you, Tristan. Always has been, always will be. Doesn't matter where we are."

"At least I still have my luck with women."

"Yep, you found El Dorado when you got Lucy," I say.

Tristan grins. "I did, didn't I?"

"We should all be so lucky," I mutter.

"Luck? You call this luck?" Tristan fumes, and looks like he wants to throw a punch. He chucks his pole instead, and it splashes into the water, shattering the dream lake's serenity. "We're the ones that died."

I grimace. "Like I could ever forget."

Reece shakes his head. "You have one life, and you're wasting it."

"I wonder what you'd do in my shoes," I say, my own voice rising. "Would you be any different?" My gaze slides to Tristan. "You would've had Lucy. You would've had a woman to love you back to life. I don't have that. I've got a bottle of bourbon, a mandolin, and the need to keep moving."

Tristan looks at me. "That's what you think. Your life can change in a heartbeat."

"I know that," I state.

"You ready for it?" Reece asks.

"Won't matter if I am or not. What do you guys know that I don't?"

"Not a damn thing," Tristan answers.

Chapter 6

Sage

I pressed my forehead against the cold window of the airplane. Sighing in exhaustion, I pulled the seat belt tight against my stomach and attempted to tune out the flight attendant's chirpy voice filtering through the intercom.

I took out the *Sky Mall* magazine, flipped through it, and marveled at the things people could be coerced into buying. Who wanted a *Lord of the Rings* chess set, a washroom for their cat, or a hideous frog fountain?

People are deranged.

I put the *Sky Mall* catalog back and took out the airline's safety brochure. The first page I turned to had an illustration of an airplane floating in the middle of the ocean with no land in sight, complete with smiling passengers hopping into life rafts as though they had reached their destination.

Right.

I shut the brochure and closed my eyes, anxiety curling in my belly at the thought that I was about to cross the Atlantic Ocean in an aluminum death trap.

"Nervous?"

I looked over to see a middle-aged, matronly woman who reminded me very much of my mother. It suddenly hurt to breathe. I didn't respond.

"Is this your first time going to France?"

"Yes," I replied, answering both questions simultaneously. I turned my head back to the window and gazed out at the runway. In the darkening light, men in orange jumpsuits sprayed down the plane, trying to scrape off ice and snow in preparation for takeoff.

I tugged at the collar on my thick, black sweater as a cold chill trailed down my neck.

"Vacation?" the woman asked, attempting to pull me into a dialogue.

"Sure." I closed my eyes again, hoping my obvious desire to be left alone would stop the woman's attempt at chitchat.

It didn't.

"Are you going to Paris? Paris is so romantic, even in this kind of weather. French winters are more rainy than snowy, but it's still a wonderful city."

I made a vague sound in the back of my throat. The flight attendant finished her safety demonstration, and the pilot announced it would be a few more minutes until takeoff.

The woman droned on, "You look like you're in college. Is this your Christmas break?"

I should have been flattered that I still appeared young after all I had been through. I swore I looked like a haggard old woman at the end of my life, a crone that had seen everything. "I'm not in college."

"Are you from New York? I don't know how people live there. The huge buildings, the subway—the homeless."

What would it take to shut her up? Her enthusiastic prattle grated on my last nerve. I thought about recounting my most horrific subway story that featured a homeless man exposing himself, wondering if it would stun her into silence. All I had hoped for after weeks of emotional upheaval was a long, quiet flight without having to engage with anyone.

"Excuse me," I uttered, unbuckling my seat belt. "I need to use the restroom."

The woman's eyes widened. "But you can't go now, we're about to—"

"When you gotta go, you gotta go."

A perky blonde flight attendant, perhaps the one who had spoken over the intercom, appeared in the aisle almost instantly. She must have had a sensor for recalcitrant passengers. "Excuse me, ma'am, you have to sit down."

"I need to use the bathroom for one second," I whispered, my voice beginning to tremble. Emotion flooded my veins as I tried to remain collected. It was everything I could to do to keep from screaming.

"Ma'am, we will be in the air in a moment. The captain will turn off the seat belt sign when it's safe, and then you'll be able to use the restroom." The attendant's voice was firm, her stance pugnacious.

I could only imagine how I appeared—gray eyes stained red from non-stop crying, my face white with pain and anger. Matted, dull chestnut hair I couldn't be bothered to brush because it didn't matter. Nothing mattered; especially not appearances.

It was all bullshit.

The flight attendant's tone turned combative. "Please sit down."

For one long moment, I didn't move, didn't breathe. With reluctance, I took my seat and buckled myself in. The flight attendant nodded and then continued moving down the aisle, closing compartments in rapid succession.

The woman next to me remained blessedly silent.

As the plane began to pull away from the gate, I shut my eyes. I didn't watch as I flew away from the city I had once called home.

———

"Would you like something to drink?" It was the flight attendant whose pleasant mask was back in place. How did she do it? I wore my emotions like a sweater, and I didn't have any acting talent to conceal my grief.

"Coke, please," the woman next to me answered.

"And for you, ma'am?"

"What scotch do you have?" I inquired. It was an evening flight, but if it had been eight o'clock in the morning, I might have asked for it anyway.

"Canadian Club, Dewar's, and Glenlivet."

"Glenlivet, please," I replied, handing the attendant my credit card and ID.

"Want anything in it?" She glanced at the ID and swiped the credit card before returning them.

"No, thanks." I opened the mini bottle of scotch, pouring it into cup I'd been given. She rolled her cart along, serving other passengers.

"You don't look old enough to drink." There was a dose of protective concern in my companion's voice.

It made me hesitate ever so briefly. "Well, I am. Would you like to see my ID, too?" Inhaling a shaky breath, I took a liberal sip, feeling warmth blast through me. "Consider it a sedative," I said, trying for levity and failing.

"You're afraid to fly, right?"

I didn't answer as I gazed out the window into a bank of clouds. I wanted to forget the horror of the last couple of weeks, the endless days and nights of my mother's pain, and then what came after.

The tears fell unchecked down my face, and I sniffed.

A tissue appeared, and then my compatriot put a hand on mine and squeezed in sympathy. It only made it worse, and I wondered if I would ever be able to take a deep breath without feeling like I was dying.

———

Eight hours later, the plane landed at Charles de Gaulle Airport.

Tired passengers unhooked their seat belts and stood, wanting to stretch their legs and disembark.

I didn't move, waiting until it cleared. When half the plane was empty, the woman next to me rose and pulled a bag from the overhead compartment. With one final look at me, she inclined her head and left.

We had come to an understanding somewhere over the ocean.

I trudged through the airport, looking for baggage claim signs through bleary eyes. I wondered how tourists ever found their way through the labyrinth of French confusion. Even I, who spoke and read French, had trouble.

Only a few pieces of luggage remained when I arrived at the carousel. Celia, with her sleek brown bob and willowy form, waited for me. Had it really been a week since I'd seen my mother's oldest friend at the funeral? Grief moved differently through time—it wasn't linear; it was everywhere, relentless and constant.

"Hello, Sage."

"Hello."

"Want me to wheel those for you?" Celia didn't wait for an answer. Reaching out, she began to drag my suitcases behind her, walking in silence to the car park. Though it was only ten in the morning, it was dark, and drizzling winter storm clouds hovered overhead. I hunched in my coat in a meager attempt to keep the rain off my neck.

"How long is the drive?" I asked, when we were on our way in Celia's tiny car.

"About three hours," Celia replied. "I'm sure you're sick of sitting."

I was sick of many things, but I kept quiet.

"Are you hungry? We could stop for something." She maneuvered through the streets of Paris, channeling the energy of a New York City cabbie. I found it amusing as she cursed in French when a bout of road rage overtook her.

"Sorry, that's the worst of it, I promise. The roads are a little wider once you get out of the city."

"No, I'm not hungry." I watched the countryside speed by.

Everything was dull, and it was hard to imagine what it would look like dressed in the green of spring. I'd lived in gray, long before Mom got sick, trying to convince myself I needed everything on mute. Stupid, stupid, stupid. "Thank you, for letting me come here."

"You're welcome," Celia said. "Sometimes you need to get away."

I glanced at her. It was impossible to miss her tired, red-rimmed eyes. She was grieving too; for an old friend, or a future without my mother—I didn't know which. I turned my head, not wishing to see Celia's pain.

Mine was enough.

We drove in silence; it could've been a three hour or a twenty-minute drive for all I knew. In that moment I existed in a state of in-between, a misty nothingness.

Celia parked the car in a narrow spot across the street from the bed and breakfast. The lobby walls were whitewashed stone. It was quaint and charming in all the ways that weren't annoying. Guiding me past the spacious dining room, comfortable library, and surpris-ingly modern kitchen, Celia chattered about nothing. The property was surrounded by a ten-foot stone wall, and we trudged through the courtyard to a small cottage.

I walked inside and found myself in the living room. There was an unlit fireplace in the corner, and a rustic burnt-orange couch up against a wall. Just past it was a kitchen, small but serviceable.

"The staircase at the back leads upstairs to the bathroom and bedroom. Take your time, get situated. Come over for some food, if you want."

The door clicked shut, and I stood in the center of the room, attempting to adjust to the place I was now supposed to call home.

Thunder rumbled in the distance, and I went to the window and pulled back the curtain to reveal the dark sky. Threatening clouds curled and lightning flashed.

I watched the storm unleash Hell. It was strangely comforting.

There was a knock, and it took me a moment to realize I should answer it. I opened the door to a young man with a charming grin and ruffled sandy blond hair. He looked to be about my age, but his face was unlined, smooth and pristine. No grief had touched him. I felt so much older.

"I'm Luc," he said with a Gallic smile, which was a cross between a smirk and a pout. "Celia and Armand's son. *Maman* sent me to light a fire." He peered at me in curiosity.

I let him inside. Luc squatted by the fireplace, rearranging logs of wood into a pile. Striking a match, he lit the kindling, and soon flames were blazing. It felt homey—almost.

"Thanks," I said.

Luc stood and smiled. "You coming over later?"

"Don't think so." I was tired—I wanted to take a hot bath and then maybe try to sleep.

"You're not hungry?"

I shook my head. My stomach had withered—eating was a nuisance, and I couldn't remember the last time I'd had a solid meal, or wanted one.

"We'll have wine," he said, attempting to entice me. "From the vineyard. You won't be disappointed."

"Maybe," I said, though I had no intention of going. I saw him to the door and closed it after him. Grabbing my suitcases, I went up to the bedroom, and I could feel the warmth of the fire from downstairs.

I set my bags down on the double bed and opened them, staring at my clothes as if I didn't know how they'd gotten there. I shoved them into drawers of the dresser, not caring that everything was jumbled.

Dipping out into the hallway, I walked a few feet to the bathroom. In the linen closet, I found a set of faded blue towels that had seen many washings. Some things managed to last through time, no matter how tattered and faded they became. It made me wonder about people. How many tragedies did it take to tarnish them like old pennies?

I placed the towel that smelled like jasmine and mint on the counter and examined the tub. It was a porcelain claw foot and for some reason it made me weep.

I turned on the faucet and the sound drowned out my sobs. I don't know how long I sat on the edge of the tub, crying for nothing and everything, but eventually the tears subsided. Stripping off all my clothes, I sank into the scalding water, hoping it would do something for the chill that lived in my bones.

Chapter 7

Sage

The next morning, incessant knocking dragged me from a drugged sleep. Rising from the bed, I swiped a hand across my parched lips. I shivered as I pulled on sweats. Winter in the Loire Valley was not temperate.

I trudged down the stairs, noting the embers in the hearth. I had fallen asleep with the warmth of a raging fire, but now I was cold once again. I opened the door to Celia standing on the steps, holding a cup of coffee.

I let her in. Without a word, she handed me the mug and went to stoke the fire. As the flames came back to life, I shuddered with relief.

"You didn't make it over for dinner."

"Jet lag."

"I figured."

I sat on the couch and leaned my head back against the cushion. "What the hell am I doing?" I said, more to myself than to Celia.

Without hesitation, she sat and wrapped her arms around me.

Burying my head in her shoulder, I began to sob. She made soothing noises against my hair, but then I realized it was the sound of Celia's own crying; we grieved together. When the storm of emotion passed, I pulled back and dried my face. She did the same and smiled in self-conscious understanding.

"You don't have to have anything figured out. Right now, all you have to do is come over and let me make you pancakes. Think you can do that?"

———

I sat at the table, drinking another cup of coffee and taking small dainty bites of fluffy pancakes. In my state of grief, everything was muted; colors, tastes, smells. All my senses were drowning in an ocean of anguish.

"So, I run the bed and breakfast," Celia said, taking a seat. "Man the desk, cook, set up tours that sort of thing. Luc and my husband handle the vineyard. When you're feeling situated, would you be interested in helping? Might give you something to do."

"Sure." I stood up. "I need to send an email. May I use your computer?"

Celia led me to the front desk and logged on before stepping away to give me privacy, though I hardly needed it. Opening my inbox, I filtered through the junk mail, disregarding Connor's emails, pleas for me to return to him and my sanity.

I typed a message to Jules that read simply, *Arrived*. I pressed send and logged out. It wouldn't hold her at bay forever, but it would give me a momentary reprieve.

"I was thinking Luc could show you around *Tours?*"

"What can I do?" Luc asked, strolling into the room.

"Show Sage the town."

Luc looked at me. "Sure. That okay with you?"

I nodded. "Let me shower real fast."

We drove twenty minutes to downtown and parked in a narrow alley. I was tired, drugged, and spacey, so I let Luc lead me. He pointed out landmarks, the train station, and the university. We walked along the main drag, and he took me to a cell phone store, where I bought a serviceable phone as opposed to a gadget. I sent a quick text to Jules and then turned it off.

There weren't many people who needed to know my where-abouts. I liked being off the grid. I wanted simple.

"I've never been to New York," Luc said, attempting to engage me in conversation. "What's it like?"

Until a week ago, it hadn't just been a city—it had been my home, and a place to build memories. I'd become an adult there, yet the idea of ever returning burned a hole in the cavern of my belly. "It's a bizarre place."

He laughed. "How so?"

Tilting my head to one side, I thought about it. "I used to love the hustle—I thrived on the energy, but things change. What was it like growing up here, in this idyllic, postcard-perfect place?"

Luc smiled. "Couldn't imagine living anywhere else."

"Have you traveled?"

He nodded. "All over Europe. Australia. I've seen enough to know this will always be home."

It started to rain, and though I had an umbrella that kept me dry, the cobblestone was slick, and I slipped. I sat still, water soaking into my jeans, the cold of winter seeping into my bones.

"What are you doing?" Luc demanded. "Get up."

When I didn't move, he hauled me to my feet. Our umbrellas clashed against one another, dribbling rain on his coat and neck. "I think it's time to go home."

We drove in silence, and my eyes began to close. I was tired, always tired. When we got back to the cottage, I let Luc build a fire as I stripped off my coat and boots. I went upstairs to change into dry clothes, then came back and reclined on the couch, throwing a plaid blanket over my legs.

"Do you want to talk about her?" Luc asked.

"No." I glanced at him. What did he see when he looked at me? I knew the bags under my dull gray eyes threatened to take over my entire visage, and my wan skin was drained of the blush of life. My cheekbones were grotesque arrows pointing to my frozen anguish. I was a canvas of flaws. "You don't have to stay with me."

"I know," he said, "but I thought you could use some comfort."

Comfort. I'd forgotten the meaning of the word. Connor hadn't given me much in the way of it—he hadn't known how. And Jules... well, she had her own idea of what it meant.

My head throbbed, crammed full and threatening to burst open. Maybe I should talk about my mother. Maybe that would make me feel better, though I doubted it.

"I wish I had a drink," I muttered. "These things are easier with a drink."

"There's some wine in the main house."

I shook my head. "Wine will not do for this kind of conversation."

"What then?"

"Scotch. Or tequila. Something that numbs." I placed my head in my hands.

"Just talk, Sage."

I sighed. Defeat was ubiquitous. "I felt relief when she died. She was in so much pain; I just wanted it to end. We put pets to sleep when there's no hope, but we watch our loved ones linger in their misery. Her suffering became my suffering." I lifted my head, heavy with guilt. "I know how I sound."

"You sound human."

"Humans are heartless."

"Or, maybe, they have too much heart. Ever think of that?"

"She was a writer."

"I know. We have her books in the library."

"Ever read them?"

He shook his head. "Not my genre. *Maman* has read them, though."

"What did she think?"

"Good stories. Your mother was very successful."

"Yes, she was." I paused in thought before asking, "What is the one thing that defines you, Luc?"

"I'm not sure I understand."

"You're a winemaker. Is that how you see yourself?"

"Ah. No, I'm other things too."

I sighed. "I'm worried I'm only a writer—we define ourselves because we have to, and I don't want to be defined. If I say 'writer', what does it really mean?" I felt drunk, but I knew it was just exhaustion. I wished I was drunk, so drunk I couldn't form a coherent thought. "It's fitting, you see, that Mom died when she did."

"What do you mean?"

"The last book she wrote was her best work; she strived for it her entire life. It was the pinnacle of her creativity. After that, there's nowhere to go but down," I whispered. "It never would've happened for her again, and she would've spent the rest of her life cursing herself for that one moment of brilliance, because it would've set the bar so high she'd never be able to surpass it."

"You weren't lying, were you? About needing a drink?"

I couldn't swallow my startled laughter.

"Come on. That's enough for one day."

Tugging me off the couch, he led me to the door. We ran to the manor in an attempt to stay dry, entering through the back door. We went into the kitchen, where Celia was placing ingredients on the counter.

"How was your day?" she asked.

"Rainy," I replied.

Luc went to the cabinet and pulled out wine glasses. "Is *Papa* home yet?"

Celia nodded. "Showering, and then he'll be down."

"Good." He opened a bottle of wine and poured me an overly full glass.

I wanted scotch, but wine would have to do. I took a sip and choked in surprise. I wasn't expecting the sharp burst of fruit on my tongue. It made me think of hot summers, picnics under trees and the hum of bees. "Oh."

Luc grinned and shot his mother a glance.

I felt like I was borrowing a memory that didn't belong to me.

"Wow. Just—wow." I used to have a way with words. How ironic that they failed me in that moment.

"Glad you like it," a man said, entering the kitchen. He had the same color eyes as his son, but he was a good five inches shorter. His face was weathered and ruddy, a testament to his time spent outdoors. "Armand," he introduced.

"Sage." I took another sip. "I've never tasted anything like this."

Armand grinned like he wasn't surprised, and then went to kiss his wife before pouring himself a glass. "It's good to be home. I'm tired."

"How's *Grand-mère?*" Luc asked.

"Stubborn, but settled in her new place. I wish she would move back."

"Never going to happen," Celia said. "Your mother is far too independent." She unwrapped a wedge of Camembert and placed it on a platter. Washing a cluster of purple grapes, she put them next to the cheese and then brought it to the table. Luc and Armand sat down while Celia stayed at the counter and began dicing an onion.

"Would you like some help?" I offered.

Celia smiled. "Sure." She pulled out a large pot and filled it three quarters of the way with water. After dumping in a palm full of salt, she covered it with the lid, turned the burner on high, and transferred chopped pancetta into a sizzling frying pan. She threw the onions into another skillet and slowly caramelized them, and then combined them with the crispy pancetta and stirred.

"What are we making exactly?" I asked as I watched her break four eggs into a bowl of cream and whisk them.

"Spaghetti Carbonara."

I paused. "Isn't that Italian?"

"It is," Celia agreed. "Oh, were you hoping for a French meal?"

I wasn't hoping for anything at all. And that was the truth of it. "No, it's fine. It smells great."

The timer buzzed, and she tested a noodle and then gave me one. "Al dente—perfect."

She divided the pasta onto four plates, added the cream of eggs, shaved Parmesan, and then cracked fresh black pepper.

"Where did you learn to make this?" I wondered aloud when we were all seated around the table.

"My mother," Armand interjected with a smile.

"Go ahead, everyone," Celia said.

I hesitated and then took a bite. The creamy, bacon and egg dish glided over my tongue, and I felt true hunger for the first time since Mom died.

As I listened to the laughter and conversation around me, I realized that life would continue whether I wanted it to or not.

I pushed back from the table. "Excuse me—I'm not feeling well." I ran from the room and rushed out the back door into the cold, rainy night, unraveling like a loose spool of yarn.

Ducking into the cottage, I stood in front of the fire as I dug into my purse for pills to help me sleep.

———

It was still dark when I opened my eyes. The rain had stopped sometime in the night, and despite the medication, shadowy thoughts had moved throughout my subconscious and infiltrated my dreams. I was tired and shaky; it was a usual post-burial morning.

Trembling, I got up from the couch where I'd fallen asleep and wrapped the blanket around my thin, scarecrow-like frame. Since my mother's diagnosis I'd lost a good fifteen pounds, and I hadn't had it to lose in the first place. Every time I looked in the mirror, I bit my lip to keep from gasping—what I saw scared the hell out of me.

There was a soft knock on the door. I knew it was Celia; she seemed to be making it her mission to care for me, but I busy being at war with myself.

Celia came into the cottage and handed me a loaf tin covered in aluminum foil. "Homemade bread."

I sniffed, and my stomach rumbled. I was in momentary shock that my mouth filled with saliva, my taste buds enticed by aroma alone. It made me yearn for all the comfort that food gave. I could use the calories. Maybe I'd find a way back to life through my stomach, since it didn't yield to heartache—not anymore—it was an angry baby bird wanting to be fed.

"I'm sorry…about last night," I apologized, taking a seat on the couch and tearing off a corner of the warm, yeasty loaf. I stuck it in my mouth and chewed.

If only my misery wasn't worn on my face. I wished I could bury it deep inside.

"Don't apologize," Celia said. "You'll come out of your shell when you're ready. In the meantime, I plan on feeding you and checking in on you, whether you want it or not. I'm here as a friend."

Celia didn't ask anything of me, and I exhaled a sigh of relief I hadn't known I held. "Thank you."

"Get dressed. Armand wants to show you the vineyard."

———

Thirty minutes later, I walked with Armand through acres of rolling hillside, covered in well-groomed rows of vines. The day was overcast, but it didn't look like it would rain. Everything was quiet, sleeping, awaiting the season of the sun. I wondered what the vineyard would be like in spring, ripe and in bloom.

What was it like to create something so beautiful? Armand was a maker of wine. My mother had been a maker of books. The need to create was inherently human, and strong within me. How I managed to settle for such an empty career was beyond me.

"How long has your family owned the vineyard?"

"Generations," Armand explained. "When my mother and father married, she moved here. After my father died, she returned to Italy."

"Italian to the core?"

"Without a doubt."

"What was my mother like? Back then?" I asked before I could take it back.

47

Armand looked at me. "Headstrong. Always knew what she wanted and where she was going. She's the reason I met Celia, did you know?"

I shook my head.

"It was their junior year of college. Summer. They were traveling all around Europe, and Celia wanted to go to Belgium, but Penny insisted on France. They got here, and the rest, they say, is history."

"Love at first sight?" I smiled.

"God no!" Armand laughed. "Celia detested me, but I knew what I wanted, and I pursued her—relentlessly."

"She finally gave in?"

Armand's blue eyes twinkled. "Celia saw me flirting with Penny one night, and it made her realize she wasn't indifferent after all."

I laughed. It sounded exactly like something Mom would have done, and in that moment I almost felt like she walked alongside us. Those we loved would be immortalized in our memories, until we too, were gone.

Chapter 8

Kai

I wondered where I was as the countryside whizzed by the train window. I unscrewed my flask, took a long sip, and tapped my foot to the beat I heard in my head.

The prostitute in the Red Light District had been nice. I'd paid her, only to realize I didn't want to sleep with her. Instead, we'd reclined in her bed, not saying a word. After my hour was up, I went down to a café, bought a blunt and smoked it.

Tristan would've told me I was crazy. Dream Tristan *did* tell me I was crazy. Dream Reece, softer, gentler, didn't judge me aloud.

I'd seen and done so many things after they died. I started with the Great Wall of China and then journeyed to Hong Kong. The pollution in the air made the sun appear blood red, and had made me feel like I'd landed on an alien planet. The Great Pyramids of Egypt were hot and dusty, and I'd almost gotten spit on by a camel. Camels were mean bastards. I drank beer in mass quantities to combat the dourness of Prague. One night I'd even stripped and went for a midnight swim in the Vltava River. I'd gone sport fishing off the coast of Croatia, fallen off the boat and almost drowned. Almost.

None of it had made an impact.

I hadn't made my way to South America yet. Maybe I'd go see the Mayan ruins and offer a blood sacrifice—to what end, I didn't know.

The train stopped, and I got off. It was raining. God, did every place I traveled have to rain so much? I should visit an island with nothing but sun and white sand, and an endless supply of rum.

My baseball cap was sodden, and my clothes stuck to me; it's what I got for not carrying an umbrella. Maybe I'd get pneumonia and die. A guy had to have dreams, didn't he?

I walked around the old cobblestone square, dried off in a pub, and then soaked my blood in alcohol. I supposed I should find a place to sleep, if I didn't want it to be a park bench.

Everything was written in French. I was in France, or so I believed—for the time being anyway.

———

I picked up the mandolin and stroked its body like I would a woman. My fingers glided over the strings; it was familiar, comforting. It hadn't always been the case. My grandfather had been relentless when teaching me to play. I remembered the hours of practice, the anger when I couldn't move my hands the way they needed to, until one day everything connected.

My grandfather had been able to pick up any stringed instrument and master it, given enough time—it had been one of his many talents. I hoped I had inherited some of them, but I doubted it. The mandolin was the only thing I stuck with; nothing else held my interest. I was decent at many things, but proficient at few.

I was too smart for my own damn good—my parents had said it often enough. I'm not sure I believed them, since I felt steeped in mediocrity.

The moon shone through the window of the tiny studio I'd found in place of a park bench. No lights were on—not because I didn't have electricity, but because I found the dark comforting, like this little town somewhere in the Loire Valley.

The notes came out mournful, poetic—a eulogy for the friends I'd lost. I'd played them many eulogies.

I uncorked the bourbon and drank straight from the bottle. When I was drunk enough, I asked, "Tristan? Reece? It's your turn. Take a swig."

But there was no answer from the ghosts that followed me; silence was the only reply—the bottle of bourbon and an old, scarred mandolin my only companions.

———

"How did you get a girl like Lucy?" I demand, casting into the lake. Tristan catches his first fish while I reel in my fifth.

"Son of a bitch," Tristan curses. "How am I supposed to win this competition?"

"My dream, my rules, remember?"

"Right."

"Tell me about Lucy."

"Fuck if I know. She's the perfect woman. Not only did she knock beer bottles out of my hands, but she knocked sense into me on more than one occasion." Tristan grins.

"You'll find it, you know."

"Will I? I'm not sure."

"You won't wander forever. You'll find a reason to stay somewhere."

"You were closer to her than you were to us, weren't you?"

"It's different," Tristan explains. "When you meet the woman you're supposed to spend your life with, you'll understand."

I shake my head. "You grew up, didn't you? I didn't even notice."

"Happens to the best of us. It's going to happen to you."

I laugh. "Not if I have anything to say about it."

Chapter 9

Sage

One night, when I'd been in France for a little over a week, Luc came to my door and demanded I get dressed. "Where are you taking me?" I asked, even as I grabbed my coat.

Luc grinned. "A dive."

Dive was a generous description of the bar. It was a seedy hole-in-the-wall with an old jukebox and a few scarred, un-level pool tables. It was stuck in the '80's, but as I was learning, *Tours* was a mishmash of culture from the past. That was part of its charm.

"What are you having?" Luc asked.

"How about a beer and a game of pool?"

"Rack 'em."

I kicked his ass in pool, or he let me, and I introduced him to "Eye of the Tiger". I didn't think I would laugh again, not so soon after losing my mother. But laugh I did when a ridiculously drunk Luc played the song over and over on the wailing jukebox, singing along off key and annoying the other patrons.

Taking pity on them, I selected a Tom Petty song, hoping Luc didn't know the lyrics. I set down the pool cue and headed to the middle of the dance floor. I wasn't a dancer by any means, but tonight, I wanted to move. It was probably the five beers I'd consumed, but still, I felt *good*.

I was paying homage to Mom. She had loved classic rock, and had hundreds of compilation playlists on iTunes. Some days it had been nothing but Zeppelin, on others it was Simon and Garfunkel. I could always tell her mood by what music was playing.

Neon lights from beer signs painted my skin in a medley of fluorescent glow. I drank and danced until the world spun, and then I let Luc cart me out into the crisp night.

"You're beautiful—did you know that?" he said, his hands steadying me while I stumbled like a clown on stilts.

"It's not polite to lie to a woman," I teased.

"I'm not lying."

"Thanks for being here. You're a good sport to put up with me."

He gazed down into my eyes. "Sage, I—"

I stopped him from speaking by placing a hand on his chest. "I just need a friend, okay? I'm not ready for anything else."

Luc squeezed my shoulder gently before turning me in the direction of home. "Okay."

———

The next morning, I threw on a pair of old sweats and a sweatshirt, and went in search of coffee and Luc in the main house.

Luc seemed to be a relationship kind of man. Until recently, I had been a relationship kind of woman, but I had been down that road with Connor, becoming entrapped in a loveless relationship. I didn't want to make the same mistake again, and I needed time.

"Where's Luc?" I asked Celia, who was at the desk sending an email. After typing something, she looked up.

"He went to visit his grandmother early this morning."

I frowned.

"Do you want to tell me what happened? Don't think of me as Luc's mother."

I smiled. "But you are, and I'd never say anything that would make you—"

"Look at him differently? You think I'm blinded by the love I have for my son?"

"Not if you're anything like my mother."

My mother's revelations about me had often left me breathless, my feelings casualties in her war with truth.

Celia came out from behind the desk and led me into the kitchen. She poured me a cup of coffee and made me sit down. I began to talk. She had that look about her; her face was the blank page of a journal I wanted to fill.

I'd ruin Luc. My pain nearly smothered me—I wouldn't willingly invite him in to share the weight of it. He deserved a woman who had things figured out, and that wasn't me.

I never expected my mother's death to be my release from a life on autopilot. Why did it take her dying for me to realize what life *wasn't* about? Floating through experiences that failed to shape me was something I never wanted again. Would I ever want to be a writer? Did I really have a choice? The battlefield of life was strewn with shattered dreams. In my own war, would I triumph or fall?

———

A week later, Luc still hadn't returned. Though he had been graceful about being denied, it appeared I had wounded him deeper than I knew.

I started helping Celia work the front desk, putting my fluent French to good use, answering emails and phone calls, and giving directions to guests. Nights were spent holed up in my cottage with a bottle of wine.

Some days, my sadness was an annoying buzz in the back of my head and I managed to compartmentalize it. On other days, it was an unchained beast snapping its ugly jaws around my heart. Tears caught me at strange moments, and at times I couldn't contain them. I lost hours trapped in sorrow with no hope for escape.

One afternoon, Celia said to me, "It's time for you to go."

Startled, I looked at her. "What?"

She grinned. "Go enjoy *Tours*. You've hardly seen the city. Don't you want to explore?"

"No, I don't. I'm not ready."

"Yes, you are. Go. I'm serious."

I'd been hiding, but it seemed I wouldn't be allowed to anymore. With no choice, I did as commanded.

———

I wandered through the heart of downtown. Compact cars littered the main drag of the idyllic city. The streets were nearly empty of pedestrians due to the impending rain, and it felt like I had the town to myself. I passed *pâtisseries*, and the tantalizing aromas of freshly baked goods pierced the damp winter air. I ambled along curvy, cobblestone streets, and found myself in front of an inconspicuous bookstore. Before I could stop myself, I went inside, and a tiny brass bell announced my presence to the shopkeeper. The aisles were narrow, and the store seemed to be bursting with books from floor to ceiling, yet there was a certain efficiency about the quaint shop. I spotted a section containing pens and notebooks, picked up a dark brown leather journal and held it in my hands. I brought it to my nose and inhaled the scent of *Tours*.

It was afternoon when I entered a café and sat at a small table, ordered a glass of wine, and pulled out my new journal and pen. I wanted to put down words, but nothing came. Had they finally abandoned me, or had I forced them away?

Staring out the window, I watched evening come. A waiter moved around the restaurant lighting candles on the tables. Customers, eager to be out of the cold, filled the doorway and began to take seats. I studied the menu and thought about ordering three entrees when I heard a voice in English say, "You're what Michelangelo hoped to create."

I looked up, a wry grin on my lips. I saw a stubble-spattered jaw, dark hair sticking out from under a University of Tennessee cap, and wounded blue-gray eyes. Sitting back in my chair, I projected lazy insolence, hoping it would scare him off. "Does that line *really* work?"

"You tell me." He plopped down in the vacant chair across from me without invitation.

I frowned. "I'm waiting for someone."

"No, you're not."

"I'm not?" I tapped the pen rapidly on the table.

"Nope, because I'm here." He pushed back his hat and smiled.

I sighed. "Why did you speak English?"

He plucked the pen from my fingertips and moved it through his knuckles like I'd seen musicians do with a guitar pick. I hated that I was mesmerized by the action. Shaking it off, I realized he was just another careless, handsome man who knew that he was universally adored by women.

But not me.

"Look around you," he said. "You dress differently than the rest of this lot. I took a gamble and spoke in English. And I was right, wasn't I?"

"So what? You spotted an American in France. Big deal."

His joking demeanor disappeared as he said, "You're sad."

His accurate assessment took me completely off guard. "No, I'm not."

"Yeah, you are."

"What makes you say that?" I crossed my arms over my chest in a subconsciously defensive gesture.

He peered at me before answering. "I've traveled the world. I know sadness when I see it."

All my effort at hiding my anguish in plain sight had been for nothing. Unbidden tears began to flood my eyes. I was starting to cry in front of a complete stranger.

His hand reached for mine in a gesture of comfort that Connor never could have mustered. Despite not knowing my new companion, I didn't pull away. I was lost in an ocean of feeling, but I managed to pull myself together. I finally withdrew my hand, grabbed my pen and journal, and shoved them into my bag.

"Wait," he said, realizing I was about to depart.

With great reluctance, I glanced at him.

"I'm supposed to play here tonight. Will you stay for just one song?"

Without waiting for my response, he rose and went to a stool at the back of the restaurant. He picked up a mandolin resting in the corner, and I watched his fingers press against the strings as he struck a chord. He began to play a song that made me feel more alone than I thought possible. It evoked a memory so powerful, that it made me rise from my seat and rush out into the night.

I was light-headed, shaky, and terrified.

The song was a trigger, a broken melody of a summer long ago in Prospect Park when Béla Fleck had given a concert. My mother and I had sat on the grass, a picnic basket between us, drinking wine out of plastic red cups. When I heard that song for the first time, it stuck in my mind, lingering like a hazy dream. For months after, I repeatedly listened to the song on my iPod while words spilled from my pen, forming into a manuscript.

It was the manuscript my mother had found.

Needing to escape my feelings, I walked through the rain, unmindful of where my legs carried me. I wanted to find a liquor store so I could drown my emotions. I entertained the idea of getting a bottle of my mother's favorite scotch, but this was no celebration. It was a time of forgetting, so a bottle of anything would do.

Back in the cottage I lit a fire, but left the rest of the lights off. I opened a bottle of cheap bourbon and didn't bother with a glass. I found my iPod, plugged in headphones and listened to the song on repeat. Grief was a strange entity, and like the moon it waxed and waned. I'd never felt more alone than in that moment, and I drank until I drifted off to sleep.

Chapter 10

Sage

I sat in the corner of the café, close enough to see the dark, careless stubble on his jaw. Sounds of the mandolin soothed me, like a salve reaching all the way to my bones.

He was talented.

When he played, he brought tears to my eyes, and I wondered what sort of magic he held, a true master of emotion. The song ended, and the sudden silence left me feeling empty.

I glanced up to find a blue-gray stare raking over me. The player inclined his head in acknowledgement. I did the same—and then, without hesitation, he began to play the song that had caused me to leave the previous night.

But this time, instead of running, I leaned towards him, wanting to soak up the notes. When he finished, he set his mandolin down in its case and walked towards me, dressed in faded, ratty jeans and a black t-shirt. I could see the tempest in his eyes. He sat on the stool next to me, a careless smile spreading across his face. I raised an eyebrow, his grin widening.

He flagged down the bartender and ordered two shots of bourbon.

"Cheers," he said, holding up his glass. We clinked and downed them; I didn't even flinch.

"You're quite impressive," he murmured.

"Glad you think so." I ordered another round.

"So, stranger. You have a name?"

I bit my lip. To tell him would make me real. "Does it matter?"

"I can call you Lady Magnolia."

I stared at him for a moment. Suddenly, my name didn't feel like it belonged to me anymore, so I told him. "Sage."

He held out his hand. "Kai."

I took it, noting both the warmth and calluses. When I tried to pull away, he tightened his grip. "May I have my hand back?"

"In a minute."

His thumb weaved a sensuous stroke across my knuckles. He stared at me, but I didn't feel like squirming. The power of his eyes entranced me, and my heart pounded as he continued to hold my hand. He was a stranger in so many ways, and yet I saw something in him that I had in myself.

His sorrow was a mirror into my heart.

I knew instinctively that Kai was reckless, and I wanted to throw myself into the eye of his storm. I wanted experiences that would forge and inspire me, and I knew that could only happen with him, but I couldn't say why.

"Sage..."

"Yes?"

"May I kiss you?"

I couldn't speak past the emotion in my throat, so I nodded.

As Kai's face came close to mine, I thought he was going to kiss my lips—instead he pressed his warm mouth to the flickering pulse at my throat.

"Will you come home with me?" he asked.

"That depends."

"On what?"

Without taking my eyes off him, I plucked the glass from his hand and drank the bourbon in a few long swallows. Setting it down on the bar, I reached for my purse to pay for our drinks, but he stopped me by pulling out his wallet and throwing down some Euros. "How many women have said *no* to you?"

"None."

"You're honest."

"I don't think you're the kind of woman that can stomach lies." He stared at me. Relentless. Feral. "You're coming home with me, aren't you?"

"Yes." There was intensity in him, and I liked it.

His hand squeezed my arm. "Stay here—don't move."

I pulled on my coat while he went to get his mandolin. We left the bar and walked into the night. Without asking, he laced his fingers in mine.

"Have you ever been so cold, so weary, you wonder how you'll ever make it back?" His voice was soft, and I wasn't sure I heard him.

"What are you trying to come back from?"

"What are *you?*"

I didn't answer.

We stopped when we came to the *Tours* Cathedral. The old Gothic building was austere in the moonlight, and seemed to block out the entire sky.

"Have you been inside?" I asked.

He shook his head. "Look." He pointed in the direction of an ancient, knobby tree as we strolled towards it. Moonlight bathed naked, twisted branches in a silver glow.

"It belongs in the realm of fairies," I said. "Imagine all the stories that tree could tell if only it could talk."

I leaned over and pressed my lips to bark. I closed my eyes and leaned my forehead against it, wanting to pay respect to something that had withstood the test of time, far longer than any single human life. I glanced at Kai, and he watched me with a steady gaze. I gave no apology for my moment with the tree. Grabbing a low-hanging limb, I hoisted myself up into the canopy. "You coming?" I called down.

A moment later, he sat on a branch across from me.

"Do you have a place where time stops for you?" I wondered.

"I used to, but it's gone now." He turned his eyes to me; they were haunted with despair.

I hadn't expected the weight of his emotion, and so I jumped down to escape the moment. Kai followed, landing next to me. Without a word, he took my hand and led me away.

———

We arrived at a narrow door on a cobblestone street, lined with dull grass peeping between the cracks. I trailed after Kai up the stairs. Jiggling the key in the lock, he let me inside. The studio was sparse —twin bed in the corner, a rickety circular table with two wire chairs, and a small refrigerator making a faint humming noise, attesting to its age.

Kai set his mandolin case down as I walked to the window and looked out over the quiet path. I could almost imagine the color of the flowers that would appear in spring. Turning back to him, I smiled.

"What?"

"It seems just the sort of place a musician would live."

He grinned as we perched on the bed. Holding my hand, he traced the back of it. "Anyone tell you that you have elegant knuckles?"

I laughed. "No."

He brought them to his lips. "This—," he gestured to the studio, "is just a place out of the rain."

"You don't like being owned by things, do you?"

He shrugged. "Obligation is a bitch. What about you?"

I thought of Connor; I had let myself be owned by people. I nodded.

Kai reached out with his free hand to touch my face. "Where's your home, Sage?"

"I don't have one." My voice was full of bone-jarring loss, an endless reservoir of sadness.

Further words were unnecessary as he turned his body towards me. Sinking his fingers into my hair, he pulled my face close to his. His mouth covered my lips in an urgent kiss, and I gave into his need, fueling my own. With gentle insistence, he pushed me back, and his body melted over mine. His hands and lips were everywhere; it was a struggle to breathe and when I did, the scent of sunshine and pine filled my nose.

Perhaps I didn't have a home, but in that moment, I felt like I did. In his arms, my aching spirit calmed. He was summoning a feeling I had long thought dead.

We struggled out of our clothes, and I watched as Kai's eyes roamed over me in reverence. I touched him, my fingers colliding with an angry scar on his chest. It looked like a burn.

"What is—"

"Not yet," he interrupted. "I'll tell you, but not right now." He silenced me with a kiss.

I swallowed questions as my hands glided over his skin and played with the dark hairs on his chest.

His fingers tickled their way down my body, and I shivered in delight, not wanting to wait any longer. The aching loneliness disappeared like mist late in the morning as our bodies joined as one.

I rocked against him, my mouth seeking his. I bit his lip and then soothed the pain with my tongue.

He groaned, but it wasn't in despair.

Everything made sense, and the only thing that mattered was Kai's mouth on mine and the feeling of his warm, flushed skin against me. We moved in a frenetic pace—a moment too brief in time.

Our breaths mingled as our hearts beat in a synonymous, steady rhythm. Kai's face nestled into the crook of my neck, and my hands gripped his hair as we attained the deepest release possible. I was fulfilled and at peace, but when Kai eased out of me I felt empty again.

"Come on," he said, taking my hand and leading me towards the tiny bathroom. The narrow shower stall would force us to remain close.

We showered in easy silence, our hands still finding a reason to touch one another. I pressed a kiss to his scar, which I could now see in the light.

"It looks like a brand." A tragic T&R marked forever on his body, remembered by his flesh.

"It is."

I didn't ask about it again.

The hot water beat down on us, and I closed my eyes and leaned against his slick shoulder. His arms came around me and squeezed. I fit into him—I belonged. We dried off, and Kai gave me one of his t-shirts.

"You're staying."

"I am?" I asked, even as I reached for the shirt and pulled it over my head. "You don't seem the type that spends a whole night with a woman."

"I'm not," he admitted, "but I want to spend tonight with you."

I did as I was bid, climbing into his bed and scooting over, making room for him. He slid in next to me, putting a warm, heavy leg across mine. My eyes drifted closed, even as I thought again that I shouldn't stay.

Comfort is a powerful sedative.

Chapter 11

Kai

I bolted up, gasping, my body slippery with sweat. I had dreamt of the crash again, the smell of burning metal in my nose, the taste of it at the back of my throat, threatening to choke me.

I looked over at Sage. It was strange to see her there. I'd never brought a woman home with me. I'd left all of them in the middle of the night at apartments or houses I'd convinced them to bring me to, but this was a woman I didn't want to leave.

I wasn't sure why.

Her hair flowed across the pillow like a mermaid under water. Her face was turned away from me, and her breathing was even and deep. Sage was exceptionally beautiful, but it wasn't her looks that intrigued me.

I got out of bed, careful not to disturb her.

When Sage came into the café for the first time I thought she appeared tragic. I noticed a sadness about her, and wanted to play her a song that would make her smile. I had no idea the song I chose would cause her to leave.

When she came back the following night, I felt something. Hope, maybe.

I'd been traveling for years, with no desire to stay put. One woman had been as good as the next, but I wanted Sage for more than a single night.

I scratched my chest as I opened the cupboard, pulled out a cup, and filled it with water. Taking a drink, I turned when I heard footsteps behind me. My shirt covered the tops of Sage's thighs and clung to her breasts, and I could see her nipples, the color of a coral starfish. Her long hair hung down her back in soft waves, fair skin flushed pink. She walked to me, and I wrapped my arms around her as she placed her head in the crook of my neck like she was made for the spot. I breathed her in—she smelled warm, like a spring afternoon in Monteagle.

"Did I wake you?"

"No," she mumbled into my chest, her mouth close to my brand.

All the women I had slept with asked about it—I gave them different answers every time, but for once, I wanted to speak the truth, wondering if I still could. But not now.

I cupped her head in my hands, tugging on her hair to make her look at me. My mouth claimed hers; I needed to feel her moving beneath me as I lost myself in her. Only then were my demons at bay.

I wondered about hers.

I took her back to the twin bed, laid her down, and covered her with my body. Her fingers trailed down my arms and gripped my shoulders as I thrust into her, making us one.

This time, we made love, the savage beast of guilt slumbering. This time, it was just for us.

———

"Don't you guys get bored?" I ask.

Tristan and Reece exchange a look as Tristan passes Reece the hand rolled cigarette. "Bored?" Tristan queries. "What do you mean?"

"I hate shoes," Reece grumbles, wiggling his bare toes.

"Why do we keep meeting here?" I wonder aloud.

"You tell us," Tristan says.

"I thought this was your favorite place?" Reece points out. The sun glides up over the mountains. It's quiet, serene—the silver lake is always placid.

"It is," I state. "But it's—"

"A painful reminder of home?" Tristan finishes.

I nod, picking up a twig and snapping it.

"You going to tell us about the girl?" Reece demands, taking another long drag of the cigarette.

Tristan raises his eyebrows. "Yeah, is it serious?"

"We just met."

"That's a 'yes'." Tristan grins.

"Think she'll make you happy?" Reece asks.

"Yeah."

"Think she'll make you a better man?"

"Hopefully."

"Does she make you reflect?"

"She is my mirror."

Tristan is thoughtful, and then he smiles. "I don't have a reflection anymore."

"Time to go," Reece says, rising. "Take it easy, Kai."

I watch my two best friends walk down the path, their bodies disappearing before my eyes. Sighing, I look at the sky and then descend the mountain.

Chapter 12

Sage

We were a mesh of tangled limbs. Kai's leg was thrown over mine as he held me in his arms. We faced one another, my head resting underneath his chin. I traced a finger in the dip between his collarbones and wondered about the illusion of intimacy. I had never had a one-night stand before, and I had been prepared for awkwardness, yet all I felt was comfort.

He sighed.

"You awake?" I whispered.

"Yeah."

I pulled back, wanting to look in the direction of his eyes. One of his hands came up to caress the curve of my cheek. He kissed me. It was a feathered dance across my lips, but not a plea for more. It was a statement of feeling, of knowledge that I rested next to him.

"Am I hogging the bed?" he asked.

I snorted. "It's barely a bed. How can you hog it?"

Kai attempted to move over. "I'm not used to sharing a bed."

Not to sleep, I thought dryly, but didn't reply. His statement made me think of Connor—the last person I wanted in bed with me. But still, I couldn't expel him from my mind. I'd broken our engagement only a month ago, and I was already in bed with another man. I shoved thoughts of Connor aside, and the guilt that came with it.

"What are you thinking about?" Kai asked quietly. His hand ran down the knobs of my spine, lingering at my tailbone.

"Nothing."

"I don't believe you."

"What are you thinking about?" I countered.

"Fishing."

"Fishing? I feel like I should be offended."

I could hear the smile in his voice when he said, "If I was back home, this is the time I'd be getting up. I'd put on my waders, grab my pole and head out to the lake." "I've never fished before."

"No?" he asked in clear surprise.

"I'm from Brooklyn," I said as if that explained everything.

"Aren't you close to water?"

"The East River doesn't count."

He laughed.

"Actually, you can fish in Prospect Park. Have to throw the fish back though. Seems kind of like a waste."

He made a vague noise of agreement. "I always eat what I catch. Are you tired? Do you want to go to sleep?"

"I'm kind of hungry," I admitted. As if on cue, my stomach moaned.

"Come on, I have some food, I think."

We got up and he slipped into boxers and I threw on his discarded t-shirt. Kai opened the refrigerator and pulled out a block of cheese, smiling in triumph. I peeled an orange that rested on the counter and set it onto a plate.

"Want some cider?" he asked.

"Sure."

He opened a bottle of brut cider and poured it into one glass. He gave me a lopsided grin as he handed it to me. "I figured we could share. I don't have cooties. Promise."

My lips twitched into a grin. "I don't believe you."

We took our snack to the kitchen table and ate in comfortable silence. The crisp cider went down a little too easily, and soon I was feeling drowsy. I got up, set the empty dishware in the sink and turned to him and smiled.

"Are you any good? At fishing, I mean."

"Not bad," he said, though it sounded like feigned humbleness.

"How many fish have you caught in one trip?" I asked as I climbed into bed. Kai got in next to me and settled the covers over us before spooning me.

"Ten. All before dawn. Once the sun comes up, it's like the fish know you're trying to catch them." He swept his lips across the skin below my ear. "Good night, Sage."

"Good night, Kai."

I dreamed of lakes.

———

I woke just as the sun was rising, but when I attempted to get out of bed, Kai's arm shot out and grasped my wrist.

"Don't even think about it," he mumbled into the pillow.

"Think about what?"

"Leaving."

"Wasn't planning on it."

He chuckled as his arms wrapped around me, and I turned towards his embrace. His eyes were open; they were clear, serene, magical. "You're a shitty liar, you know that?"

"Let me up," I protested, struggling against his arms.

"Not until you promise you won't bolt."

"I promise. Now let me make some coffee, or you'll wish I had left. You do have some here, right?"

"Yeah." He released me, and I scrambled out of bed, giving him a view of my backside. He pulled on a pair of shorts, but left his chest bare. "You don't do this a lot, do you?"

I moved around the kitchen and made coffee as we conversed. "What, sleep with strangers? How could you tell?"

"Just knew."

"Am I just another notch on your belt?"

"Would it bother you if you were?"

I shrugged. "What can a girl hope to expect? It's not like we spent a lot of time getting to know one another."

He smiled. It was slow, heated. "I know you fine, but I'd like to know you better."

I looked at him, amusement stamped across my mouth. "We don't have to do this."

"Do what?"

"Let's call this what it is and leave it at that."

"Are you telling me you used me for sex?"

I laughed. "What if I did?"

"I feel so used," he teased.

I pulled out two mugs and handed him one. I had no idea how he liked his coffee, and I didn't want to pretend I did, so I poured it black.

"Let me take you to dinner."

"Are you promising to buy me food before we have sex next time?"

"Well at least I know there will be a 'next time'." He grinned. "I win."

I looked at him for a long moment, sipping my black coffee. It was hot, and it scalded my tongue, so I set it down. I went to grab my belongings, shimmied into my clothes, and then put on my coat. I was willing to give him the benefit of the doubt—at least for one more night. "Come to the *Château de Germain* tonight. I live in the small cottage behind the bed and breakfast."

"You live on a vineyard?"

"Yes. Bring a bottle of bourbon. I'll take care of the food."

"Can't argue with that."

———

"Someone got in early this morning," Celia said with a wry grin as I joined her at the front desk.

My face heated, but I said nothing.

"It's okay, you know."

"What?"

"Moving on with your life."

"Is that what I'm doing?"

"Don't think too much about it," Celia said, pulling me from my thoughts. "Enjoy it."

Even after my night with Kai, I was still in a river of grief. What did I expect after a month in France? A miracle?

"What's it like for you?" I queried. In all this time, I never thought to ask how Celia was dealing with the loss of her oldest friend—I felt heartless.

"Nothing like what you're going through," Celia said. "Losing a friend weathers differently; losing a parent...nothing compares."

"Loss is loss, isn't it?"

"I suppose so. You want to tell me about the guy?"

"Nothing to tell. A ship in the night—he'll be gone before you know it."

"Don't be so sure." Celia sounded like a cryptic fortune-teller.

"What do you mean?"

"Things have a way of finding us and sticking when we least expect it."

————

I pulled the door open and stood back, letting Kai inside. I wore a pair of black leggings, a slouchy white sweater and house slippers. The roaring fire swallowed the chill from the air, lending a comfortable ambiance to the room.

"Cozy," he said, leaning in and grazing my cheek with his lips.

"Let me take your coat."

He shrugged out of it, and I hung it on the rack as he set a bottle of bourbon down on the coffee table.

"What have you got planned?" Kai asked, his gaze straying to the pillows and blankets in front of the fireplace. The coffee table was set with two whiskey glasses and platters of cheese, bread, olives and fruit. "Is that going to be enough for both of us?"

"Used to bigger portions?" I teased.

"Yup. Must be the Southerner in me."

"Ah, I had an inclining you were from the South. You've got that lazy drawl—it's like whiskey and lemonade on a hot summer day."

He grinned. "You like my accent?"

"Maybe." I paused. "Where are you actually from?"

"Monteagle, Tennessee. What about you?"

"I'm from New York."

"Yankee!" he said, feigning shock. "Don't worry I don't discriminate." He winked.

"Thank goodness for that. Take off your shoes. Stay a while."

He grabbed the bottle of bourbon. "Ready to crack this open?"

"Sure. Ice?"

He nodded, and I went into the kitchen with the two glasses. A moment later, I returned and we sat down on the pallet and took a sip of our drinks.

"Hi," he murmured, leaning closer.

"Hello." I let him kiss my lips, enjoying the warmth of the fire and him. He pulled back, picked a grape off one of the plates, and popped it into his mouth.

"I was surprised you opened the door."

"Were you?"

"I thought I might've scared you away. I'm glad I didn't." Though his tone was light, his eyes blazed with intensity.

I took a large swallow of bourbon, but said nothing.

"It feels easy, you know? I want to be myself around you."

"Thank you for that," I said in sincerity. Unveiling ourselves to strangers was never an easy task. There was always the fear that the other person wouldn't like what they saw.

I picked up the bottle and topped off our drinks.

"Are you ready to tell me why you ran out of the café when I played that song?"

I peered at him over my amber liquid. "Only if you tell me about your brand."

"I was going to tell you about that anyway."

I raised an eyebrow. "You first."

Kai clenched his glass, turned somber eyes to me and said, "Two years ago my best friends died in a plane crash. Now I wear their initials."

The air left my lungs, and I blinked several times—whatever I had been expecting, it hadn't been that. We were both fluent in the language of grief.

His hand came up to stroke the side of my cheek. "What happened to you?"

I sighed. "The first time I ever heard the song you played was at a concert with my mother. And she died—a little over a month ago."

It was his turn to be speechless, and then he cleared his throat. "A month? Wow."

I nodded. "Ovarian cancer."

"Fuck." He shook his head. "What brought you here?"

"My mother's oldest friend married the man who owns this vineyard."

"Had to get away?"

"Yeah, you?"

"I left home right after they died, and I haven't been back since."

I leaned into his touch. "Have you been in France the whole time?"

Kai shook his head. "I started in Asia, and I go wherever, whenever."

"Playing your mandolin in cafés?" I smiled. His hand moved to my hair, and he twirled a strand around his fingers.

"That's a fairly recent thing."

"Is it?"

"Only since I came to France."

"Which was when?"

Kai laughed. "About a month ago."

"Interesting timeline," I noted.

"Isn't it?"

I kissed him, and as I did there was a knock on the door, startling us apart. "Sorry, I don't know who that could be."

"No?"

I stood, and answered the door with a slight smile on my face, not at all prepared for Luc to be on my front steps. "You're back?" I blurted out.

He nodded. "Just now. Listen, can we talk?" His eyes widened when he saw Kai, who rose and came to stand behind me. I felt Kai's heat through his shirt, and I wanted to press into him, but that would give them both the wrong idea.

"Now is not really a good time," I said.

"No kidding," Luc replied, his gaze trained on Kai. "Who are you?"

Luc asked the question like he had the possessive right, but I didn't know how to get around introducing them. "This is Kai. Kai, this is Luc. He's the son of the owners."

Kai held out his hand, ever the Southern gentleman. Would Luc be as refined? He was French after all.

When it was clear that Luc was not going to take Kai's hand I asked, "Can we talk tomorrow?"

"Sure. Whatever," Luc said before leaving.

I closed the door and turned to face Kai. His blue-gray eyes narrowed and his jaw clenched.

"Did you sleep with him?" Kai asked, his voice tight.

"Not so good with beating around the bush, are you?"

"Sage…"

"If I did?" I challenged.

Like a jungle cat, he was on me, pushing me against the door, his mouth covering mine. It was a brutal tempest of emotion, and I held onto him like a castaway in a life raft.

"I didn't," I murmured once Kai's kisses calmed. He bathed my forehead with tender lips as if apologizing for his irrational behavior.

"What happened between you two?"

"Is this really any of your business?"

"I'm making it my business. What happened?"

"Nothing."

"It doesn't look that way."

My sigh was weary, but I gave in. "I didn't lie to you."

"Do you want him?"

"No," I stated. His eyes poured into me, filling me up with the depth of his feelings. I wanted to shake in fear. "Don't make claims, and don't ask for promises."

"Okay," he said in reluctant acceptance.

I raised an eyebrow. "You ready for dinner?"

"No."

"More bourbon?"

"No."

"Should we go upstairs then?"

"Yep."

———

I watched Kai sleep on his stomach, like a baby that wanted for nothing. The fairy moon outlined his fair skin in a silvery glow, a demigod gilded in shadow. He stirred. Pain rarely slept, even in dreams, but tonight we'd both rested peacefully. I had awakened only moments ago, needing to see him with my own eyes, to remember he was there.

"We should get candles," he mumbled into the pillow.

I trailed a hand down his back, loving that he shivered at my touch. "Candles? Candles are cliché," I whispered, placing my head next to his so our breaths mingled.

"I want to see you golden." He rolled over. "That first night you came to the café, I couldn't help but notice how you looked in candlelight."

"You're like a wandering bard, you know."

"I'm no bard."

"But you *are* a wanderer."

We never made it back downstairs for dinner, choosing instead to spend our time in bed—touching, sharing, exploring.

"Would it really have bothered you if I'd slept with Luc?" I asked.

He inhaled deeply as if he was stalling for time so he could choose his words carefully. "I know it's hypocritical since you know my history, but yeah, it would've bothered me."

"Luc? Or the idea of Luc."

"I don't know," he admitted, "but I'm glad nothing happened between you two. It's one thing to know you've been with other people—it's another to have to see them."

"That's fair, I guess."

I kissed his collarbone and wondered how he'd played his way into my blood. He held me like his mandolin, cradling me so that I felt like a cherished possession. Kai had learned the corners of my soul, and it had occurred in the darkest part of the night, when the stars peeked out from the clouds and a sliver of moon rode high in the sky. I felt both aged and reborn.

He would have to leave me in the morning, when the sun would rise and time would start again. But for now, the sleepy minstrel sheltered me in warmth. I fell asleep with a smile on my face.

———

The next morning I was not at all surprised to find I was alone in bed, but I was stunned by the wash of bereavement. I was supposed to be glad I had my space back, but when I breathed in, I no longer detected the scent of sunshine and mountains—the smell of Kai.

Stumbling downstairs, I halted. Kai was in the kitchen, standing at the counter having a cup of coffee, like he belonged there—like he lived with me. Taking a moment, I consumed him with my eyes. He wasn't very tall, close to five-ten maybe. His body was sturdy, almost compact, and when I was in his arms, I didn't know there was a world outside just the two of us. His hair was dark brown and a bit too long; it fell into his face. I didn't know if he owned a razor, but I liked his gritty jaw. He was careless with his appearance, but it didn't matter; all I saw were captivating eyes and a kindred spirit.

I moved behind him and pressed my cheek to his back. He stiffened and then relaxed. Setting down his coffee cup, he turned to me, pulled me into his arms and lifted me onto the counter. He stood in between my legs, which I wrapped around him. He was in boxers and a white undershirt, his hair sticking up on end. I smiled and smoothed the most endearing, irreverent cowlick I had ever seen.

Placing my hands on his chest, I closed my eyes. "You're still here."

"Where else would I be?" His voice was husky with sleep and something else. Desire, maybe.

"I don't know," I answered, talking into his neck. "None of this seems real."

"The most surreal moments are often the most genuine."

"I didn't believe it when my mother died, but it turned out to be the only truth of my life."

"This is truth, too."

"Is it?" I still wasn't sure.

His arms tightened, but he didn't speak. I let him hold me before pulling back and stealing his coffee. Touch of cream was how he took it, I noted.

After we showered and dressed, Kai walked me to the back of the bed and breakfast, kissing me on the lips and saluting before walking away. He didn't tell me he'd see me that night; it was already a forgone conclusion. Whether I wanted him or not.

Ship in the night, I reminded myself, seed in the wind. And I'd let him go when the next place called to him.

———

I spent the morning at the desk with Celia, but by the time after-noon rolled around, I knew I couldn't put off the confrontation with Luc any longer. I found him drinking a beer on the balcony that overlooked the vineyard. It was cold and quiet, but the sky was clear.

He didn't turn as I approached. Perhaps he was expecting me all along.

"You're with Kai."

"No," I said.

"Certainly looked that way to me."

"I was engaged, Luc. Not long ago."

"Oh. I didn't know."

"That's why I'm telling you. I don't know what I want," I admitted. "All I know is what I *don't* want."

"And that's me?"

"This isn't about you. This is about *me*. Let me breathe, Luc."

He picked at the corner of the beer label and peeled it. He still wouldn't look at me.

"You don't want me, not really. You think you do because you don't know the real me."

"Do *you* even know the real you?"

I glanced at the vines, my gaze landing on a rut of dirt. "No, I don't. I thought I did, once. It was all a lie. Do you want me to lie to you, Luc?"

When he wouldn't answer, I walked away.

———

"I haven't talked to my family in two years," Kai said. His voice was quiet, his hand sliding up and down my arm. Lying in the double bed, my head resting on his chest, I stroked his brand. It was jagged, like my heart.

"Do you miss them?"

"No."

"Liar."

"No, it's true."

"Do you miss anything?"

"My favorite fishing hole," he admitted. "I miss the hours I'd lose up in those mountains. I miss Reece and Tristan, but that goes without saying. I miss Alice and Keith, Reece's parents, who are more my parents than my own. I miss my grandmother. But I don't miss my Mom and Dad, or brother."

"Why not?"

His sigh was labored. "My parents want me to be a certain way, and Wyatt…"

"Wyatt?"

"My brother. He's everything I'm not."

I mulled over his words before asking, "Do you plan to go back?"

"No. What about you?"

"What about me?"

"You ever think of going back to New York?"

"To what?" I sat up, my tangled hair falling across my shoulders.

"What did you leave behind?" He sat up too, the moonlight turning his skin silvery blue. Somewhere far away the sky rumbled.

"Nothing—there's nothing there."

"A girl like you always has someone waiting."

Without thought, I glanced at my ring finger.

"Sage, are you married?"

"Would it bother you if I was?"

He didn't answer, he just continued to stare at me.

I sighed. "No, I'm not married."

"Engaged?"

"I was." There was no apology, no sadness in my voice. It all seemed so long ago, my relationship with Connor. "None of that matters now."

"How could it not matter?"

"The same way it doesn't matter that you've been with a bunch of women."

"It's different," Kai insisted. "I wasn't planning to share a life with any of them. Did you leave him?"

"Yes," I explained. "It needed to end. So I ended it." I examined him, trying to see all the little parts that made him who he was. "You're afraid I'm going to leave you, too."

"No, I'm not." He climbed out of bed and went in search of his pants.

"Like hell you're not," I said, watching him. "You think I abandon people."

"Do you?"

"No. It looks that way, maybe, but it's not true. I know what you're doing."

"What?" His voice was strained with hurt and rage.

"You're leaving me before I leave you, before you're in too deep."

"Don't you get it?" He stalked to the side of the bed and hauled me into his arms. "I'm already in too deep."

"This has to be enough," I begged, "please, this has to be enough." It was a broken plea.

"For now."

His mouth came down to claim mine in fierce possession. I ripped at his clothes, tearing into him, wanting him to brand me until I knew him in my bones. It scared me—our intensity. I wondered what we would leave in our wake, but I was straining towards it anyway.

Maybe not a passing ship after all.

Maybe the seed had settled and taken root.

Chapter 13

Kai

I came to, knowing it was morning. I inhaled—Sage was near; she shifted closer, and the tickle of her long brownish-red hair joined her smell.

"You want a lot from me, don't you?" she whispered.

"Yep."

"Why?"

"It would terrify you if I told you."

"Get out," she commanded.

I forced her to meet my gaze. "No."

"What do you mean, *no?*" she demanded, throwing her legs over the side of the bed.

"Exactly as it sounds. I'm not going anywhere."

She moved away, and I watched her from the confines of the covers, staring at the woman who was doing everything in her power to retreat. It was too late for that; I'd follow her. Maybe I could be relentless when I wanted something. Who knew?

"I'm not ready for this—whatever *this* is."

"Okay."

"I mean it, Kai. Don't placate me. I'm not ready for anything serious."

"Is that what you told Luc?"

She didn't reply.

"Why did you come home with me that night? There was a guy right under your nose you could've been with."

"I knew Luc would want more. I didn't think you would."

"You thought you were safe." I sat up and stretched, glad she watched my every move. "Hate to break it to you, darlin', but you're not safe. Not from the way I make you feel."

"Stop it."

"Stop what? Do you think I like knowing I want you, and there's nothing I can do about it?" Tears fell down her magnolia cheeks. "Your mother just died," my voice was a whispered caress, "let me be here for you."

She collapsed onto the floor, and I went to her, wrapping my arms around her. Leaning against me, she shook with sobs. When she cried, she put her whole body into it—nothing about Sage was passive.

"How can you be here for me? You're not even here for yourself."

Was she right? I'd been running for so long I didn't feel winded anymore.

"I was drinking a lot," I admitted, "before we met." It was an extreme understatement. How would she react if I told her there were weeks, months that were nothing more than a blurred recollection?

"It's only been two weeks since we met, Kai. Do you see such a drastic change in yourself already?"

I cocked my head to the side. "Do you?"

We were at a standstill—she wiped her face, slid out of my embrace, and stood.

"Nothing can be resolved in a day, Sage."

"So what do we do?"

I grinned. "We eat breakfast."

———

I didn't want to leave, worried that if I did Sage would disappear like a thought just out of reach. I needed her.

I loved her.

When her hand lingered on my shoulder and she leaned into my mouth, I swallowed the words and almost choked on them. They didn't go down easy. I touched her hair and then left.

The winter day was crisp but clear as I walked to my studio. Grabbing my mandolin, I went into the café, ate a croissant, and washed it down with an espresso. I played until late afternoon. As I packed up, a man in his late twenties approached me.

"You're good," he said in an Irish lilt.

I looked at him. "Thanks, but why did you speak to me in English?"

The man gestured to my University of Tennessee baseball cap. I wondered if I should start carrying around a hotdog, so I could drive home the point that no one could be more American than me.

"Dorian," the man introduced, and I shook his hand. "A friend of mine and I have a band. Wondering if you wanted to jam with us."

"Two man band? What kind of music?"

Dorian grinned. "Irish, of course."

"Of course," I said with a smile.

"I play the guitar, and Finn plays the fiddle. I thought a mandolin might be a nice addition."

I didn't have to think about it. "Sounds like a good time."

"Do you know McCool's on *La Rue du Commerce*? We jam there. Patrons are pretty forgiving, especially on the weekend. You free tonight?"

"I am."

"Seven sound good?"

"Sure."

———

I wander through the forest, the sound of trickling water reaching my ears. Leaves crunch under my feet and my hands are cold as I shove them into pockets. The trees are slick with frost, but the familiar noises I associate with nature don't exist. No chirping birds, no humming insects—only my breath. When I come to the clearing, I stop.

"About time you got here," Reece says.

"Sorry, this is a new path."

"You were annoyed that we kept meeting at the lake."

"True. This is a nice change of scenery." I take a seat next to my old friend, blood turning to ice—my heart is in danger of bursting. "Were you afraid?"

"Of death?"

I shake my head. "Of life."

"The unknown scares you, doesn't it?" Reece hops off the rock and walks around barefoot, the cold not affecting him.

"What's the point of it all?" I ask him.

"Going all existentialist on me?"

I laugh. "It's been on my mind lately."

"Tell me about the girl."

"Sage."

"Tell me about Sage. She's different, isn't she?"

"Very."

"So you meet this woman, and suddenly you're wondering what life is about?"

I breathe deeply. "I feel like I've found someone special, and I'm worried she's going to leave me."

"You're allowed to be happy. Don't waste time worrying about things you can't control."

"Is that what I'm doing?" My tone is callous.

"Just live, Kai."

Chapter 14

Sage

I couldn't stop the grin from spreading across my face as I stepped into the Irish pub. It looked like a bar straight out of Dublin, yet it was nestled in the Old Square of *Tours* in the heart of the Loire Valley.

I was ordering a glass of Bushmills when I felt a body sidle up next to me. Swiveling my head, I smiled. "Hello, stranger."

Kai greeted me by pulling me close and running his hand along my jaw. His blue-gray eyes were flinty with promise. Our familiarity knew no bounds—eyes and bodies spoke when words weren't enough.

"I wondered when you'd show up. We're almost ready to go on."

I looked past him towards the two men on stage. I had met Dorian and Finn a week ago; they were charming Irishmen with easy smiles. The crowd was growing eager, and I didn't want to keep him. "Maybe I should find a seat?"

He winked. "I found a spot for you, come on."

Grabbing my drink, I followed. He sat me at a small table off to the side of the stage so I would have a perfect view of the band. I kissed him and whispered, "Break a leg."

While the musicians were tuning their instruments, my gaze wandered around the bar. A young man with a group of friends peered at me with unconcealed interest. I broke eye contact, focusing my attention on Kai. I was grateful when the music started.

Kai's smile brought a pool of tears to my eyes—I felt his joy. This moment, this happiness, was all for him. Was this how he looked when he was fishing, or when he was with his two best friends, who were now gone? When we were together, did he feel the same way?

The band played a fast paced jig, and the crowd roared in delight. Dorian, the singer, had a strong, clear voice. Throughout their set, Kai's gaze would find mine and linger, making me warm all over.

In the middle of a song, I rose to fetch another drink. I attempted to catch the bartender's attention, but he was busy flirting with a blonde at the other end of the bar.

"Buy you a drink?"

I turned to the voice—it was the young man who'd been watching me. He was tall and thin, with a wide, crooked smile. His brown eyes looked their fill, and liked what they saw.

"No, thanks," I dismissed.

"You have a boyfriend?"

"Yes." It was a lie. Kai and I hadn't talked about it, but even if we had, Kai didn't encompass the word—he was more, but I wasn't ready to admit that to myself, let alone to a stranger.

"I don't believe you."

"Your choice."

"Let me buy you a drink," he insisted.

"I'm just here to enjoy the music."

"Dinner then—let me take you to dinner."

His persistence annoyed me. Resolute that I wouldn't be able to get another drink, I went to leave, but the man grabbed me by my upper arms. "What the hell?" I yelled, attempting to fight him off.

He kissed me, and I gagged on the taste of beer and street vendor food.

The young man pulled back, looking pleased with himself even as he swayed, barely able to stand upright. "Now you want to go out with me, don't you?"

The band played on, but the sounds of Kai's mandolin were suddenly absent. Before I could register why, a fist came out of nowhere and collided with the Frenchman's jaw. My head whipped around to find Kai shaking out his hand and cursing under his breath. The drunken Frenchman slumped against the bar, his tongue lolling in his head. I might have found it comical if I hadn't been in outright shock.

The bartender started yelling for us to leave, and I managed to coerce Kai out of the pub before the Frenchman's friends came after us. "What the hell were you thinking?" I demanded, my voice booming across the cobblestones.

"I wasn't."

"Clearly." I glared at him. "I was about to slap his face."

"Really?" Kai raised his eyebrows, the set of his shoulders taut with anger.

"Really. I know you're Southern, but *come on.*"

"His lips were on yours," Kai said through a clenched jaw.

"I'm well aware of that fact, and I didn't like it any more than you did."

He took a step closer to me, his face harsh, almost grotesque in the moonlight. "Don't pretend to be offended by what I've done. Do us both a favor and admit you liked it—liked me fighting for you."

"Fuck you!"

He yanked me into his arms and kissed me. The breath left my body, and I wrapped myself around him, hating him for speaking the truth, and hating myself for knowing it. I shoved him away and wiped my mouth with the back of my hand, as if I could remove the taste of him. I had pieced a life together around a man, and I hadn't been aware I'd done it. I'd stopped thinking of Kai as something temporary. When had it all changed?

He took my chin in his hand, compelling me to look at him. Kai with a steady gaze was more unnerving than Kai with unknowable intensity. Unable to say all the things I wanted to, I said instead, "You're were supposed to be a seed and blow where the wind carried you. You weren't supposed to stay."

"I wish you'd show me what you write in those journals. The ones you talk to when you can't talk to me."

"Why?"

"I want to know you."

"You know me fine."

His stare was unflinching. "I want to know your heart, and I think you put it in those pages."

I took a deep breath and forced myself to admit, "I'm not some great mystery, Kai. My mother's death wrecked me, and I barely survived. You'll wreck me, too. Maybe forever."

"You think I'll continue to wander, don't you?"

"When was the last time you felt the urge to stay?"

"I've never spent more than one night with the same woman. Don't you get that?"

I couldn't tell him he was a love ballad, a song that would play in my blood long after he'd left me for someone else.

"I need some ice," he muttered.

"Don't you have to go back in there and continue?"

"I effectively ended the set. Besides, I don't think I can flex my fingers to play."

We began to walk in the direction of my cottage.

"You're falling in love with me," he stated, putting his arm around my shoulder. "That's why you're upset. Not because I punched some guy who deserved it."

I didn't reply because I wasn't falling in love—I'd crashed into it, and it gripped me in an unyielding embrace.

I was already there.

———

Kai was on the couch, cradling his hand in his lap while I filled a bag with ice. Handing it to him, I sat and stared into the blazing fire

I'd lit upon arriving home. The bottle of bourbon on the coffee table was open; we didn't bother with glasses. I took a swallow out of it and then handed it to him.

"It's a good thing people can't die from guilt," he said.

"You don't have to feel guilty anymore—I forgive you for treating me like a trophy." My tone was full of brevity.

He grinned in sardonic humor. "I'm not talking about that." He took a long drink from the bottle. "I was supposed to be in the plane."

"What? What are you talking about?"

Kai was silent for so long, I didn't know if he'd speak again. "It was a little two-seater, and Tristan was flying. We were celebrating because he'd gotten his pilot's license. I won *rock, paper, scissors*, but Reece looked so depressed I let him go instead of me."

"Holy shit," I whispered.

Flames danced in his eyes as he leaned over and pressed his lips to my throat, saying words against my skin. "Please don't leave me out here alone. Let me in."

I placed a hand on his chest, the steady beating of his heart solid and reassuring. Kai covered my hand with his and then brought it to his lips. My breath hitched, and I tried to hide my tears, but they came and I couldn't stop them. "I already have, Kai."

He pulled me to him. "Damn, what you do to me."

"Do you regret leaving?"

"I regret *how* I left."

"What do you mean?"

"I didn't even leave a note. I just…left. Do you judge me for that?" His gaze was open, honest, and he hid nothing, including the blackest parts of himself.

I shook my head. "I'd be seven shades of hypocrite if I did. I haven't spoken to my best friend in weeks. I silence her calls. I ignore her emails."

"Do *you* have any regrets? About leaving New York?"

"No. I left a job that meant nothing. I couldn't stay with Connor and pretend my mother's death didn't change everything," I touched his face, "but you left behind your entire family. How are you supposed to come back from that?"

"I don't know. I don't know who I am anymore," he said, like it was a revelation.

"Would your friends want this? You feeling guilty because you lived and they died?"

"Don't tell me they would have done any better if I had been the one who died. You'll never know them, and they'll never know you."

"Tell me about them. It will only give me a vague idea, but tell me anyway."

He took my hand. "Reece was quiet until you got to know him. He liked to watch things…people. Tristan though—that kid jumped in knee-deep before any of us decided to follow. He got into so much trouble."

"What kind of trouble?"

"He smoked and drank—bought a motorcycle, that sort of thing. Ran around with a bunch of women, but then he fell in love with Lucy."

"Lucy?"

"His wife. Life is so unfair."

"It is," I stated. "How did she manage to get Tristan to settle down?"

Kai laughed; it was the first genuine sound of happiness that had come out of his mouth all evening. "We met Lucy in fourth grade. She was this gangly girl with freckles covering every inch of her face, huge glasses, and hair more orange than red. But she got super hot around the time we were in high school, and she understood Tristan like no one else. She didn't berate him for drinking or smoking, and when he found acceptance in her, he fell hard and fast. I didn't understand it…not until now." He touched my cheek and smiled. "If this is what healing feels like, I'll take it."

I wanted to crawl into him and bury myself. I could no longer hold back the tears.

"Ah, darlin'," he mumbled into my hair, letting me sob out my anguish.

Hope, tinged with despair permeated my voice as I asked, "Do you think we have a chance at happiness? We've both lost so much."

He smiled before capturing my lips, demanding and greedy. We were rough, clawing at each other in zealous passion. It was devastating, so complete, leaving nothing but heated breaths and desire. When we lay together, spent and exhausted, Kai pulled the blanket from the couch over us.

"Tell me," I demanded, knowing he would know what I needed.

"I love you."

His declaration was my salvation.

Chapter 15

Sage

"Where are you going?" I whispered the next morning.

Kai grinned and pressed a kiss to my exposed shoulder. "My, how the tables have turned since we first met."

"I don't know what you're talking about," I teased as I stroked his face. "Don't even think about shaving."

"Yes, ma'am."

"So where *are* you going?"

"I want to track down Dorian and Finn and apologize for last night. See if I ruined our place to jam."

"Can I convince you to shower first?"

He raised an eyebrow. "Will you join me?"

After, I kissed him on the lips and saw him off, then went in search of Luc. We would have to coexist, and I refused to avoid him any longer. I found Armand instead.

"Walk with me," he said. We ambled through vines that were still quiet, still waiting for spring. I rolled my shoulders, wanting to stretch and open like a new flower.

"How are you settling in?"

"It's weird. I feel like I've been here forever."

"Magic of this place," he agreed with a grin. He turned serious. "You can talk to me. I mean, I know it's probably easier with Celia, but I knew your mother, too."

It was a knife to my heart, a reminder that I'd gone on living. I'd told Kai that Tristan and Reece would want him to find peace, find happiness. Would my mother have been any different?

Death was hardest on those left behind.

"Tell me a story about my mother."

"Did she ever tell you about the time she wanted to learn to work in the fields?"

"No, she didn't."

"She got so sunburned, she looked like a crispy chicken."

We laughed, and I sighed knowing I had people to help me remember her.

"Is my son still avoiding you?"

His question jarred me. "You know about that?"

"Celia might have said something, and Luc isn't here."

"Where is he?"

"Visiting friends in *Marseilles*. You didn't notice he was gone?"

My cheeks bloomed. "Ah, I've been sort of…occupied."

"We've noticed. You both should come to dinner tonight."

"Dinner?"

He nodded. "I think it's important we get to know the man you've been spending time with."

"Wow."

"What?"

"I have a family."

Armand grinned. "Whether you want us or not."

"I do want you," I said, not at all surprised to find my eyes burning with emotion. "It's nice to be cared for."

"Not cared for, Sage. Loved."

———

"This isn't 'meet the parents'," I explained.

"It feels that way," Kai said.

"I don't have parents, remember? But Celia and Armand have become family to me."

"And what am I?"

"Too soon to tell," I lied.

We walked into the kitchen; Celia covered a pot of water with a lid, and Armand sat at the table with a glass of wine.

"Do you ever cook?" I asked Armand, who grinned at the question.

"Not if I can help it." He stood and went to shake Kai's hand. "Get you a glass, Kai?"

"Sure. Thanks."

Celia watched Kai with an unnerving stare, and I had a brief glimpse of what it would have been like if my mother had met him. Mom had barely been able to tolerate Connor. Would she have accepted Kai? Would she have liked him?

The tension grew insurmountable until Celia said, "Kai, how are you at making salads?"

"Can't hurt to give it a try." He went to the sink and washed his hands.

"Stuff's on the counter." Celia's gaze slid to the doorway. "What are you doing here?"

"I live here." Luc sauntered into the kitchen and looked at Kai. After a moment he glanced in my direction and asked, "Can we talk?"

Impeccable timing.

"Please?" he pleaded.

Kai's face was unreadable. Shrugging, I followed Luc into the courtyard. The sun had set and it was cold, so I wrapped my arms around myself and bounced from one foot to the other.

"I'm sorry, I've been an ass."

"Yes, you have been," I agreed, "and you've been avoiding me."

"You're happy with him, aren't you?"

"Yes."

"Then I'm glad for you."

94

"*Really?*"

He shrugged. "Not yet, but I'll get there."

"How long do you expect that to take? Kai's in your kitchen."

"So he is."

"I don't need you to like him, but what about us? Can we be friends?"

His eyes were hopeful. "I didn't blow it?"

"Of course not. We were well on our way. I emoted all over you when I first got here, if you recall. That makes us friends, right?"

He laughed in relief. "Do you mean it?"

"I do. Let's just forget everything, okay?"

"You can do that?"

"Why not? What is there between us, Luc, except friendship? In time, you'll realize I wasn't right for you."

"Don't patronize me."

"I'm not trying to."

We stared at each other, and Luc's shoulders lost their tension.

"Let's go eat. Maybe pretend you like Kai?"

We went back inside to a quiet kitchen. Kai diced vegetables, and the only sound in the room was of the knife hitting the cutting board. Celia enjoyed a glass of wine while Armand rubbed her shoulder.

Luc and Kai stared at one another, not saying a word. My eyes dodged back and forth between the two of them, wondering how things were going to play out. Luc inclined his head, and Kai did the same. I didn't know what it meant, but they seemed to have come to an understanding.

"How long have you been traveling?" Celia asked Kai.

"Couple of years."

"And you've been in France how long?" Armand pried.

Somehow I'd acquired surrogate parents. I smiled into my wine.

"Close to two months now."

"Plan to stick around?" Luc wondered.

Kai glared.

"I'm asking as a friend," Luc defended. "Sage has had a rough go of it. I don't want her hurt."

I raised my eyebrows and looked at Kai inquisitively.

Kai took my hand and grinned. "Just try and get rid of me."

———

"Have time for a quick chat?" Celia asked me the following morning.

"Sure." I poured myself a cup of coffee and sat at the kitchen table. Armand and Luc were running errands around town, and Kai had already left.

"I like Kai," Celia began.

"Oh, boy. I'm sensing a *but.*"

"Not a *but,*" Celia said with a shake of her head.

"You're worried."

"Concerned."

"Same thing in the eyes of a parent."

"I'm not trying to replace Penny."

"I know."

"But, I've come to know you, Sage. And not just as my friend's daughter. I want to look out for you."

I smiled. "I know."

"This thing with Kai is happening really fast."

"It is."

"You just lost your mother, ended things with a fiancé, and left your entire life behind. Are you ready for this?"

I tapped the rim of my mug. "I've felt more alive in two months with Kai than in one year with Connor." I stood, wanting to put an end to the conversation. I respected Celia, but this was my decision to make. "I know how this looks, but you don't know what's between two people unless you're one of the two. Do you know the things we say to each other late at night? Do you know what it's like to wake up in the morning and feel like you've been given your life back? I do."

"You're angry."

"I'm not," I said, meaning it. "I appreciate everything you have done for me. Letting me come here, giving me your shoulder. But I love him."

"Is he a crutch?"

"I don't know. Maybe. Probably. But my heart went to him before I could consciously give it."

Celia stared at me for a long moment, her eyes full. "Will he hurt you?"

"No."

"How do you know?"

I smiled. "I just do."

———

We were lying in bed, the clear night shining through the window when Kai said, "I was thinking…I should move in here."

I snorted with laughter.

"What?" he demanded. "The idea of living together is *funny*?"

I laughed harder and threw a hand in the general direction of the corner. "That's your mandolin, right? And those are your pants? When was the last time you went to your studio?"

He laughed, too. "I guess you're right."

"Might as well move in the rest of your things."

"There's not a lot."

"Makes packing easy."

"Can we have a party?" Kai asked.

I turned in his arms and pressed a kiss to his collarbone. "Any kind of party you want."

His lips touched mine. It didn't seem to matter, day or night, I wanted him. I wondered if it would ever wear off.

I hoped it wouldn't.

"Tell me—what kind of foods will we have?"

"Sweet things," he said as he nibbled my shoulder.

"What else," I demanded.

"Will you let me distract you already?" he pleaded, his voice husky.

Desire fizzed under my skin like a thousand champagne bubbles popping.

Later, when he climbed out of bed and went in search of his clothes, I asked, "Where are you going?"

"To get the rest of my things."

"Now?"

He grinned. "There isn't much. I want to live with you, Sage."

"I'm coming, too."

When we were strolling hand in hand towards his studio, I took a deep breath and said, "Smell that?"

"What?"

"It will be spring soon."

"How can you tell?"

I smiled. "I've lived in New York my whole life, I know the scent of snow. There's no bite to the air right now. Spring is close." I felt joyful, young. But when was the last time Kai had been carefree? His guilt tethered him like a kite.

"I can't wait to walk around barefoot," he said. "It's been so long since I've felt the grass between my toes."

"Wild child," I teased.

"You never walk around without shoes?"

"In New York? And get hepatitis?"

We laughed, and it warmed the dark corners of my heart. We arrived at his studio a few minutes later and climbed dingy stairs toward the front door. Kai slid a key into the tattered deadbolt, turned it sharply and eased the door open, letting me through. The refrigerator hummed in the corner of the small kitchen, drawing attention to its chipped, enameled body. Everything was bathed in fluorescent light, and as Kai began to gather his things I realized that this place had never been Kai's home—and he had never wanted it to be. I crossed the room to help him pack and he looked at me, his smile wide and easy. And in that moment, without a word, I knew we were both thinking about starting a new life together.

"What was it like? Living with your fiancé?" Kai asked, jarring me out of my thoughts.

"Why do you want to know?"

"I'm curious about Connor and your life before you came here —tell me about it," he demanded.

"What am I supposed to say?"

"I don't know."

I bit my lip in thought. "I hated his socks and all they stood for. Rigid, confining. When he proposed, I should've broken it off, but I didn't. Instead I complacently accepted him." I stared at Kai, my mouth tight with remembrance. "I don't want to talk about who I was. I was scared to dream. Scared to think I could be different, or have something different. I settled, and I don't want to talk about it."

"It's the flaws that make us truly love someone."

"That's far too poetic, even for me, Kai."

He smiled.

"Can I tell you some things I want you to know?"

Kai nodded.

"I love that we stay awake late into the nights, learning the outlines of one another. I love that I've learned you by touch. I love that the small crinkles at the corners of your despondent, troubadour eyes tell your life story. And when I'm in your arms and you're inside me, I feel a connection deeper than words can describe."

He embraced me as I continued to speak, "I know your heart has been broken, but I want to help you stitch it back together... Will you let me?"

Kai's hands cradled my cheeks as he stared into my eyes. His lips covered mine, and we fell into the moment—and each other.

Chapter 16

Sage

Winter turned to spring, and the grapes in Armand's vineyard ripened. I helped out around the bed and breakfast, deriving a primitive joy from being productive. I didn't think about the future —choosing instead to live in the present, wanting to soak up every experience, every moment.

Most of my reflections found their way into a journal. Every once in a while I'd share something I wrote with Kai before putting it under the mattress, like I had been doing for years. It was the only routine I followed.

One warm May afternoon, I was manning the desk alone when Kai tore into the foyer, animated and happy. "I have a surprise for you. Can you sneak away this weekend?"

It was the sort of spontaneity I'd grown to love. "I don't see why not."

Twenty minutes later, we were packed, seated in a small black rental car, and driving out of the city. "Will you tell me where we're going?"

"Nope."

"Will I like it?"

"Yep."

"How long do I have to wait until I find out?"

"About three-and-a-half hours. Turn on some music."

"What do you want to hear? Jazz? Bluegrass?"

Kai grinned. "How about some Creedence?"

I smiled back. "Perfect road trip music." I peered out the window, enjoying the scenery. The countryside was in bloom, and the lush rolling hills reminded me of a postcard.

"It doesn't look real, does it?" Kai asked.

I glanced at him; he smiled, but his eyes were on the road. "I still can't believe I get to call France home. Is it home for you?"

"Home is wherever you are, Sage. Does that scare you?"

"Not anymore," I admitted. "What are your dreams, Kai?"

"To feel the way I feel right now—forever."

I caught my breath. "And you call me the writer."

He sighed. "I never thought this was going to be my life. I didn't think I deserved this; to feel all I feel for you, to want to laugh and cry in your arms." His throat tightened with emotion.

I brushed tears from my eyes. I could tell he was trying to shake off the heaviness of our conversation. We needed light, so I steered the dialogue somewhere else. "Favorite Ben and Jerry's ice cream flavor?"

"Phish Food. You?"

"Boston Cream Pie."

"Hmm," he said, running his tongue across his lips. "Favorite book?"

"*The Thornbirds.*"

"Never read it. What's it about?"

"Forbidden love, for one. The story follows three generations of women. They made it into a really good miniseries."

He snorted with laughter. "I'll read it if you read my favorite book."

"And that is?"

"*A River Runs Through It,* by Norman Maclean."

I smiled in arrogance. "Already read it."

"Have you now?"

"Okay, next question, if you threw a dinner party, who would you invite?"

"Do I have to cook?"

"No."

He furrowed his brow. "Do the guests have to be living, or can they be dead?"

"Either."

"Fictional or real?"

"Just answer the question!" I said in exasperation.

"Captain Hook."

"Captain Hook? *Really?*"

"Yeah, I bet his side of the story is more interesting."

I chuckled.

"How about you?" he asked.

"Wild Bill Hickok. I want to know if he really had a premonition that he was going to die, and if he did, why he didn't try and change his fate."

"Can you really change your fate?"

I shrugged. "I like to believe anything is possible. If you could be Scarecrow, Tin Man, or Lion, who would you pick?"

Kai thought for a moment. "Scarecrow. He has the best song. You're Tin Man though."

"How do you figure?"

"You're all heart."

Three-and-a-half hours later, we reached our destination, and I pressed my nose against the car window. "A vineyard? We *live* on a vineyard!"

"It was Armand's suggestion. Welcome to the *Château La Piolette.*"

Kai parked, and we walked into the *château*, where we met the owners, a middle-aged husband and wife, who reminded me of Celia and Armand. It made me wonder about the institution of marriage. Was it another box I tried to fit into? Another lie I'd been told I wanted? I looked at Kai as he conversed with the couple. His smile was deep and hearty. I wanted him, any way I could have him —odd, how that became the only truth I knew.

After we set our bags down in our room, I asked, "What should we do first?"

"We have a few hours before sunset. Want to walk around?"

"Yeah, let's eat and then explore."

He called and requested a picnic basket. We found a pristine spot underneath a large tree, spread out a blanket, and began to unpack. Kai pulled out a small half bottle of wine and twisted off the cap.

We laughed and talked, late afternoon sinking into twilight. Moments like these made me feel suspended in time, like there was no other place I was meant to be. Everything before Kai seemed so far away, so trivial. He heightened all my senses; for the first time, I tasted life, and I wanted to chew it up like a ripe, sweet peach.

My thoughts drifted to Kai's home in Monteagle, wondering what it would be like to go there with him. Would I ever find out? Did I want to? Would he consider returning if I said I'd go with him? Did I have the right to ask?

Wanting to change the direction of my unspoken questions, I leaned in to kiss him, cutting him off in the middle of a word. I knew his lips like they were my own. His hands were in my hair as we strained closer to one another. Desire whirled through me, awakening everything inside—I was consumed and reborn in my passion.

I led him back to our room. I undressed him and ran my fingers along the planes of his body. The sheet was cool beneath my heated skin. I grazed my fingertips along the slope of his back, and his shallow breathing turned heavy. His desirous eyes peered into mine, and I gave a part of myself to him I didn't want back. I cried out as Kai filled me—I wasn't cold, not when he was with me.

Lying in bed with our arms and legs entangled, I closed my eyes. Kai rested his chin on my breastbone. It was dark, and the curtains were pulled back to reveal the face of the moon.

I traced his ear with my finger. "My thoughts and feelings, they're all of you. I'm sad for what I've lost, but knowing I have you makes it bearable—so bearable." I kissed him. "I think we are what ballads are written of, what bards sing of. We are epic, you and I." I sat up and put on a shirt over my naked body.

"What are you doing?"

"Come with me." Holding hands, we walked into the intoxicating evening. Countless stars hung in the net of the endless universe. I picked out Orion, wondering what it would be like to be forever in the sky, watching, waiting.

Kai pulled me into his arms and I placed a hand on his heart, my face in the crook of his neck. "You remind me of this poem I read once," he whispered.

The smell of him was in my nose, my brain smoky with comfort and peace.

"How familiar are you with Yeats?"

"A little."

He told me about "The Song of Wandering Aengus". It was about a man who had caught a silver trout that turned into a beautiful woman. She disappeared, and he spent the rest of his life wandering the hills in search of her.

"That will not be us," I said when he finished. "I will not leave you in the night, and you will not have to look for me."

"It was dark for so long, Sage, but you're my light."

I pressed a kiss in the dip at the base of his collarbone.

"How long will it last?" I asked.

"What do you mean?"

Staring up into his eyes, I wished I could see the stars reflected in them. "The light goes out, Kai. Always."

———

"Wake up, darlin'." Kai brushed his lips across my cheek as I struggled to open my eyes.

"What time is it?"

"Just before sunrise."

I rolled over and hugged the pillow. "Wake me up in a few hours." I attempted to go back to sleep, but with gentle insistence, Kai tugged on the sheet, so I was nothing more than skin.

"Come watch it with me."

Growling like a bear cub, I searched for his t-shirt. We sat outside, my legs thrown over his while I yawned. The sun crept up, lighting the dew-covered leaves, making them sparkle.

"You are so beautiful when you first wake up," Kai said. "Your skin is flushed and you smell like powdered sugar."

I smiled. "That just tells me that you want a donut in the morning."

We laughed, the air teasing the hair at our temples. After a quick breakfast in the main house, we visited a bee farm, then rented bikes and rode to the small town that hummed with life. We walked hand in hand as timeless lovers.

When we returned to the vineyard it was evening, and a celebration was in full swing. Musicians with guitars and hand drums were playing as people danced. Children ran around, engaging in games and trickery. Bottles of wine were broken out and flowing. Laughter blanketed us in a joyful sound.

His hand was warm and steady at my waist, and I longed to breathe in the scent of him and touch his skin. When the moon was at its zenith, I felt like a fairy woman; my chestnut hair shining in the moonlight, and Kai, my human lover, entranced by my beauty was caught in my magical web. I led him back to our room, needing to possess him and lose myself.

Unable to unbutton his shirt fast enough, I pulled it apart, small white buttons scattering like seeds in the wind. Kai pushed me against the wall, lifted my skirt, and sank into my depths.

I welcomed him home. His hands wove into my hair, and his breathing became labored. As I scraped his back with my nails, I felt the sob of release in my throat. Our hearts beat in a codependent cadence, and still he stayed against me.

Kai looked into my eyes, lifted himself off me, and moved us to the bed. We lay down face to face. "I'm sorry—did I hurt you?"

Shaking my head, I put a hand to his cheek. "I needed you, like I've never needed anything."

He caught my escaping tears with his lips, kissing the corners of my eyes. His voice was a distant magical chant as he said, "You're enough to make me believe there's a God."

I smiled, listening to the night settling down, inhaling the fragrant breeze drifting through the room. I didn't want to move, wishing to remain frozen in time, my lover next to me for all eternity.

———

"This was a perfect weekend," I said the following morning as we loaded the car. "I'm glad we came. I love living life in the moment."

"You've never done that before, have you?"

I shook my head.

"But you left New York and moved to France."

"That was different—it was not a whim. It was necessary." Kai started the engine and I buckled myself in and said, "It's how you live your life, though, isn't it?"

He shrugged. "For a while, it was the easiest thing to do. No demands, go where I wanted, when I wanted."

"Do you ever plan?"

"I planned this trip, sort of. What would you do if money was no object?"

"Money isn't really an object for me. My mom did okay as a writer, you know, and she left me everything. And I haven't figured out what I want in life."

"No?"

"Have you?" I asked.

"Can't say that I have," he admitted.

"You and me. That's it, that's all that matters."

"You don't want more?"

"More what? I had the career and the guy. Both were the *right* ones, I guess, but I'd lie awake at night feeling empty. I didn't know what I was supposed to do about it, so I did nothing."

"What about writing?" he asked. "You ever going to pursue it?"

"I don't know. It's all wrapped up with my mother. Like my talent is tainted. What happens if I give in?"

"What happens if you don't?"

I was silent as I pressed my head to the window. "I used to laugh at all those women who wanted nothing more than a house, a husband, and kids. I thought they weren't ambitious, and I could never understand why they thought that stuff was enough. Now I'm thinking they might be on to something. It's the simple things, isn't it? When your days are spent laughing and loving, what more is there? What are we supposed to need?"

"If your mother hadn't died, would you feel this way?"

I shrugged. "I don't know."

"I've been wandering for years. I have no drive, no ambition except for the next beautiful place, the next breath of peace."

I stared at him, and a missing key of understanding sank into its lock. "You come from money, don't you? Serious money. That's what this is about?"

He nodded, his mouth full of resentment. "Are you angry?"

"Why would I be? It explains how you've been able to travel the world without worry."

"I didn't share it with you. Should I have told you sooner?"

I shook my head. "I don't think so."

"It doesn't change anything for you?"

I smiled. "It doesn't change how I see you."

"Coming from a family with money is such a burden. There was always this expectation that I had to do something with my life. Go to law school, become a doctor—live the dream my parents hoped would come true for me."

"You never wanted that life?"

"No. Not before Tristan and Reece died, and definitely not after."

"Strange, how you recognized it for what it was. I never saw things clearly. My mother always wanted more from me—for me to publish my works, but I didn't see it like you did." I was thoughtful. "Are you ever going to face your family?"

"Don't call me a coward."

"I wasn't."

"You were."

"I don't think you're a coward," I insisted, "but you've got to deal with this, Kai. If you don't, it's going to swallow you—swallow us. Is that what you want?"

"I didn't know I could live again. *You* make me live again." He paused. "Marry me."

"*What?*" I asked, startled. "You don't mean that."

"I do," he said. Then in a stronger voice he said again, "Marry me." He pulled over onto the side of road and cut the engine. With an intense look, a fire in his eyes, he dragged me to him, his fingers in my hair, and his mouth close to mine. "I can face anything knowing I have you. I *will* face it," he vowed. "Marry me, Sage."

I traced his jaw with a finger. The stubble was rough, like the sandpapery tongue of a feline. Tears welled in my eyes.

I nodded, and Kai smiled deeply. It was pure, effortless, like I had given him the world.

Chapter 17

Sage

"What was your wedding to Connor going to be like?" Kai asked, later that night when we were in bed.

I sighed and snuggled into his arms. "Big, grandiose. It was supposed to be on Long Island."

"That doesn't sound like you."

"It wasn't."

"What kind of wedding *do* you want?"

"Small, and over fast."

He chuckled. "Think I'm going to run?"

"It actually has nothing to do with you. A wedding isn't what's important. It's the marriage."

"Wise words. Are you going to invite Jules?"

"I don't know; I haven't spoken to her since I got here. Do I want the first conversation to be, 'Hey, I'm getting married, and, no, I'm not crazy'?"

"Valid point, but she is your best friend."

"I want to be happy on my wedding day, Kai. I'm not sure I can be if Jules comes. I don't want to have to explain myself. Even to her."

"I can understand that. What happens when she finds out, though? After the fact?"

"I'll deal with it, but for now, I want to revel in us, and continue to shut out the world."

"You're a bad influence," he teased.

"Let's hope."

"Were you planning to take Connor's last name?"

"Yes."

"Are you taking mine?"

Reaching up, I stroked his hair. "Yes."

"Would your mom be mad about that?"

"No. She took my dad's name. Even though she already had a successful writing career by then." I laughed in wry humor.

"What?"

"I'm thinking about a fight we had—she told me to publish under a different name if I didn't want to be associated with her. I can do that now, if I ever…" I shook my head and kissed his brand. "Irony, huh? Life's a satire."

"A series of them," he agreed.

———

We were married a week later, standing among the vines and tucked away in a pocket of serenity. I wore a simple white gown, the sun heating my skin, a crown of dandelions resting on my head—it was a crown of wishes yet to be made.

The lines around Kai's eyes wrinkled as he smiled, and I envisioned how he'd look in middle age. It was a moment of my life I'd remember forever—those lines would become deeper and more meaningful as the years went on, like a mountain pass forged by a river.

Kai clasped my hands and vowed to be my roof out of the rain, to keep me going when I didn't have the strength, and to be everything to me when I felt like I had nothing.

Only Luc, Celia, and Armand attended. When we toasted to our marriage, Kai and I looked at one another and silently gave tribute to those we'd lost. This day that meant so much to us was tinged with unspoken sadness, the beauty of our marriage smudged with darkness like the corners of an old photograph.

We sat outside at the table that had been set with simple china. I touched Kai's hand, loving that when we retired for the night, I would be sleeping next to my husband.

"I found something, and I'd like you to have it," Celia said when the wine bottles were empty and day descended into night.

It was a discolored Polaroid placed in a thin black frame, a portrait of my mother and Celia in their early twenties. The girls had their arms around each other's shoulders, looking jubilant, hopeful, before they knew what life would throw at them. In the background was the vineyard.

"You said no presents," Celia remarked as I continued to stare at it, "but I found this in an old shoe box."

I looked at Celia, who peered at me like a mother. "Thank you."

"She would be proud of you for living your life and finding love."

I was about to answer, but emotion gripped my throat, so all I did was nod.

"Sage?" Kai called. "You ready?"

Embracing Celia, I closed my eyes. I wished Mom had lived long enough to see this milestone. But if she had, would I even be here, or would I be married to someone else, trapped in a life of my own foolish, rebellious making? Something to think about—later, when I was ready.

We walked into the cottage, breathing in the night air wafting through the windows. I set the frame on the mantle, took off my wreath of wishes, and placed it next to the photo.

"You look like her," Kai commented.

"I know." I smiled. "Genes don't lie."

"I'm sorry she couldn't be here."

"I'm sorry they couldn't be here, either."

I reached for him, not wanting to think about our pasts and all we'd lost. I wouldn't think about our future either—I only needed time in the present, because it too, would flee from us before we were ready. "Take me to bed, Kai."

He did exactly that.

———

"Good morning, darlin'," Kai whispered.

I rolled over, my arms encircling him. I snuggled into his chest and kissed his skin.

"Morning," I answered, opening my eyes and smiling. "We got married yesterday, didn't we?"

He looked smug. "Yep. Tricked ya; now, you're mine."

I laughed as he pressed his lips to my ear and then moved his way to my mouth. "We get to do this every morning," I said.

"How lucky are we?"

"Promise not to get sick of me?"

"Stupid promise to make, Sage. I could never get sick of you."

"You say that now, when we're fresh and new. What happens after fifty years? You may hope to go deaf so you never have to listen to me," I teased. He ran a hand across my body, making me tingle from his touch. I wanted him to sink into me and stay, so we'd never be separated again.

"Fresh and new are for others. Others without pasts, others without heartache. You and I, we're old already. We'll grow older still—and maybe a little wiser."

"Do you feel wise now?" I asked. "Can I borrow some of that wisdom?"

He raised an eyebrow. "Married you, didn't I? That may be the wisest thing I've ever done."

———

"Go to Paris for a few days," Celia said.

"Maybe."

"You should have a honeymoon—even if it is a short one."

"We live in France. Every day is a honeymoon," I said with a laugh. "When was the last time you went on a vacation?"

"Valid point."

"I'm enjoying living in the present. If we go on a honeymoon, we'll just pack and head to the airport and decide our destination when we get there."

Late that afternoon, Celia left to begin dinner preparation. I was getting ready to head back to the cottage and wait for Kai, who was helping Luc and Armand around the vineyard. The front door of the bed and breakfast opened. I looked at the entrance, expecting to see guests returning for fruit and wine.

I gasped.

Jules' long, black curls were cut into a bob, and her blue eyes stared at me with resolute intensity.

"What are you doing here?" I gaped like a fish.

"Some greeting after five months of no communication." Jules crossed her arms over her small frame.

"Sage?" Kai called as he came into the lobby from the back.

Jules' gaze snapped to Kai, who was covered in sweat and dirt. "Who's this?"

"Kai," he said, putting out his hand. He looked at it, saw the grime, and pulled it back.

"Kai, this is Jules."

"*Jules* Jules?"

I nodded. "This is Kai."

Jules rolled her eyes. "Yes, I know, he already introduced himself."

"My husband."

The ticking of the grandfather clock let me know time passed, even as Jules continued to watch me in mute horror.

Kai made an instinctive and hasty retreat.

"*Husband?*" Jules squeaked. "You got *married*? To a fucking stranger?"

"He's not a stranger," I said, my voice rising.

"What did you do—marry the first guy you got into bed with?"

My hand reared back, and I slapped Jules across the cheek hard.

I didn't know who was more surprised. I looked at my palm, wondering if it had found a mind of its own. My gaze snapped to Jules, and my voice shook when I said, "You don't know shit. Don't pretend otherwise." I turned to stalk out of the room.

"Sage Eleanor Harper. Stop. Right. There."

"My last name is Ferris, and what have I told you about calling me by my full name?" I yelled, spinning around. I didn't care if anyone heard us.

"You slapped me!" Jules bellowed, a bright red handprint across her face. "You fucking slapped me!"

"Why are you here?"

"What reason do you want? You wouldn't answer my emails or calls, so I came, knowing you'd have to talk to me if I got in your face. And then you *slapped* me. Who the fuck are you right now?"

I didn't want to explain myself, so I said nothing.

"Have you told Connor?"

"Why would I tell him anything?"

"You don't think you owe him any sort of explanation?"

"No, I don't."

"How long have you been married?"

"Stop hurling questions at me!"

"Answer me!"

I felt weary and defeated. "Few days."

Jules' voice softened, "Can we do this sitting down?"

"You think I'd invite you into my home? Now?"

"I flew across an ocean to see you."

"I didn't ask you to do that."

"Just...let's sit down. Please?"

Once we were seated in the cottage, two glasses of bourbon poured but untouched, Jules said, "I can't believe you got married. I can't believe you got married without *me*."

I heard the distress in her voice; it cleared the last of the anger from my mind. "I'm sorry."

"Are you?"

"Yes. I didn't do it to hurt you." I was adamant. "And I'm sorry about the slap."

"I deserved it—I was mean."

"Astute of you." I smiled and took a sip of my drink.

"Was marrying Kai another one of your so-called symptoms? Are you still reeling?"

"*This*—this is why I didn't invite you. You think I'm broken and damaged, and moving to France was a mistake." Jules opened her mouth to speak, but I silenced her with a hand. "Don't bother. I'm well aware of how this looks. I didn't want to hear it—not from you. I still don't."

Upstairs, the bathroom door opened, and Kai's footsteps echoed across the wooden floor. I looked up as if I could see him through the ceiling. A smile with a volition of its own drifted across my face, like a puffy white cloud making its way in the blue sky.

"Holy shit."

My attention snapped back to my friend, and the smile faded from my lips. "What?"

"You're really in love with him—in a way you never were with Connor."

I paused. "Yes."

Jules stood, walked to the mantle, and stared at the photograph. "Is this Penny?"

"And Celia, from days gone by."

"She'd be happy—that you married Kai after such a short time."

"You think?"

"She was always worried you'd find yourself trapped in a loveless marriage. Worried you loved the idea of security more than you'd love the man you chose. She would've approved of you marrying for love."

"Kai and I, we're real."

She caressed the drying dandelion crown.

"I wore that at my wedding," I said.

"You *are* different. New York Sage would never have worn such a thing."

"New York Sage wouldn't have done a lot of things."

Jules took up residence in the chair again and said nothing.

When Kai came down the stairs, he seemed hesitant. I scooted over on the couch, making room for him and patted the seat cushion. He sat next to me, lending his silent support. I curled into his side and then looked at Jules, who watched us with keen interest.

"I don't forgive you, you know," Jules said, pretending Kai wasn't there. "For ignoring me these past few months, and for not inviting me to your wedding."

"But you understand?" I asked.

"Yes."

"I apologize, but I stand by my decisions."

Jules nodded. "Okay then."

"I'm glad you're here."

"No, you're not."

"I am," I said, "but I was afraid."

"Of what?"

"I thought if I saw you, I'd feel my mother's death all over again."

Jules picked up her glass of bourbon on the rocks and took a sip. "This is terrible."

"Careful," I warned. "You've got a Southerner sitting not five feet from you." Jules held the cold glass to her cheek, but I was the one who winced. "I'm a shit."

"Yep, my cheek is throbbing."

"You deserved it."

"Yeah, I did."

"You guys act like you're sisters," Kai noted.

Jules and I laughed. "You have no idea," we said at the same time, and then laughed again.

The three of us talked long into the night. After a few hours, Kai stood up and kissed me on the forehead, leaving Jules and me alone.

"More tea?" I asked, grabbing our cups. We had switched from bourbon to avoid getting too drunk.

"Sure," Jules said, looking thoughtful. "Your life is here now, isn't it?"

I nodded as I filled our mugs with hot water.

"What about Kai?"

"What about him?"

"Will he ever visit his family?"

"I don't know. I won't force him."

When we were too tired to carry on, I made up the couch and Jules settled down for the night. I crept upstairs and slid in bed next to Kai, who snored lightly. In his sleep, he wrapped his arm around me and patted my rump. I smiled, scooted closer and fell asleep.

Chapter 18

Sage

The following morning, we took Jules to the main house and introduced her to the Germains. Celia insisted on making a breakfast that lasted until lunch. Armand left to tend to the vines, but Luc lingered, and I didn't miss the interested glances in Jules' direction. It reinforced what I already knew; Luc had never had any real feelings for me. If she found him charming and interesting, then I'd give them my blessing. Every woman needed to have at least one torrid love affair while in France.

"Where are we going first?" Jules demanded after we finished eating.

"How about a tour of the vineyard?" Luc asked.

Jules smiled and took his arm. "Lead the way, and thanks for speaking English for my benefit."

I watched Luc guide Jules outside and then glanced at my husband. "That looks promising."

"I'm glad he's over you."

I stifled my laughter. "There was nothing to get over. Not really."

"Didn't he go to Italy for two weeks because you shot him down?"

"Jealousy becomes you," I teased. "Luc didn't know any better."

Kai looked thoughtful. "I bet Connor is still tortured."

I sighed. "Do you think Jules is right? Should I contact him?"

"Do you respect what you had together, even though it didn't work out?"

"I suppose so."

"There's no good way to tell him, but yeah, I think he deserves to know. If a woman I loved broke off our engagement, moved across an ocean, and remarried before the year mark, I'd be a wreck."

"*Any* woman, or a specific woman?"

He looked at me. "You. He's not the same after you; he can't be."

I smiled. "Are you the same?"

"Not even a little bit."

"Did I make you a better version of yourself?"

"Maybe," he joked. "Maybe even the best version of myself. How do you like that?"

Sighing, I tugged on his arm. "Come on, let's catch up with them."

"Think they'll do something crazy?" Kai gestured with his chin.

"Who knows?"

"How did you guys forgive each other so easily after not speaking for so long?"

"How did you and your friends handle stuff?"

"We punched each other."

"Well, I did slap her, but I apologized. I guess, sometimes, friendship is more than just years of history."

After the tour of the vineyard, we hopped into Luc's compact car and drove to downtown *Tours*. We walked around the Old Square, eating gelato, and Kai pointed out the Irish pub where he played.

"Will I get to see you in action?" Jules asked.

Kai smiled. "Absolutely."

Before the sun set we ducked into a café, squeezed ourselves around a small table and ordered two bottles of wine.

"How is it that the table wine in France is better than most wines in the U.S.?" Jules wanted to know.

"Because Americans don't know the first thing about wine. Among other things," Luc said with a grin.

"Your mother is American," Jules pointed out.

"But she married a Frenchman and became an expatriate."

"Touché."

Kai whispered to me, "I bet you five bucks he'll get her into bed by the end of the week."

I turned my head, my lips grazing his ear. "You kidding? She'll get *him* into bed by the end of the night."

Kai pretended to be scandalized. "You New Yorkers move really fast."

I put a hand on his leg and grinned. "*We* move fast? When did *you* propose?"

"Point taken."

———

Three days later, we were in McCool's watching Kai and his band play. A smattering of empty glasses sat in front of us, attesting to the length of time we'd been there. I had a nice buzz going, and I was getting itchy feet, wanting to dance.

"Your husband is kind of hot," Jules commented.

"Tell me about it," I said.

"You know, I'm sitting right here," Luc said, his arm around Jules. She looked up, smiled, and moved closer to him.

I grinned into my pint of cider. I'd been right about their time-line for getting together. Jules was only in town for another week, and there hadn't been time to wait—Luc wasn't complaining. I was happy for them, and I wondered if it would turn into something more permanent.

When the band stopped for a break, Kai sat down next to me and took a drink from my glass.

"You guys are good," Jules commented.

"Thanks."

"Do you plan on doing anything with it?" she pressed.

"Doing anything? I don't follow."

"Is this for fun, or are you hoping it goes somewhere?"

"God, you New Yorkers are so driven, aren't you?" Kai laughed. "Whatever happens, happens."

"How Southern of you." Jules stood up. "I need another drink."

"I'll come with you." Luc trailed after her.

"Ah, drive. I wonder what that feels like," Kai joked.

"I'm not sure it's all that it's cracked up to be," I answered.

"What do you mean?"

"Driven people always want more. They never know contentment."

"You sure about that?"

I smiled. "Nope."

I thought of my mother. She hadn't been happy unless she was writing, and even then her happiness was tainted with frustration and insecurity, wondering if she was going in the right direction. Maybe there was no *right* direction, only forward.

Jules and Luc returned, and I kicked Kai out of the booth. "I want to dance," I said. "So make it a quick jig."

Grinning, he rose. "Whatever you say, ma'am." He touched the brim of his hat, sauntered to the stage, and picked up his instrument. I stood and chugged the last of my pint.

"What are you doing?" Jules asked, when I grabbed her hand and tugged her towards the floor, forcing her to relinquish her newly acquired drink.

"We're dancing," I informed her.

"Who the hell *are* you?" she shouted over the din of music, but she was smiling. "You hate dancing!"

"Not anymore."

Jules must have learned her lesson—she no longer asked questions about my newfound sense of crazy, she just went along with it. The crazy wasn't going anywhere.

———

I dropped the letter into the mailbox before I could think better of it. I sighed, wondering how it would change Connor's life. I hoped it liberated him.

"He'll appreciate the gesture," Jules said, linking her arm through mine. We walked to a café for a quick bite alone before Luc drove Jules to Charles de Gaulle for her evening flight.

"You think? After he reads it, there's a very good chance he'll be performing Voodoo on a doll that looks like me." We settled into chairs, and I ordered for us in rapid French. "I'm sure he gave up thinking he'd hear from me ever again."

"Ah, no, he hasn't." Jules stared at a spot on the table, running her thumbnail in a groove of a wood seam.

"You talk to him, don't you?"

Jules continued to evade my gaze. "Every now and then. He's called to ask if I've spoken to you."

"You told him I'd come back, didn't you? That's why you've been on my ass to contact him."

"I'm sorry," Jules said, finally looking at me. The waiter dropped off our coffees. Jules reached for her cup, took a hasty sip, and then made a noise.

"Scald your tongue?"

"Little bit." Jules sighed. "What did you say in the letter?"

I rubbed a tired hand across my face. It had been a late night, but after everyone else had gone to sleep, I picked up a pen and wrote to my ex-fiancé, thinking uncomfortable words might be easier to write in the dark. Turns out it wasn't the dark that helped, but the liquor.

"I'm not sure it was entirely coherent," I admitted. "There was an apology woven in there—about breaking the engagement, but I also wrote that I should never have accepted his proposal in the first place."

"Oh, Sage…"

"Yeah, I was a little too honest, maybe. I told him he was a wonderful person, and he would make someone else very happy—though hopefully it wasn't as generic as all that."

"Did you tell him about Kai?"

"I told him I found someone, but not that I got married. I didn't think it would be nice to clobber him with that information. Maybe that can come later."

"You mean from me?"

"If you're so inclined. I'm sure he'll contact you as soon as he gets the letter."

"I'm sorry for this mess, for making him think you were just on a bender and you'd return to your senses."

I waved my hand, dismissing Jules' apology. "How were you to know? How were any of us to know? I should've contacted him long before now."

"Can I change the subject?"

"Please."

"Luc wants me to come back. Maybe at the end of summer. Is it okay that I'm with him? He told me he had thing for you when you first came here."

I smiled. "It was fleeting and nonexistent. He's a good guy, and you're a better fit for him. You both have the same outlook on life. You get each other. Just makes sense, y'know?"

"You mean that?"

"I do. Without a shadow of a doubt."

We finished our meals, and when it was time for Jules to leave, Luc loaded her bags into his car and got in to start the engine. Jules hugged Kai goodbye and whispered something in his ear that made him nod solemnly. I opened the passenger door and then put my arms around my oldest friend.

"You better email and call more, or I'll fly back over here just to kick your ass," Jules threatened.

"I promise." As they drove away, Kai and I watched them disappear down the road towards Paris.

"Everything okay?" Kai asked, rubbing a hand across my back.

"I miss her."

"She'll be back."

"I know."

"We can visit her in New York. Any time you want."

"You're so good to me."

He smiled, but it was sad. "I know what it's like to have friends that mean the world to you."

"Things are changing, aren't they?"

Kai took my hand and squeezed it. "Haven't they changed already?"

I squeezed back. "Yes. I suppose they have."

———

"Happy Birthday, Sage," Kai whispered. The windows were thrown wide open, and the June country air swirled around the room. After a light supper of fruit, bread and cheese, we had gone to bed but not to sleep. We had stayed awake, laughing and talking, not caring that dawn was close.

I snuggled deeper into his arms, relishing the feel of his warm skin beneath my cheek. "Twenty-seven. Wow."

"Do you feel old?"

"No. I feel like I'm getting younger. Is that weird?"

"Kind of. You ready for your present?"

"You didn't have to get me anything." Kai moved, and I groaned. "Come back." I heard the bedside table drawer open and the clanking of metal, and then Kai handed me a set of brass keys. Sitting up, I looked at him for an explanation. "What are these for?"

"I bought us a house."

My eyes widened. "*You bought us a house*—just like that?"

His smile faltered. "I wanted to surprise you."

"You bought a house? Without even consulting me?" No matter how many times I repeated it, I couldn't believe it. I shot out of bed and reached for my clothes. "I want to see it. Now." People didn't just buy a house on a whim, but Kai was a whim kind of man. I loved that about him—but a house?

Kai didn't argue. We borrowed Celia's car and drove in silence for twenty minutes before pulling up in front of a modest stone farmhouse. Most of it was swaddled in darkness.

I strolled to the quaint, red front door and touched the golden lion knocker, curious about my new home. Using my shiny new key, I stepped into the foyer, fumbled for a light switch and watched as the hallway blazed to life.

I ambled through the house, learning it like a lover. Kai followed at a discreet distance, allowing me time. I ran my hands over the whitewashed walls of the living room, noticing the open feel of the home. I went into the modern kitchen and marveled that it didn't detract from the rustic beauty of the rest of the house. Opening the back door of the kitchen, I saw moonlight glinting off a small lake and watched grass dance in the gentle summer breeze.

I took the spiral stairs to the second floor turret and found a large bay window that overlooked the property. It was the perfect room to write. Writing for me was inevitable now, like taking my next breath. To keep denying it would be to deny myself. Maybe I would get a typewriter, an old one. It would mean more when I finished whatever I decided to create. I would feel like I'd earned it through each punch of a sticky key.

When I came to the master bedroom, I pulled open the French doors and went out onto the balcony, cool predawn air caressing my skin. I sat on the stone floor, stretching my legs out. Kai crouched next to me.

"It's—"

I held up a hand, willing him silent. We sat in quietude, long enough for our bodies to grow numb, but still we didn't move.

By the time the sun crept up on the horizon, I had managed to find my voice. "The sky looks different here—it's golden. No, not golden exactly, butterscotch. And lavender, the color of cotton candy." I smiled in whimsical thought.

"Sage?"

"It's perfect." My voice turned to a muffled whisper. "You didn't ask me because you knew this house was perfect for us—it's a dream."

Moments we hadn't had yet flashed in my mind. Making love by the fireplace on cold winter nights; Kai standing in the doorway of the nursery while I watched him soothe our child in his arms. And years later, his temples stained gray with age and wisdom as he chased our children around the lake. Would five be too many?

"Do you want kids?" I blurted out.

He looked at me. "I think so, but I never thought much about it."

"I know we should've probably talked about this sooner, long before we got married."

"I always assumed I would, but it was a vague idea. What about you?"

"I thought I had a lot of living to do before I made that happen. The idea used to terrify me."

"And now?"

I shrugged.

"I'll give you anything you want. Making you happy is my reason for living." He took my hand and brought it to his lips. "Let's make a baby."

I inhaled a shaky breath. "We already have—I'm pregnant."

———

We drove back to the cottage in silence, the shock of my news infusing the air. It wasn't until we tumbled back into bed and held each other that he spoke.

"How far along are you?"

"Six weeks." I sighed.

"Why didn't you tell me sooner?"

"I wanted to be sure. I didn't plan this."

He laughed and laughed until he cried.

"What?" I demanded. "What's so funny?"

"You and me. Flying by the seat of our pants. Of course this would happen to us."

"You're unhappy about it, aren't you?"

He shook his head, pulling me close, so I couldn't leave. "No,

I'm sorry, darlin'; you misunderstand. Did you plan to marry a man you'd only known for a few months?"

"What does that have to do with anything?"

"Look at our relationship up until this point. Should I really be surprised you're pregnant?"

"I didn't trap you, I swear—"

"Oh, is that what you think this about?"

I nodded.

"I know you'd never do something like that."

I exhaled in relief.

"Things change all the time, Sage."

I looked up into his eyes; they were soft with emotion though there was nothing soft about him.

His hand touched my belly. "I didn't think my life could be this full. It all seems possible, now."

"What does?" I asked.

"Everything."

———

We moved into the farmhouse that week. I sat on the bank of our property, my bare feet in the cool water of the lake. Tilting my face up to the sky, I felt the sunbeams mark me. I could already feel my skin turning pink, but I didn't care. Let the perfect day stain my body.

"You look like a Baroque painting," Kai said from somewhere behind me. I turned my head and looked over my shoulder at him. He was shirtless, his red brand bright against the fair canvas of his chest. He wore a pair of old khaki shorts and his baseball cap; his hair was long and falling into his eyes, and he hastily brushed it off his forehead.

"What would the title of the painting be?" I asked, as he came and plopped down next to me, sticking his feet into the water and brushing my toes with his.

"*A Content Woman.*"

"Hmmm." I leaned my head against him. He was warm, familiar, like I had known him before this life. "We are defined by the joys as much as the tragedies."

"I want to give you so much joy you forget you ever had any tragedy. Fill you with so much light that it shoots out of your fingers and toes."

"Now, that would be an amazing painting."

"Maybe we'll have it commissioned, and we can hang it over the fireplace in the living room."

"And when our children ask what it means, what will you tell them?"

He pressed a kiss to my collarbone and said, "I will tell them you are my sun and the keeper of the light."

I sighed. I was a yellow balloon in danger of floating away. "Content doesn't seem right."

"No? What then?"

"*A Woman in Joy.*"

"*A Woman in Joy,*" he echoed. "A true masterpiece."

———

We were naked on a pallet of blankets in front of the unlit fireplace of the farmhouse. It was early evening, just past twilight. We owned a bed, but I was a bigger fan of the floor at the moment.

"Is this what you had in mind when you saw the house?"

I grinned. "Maybe. I definitely thought we'd be doing this in winter." Kai's fingers drew circles on my belly. "I was thinking we could paint the nursery green. None of that pink or blue crap."

"Green is good."

"Not mint green—forest green."

"Sage green?" he teased.

I laughed. "Do you want to find out the sex when it's time?"

"I already know."

"Do you?"

"It's a boy," Kai stated.

"You seem pretty sure of that fact. What happens if it's a girl?"

"Then it's a girl. I'd be happy with that, too."

"You want a son though, right? Don't all men want a son? A legacy?"

"Some legacy I am," he said, bitter resentment coating his tongue.

I touched his arm, but did not placate him with empty words. I doubted he'd listen to them anyway.

Kai sat up and gazed at the mantle. "I think I have to go back."

I stared at him; his revelation was a hammer on a glass window. "How long have you being thinking about this?"

"Ever since you told me you were pregnant. It changes everything. I can't look our kid in the eye and tell him I was a coward. I've got to go back and deal with things—finally deal with things."

I'd been dreading and hoping for this moment. How long could we have kept pretending that we were enough for each other? I wanted to tell him I was afraid, that our life wouldn't be the same after we went to Monteagle, but what did we have if we couldn't face his past? It would be a labyrinth, hedged with brutal emotions and unspeakable truths, but at least we'd find our way together.

"Okay." I wished I felt stronger. "We'll go."

He leaned over and placed a kiss on my stomach before wrapping his arms around me.

"It's always something, isn't it?" I said.

He pulled back, brushing his thumbs across my cheeks. "I think they call this *life*. I have to do this."

"I know." There wasn't just one moment that defined adulthood. Our lives were a series of rebirths. Some of us were born with indomitable spirits that ensured we got up, checked for broken bones and then started again.

He made me proud.

With one arm around me, Kai reached for his cell phone and held it, weighing it in his hand. He took a deep breath and dialed. After a few moments he said simply, "It's me. I'm coming home."

Chapter 19

Kai

Sage rested against my shoulder, sound asleep, and I brushed my lips across her forehead. We were somewhere over the Atlantic, and I knew that if I opened the airplane window shade, all I'd see would be darkness and gray clouds.

I felt like I was returning to my own funeral, so heavenly judges could weigh the balance of my life. I wondered if my faults outweighed the good deeds.

Sage made a whimpering sound and twitched before settling down. It'd been a week since we decided to face my family. Celia had put up a fight, telling us that Sage could travel now, but when she was in her third trimester it would be unsafe. I told Celia we'd be back long before then—I didn't want to linger in Monteagle. My life was in France with Sage, and soon our child, but I had to face my family.

My guilt had been a constant companion, and though I thought I had shut the door on my past, it came at me with a vengeful axe. It would find me no matter where I went. I couldn't run anymore; I had to stand and accept it. It would be harsh and ugly, but maybe it would give me peace. Maybe it would give everyone peace.

Sage finally stirred and awakened. Turning to me, she offered a sleepy smile. It seemed the woman held secrets and mystery in the corners of her mouth—more so than even the Mona Lisa. I didn't think I'd ever fully understand the quirk of those beautiful lips, even if I had years. And I would have years. *We* would have years. So many.

I wanted to protect her from everything, even myself—and most definitely my parents. I was about to subject Sage to my family— they were like angry bears. *Don't feed the animals, folks; they aren't tame!*

"Want some water?" I reached up and pressed the flight attendant call button.

Sage nodded. "I cried most of the way to France, you know."

"I'm crying on the inside," I drawled. "I wish I didn't feel compelled to do this."

"Blasted adulthood."

"Blasted reevaluation," I said. The flight attendant came, and I requested a bottle of water.

"Maybe some pretzels?" Sage asked. "Please?"

The woman turned off the call light and left.

"Are you going to tell me the plan, or are we winging it?"

"We're seeing Reece's parents first."

"It doesn't seem fair to just show up on their front porch."

I paused. "They know I'm coming."

"Yeah, I know you called them to let them know."

"I called them again."

"Oh. Do they know about me?"

"No, not yet."

"What about the baby? Are we going to tell them?"

"Eventually."

Sage turned her eyes to the closed window and lifted the shade. "I wish we were already there. The waiting is killing me."

"They'll love you."

"Will they?"

"Of course."

"What about your family? And don't lie to me."

"My grandmother, father, and brother will adore you."

"But your mother?"

"My mother hates *me* right now, so there's a good chance she'll hate you too." My tone and words had the desired effect I wanted—Sage laughed. I was kidding, sort of. I hadn't spoken to my mother, but I didn't need a crystal ball to know how she would react.

————

It was just past lunchtime when we climbed the porch steps of Reece's parents' ranch house. We were tired and nervous. I'd had so much coffee I was jittery, but Sage remained calm.

The screen was closed, but the main door was open; I could hear pans clattering in the kitchen and running water in the sink.

I stared at nothing for a long moment, Sage's hand gripping mine. I wondered if I ever would've found the courage if it hadn't been for her. Probably not.

With a deep breath, I finally rang the bell.

A middle-aged woman with graying blonde hair and a flour-smudged face appeared through the screen. She opened the door and then threw herself at me, the sound of her crying in my ears. I hugged and patted her back as I rested my cheek against her head, closing my eyes. She dropped her arms and swiped the tears off her cheeks as she turned her curious gaze to Sage.

"Alice, this is my wife, Sage."

Alice blinked. "Wife?"

"It's nice to meet—" Sage began, but was clearly caught off guard when Alice enveloped her in a strong hug.

Pulling away, Alice smiled. "It's wonderful to meet you, Sage. Go on into the kitchen. I'm going to run out to the barn and grab Keith."

"No doubt to warn him," I said. Alice threw me a look, raised an eyebrow, and went to find her husband. It was good to know that some things hadn't changed with time. She still had a sense of humor after everything she'd been through.

"What was that?" Sage demanded. "I expected anger when you told her about me."

"She doesn't think it's out of character," I explained with a wry grin, "even for me. I'm the kind of guy that leaves in the middle of the night on a whim, remember? It almost makes sense that I'd return with a wife."

We walked into the kitchen, and Sage settled into a worn chair while I opened the cupboard. Taking out two glasses, I went to the refrigerator and pulled out the carton of orange juice.

Sage laughed. "You're certainly at home here."

I smiled; it was both in pleasure and pain. The back door crashed open, and Keith Chelser stormed into the kitchen, his face wreathed in disbelief as if needing physical proof of my existence. The man was huge, a modern John Wayne, filling the kitchen with his height and breadth. He was what a cowboy hoped to look like.

When I was a kid, I thought he could crush me. But I'd seen his bear-paw hands deliver foals. I'd wanted to be him. Keith had heart and a moral code that ancient warriors could have lived by. Being near him now made me realize my own code was at the bottom of a lake. I'd have to hold my breath, swim down to the dark muddy goop and retrieve it if I wanted it back.

Keith embraced me, and then promptly withdrew and decked me across the jaw. I collapsed on scarecrow legs, but he immediately reached down to help me off the floor. I staggered like I was drunk, and Keith steadied me like I was a toy.

There was that moral code.

Looking at Sage, I grinned. She hesitantly smiled back, but then she stared at Keith, shooting him an angry glare.

She stood and craned her neck to peer at him. The cowboy towered over her, and it made me swallow a laugh. A fight between Sage and Keith?

I'd bet on Sage—always.

"You punched my husband."

"Yep," Keith said without apology. "Sage?"

"Yeah?"

He grinned. "Welcome to the family."

———

After a dinner of meatloaf and potatoes, and many hours of talking, Alice insisted we stay with them. She didn't take *no* for an answer. I didn't want to stay anywhere else anyway.

The window drapes of the guest room were open, letting in the moonlight. Sage burrowed close to me.

I inhaled deeply, and the muscles of my back relaxed as I exhaled. "You smell that?" I mumbled, pressing my head against hers. "It smells like sugar and nutmeg. It smells like home."

"It wasn't as bad as you thought it would be, was it?"

"No. They make it easy. Well, not easy, but they don't make it worse." The shock of seeing Alice and Keith had nearly felled me. I hadn't been prepared for the tiny lines of pain at the corners of Alice's eyes, put there by the grief of losing her only child. But she was like a rapier forged in fire now, hardened and almost unbreakable. Keith, on the other hand, looked like a tired, worn out saddle at the end of its life.

"When are you going to see Lucy?"

My voice was laced with guilt when I answered, "Soon. It's going to be rough. I left her alone to deal with everything—she doesn't have parents like the Chelsers. There's no home for her like this…she's alone."

"What about Tristan's family?"

"The Evanstons are proper, concerned with appearances. They're the kind of people that retreat into themselves when bad things happen. Lucy might as well have been by herself."

"I can't imagine what that must have been like for her," Sage said. "I don't think I could've been that strong."

I pressed my lips together in bitterness. "She shouldn't have had to be that strong. I should've stayed."

She ran a hand through my hair, but said nothing. Sage didn't try to absolve me, and I doubted I would've accepted absolution anyway.

———

The next morning, Sage lifted her head from the toilet and glared at me. "You rat bastard."

"I asked if you wanted me to hold your hair—you said no."

Rising from her spot on the bathroom floor, she went to the sink and washed out her mouth. "It's bad enough I've had to give up coffee and scotch, but the constant puking? Not fair. I feel like I have chronic sea sickness."

"You're beautiful."

"I'm green," she snapped. "I look like Kermit the Frog."

I rubbed a knuckle against my lips, trying to hide my smile.

"Fuck you."

I laughed.

We went downstairs to the kitchen, and Sage sank into a chair. Alice was at the stove, flipping bacon. Keith sat at the table, enjoying a cup of a coffee and reading the newspaper.

"Good morning," Alice said. "You guys hungry?"

"Famished," Sage said. I stared at her and raised an eyebrow. She shrugged.

"Famished?" Keith asked, lowering the newspaper. "I could've sworn I heard you throwing up right before I came downstairs."

Alice looked over her shoulder at Sage. "You feeling okay? Are you sick?"

Sage glanced at me, and I nodded. She announced, "I'm pregnant."

Alice made a noise in the back of her throat, and Keith's eyes widened.

"Can you not tell my parents?" I asked.

"You sound like a teenager," Alice said with a grin.

I rolled my eyes. "I'd just rather tell them in person."

"Like waiting to tell us about Sage until you were on our doorstep?" Alice teased. She patted Sage on the arm, and I knew I was right. Alice and Keith liked her. How could they not?

Alice set a plate of food in front of Sage. "Congratulations, but eat slowly. Trust me."

Keith laughed. "Congratulations—to the both of you."

After we ate, we showered and headed out. When we were on

our way, Sage looked at the colored bruise on my jaw and said, "God, he really decked you."

"Yeah, it hurt like a son of a bitch. He didn't hold back."

"It gives you a dangerous look. Not going to lie; I kind of like it."

"Then it was all worth it," I said with a wry grin.

Lucy lived in a small cottage along the edge of a glade in the house she had shared with Tristan. We parked the rental car and got out, but before we even reached the front door, it opened. A tall, slender, red-haired woman stepped out onto the porch.

She held a toddler.

My steps faltered. The baby made a noise, a cross between a squeal and a gurgle. His brown hair was mixed with traces of red, but his eyes were green.

Like his father's.

"Hello, Kai." Lucy's voice was weary, resolute.

I tried to speak numerous times before finally spitting out, "Why didn't you tell me?"

Lucy's face was pale, her eyes wide. "I didn't know for sure until after you were gone, and then there was no way to find you."

The guilt of leaving washed over me, compounded by coming face to face with Tristan's son for the first time. Lucy had needed me, and I'd left her. It was another reason to hate myself.

The toddler reached out, and without saying a word Lucy plopped him into my arms.

Tristan's son.

I looked into the boy's eyes, and my heart shattered into tiny shards of glass.

Fuck.

"You must be Sage."

"News travels fast," Sage said.

"Alice called, but I didn't believe her at first," Lucy explained. "Come in."

"Christ," I muttered. "If Alice called you, then she definitely called my mother."

Sage took a seat on the couch, and Lucy made her way to an old scarred recliner and collapsed into it. I saw exhaustion in the grooves around her mouth, the bags under her eyes. How much of it was heartache, and how much of it was raising a child alone?

I bit my tongue hard, stopping myself from asking her all the questions I didn't deserve answers to. "What's his name?" I sat down next to Sage with the baby on my lap.

"Dakota." She peered at her son. "He doesn't usually take to strangers."

I stared at her—I wasn't supposed to be a stranger, yet I was. "I should've been here."

"Yeah, you should've been," she stated. Dakota cooed and turned big green eyes to Sage, luring her attention.

"May I?" Sage looked to Lucy, asking for permission to hold Dakota.

Lucy nodded and without hesitation, I handed Dakota to Sage. I became mesmerized by the sight of her entertaining the toddler. It gave me a glimpse of our future—it was closer than I thought.

"So you're back."

"We are, but only for a little while," I explained.

Lucy closed her mouth, but her cheeks suddenly flushed red with anger. "Damn you."

I looked at Sage, who nodded in tacit understanding, stood up, and took Dakota out onto the porch. The front door clicked shut, and I was left alone with Tristan's widow.

Widow.

The word was supposed to be reserved for old women, wrinkled by time and with many years of love in their lives. Widow was not a word for Lucy. Vibrant, passionate, warrior—those were the words I would've called her.

"I'm so mad at you I can barely see straight," she seethed. "How could you—"

"I had to."

"You have no idea what the last two and a half years have been like for me."

"You have no idea what they've been like for me either."

"You should've stayed."

"Why? To be constantly reminded that they're gone?" I stood and faced her, no longer shying away from Lucy and all that I had run from —we dueled with words and hurt feelings. The years of grief burdened us both, but I wanted to claw my way out—I had too much to live for.

"When they died, everything was dark. All I saw was the next bottle of bourbon, the next place to move. I never thought I'd meet a woman I wanted to marry. She's more than that, Lucy. She's the reason I came back." I sighed wearily. "She's pregnant."

Lucy's ire diffused, replaced by shock. "You're kidding?"

"Nope. We're going back to France."

"Why?"

"What do you mean, *why?*"

"What's keeping you there?"

"We bought a house."

"So sell it. *This* is your home."

"No." My voice was unyielding granite. "I can't, Lucy. I can't walk around every corner expecting to see my two best friends. If I moved back here, I'd never sleep well again. I don't get how you can stand it here."

"Where else am I supposed to go?" she demanded. "Take my son away from his grandparents? Away from the Chelsers? Away from—"

I looked at her, sharp and assessing. "Away from who?"

She took a deep breath. "Wyatt."

The name was like being thrown into an avalanche of snow; the air left my lungs and I felt cold and buried. "Wyatt? My brother?"

Two patches of red appeared at the top of her cheekbones, only this time it wasn't anger coloring her. "Yes."

"I'll kill him."

"I love him, Kai."

"You love *Tristan*," I gritted out.

The sharp contours of her face softened. "Of course, I do, but am I supposed to be alone the rest of my life? Am I supposed to never love again?"

"How long?"

"*What?*"

"How long did you wait before you got together?"

Her blue eyes were stormy. "Fuck you, Kai."

"How long, Lucy?"

"None of your goddamn business!"

We glared at one another. I wondered if learning to love again was a betrayal. But Tristan was dead; he'd left behind a wife and a son. Didn't Lucy deserve some measure of happiness? If I'd been here, would it have happened? Thinking about the what-ifs of my life would sink me. I couldn't change them.

"He's loved me for years. Did you know?" Lucy asked.

"No, I didn't."

She paused before saying, "A year—nothing happened for a year. Dakota was sick and in the hospital. Wyatt had been coming around, checking in on me. I called him, and he came. I could depend on him; he's been solid, steady."

It didn't sound at all like the kind of love she'd had with Tristan. Theirs had been a wild, tempestuous, burn-everything-to-the-ground kind of love.

Which kind meant more?

While I reeled from revelations, she wasn't through giving them. Lucy took a deep breath. "He's asked me to marry him—and I've said yes."

———

A car door slammed, and a moment later, I heard my brother's voice on the porch. I stalked outside, ignoring Sage and Dakota, eager for a confrontation with Wyatt.

"You," I fumed, the full force of my wrath directed at Wyatt. I heard Lucy moving behind me.

"He knows?" Wyatt peered at Lucy for confirmation, his face wreathed in calm acceptance.

"Yes." She strode towards Wyatt to stand near him in a show of solidarity.

"Knows? Knows what?" Sage asked in confusion, handing off Dakota to his mother.

"Wyatt asked Lucy to marry him." My voice was full of outrage on behalf of my dead friend. I took another menacing step towards Wyatt, my fists clenching for a fight.

Sage moved between us to ease the tension. Her voice was low, but solid like steel as she said, "Don't do it. It'll make things worse."

I glared down at Sage, "Lucy is—"

"Not yours to defend."

I was in no mood to be placated. Cursing violently, I stalked past my brother and trekked into the woods, wanting to leave it all behind.

"He just needs some time," I heard Sage say right before I was out of earshot.

I wanted to hit something, but I was afraid I'd never stop, so I let my feet carry me instead. The sound of swishing trees filled my ears, the smell of warm earth in my nose; I knew where I was headed.

The cemetery was empty of mourners as I strolled to Reece's modest headstone. Next to it was Tristan's, and I grimaced when I looked at it—it was a monument, colossal and grotesque, nothing like Reece's. *Appearances*, I sneered. The Evanstons would never have let their son's death go unnoticed.

My friends should've been buried in the mountains in unmarked graves, part of the earth they came from. It's what they both would've wanted, but at least their parents had done something right, and had laid them to rest next to one another. It made it easy for me when I paid my respects. I snorted. *Easy.* Nothing about this was easy.

"What the fuck," I said to the ground, knowing I wouldn't get a reply.

Wyatt would marry Lucy, and he would be the only father Dakota would ever know. My brother was a good man, but could he love Lucy the way a woman with heartache and darkness needed to be loved?

I swam through my thoughts with a powerful breaststroke, but I didn't find any peace.

Afternoon wore on, and I did not return. Instead, I took up vigilance, sitting with my back against a tree. The sun traveled across the sky as I talked to the ghosts of my two friends, trying to rectify my past so I could have a future.

I wondered how Sage was getting along with Wyatt. What was he telling her? Scaring her, no doubt, about what she was about to endure when she faced our parents.

A car door slammed in the distance, and a few moments later Sage ambled through the cemetery. The headstones looked bare, solemn in the green lawn. Gold rays glinted off the leaves, aiding in the serenity where bodies rested eternally, their souls long gone.

Without a word, she eased down next to me and plucked at the grass. A slight breeze played with her hair. "How are you doing?"

I shrugged, surprised that I no longer felt anger. I was resigned. "Life's odd, you know? I should've been prepared for things to be different when I came back. My life is different, why wouldn't Lucy's be? Wyatt's?" Looking at her, I grinned in wry humor. "Time didn't stop while I was away."

She stood up and reached a hand down. I grasped it, rose, and pulled her into my arms. "Be happy for them," Sage whispered.

"I am—sort of."

I hoped that Wyatt loved Lucy the way I loved Sage. Perhaps Wyatt and I were more similar than I had thought, and maybe our tension had no place in adulthood. We were men now, hardened in the fires of life.

Sage laughed. "No, you're not."

"You've got to understand…Wyatt is my brother. A brother I never got along with, never felt any sort of kinship with. He's in love with Lucy, Tristan's wife. Tristan—my brother in every way except blood."

"He loves her, and he loves Dakota too," she pointed out. "If you can't be happy for Wyatt, be happy for them. Wouldn't Tristan want this for her, for his son?"

"Part of him would want her to move on, find someone, love again," I conceded.

"But the male part of his brain would demand she love and pine for him forever?"

"Something like that. You understand them, don't you? My friends you've never met."

"You've painted a vivid picture of them." She stared into my eyes. "I'd want you to find someone."

My arms tightened around her, unable to fathom such a horrible idea as living a life without her. "Nothing is going to happen to you."

"You're right." She pressed her lips to mine. "We're going to grow old and wrinkly together."

I sighed in contentment.

"I told Wyatt I'm pregnant. Think he'll tell your parents?"

"Not if he knows what's good for him."

She smiled. "He picked Lucy. I think he has a fair idea of what's good for him. He invited us to a family dinner with your parents."

"When?"

"Tomorrow night."

"You mean we've got a whole day before entering the lion's den?"

"That gives us twenty-four hours to prepare."

"Hate to break it to you, darlin', but twenty-four hours isn't enough. I've had twenty-nine years, and I'm still not ready for this moment."

"It's time to face them," she said. "You can do this; I know you can."

The faith she had in me was staggering. *Nothing like the love a good woman, right?* I didn't know why she loved me, but I'd take it. "You don't know what you're getting into," I warned.

———

I open my eyes, watching the sun rise over the lake as I perch on a rock. Tristan is on the bank, fishing pole in hand, casting away.

"Any luck?" I ask.

"With life, or fishing?" Tristan answers with a question.

"Aren't they the same thing?"

Tristan's smile is wide, devilish. "No point in life if you can't fish."

"You're so Norman Maclean right now."

"I prefer David James Duncan."

"You would."

"So Lucy and Wyatt…"

"Ah, you know."

"I do."

"You're not mad."

"I was, for a while. Reece got to hear all about it. I'm okay with it now."

"How?" I demand. "How can you be okay with it?"

"You wouldn't understand."

"Explain it to me."

Tristan's gaze is steady. "You left voluntarily. You just…up and left. You went somewhere else, and you didn't look back."

"I didn't have much to keep me here." I defend myself, but there's no anger in my voice.

"But still, you left. I was forced by fate. I left a wife behind. She was alone, terrified, grieving—and pregnant. If she'd been the one to die and I had to go on…" He shudders visibly at the thought. "There were countless nights she cried non-stop, curled up in our bed. Do you know what it's like to leave the woman you love, and watch her live without you, hoping she finds the strength because you're not there to give it to her? Only death was powerful enough to make me leave her."

Tristan's haunted eyes lock on mine, and I see my own heart reflected in them —twisted, ravaged, then stitched back together but barely beating.

"Wyatt gives Lucy the strength she needs to go on. He protects her, and loves my son as his own. Life never looks the way you think it will. Never in a million of my dreams did I think my wife would end up with your brother. But I never thought I'd die, either—unable to touch her, hold her, wipe the tears from her eyes. I don't get to be there when our son grows into a man. Wyatt will have that honor. Do you know what that feels like?"

"Are you in Heaven?" I wonder, my voice gritty, my throat tight with regret and pathos.

"Technically, spiritually, or hopefully?"

"All of the above."

143

Tristan's mouth curves into a ghoulish, gruesome smile. "I'm in limbo, waiting until I can see Lucy again. But she has a long life to live first. A life without me."

"Do you know that for sure?"

He laughs in sardonic humor. "Nothing is for sure, Kai."

Chapter 20

Sage

The Ferris' library was quiet, the air salted with strain and implied accusations. I sat next to Kai on a black leather couch while Claire Ferris stared at her wayward son as though she didn't recognize him. To his credit, Kai didn't wear the University of Tennessee baseball cap that was usually glued to his head. He had even combed his hair for the occasion. I wanted to mess it up. It made him look like someone else, someone orderly, not my Kai.

Wyatt was in the corner, clutching his drink and sending me subtle looks of support. I liked Wyatt. I liked any man that went after the woman he wanted, despite insurmountable obstacles.

George stood by the liquor cart, putting ice cubes into glasses. I studied Kai's father and I struggled to see any family resemblance. It was Wyatt who favored George in looks—blond hair, blue eyes. Kai really was the black sheep of the family, it seemed.

I turned my attention to George's mother. She smiled wide, and I felt myself relax a bit. I recognized that smile instantly. It was Kai's. Memaw just might be a kindred spirit.

"Can I get you a drink, Sage?" George offered.

An entire bottle of scotch, I wanted to say. Instead, I said, "Club soda, please."

"Kai?"

"Bourbon on the rocks."

After George handed us our glasses, he took a seat next to his wife on the couch facing us. I was in the front row for the Ferris family fight.

"So, you're staying with the Chelsers?" Claire asked, smashing the silence.

Maybe I can hide behind that big desk over there...

"You already know the answer to that, Mom."

"And you've seen Lucy?"

Kai's sigh was labored. "Yes."

"So, we were your last stop?" Claire's voice was frosty, like Superman's Fortress of Solitude.

"Saving the best for last," Kai said in a sarcastic voice.

Memaw almost spit out her drink, but managed to contain her laughter.

"What took you so long to come back?" Claire demanded, ignoring her mother-in-law.

"Claire," George warned.

"No. I have the right to know why my son decided to visit everyone before his own parents."

"Yeah, I know this is bad—" Kai looked pained.

Claire glared as she went on, "And why he stayed away without a single word for two-and-a-half years before coming home."

"Home—is that where I am?"

My husband could play mean when he wanted. This wasn't going well. Not at all.

"Kai," I pleaded.

"No, let him speak. Are you planning on continuing your little jaunt across the world, or are you going to stay in Monteagle, be an adult, and live up to the Ferris name?"

"I *am* an adult."

"Well, you're not acting like one," Claire snapped.

"We bought a house in France."

"Doesn't make you an adult."

"We are going to raise our baby there."

It was like a vacuum had sucked all the air out of the room. The ice in the drinks clinked against glass. Kai's breathing was heavy, like he'd run some great distance.

"Baby?" Memaw asked. "You're having a baby?" She looked at me, and I nodded slightly. All at once they seemed to remember that I sat among them.

"Did you know about this?" Claire stared at her oldest son. Wyatt's jaw clamped shut, but he inclined his head. Claire turned her attention back to Kai, her eyes narrowing. "You can't live in France. Especially not now. Now that she…"

I wondered why Claire couldn't finish the sentence. She didn't believe it, maybe, or didn't want to believe it. Well, if I had any doubts about what she thought of me, I didn't need to wonder any longer. The woman couldn't even say my name. We'd just told her she was going to be a grandmother, and yet there was no joy in her voice. If my mother had been here, there would've been hugs, tears, and celebration. There would've been so much happiness it would've felt like a gift from the stars.

Mom. Someone would be calling me that one day. One day soon.

"Why can't we live in France?" Kai demanded.

Claire made a sound of exasperation. "What will you do there?"

Kai shrugged. "Whatever I want."

I was exhausted, even though it was Kai fighting each round. No matter how many verbal fists he took to the jaw, he got up, ready for more. I fell deeper in love with the tortured man I had married. The father of my child. My husband. My strength.

"Sage, do you want to come sit outside with me?" Memaw asked. I looked at Kai who nodded and squeezed my hand. A reprieve. I'd take it.

"I'll just…" Wyatt said, moving towards the door. "Oh hell, I'm getting out of here."

I snorted with surprised laughter as I let Memaw lead me out of the library and through the house. The photographs on the walls were exhibits of memories from Kai's childhood. As we walked past a pristine kitchen occupied by a private chef, I understood more about the Ferris family than I ever would from any line of questioning.

"Let's go out back," Memaw suggested. "It's the only redeeming quality of this otherwise cold house." Once we were on the porch, we settled into plush chairs and looked up into the dark purple sky; the sun had set, and the night was soft and quiet. "So, you're pregnant."

"I am."

"Are you excited?"

I looked at her, and Memaw shrugged.

"Inane question, I know."

"I am excited." It was the truth—children no longer terrified me. I had Kai. What did I have to be scared of? I rested a hand on my belly, breathing in the heady mountain air.

"Y'all didn't wait…"

"Ah, no, we didn't."

"Planned?"

"Nope."

"Most things aren't."

"Death never is, so why should conception be any different?" My voice came out hard and warped, like twisted steel. I didn't mean it to, but I felt I had the right to be defensive.

Memaw glanced at me. "I wasn't judging you—either of you."

"Okay."

"As long as you're both happy."

I smiled. "My mom used to say fitting yourself into a box is like wearing shoes that are too small. Convention is a box people put themselves in because they don't know where else to go."

"Your mother sounds like a wise woman."

"She was."

"Was?"

"She died—not even a year ago."

"I'm sorry."

"I know what you're thinking."

"Do you?"

"You think we jumped into this too soon, don't you?"

"That's Kai."

I looked at her in confusion. "You're not upset?"

Memaw chuckled. "Let me guess; he decided he wanted you, whether or not you wanted him back."

I laughed. "You know your grandson."

"I do."

"I chose him, too. Not right away, but—"

"He's Kai."

"Exactly." I had been cold before I met Kai—barren, empty. He had been the sun, and I the dying bloom. Maybe we were both and neither. I rubbed my stomach in thought. I didn't like to think about what turns my life would've made if Kai and I hadn't found each other, but we did.

"The baby sparked his conscience," I went on. "He didn't want to be known as a coward, so he came back to face…everything."

I had never called Kai a coward. That was his own word for himself. Another box.

"Part of him died when Reece and Tristan did," Memaw said.

"I know. You can't outrun your past, no matter how hard you try, and believe me, Kai tried. But he can't live here. As much as he loves it, it would be a constant reminder of all he's lost, and he wants to look to the future. Will his parents understand that?"

Memaw gazed into the sky, as if she'd find the words written in the stars. "I don't know. Kai has never done anything they wanted him to do."

"Maybe they should stop expecting him to be who they want and just let him be himself. They see him as a disappointment, the screw up, don't they?"

Memaw's non-reply was her answer. We sat in silence for a time before she finally said, "Kai never sought his parents' approval—for anything. He had Tristan and Reece and they were the only people he was accountable to, the only people he *wanted* to be accountable to. George and Claire never really understood that."

"And Wyatt? Did he understand it?"

"Wyatt grew to understand and accept it because he didn't have a choice. It's hard for him, even now, knowing he and Kai have never been close."

Resigned, I stood. "Should we go back in there? See if the smoke from the dueling pistols has cleared?"

"Are you going to rescue him?"

"You think he needs it?"

"Without a doubt."

———

Dinner was a silent, stunted affair; there was no attempt at polite conversation. There was plenty of alcohol consumption, long disdainful looks, and enough tension to gorge on. I stared at my plate most of the time, enjoying the duck in a fig reduction sauce. I didn't miss the irony of being fed a decadent meal, all the while Claire making me feel like I didn't deserve it. She observed me through dinner; her eyes trained on my hands, examining me while I ate the main course with a salad fork. I did it just to piss her off. It was cheap, but it felt good.

The minute dessert was over, we rose to leave.

"You aren't taking a plane out tonight, are you?" Claire asked.

Kai threw his mother a look and said, "No, Mom. We bought one way tickets so we can leave whenever we want."

"You might as well take your car back. While you're here," George said. "Keys are on the front table."

Kai looked at his father in surprise. "Thanks." We walked to the garage and Kai's black Mercedes sat in its spot.

"You weren't lying, were you? About the money."

"The car was a college graduation present." Kai plopped the car keys into my hand, and I had to admit I was itching to get behind the wheel. "I'm too buzzed to drive."

"Lucky bastard. If I wasn't growing a human, I'd be hammered."

Kai laughed and then hugged me. "God, I have no idea what I'd do without you."

"You never have to find out. What are we going to do with the rental?"

"Return it tomorrow. Get in."

Once we were on our way back to the Chelsers', I said, "Tell me about the showdown."

"Dad let my mother do most of the talking. She asked if you married me for my money."

I snorted.

"You're not surprised?"

"Not at all—Wyatt warned me."

"Did he? When?"

"When you were at the cemetery. He told me more about your parents than you did."

"So you didn't walk in totally blind?"

"No, I knew it was coming." I laughed.

"What?"

"Our mothers are complete opposites. My mother lived in truth. Your mother lives in denial." I pulled into the gravel driveway and parked next to Keith's green truck.

"Yeah, when she was talking I could see the disappointment on Dad's face. Doesn't matter, though; I feel great. You know why?"

"Bourbon?" I smiled. I loved this giggly drunk version of Kai. Usually, when we drank, we suffered great melancholia. Not tonight, apparently.

"Partly. But I faced my parents, told them what I wanted, and I didn't care if they supported me or not. And the thing is, I meant every word." We got out of the car, and Kai grabbed my hand and led me to the stables.

We ducked into the barn; a few horses neighed in greeting, but most ignored us. Finding an empty stall, he grabbed a couple of horse blankets, threw them onto the straw and pulled me down. I cuddled into his arms. I was drowsy from food and the smell of him. He was better than a sedative.

"I just want some time with you here."

Before I knew it, my eyes were closing, and I was falling asleep, wrapped in security and warmth.

———

"My mother wants to throw us a wedding reception," Kai said two days later. He poured a cup of coffee and sat down at the kitchen table. Keith was already tending the horses, and Alice was collecting eggs from the chickens.

"No." I eyed the coffee in forlorn longing. "I will not be paraded around in her social circle so she can pretend to accept us."

"I told her we weren't going to be in town long enough for her to put it together."

I raised my eyebrows. "I bet she didn't take that excuse."

"She had the nerve to say that I was ashamed of you; otherwise, I'd want to show you off and tell everyone we're happy and expecting a baby."

"She's good." I sighed. "You agreed, didn't you?"

"Call it a gesture of goodwill."

"Did she give you a time frame for this event?"

"September."

"That's over two months away!"

"I know, but Mom wants to have the party at the Hermitage Hotel in Nashville. It's the earliest available date."

"Joy."

"Black tie."

"Didn't doubt that for a second."

"She wants you in a wedding dress."

"*Absolutely not*," I declared. "I'm not going to be the pregnant girl in a big poofy dress. I will not look like a frosted cupcake."

Kai's lips twitched.

"This isn't funny, Kai."

He stared into his cup before peering at me with an abashed look. "I sort of already told her she could take you dress shopping."

We gazed at one another and I said, "If you weren't the father of my child…"

"Okay, I get it, I owe you big time."

"Yeah, you do."

———

I sat in the passenger side of Claire's car as we drove in silence towards Nashville. Stifling my disdain for the situation, I was determined to get through this with whatever grace I possessed, but I didn't have a lot of reserves left.

Kai had volunteered to go with us, but I refused. I wouldn't let him be the buffer—I had to endure this; I would endure this, no matter the cost. I wouldn't cower or hide, and certainly not behind my husband. He'd been through enough.

"Why are we doing this?"

"Because we have to." Claire glanced at me from behind black Dior sunglasses.

"Says who?"

"Me."

Claire was all about appearances—that much was obvious. I didn't miss her snide look as she took in my messy bun and lack of makeup. I was wearing a pressed white button-down, skinny jeans, and black flats.

I can't be that embarrassing, can I?

Ignoring her, I lost myself in thoughts of *Tours*. How were Armand and Luc doing? The vines needed pruning, no doubt. And Celia? Was the bed and breakfast full of eager guests looking for new experiences?

"You manipulated him into marrying you."

Hurled in a quiet tone, the accusation was more powerful for it. It ricocheted off the glass windows, landed in my lap, and now I'd have to deal with it. Keith had reconciled his anger with Kai by using his fist. Claire, Southern belle that she was, delivered blows in the form of verbal lacerations.

I would've preferred the fist.

I went from simmer to boil in moments. "Have you ever even met your son? He's got a will of his own—he's not a marionette on strings."

"He's a runner. He'll leave you."

I fingered my wedding ring, a simple thin band that meant more to me due to its simplicity. Every time I looked at it, I thought about how far we'd come, how far we still had to go. I knew deep inside that Kai would never leave me, no matter what anyone thought.

"You have no faith in him, do you?"

"He's proven that when things get hard he can't handle it."

"People change. I understand why you're upset. Your son left you for two years." I studied her. Her face was pinched with tension and pale with pain. "You're waiting for him to leave home again."

"He will," Claire answered tightly. "You'll go back to France and raise your child there. I'll never see my son. I'll never see my grandchild."

"Do you really think I'd keep you away?"

"I don't know. I don't know anything about you."

"All you need to know is that I love your son."

Claire pulled in front of the Hermitage Hotel, a beautiful, architectural gem in downtown Nashville. A valet took the car and drove off, and I followed Claire into the lobby. A short woman with hair in a no-nonsense bun held a clipboard and a pen, waiting for us. Claire greeted her and then turned to introduce me.

"Charlene, this is my daughter-in-law, Sage."

I wondered if part of Claire died admitting it.

"Pleased to meet you," Charlene said, shaking my hand. "If you two will follow me to the Grand Ballroom, we have some table settings for you to pick from."

The room was dimly lit; dozens of tables were adorned with different china sets and flower arrangements. I didn't pay attention to the mindless babble between Charlene and Claire as I walked around, hoping instead for one beautiful table to appeal more to me than another. It reminded me of a time, not so long ago, when I was with Connor choosing the menu for our wedding. The memory sat like curdled milk in my stomach.

"Sage, what do you think of this one?" Claire called out.

I strolled over to a round table laden with a white tablecloth and white china with gold accents. The stemware was fine crystal, and had an elegant gold band around the lip to match the china, and the silverware gleamed in candlelight. It looked royal and out of touch. I shook my head in disapproval as we moved from table to table. After a few minutes I watched as Claire and Charlene exchange a look, and Charlene walked off, leaving us alone.

"You don't like the settings?" Claire asked, her voice tight with impatience.

"No, I don't."

"What are you looking for?"

"Not these. They all look the same to me. It's all too formal."

Claire raised her perfectly sculpted eyebrows. "What would you have us do? Remove all the tables and have a picnic?"

"Sounds great to me."

I watched Claire's face turn the color of a plum tomato as she attempted to keep herself under control.

I crossed my arms over my chest. "Look, I don't care. This is *your* party. This isn't us—this is *you*, and we're doing this for *you*."

"Then why are you here? I could've made all these decisions without you and not gone through this."

"Go ahead," I allowed. "Save us both a headache; this was *your* idea."

"This was not my idea—none of this was my idea. You think I wanted this? My son married to a stranger?" Claire shouted.

"What's wrong with you? We're happy. Don't you want that for your son? What did you expect, Claire?" My emotions were cranked up high with a little help from pregnancy hormones.

"Well, I didn't expect for him to come back with a wife!" Claire's face was pinched in rage.

"But he did! And no matter how terrible you are to me, I'm not going anywhere!"

Tears of anger filled my eyes as I spun on my heel, eager to be out of the ballroom. Somehow, I found my way to the bathroom and collapsed on the long white couch. Grabbing a couple of tissues, I blew my nose. The tip turned red when I cried. It would take hours for it to return to normal. Everyone would know my mother-in-law had caused me grief.

The bathroom door opened. Claire came in, approaching the sink. She washed her hands with her back to me but said nothing. She seemed composed, calm, like we hadn't just been screaming at one another. I didn't have the strength for another confrontation, and would save my energy for the things that mattered—the wedding reception wasn't one of them. I wouldn't bother talking to her about anything else. She had her opinions and puffed up rhetoric wouldn't sway her anyway.

"The white table cloth with gold accents is fine," I said.

Claire did not reply as she wiped her hands dry.

"I'll even wear whatever dress you want," I relented.

"You will?"

"One condition—Kai and I get to have a bluegrass band for the party."

"Any dress I choose?"

"Any dress you choose."

Claire nodded. "You have a deal."

Four hours later, I cursed myself as I stood on a platform in front of three mirrors and a handful of bridal boutique attendants. My mother-in-law sipped champagne, looking very pleased with herself.

I was in a strapless ball gown with a satin corset, a full tulle skirt and tulle overlay. On the back of the dress was a peplum of organza petals. I looked like I belonged miniature sized on top of a wedding cake, but I turned to Claire and managed a smile, even though I wanted to throw up—and it had nothing to do with pregnancy.

For the wedding day, she would groom me into what she wanted. And I would let her because I loved Kai.

"Perfect," Claire said with a smug grin.

That night, I crumpled onto the couch and refused to move. Kai sat down, picked up my feet, and let them rest across his lap. "You're a sport," Kai said as he began to rub my toes.

I purred in delight. "Your mother is pure evil. You won't believe the dress she picked out. Tell me about your day. Distract me from the memory of all the tulle."

Kai laughed. "I helped Keith with the horses and tried to get Tristan's father on the phone."

"Any luck?"

"No. I left messages, but he hasn't called me back. I think he's avoiding me."

"It's all *Alice in Wonderland* right now."

"What does that mean?" he asked.

"You know when she falls down the rabbit hole and then goes through the hourglass and turns upside down? That's what you've done, coming back here—turned everything upside down."

"I should be patient, shouldn't I?"

"Yes, and you should keep rubbing my feet."

Chapter 21

Kai

I slipped out of bed, watching the rise and fall of Sage's chest. She slept soundly; I touched her hair and leaned over to kiss her forehead before I left the guest room. I drove on autopilot on a road I had driven a thousand times. The terrain steepened as I entered the mountains, and twenty minutes later I pulled into the driveway of my grandmother's small wood cabin.

Cutting the engine, I got out of the car. The stars were bright, and the night was warm—I loved summertime in Monteagle. I missed this place more than I had thought.

I tread quietly, not wanting to scare the crap out of Memaw, but then the front door opened, and she stood in the doorway.

"What are you doing here?" she demanded.

"Couldn't sleep."

"So you thought you'd pop by for a midnight chat?" She smiled.

"You're awake, aren't you?"

"I am." She pulled the sash of her bathrobe tighter across her body. "I was going to make some tea. Want some?"

I sat in the kitchen as she heated water, and when she was done we took our mugs out onto the back porch to watch the stars. "It's nice out here," I said.

"Reminds me of all those nights in your childhood when you came to stay here with me and your grandfather."

"Those were the best." My voice was tinged with fondness. "Ice cream sundaes for dinner; pitching a tent in the backyard and pretending to go camping." I sighed. "This was more than my home—it was my haven."

"What about the Chelser ranch? You spent a good amount of time there, too."

I grinned. "That was the club house."

We laughed, and Memaw reached over to touch my arm. "I'm glad we could be there for you."

"You really have no idea what you've done for me. I wouldn't have survived without you and Grampy. I'm sorry we lost two years."

"But you're not sorry you left."

I shook my head. "I met Sage."

She smiled. "We all have our own journeys, Kai. Never apologize for where yours takes you."

"How did you go on after Grampy died?"

"The same way you did. I chose life."

I took a deep breath. "I thought I had lost everything when I lost Tristan and Reece, but now I have Sage, and I'm afraid all the time. I can't lose her too."

"That's how you know you have something truly beautiful, Kai. That's how you know your love will last a lifetime."

———

I crept into the Chelsers' house, surprised to find Keith in the kitchen, heating something on the stove.

"I thought you went to bed hours ago," Keith commented as I sat at the table.

"I did—couldn't sleep, so I went for a drive. What are

you doing?"

"Warming some milk."

"No bourbon?"

Keith smiled and went to the cabinet. He pulled out two cups, poured the milk into them and handed one to me.

I took a sip of warm milk and grimaced. "This is terrible."

"Yep," Keith agreed, sitting down with his mug.

"You don't sleep well?"

Keith shrugged. "Not anymore. Doesn't matter how long or how hard I've worked, I still wake up in the middle of the night."

"And the milk helps?"

"No, but it's habit now. Sometimes Alice is awake, too, and we have a nice long talk."

"Ever try pills?"

Keith made a face. "Poison."

I was silent and thoughtful. Pills had never been my choice to help me forget. Bourbon seemed destructive enough—and the women before Sage.

"What's on your mind, son?"

"I've tried getting in touch with Tristan's dad, but I haven't heard anything."

Keith's lined face looked resigned. "Alexander and Evelyn are separated."

"What? When?"

"For about a year, now," Keith admitted. "They had problems long before Tristan died."

"Shit. Why didn't Lucy tell me?"

"She doesn't know."

"Are you kidding me?"

Keith shook his head. "They don't want anyone to know."

"How are they keeping it a secret?"

"They still appear together in public but live separately."

"Appearances, huh? I can't believe it."

"Some people can't survive the tragedy of losing a child."

"You and Alice did."

Keith smiled, but it was buried by sadness. "You haven't been here to know what we've gone through, son, and I'm glad you weren't."

"Really?"

"Yes. You can't look back." Keith shrugged. "It was rough for a while, like living with a stranger."

"You guys were stronger than the tragedy."

"We're stronger in spite of it. I wouldn't wish losing a child on my worst enemy. It goes against the laws of nature—we were supposed to go first." He sighed. "Go to bed, Kai. Crawl in bed next to your beautiful wife and hold her."

Taking Keith's suggestion, I did exactly that, and wrapped my arms around Sage, who instinctively rolled towards me and whimpered in her sleep. I felt joy mixed with sadness, and pondered if life would ever be one without the other.

———

"Do you ever wonder what your life could've been?" Reece asks.

"Sure, who doesn't?" I answer.

"Are there moments in your life where you knew that if you had taken a different path, everything would've been different?"

"I almost went to Italy instead of France."

"Really? What made you decide?"

I grin. "Train leaving first."

"That's it?"

"That's it."

"Damn." Reece pauses. "I almost didn't graduate high school."

"I know."

"If it wasn't for you and Tristan, I would've never gotten through it."

"I know that, too." I toss a pebble into the lake. "I wonder how Sage will look in fifteen years."

"Content," Reece predicts.

"I don't know if Sage and I are meant to be content—it may not be for us."

"It'll be what it'll be."

"I really miss you guys. I miss drinking beers on Tristan's porch, talking about women and life."

Reece laughs. "You never talked about women."

"Tristan's women," I correct. "Until he fell in love with Lucy. I haven't asked her if she's happy."

"Must be hard to look at Dakota and see Tristan peeking out from his eyes."

"Might give her comfort."

"It might—doubt it though," Reece says. "It's nice knowing there's a piece of him left."

"What's left of you?"

"You remember me, don't you?"

Chapter 22

Sage

I opened the door and blinked. Memaw stood on the Chelsers' porch, blue eyes twinkling, her smile wide.

"Sorry, did I wake you?"

"How could you tell?" I asked, my voice raspy. I'd been enjoying a nap on the couch when the knock sounded. Kai was with Keith, helping with the horses; it somehow gave him comfort to come home with dirt under his nails and sweat on his brow. Alice was out running errands, and I'd had the house to myself.

"First trimester. Besides, I see a pillow crease on your cheek."

I laughed, reaching up to touch my face. Sure enough, I felt a little groove.

"You want to come with me?"

"Sure." I slipped on my tennis shoes and sent a quick text to Kai. We drove into the mountains and I asked, "Where are we going?"

"I thought I'd show you the property."

"Property?"

"Mine."

We drove for a while and then parked at Memaw's cabin and climbed out the car. The day was bright and warm as we hiked, and soon I was wiping my forehead with the back of my hand. My grogginess melted away, leaving me restored. Memaw shot me a look and said, "You aren't winded are you?"

"Like I'd admit it to you?" The woman was downright spry, youthful.

Memaw chuckled. "Well, what do you think?" She gestured to the land, filled with trees, serenity and the most incredible panorama I'd ever seen.

"To say it's beautiful doesn't do it justice. Hand carved by Mother Nature herself."

"Must be strange for a city girl like you."

"I'm not a city girl. Not anymore," I said. "Hard to believe I ever was."

"You miss France."

"So much. Not just *Tours*, but the Germains, too." They'd been there for me, given me a place out of the storm, a place to weather the grief. *Family.*

Memaw touched my arm in tacit understanding. "How are the plans for the party coming?"

"You'll have to ask Claire. I'm out of it." Thank God, too, because I was fairly certain one of us wouldn't have survived. I went to fittings when she told me to. I nodded in agreement when she talked. I didn't hear anything.

We continued to walk until we came to a clearing, and then sat on gray rocks that were almost large enough to be boulders. I asked, "How are they dealing with Kai's homecoming?"

"They're not. George spends most of his time at the office, and Claire…"

"Claire is very free with her opinions."

"Don't let it get to you."

"I'll try. How did Claire wind up with George?" I wondered aloud.

"My son met her when he was too young to know any better."

"Does he love her?"

"Yes, but he also likes a challenge. It makes him feel like he's constantly earning something."

I snorted in laughter. "How like a lawyer to enjoy the take down."

"Were you a challenge?" Memaw asked.

"Maybe. Not really, I don't think. I had put up walls, but to Kai they were made of glass. He saw right through them. He was very persistent."

"He knew what he wanted," Memaw commented, "and he went after it."

"Yes, he did."

"Most of us see the truth between you and Kai. Claire will either climb on board or she won't. It's that simple."

I let out a breath, along with some of my tension. "It would be easier. On Kai that is, if she could just learn to accept me."

"It would be easier on all of us, honey. How is Kai?"

"He's okay."

"What's going on between Kai and Wyatt?"

"Not a lot. Both are in a state of mutual avoidance." I shook my head. "I like Wyatt. I like him a lot. And Lucy. I'm glad they're happy." I stood and stretched my back, unable to hide another yawn.

Memaw laughed. "Come on, I'll take you back to the Chelsers'."

I put a hand to my slowly rounding belly. "I feel like I'm sleeping all the time."

"Do you believe it yet?" She glanced at my midsection.

I shrugged. "Not yet. I don't think I'll believe it until I push the thing out of me."

She laughed. "You have such a way with words, Sage."

———

I was setting a basket of newly-gathered eggs on the counter when my cell phone buzzed. Answering it, I heard Jules' voice on the other end just as the doorbell rang. "Hold on a second," I told her.

Throwing open the door, I stared at my best friend, who grinned, held out her phone and then hung up. She held a wrapped present under her arm and her suitcase rested on the porch.

"What are you doing here?" I asked, even as I enveloped Jules in an exuberant hug.

Grinning like an imp, Jules stepped into the foyer. "Kai and I planned this—thought you might need some reinforcements for this party you told me so much about."

"Best surprise ever!"

"Where is he?"

"With Keith, leading a group on a horse-back riding trail."

"Say what, now?"

I laughed. "He spends most of his days outdoors, getting his hands dirty."

"How Clint Eastwood of him."

"You have to stay here."

Jules set her bag down by the door. "Really?"

"Are you kidding? Alice will insist. This place is like a youth hostel." I pointed to the box. "What's that?"

"A gift for you."

"For me?"

"Well, for my niece or nephew."

I grinned and took the present into the kitchen. I tore off the wrapping paper, opened the box and pulled out a stuffed giraffe. "Could this be any cuter?"

"I got it from one of those really expensive baby boutiques."

"Upper East Side?"

"You know it."

"Thanks, Jules." I set the giraffe down on the chair. "I love it."

"There is a basket of eggs on the counter."

"Observant of you," I teased. "They have chickens."

"Chickens?"

"You know, *cluck cluck cluck.*"

"I know what a chicken is."

"I collect the eggs."

Jules laughed. "Dorothy, I don't think we're in Brooklyn anymore."

"Haven't been for a long time. You hungry?"

"Starved."

I made us sandwiches and then sat at the table. "Kai's mother continues to hate me."

"Has she spent any time with you at all?"

"As little as possible."

"I really wish you weren't knocked up. What's gossiping without a bottle of wine?"

"How about some chocolate?"

"Guess that will have to do."

"I'm glad you're here."

"I wish it was under better circumstances."

I sighed. "You know when you walk into your home and take a deep breath and feel the sanctuary of it?"

"Yeah."

"Being here feels something like that, but also like I'm hopping from one rock to another, trying not to fall into molten lava."

"That makes absolutely no sense."

"There's peace here, but there isn't. I don't know—maybe it's the hormones. Or this is the place where it all collides, and when it's over, I'm left with nothing but broken pieces."

"You talk in riddles; you didn't used to do that."

"Sorry, my brain is scrambled."

"Scrambled brains, yum. What do they taste like?"

"A little bit salty. From all the tears." Shaking my head, I smiled. "Come on, let's see if we can get Memaw to bake us something. You're going to love her."

———

Kai and I had booked an expansive, cream-colored suite at the Hermitage Hotel, so we could get ready before the reception. Afterward, we'd come upstairs, soak in the Jacuzzi, and wash away the ordeal that would be this night. Kai, looking handsome in his tuxedo, had left thirty minutes ago. He was probably at the hotel bar having a drink. I was alone with Jules, who was helping me with my hair and dress.

"Stop laughing," I demanded as I ran a hand down the ridiculous tulle skirt. I turned back to the mirror and stared at my reflection. I looked like a doll—lifeless and cold. "Why did I decide to do this?"

Jules sobered, rose from her chair and tied my sash into a bow. "Because you love Kai."

"It's that simple? I love him, therefore, I suffer?" I groused.

"Just wait. You'll see."

"See what?"

"I can't tell you. It will be worth it, though."

"He planned a surprise? Another one? He's full of them." I couldn't help the smile that tugged across my face.

"He did good with the farmhouse, didn't he? Trust him."

I reached for Jules' hand and squeezed it. "Can you tell I'm pregnant in this dress?"

"Yes," she said.

"Sometimes I wish you'd lie to me."

"No, you don't. Then you couldn't trust anything I said."

"There is that."

"You look beautiful," she went on. "You've got that pregnant glow."

I shot her a look, and she shrugged.

"The dress really isn't that bad, just not your style—you can do this."

"I don't want to leave this hotel suite. It's gorgeous and safe, and down in that ballroom, I'm going to have to talk to people I don't know and smile until my face hurts."

Jules linked her arm through mine and led me to the door. "Just think about what happens after the party."

"It's not appropriate to talk about."

"*Ga-ross!*"

We laughed as we got into the elevator. I fell silent, listening to the sound of my own heart. There would be people I knew, and I'd take comfort in the small dose of the familiar. Most of my life had become the unfamiliar, but I'd deal with that, too; I always did. I was nothing, if not adaptable.

I searched for Kai, wondering why I couldn't find him in the crowd. Letting Jules guide me, I didn't know where we were going until I saw the stage. Kai sat on a stool, a mandolin across his lap.

His blue-gray eyes were devouring me, and I didn't care that everyone could see. His face was a canvas, painted in shades of love and hope. My gaze slid to the lone man walking onto the platform. He carried a banjo and sat in the other chair.

I recognized Béla Fleck, whose song Kai had performed the first night we'd met—the song that always hummed just below the surface of my skin.

They played it for me.

When they finished, they moved into another song, something I'd never heard before. I knew it was written for me, for us. Kai stared at me, his heart in his eyes; mine was in my throat.

———

I leaned into Kai, pressing myself against him as we swayed on the dance floor, our arms wrapped around each other. I sighed in dreamy contentment. "You are an incredible husband." I stared at him as I brushed a hand down his tuxedo-clad arm.

Kai smiled, the corners of his eyes crinkling. "Award-winning?"

I laughed. "Yes. When did you write that song?"

"You nap a lot now—I had some time."

"That simple, huh?"

"Ever hear of a little thing called inspiration?"

I grinned. "Starting to." My journal writings had diverged onto a new path, paved with thick mossy trees and speckled with sunlight. I wondered where it would lead, and if I'd follow.

"So how'd you get him here?"

"Béla Fleck?"

"Yeah."

"My secret. Just know that there isn't anything I wouldn't do for you."

"Good to know."

I brought his mouth close to mine, getting ready to ask him if he wanted to leave when George appeared next to us and asked, "Can I cut in?"

I swallowed my sigh of disappointment. I wanted to be with Kai, and only Kai, but our time alone would have to wait.

"Sure. I'll go dance with Memaw." Kai brought my hand to his lips, his eyes promising me joy and other things, before walking away.

George held out his arms and I stepped into them. "Thank you," he said.

"For what?"

"For going along with this."

"Did it make Claire happy?"

George's lips twitched in humor. "Does anything make Claire happy? No, I was thanking you for myself. It made my home life far more enjoyable this past month."

I chuckled. "You're welcome."

George looked over my shoulder and stared at Kai. "He used to be so restless. Now he looks happy."

"He is."

"We have you to thank for that."

"Me?"

"I don't know how I can ever repay you. What you've done for Kai, for our family…"

My eyes misted. "We're family, George. You owe me nothing."

George was about to reply when there was a shout from across the room. I turned at the sound, wondering what was happening. I saw Wyatt kneeling on the ground next to a form I couldn't make out. Breaking free of George's embrace I ran, shoving people out of the way. The crowd parted as I approached, and I saw a pale and unconscious Memaw on the floor. She looked small and frail, and the pulse at her neck fluttered like the beat of a dragonfly's wing.

Kai yelled for someone to call an ambulance. His eyes scanned the guests, and I knew he was looking for me. When he saw me, he reached out, grabbed me by the hand and pulled me to his side.

I placed a hand on the frantic beating of his heart.

———

The mood in the Ferris library was somber. George's eyes were empty, his face painting a picture of disbelief. Memaw had had a stroke. By the time the ambulance had arrived, it was too late. Her life had slipped away, like soil through a closed hand.

Everyone was still in their formal wear, a painful reminder that hours ago we had been celebrating. Now, we would have to plan for a funeral.

Is this life? From happiness and health to death in one breath?

I glanced at Kai. Solemn face, haunted eyes, but his grip was strong in mine.

"I need to lie down," George announced, his voice broken. Standing, he set his bourbon on the end table. He paused, looking unsure before leaving.

"Should we start thinking about the funeral?" Wyatt asked.

Claire nodded. "I'll start the arrangements."

George wasn't in a mental state to see to it, and now Claire was the matriarch of the family. She had duties and impossible shoes to fill.

Lucy spoke up, "Please let me know what I can do to help."

Wyatt and Lucy left, and the room was quiet with loss.

Claire looked at her son before her eyes darted to me. "Will you leave? After the funeral I mean? There's nothing keeping you here anymore."

Kai was about to answer when I interjected, "We haven't talked about it yet, but I think we'll stay for a few more weeks, at least."

He gazed at me, tracing a finger over my ear, his eyes saying everything his mouth couldn't. Turning his attention back to his mother, he said, "Get some rest, Mom." Kai stood and kissed his mother on the cheek.

"Kaplan is coming by tomorrow to read the will."

"We'll be here," Kai assured her. We were out the front door, and the cool night welcomed us, a reprieve from the subdued intensity of the library. "Want to go for a drive?"

"Sure."

Kai drove us up into the mountains and parked. We got out of the car, and he stripped off his tuxedo jacket and bowtie, and threw them into the back seat.

"I wish I could get out of this dress."

"You can." He reached for my zipper.

"I'll be in nothing but a slip."

"Who cares? No one to see you out here."

"I'll be cold." The weather had turned. It was officially autumn.

After he helped me out of the gown, I shrugged into his tuxedo jacket, and we climbed onto the hood and sat next to each other.

We watched the stars winking at us from above. I never saw them in New York due to the city's light pollution. I had settled for so little, but I had thought it was so much. But moments like these were what mattered.

"You're sad."

"Yeah, but not in the way you think."

"Explain."

"I miss her already, but I'm not sure I believe it yet. I can't help but hope she's with my grandfather."

"In a better place and all that?"

"Maybe. I think she's with Tristan and Reece, too, and they're all sitting around a table playing poker, waiting for the rest of us to join them."

"She played poker?"

"Are you kidding? She taught me the game, and she was better at it than anyone. God, I learned so much from both of them—things I never learned from my own parents."

"Tell me what you learned, tell me what you're going to teach our children."

His hand toyed with my hair as he answered, "My grandfather taught me how to play the mandolin, to hold a fishing rod, to recognize the right woman when she came along."

"How did you know I was the right one?" I asked, snuggling close to him, undoing the top few buttons of his shirt and placing my hand against his warm skin.

"I wanted you for more than one night. I started thinking in terms of forever when I met you—and I'd never been one to dream about forever. I didn't think I deserved it. You made me want to stop wandering, made me want to finish something, made me want to love you with everything that I am."

A lone tear, an elegant dewdrop, escaped the corner of my eye. "And your grandmother, what did you learn from her?"

"Everything—," his voice caught in the back of his throat, "everything else."

———

"Can I get anyone a drink?" Claire asked, ever the polite hostess. We shook our heads, except George, who didn't appear to be listening. I sat on a leather couch in the library, holding Kai's hand. Wyatt was alone in a chair, and Claire perched next to her husband, her spine straight.

Kaplan, the lawyer, picked up the document resting on the desk and cleared his throat. He read Memaw's words, "My liquid assets, including stocks, retirement funds and bank balances are to be divided evenly between my son, George, and my grandsons, Wyatt and Kai. As for my home and all properties, including land—I bequeath to Sage Harper Ferris."

"*What?*" I asked, feeling like I'd gone momentarily dumb. "Can you repeat that?" I stared at the lawyer, uncomprehending. Kai looked like he hadn't even heard the news.

Kaplan reread Memaw's will, and then Claire perused me as if seeing me for the first time.

"This has to be some kind of mistake," Claire said.

"Mom," Wyatt began.

"No, we have to contest this. She obviously wasn't in her right mind." Claire stood, her eyes blazing.

"Memaw was as sane as they come," Kai stated.

Claire turned towards Kai. "Your wife," she spat, "has been in the family for all of five minutes. This is *ridiculous*—how did you do it, Sage?"

"You think I *orchestrated* this?" I gasped.

"Stop it!" Kai pleaded. He stood, ready to defend me.

"Claire," George snapped, coming out of the daze he'd been in for the better part of two days. "That's enough. This was my mother's choice, not yours. Sit. Down."

"How can you be so calm about this?" Claire hissed.

George's eyes were dull when they focused on his wife. "She discussed it with me before she changed her will."

Claire's eyes widened. "What? What are you talking about?"

"About two months ago, shortly after Kai and Sage came home," George said, exhaustion pervading his voice.

With one last baleful glance in my direction, Claire stormed out of the room. George looked after her, his face weary, and said, "I don't have the strength."

"I'll go." Kai said, following his mother.

"Kaplan, I'll walk you out," George said.

"Thanks," the lawyer said. "The rest of the details are spelled out clearly in the will. Call me if you have any questions."

No doubt he was used to triggering emotional landmines. Perhaps this family was normal.

When I was alone with Wyatt, I said, "*I did not*—"

He cut me off. "I know."

"I don't understand. Why did Memaw do it?"

Wyatt smiled. "Honestly I think Memaw thought that if she gave you the land and house, it might give you two a reason to stay."

Setting a hand on my belly, I leaned my head against the back of the couch. I felt a ripple just below the surface of my skin, realizing my child moved for the first time. Even in my state of grief, I was overwhelmed by a surge of joy and a deeper connection with the life I carried inside me.

It reminded me that birth and death were merely front and back covers—the stuff in between nothing more than a novella.

Chapter 23

Kai

My mother and I were outside behind the house, the smell of changing leaves and wood smoke in the air.

Mom crossed her arms over her chest and refused to look at me.

"This isn't about the will at all, is it?" My voice carried across the abyss of resentment. I doubted she'd hear me.

"She's a predator."

"You're still on this? She thought I was a broke musician when we met. She thought I had nothing, and she still wanted me. Besides, she has her own money."

"What are you talking about?"

"Her mother was Penny Harper, the author. She left Sage everything when she died."

"*The* Penny Harper?"

"Yeah. Sage isn't using me. She didn't trap me, Mom. We love each other. Why can't you understand that?"

"That doesn't change how fast you two got married. You still barely know each other."

175

"You know, it doesn't matter what you think anymore. I'm a man. I wish you could see me as one."

Her face and voice were tight with pain. "You don't know what it's like—to have expectations and then have them—"

"Fall short? That's what you want to say, right? I'm a raging disappointment?" I raked a hand through my hair. "Do you love me?" It came out as an accusation.

Genuine hurt flashed across her face. "Of course I do."

"No," I said quietly, "I don't think you do. If you did, you wouldn't be trying to burn down everything I've tried to build for myself." It was devastating to realize my own mother didn't love me unconditionally.

"And what is it you think you've built? Your father and I have been married over thirty years. You think it's easy? You think love is enough?"

I laughed without amusement. "No, it isn't. But we're right for each other and I can't explain why. We're meant to be together."

"Sure, for now. Until things get too hard for you. And they will get too hard for you, Kai. You ran when Tristan and Reece died. You'll run again, and she'll let you."

My body went cold with anger. "Wow. You've got no illusions about who I am, huh?" I stared at her. "I'm guessing you had no idea I was supposed to be in that plane."

Mom gazed at me, her hawk eyes narrowing. "What are you talking about?"

I knew Alice and Keith hadn't told my parents. They, themselves, wouldn't have even known about it if I hadn't been drinking after the crash. But drunk out of my mind, I hadn't been able to hold the words in my mouth, so I'd spewed them, hoping it would rid me of the blackness. Alice and Keith had carried the truth for two years, letting me tell it when I was ready. If I had never returned, they would've gone on bearing it, but I was back now, and everyone needed to know.

"Reece and I played *rock, paper, scissors* for the first flight, and I won, but I gave him my spot. I thought I was being a good friend. I left when they died because of the guilt." I stared at my mother; she paled with my admission. "It should've been me up there—but I'm glad I lived, do you know why?"

Mom was silent.

"If Reece had been the one to live, he would've died from the guilt. He was softer than us; kinder, gentler—better. I lived through it all, because I *could*. He wouldn't have made it, Mom."

"Alice and Keith…they never said anything."

"Wasn't their secret to share; it wasn't their shame to unburden. Would you have heard them, anyway? Would it have made you understand me better? Curse at me, rant at me, yell at me if you want, but you will leave my wife out of this. If you continue on this way, you'll drive us away, and we'll never come back."

"Are you threatening me?" Her voice was as thin as a reed ready to snap.

"Sage is everything to me, Mom."

I stared at my mother before leaving her alone with her right-eousness and my confession. Seeds of bitterness didn't grow into trees overnight, and I doubted I'd be able to fell them in day.

Maybe I should stop trying.

———

Later that evening, Keith and I were sharing a beer in the kitchen of the Chelser ranch house. Sage was upstairs asleep, and Alice was getting ready for bed. Jules had wanted to stay for the funeral, but I'd told her it was unnecessary, so she had hopped on a plane that morning.

"Memaw left the house and land to Sage?" Keith asked.

I nodded. "Dad knew about the change to the will. Mom shit a brick."

"How did Wyatt react?"

"He was okay with it," I said. "The only one who can't wrap her head around it is Mom. She used it as an excuse to unload all her pent up anger at me. She's pissed I left home, she's pissed I got married really fast. She's just pissed."

"Can you blame her? Take a step back. Maybe she didn't handle her emotions all that well, but can you see her points?"

"Yeah, I can, but enough already. I'm happy. Sage and I are happy. It's like Mom doesn't believe me or something."

"Claire's a complicated woman. It must be hard for her to watch her son live a life she never could've imagined for him."

"But it's *my* life," I gritted. "Mine and Sage's."

"When you have family, it's never really your own. You're tied to other people, son, always will be. No matter where you live or where you go that tether is still there, and it can't be cut no matter how sharp the shears."

"I wish she loved me for me. I finally told her the truth—that I was supposed to be in the plane." I wiped a hand across my face feeling bone-deep tired. "I don't know if that will make a difference to her—I still ran."

"You can't expect to sort out a lifetime of hurt and misunderstandings in a few months, Kai."

"It took two years, but I ran in a very large circle, and where did I end up? Back in the mountains. There isn't enough distance from Monteagle, no matter where I go."

"This is your place, and the sooner you make peace with it, all of it, then maybe you'll begin to heal."

"I'm healed."

"You think you are, until someone pulls on a ratty thread and it all comes undone again. Maybe you should stay. For a little while, at least."

"Stay here?" The idea churned in my mind like clothes in a washing machine.

Keith shrugged. "Memaw gave you guys a house and land for a reason. I'm sure she wanted you to make peace with your soul—and with your family."

I craved a fishing rod in my hand, like an alcoholic yearned for a drink.

"Would Sage consider staying?"

"And live near my mother?" I snorted. "Can I really ask her to do that?"

"No, I mean, would she give you time here—because she loves you?"

"I don't know," I said, meaning it. "It's a lot to ask."

"Would you do it for her?"

"Of course."

"Ask her and find out."

———

I couldn't stop the feeling of déjà vu as I watched my grandmother being lowered into the ground, and I wondered if my life would be defined by these moments—losing those closest to me. My existence was a series of gray milestones, and I was constantly tripping over them.

It smothered me, the somber faces and black clothes. I turned away, my hand dropping from Sage's. I began to walk and didn't stop until I reached a mausoleum, plopping down on the marble stone steps. Looking out the corner of my eye, I saw Sage's dainty feet in black heels. She perched next to me and plucked a late blooming dandelion from underneath the steps.

"I don't understand funerals. I mean, I do, but they're for the living, not the dead. Closure and all that kind of bullshit, but do people really get closure—ever?" My voice was hushed, mindful of our location.

Sage blew the dandelion, and we watched the seeds travel. "Moments like these aren't about closure."

"What are they about then?"

"Reconciliation."

I sighed. "I can't go to my parents' house after this and sit through another one of these things."

"Don't you think you should be there for your dad? He needs you."

I pulled out a handful of grass, clutching it in my grip. The land was green, alive, in a place where the reminder of death was all around us. "Why didn't you let Jules help you through your mother's death? She's your oldest friend."

"Why do we push away those we love?" she asked instead. "You might never have the relationship with your family that you want, but it wouldn't only be their fault. You're in this, too."

"Can we stay?"

"Stay?"

"In Monteagle. Not forever, but for now? There are things that I…"

"Have to reconcile—I know."

"You're not surprised I'm asking, are you?"

Sage knew me. Like words on a page, she read me.

She smiled and leaned her head against my shoulder. "If you need to stay, we'll stay." She took my hand.

"We'll go back to France," I vowed.

"I know. One day. I love that farmhouse. That turret, that fireplace in the living room." She smiled. "But it looks like our kid will be Southern."

"Wean him on bourbon and fishing," I teased.

"Just like his father."

———

Tristan chews on a matchstick as he hands me the bottle of bourbon. Even in my dreams, I crave Gentleman Jack. I take a swig.

We are sitting on the edge of the mountain, watching the sun sink into earth. The colors are muted, like a memory that dims or turns gray.

"You say 'I do' out loud, once, but you make a choice, every day—it's active, not passive."

"Thanks for the advice," I say with a grin, but Tristan doesn't grin back.

"I know what I'm talking about."

"You? I'm supposed to take marriage advice from the guy that never saw a girl after he got her into bed?"

"That's why you should listen to me; I never played around on Lucy."

"I didn't think you did."

Tristan finally smiles. "Yeah, right. It's okay. I would've thought that about me, too."

"How did you change?"

"I just did. I'd do anything to see her happy. And she wanted me, bad boy and all."

"The heart wants what it wants, huh?"

Tristan laughs. "Man, the heart doesn't even know what it wants. It latches onto something and won't let go. It knows before the mind."

"The heart can play tricks on you. I think it's the ultimate creator of illusion."

"You don't think this is real?"

"What, talking to you? I know this isn't real."

"I meant you and Sage."

"Oh, that. It's terrifying, so I know it's real," I explain.

"Take this bottle of Jack. It feels real, tastes real, but it's still a dream. How do you know you and Sage aren't a dream in someone else's mind?"

"Because in a dream, I can do this." I throw the bottle of bourbon, and it hits the tree with enough force that it should shatter. It doesn't because the tree moves and catches the bottle in its spindly branches.

"Neat little trick." Tristan smiles.

"Our love is no trick."

"Whatever you say, Kai. Only you know the truth. I'm just a ghost."

Chapter 24

Sage

"I hate you, I hate you, I hate you," I grumbled, as I tied the laces of my tennis shoes.

"Oh come on, you'll have fun, promise," Kai said.

"I like the idea of fishing, but does it have to be so friggin' early?"

"You love me, remember? Do this for me?"

"I do love you." I sighed. "And I'll prove it by holding a fishing rod. On the upside, this is the first morning I haven't wanted to dry heave into the toilet."

I threw on a light jacket, knowing I'd strip it off later after the sun rose, but it would be chilly in the predawn air. The days were still warm, but the nights were cool.

We drove into the mountains and parked on an incline. We hiked up the hill, taking a leisurely pace. When we arrived at the lake, I said, "Okay, the view alone was worth getting up at the crack of dawn." Streaks of sun were bouncing off the water, making me think of silver fish scales.

Kai grinned and handed me a pole. He took me through the motions, but I was clumsy. Never losing his patience, he continued to teach. "No, like this." He adjusted my arm when I cast incorrectly. I watched him and marveled at his skill.

"You'll get better," he vowed, "but it's going to take lots and lots of practice."

"You're going to drag me up here day after day, aren't you?"

"Year after year," he went on.

I shook my head. "Hate to break it to you, sport, but I'm not a fisherwoman."

Kai pretended to be shocked. "Not in front of the kid!"

I laughed, the sound of it ringing through the trees. We fished in silence for a quarter of an hour, and then I spoke. "Should we move into your grandmother's house? Is it too soon?" It had only been a week since Memaw had died—it might always be too soon. If we lived there, would a lingering ghost haunt us? There were so many of them in Monteagle.

"I wanted to talk to you about that. I was thinking about building a house on her property."

"You mean tear hers down? I don't understand."

"No, leave it. Memaw put her money into the land, but her house is too small for a family. We'll use it as a guesthouse, but I want to build us our dream home. A home for our family."

"We might stay forever if you do that." My voice trembled with fear and hope.

"Forever is wherever we want it to be. France, here, New York."

"I hate New York—I never want to go back."

His eyes sought mine. "Could you be happy in Monteagle? Long term?"

"Could you?"

"I'm not sure anymore," he admitted. "Just when I think things won't change on me, they do."

He set his pole down and came to me. Taking mine from my hands, he set it along the bank and hugged me to him. "I can't imagine a life without you, Sage, and I don't even want to try. We'll change, but we'll do it together. That I can promise you."

Pulling back, I shook off the somberness of our conversation. "Now, take pity on me. Can we be done with fishing for today? I'm hungry." It was a few hours past sunrise, and I was ready for food.

Sighing in defeat, Kai packed up our gear and handed me the rods. "Can you take these back to the car? I'll grab everything else."

I started my descent, taking it slow. Though I was showing, I knew I wasn't as large as I felt. Still, I had bruises on my arms and legs because I kept bumping into things—corners of doorways, coffee tables. My mind hadn't caught up with my blundering body, or maybe it was the other way around.

After breakfast, maybe I'd get a nice soak in the tub, wash away the dirt and steep my muscles. Perhaps Kai would like to...

Momentarily lost in thoughts about steaming water and my naked husband, one of my shoes caught the root of a tree, and I tripped. I dropped the poles and tried to put my hands out in front of me, but I went down hard, landing on my stomach.

"Sage!" Kai cried, crouching down to help me. I was dazed, my vision speckled. Gently, he hauled me up, his arms steadying me.

I was wobbly and scared, and I felt stupid.

"Lean into me," he commanded as he guided me back to the car.

My heart galloped in my chest. I rested my hands protectively over my stomach, but something told me my efforts were in vain.

We were driving down the mountain when I felt the cramps start low in my belly. I moaned in pain.

"Kai? I need to go the hospital—and hurry."

———

We were alone in the hospital room, so no one was there to witness our version of rock bottom. Rock bottom had layers, and every time we peeled back another one, there were more waiting for us. It was deep and gritty—a sharp descent into nightmare.

"My fault," Kai mumbled. His arms were around me, and I felt tremors pulse through him.

"No, it's not like you pushed me. How is this your fault?"

184

"You wouldn't have been on that mountain if it weren't for me."

I held him, my tears soaking his shirt as I tried to soothe him with my hands and crooning noises.

"I'm so sorry, Sage." He said the words into my hair.

"Not your fault."

"Do you still want me?"

"More than life."

He gripped me. "Don't say that."

"Hold me, Kai, don't let me go."

"Never."

"How do we get through this?" I wondered. My voice sounded very far away, as though it belonged to someone else.

"I—I don't know."

The man I loved didn't have an answer.

"But, we have each other, don't we?" he whispered, the thread of a lifeline in his voice.

I clung to his words, a tiny raft in a vast sea of sorrow.

Chapter 25

Kai

When Sage was released from the hospital, I wasn't sure where I was supposed to take her, so I went to the Chelsers, knowing she needed a mother's care. My own was ill-equipped to handle Sage's anguish—or anyone's, for that matter. Tucking my wife into bed, I rubbed her back until she fell asleep.

Then I left.

Guilt blended with bile, and it threatened to swallow me—it was a familiar feeling.

I parked in an oily lot next to an old beat up truck and went into the shadowy dive. Approaching the bar, I ordered a shot of cheap bourbon and threw it back. It gave me no respite as it burned my insides.

Sitting down on the stool, I ordered another, attempting to drown myself.

I had taken Sage fishing—I had cajoled and pleaded because I wanted to share what I loved.

My fault.

Always my fault.

It was my burden to suffer, and no amount of absolution would make me feel otherwise.

Our baby…

But I still had Sage. She wasn't lost to me, thank fate, but the fist around my heart clenched. Why didn't it just squeeze until there was nothing left? Pulverize it already.

I couldn't swallow more guilt, so I washed it down with another drink.

Later, maybe hours, Lucy strolled into the bar and plopped down on a stool next to me. When I reached for a shot, she knocked it out of my hand. The glass clattered across the bar, spraying the old scarred wood with alcohol.

Her eyes were blue, electric, angry. "Your wife woke up to find you gone. Why aren't you at home, holding her?"

My gaze slipped away, unable to face her, too.

But Lucy would not be denied. She grabbed my chin and made me look at her, made me peer into the mirror.

I did not like the reflection.

"You didn't do this." She searched my face for understanding.

"I'm a fucking tragedy. My two best friends die in a plane crash. My grandmother dies at my wedding celebration. My baby…"

"You'll come through this—you both will." Her voice was hard, unyielding. "You need to be there for her. Drinking in a shitty dive is not being there for her."

I shook my head. "I—"

"Do you want me to split your lip? Tristan and Reece aren't here to talk sense into you, and I know you won't listen to Wyatt, so it's fallen to me. Get. Up."

Somehow, I did as I was told and let Lucy lead me out into the dark.

When had it become night?

"I'm about to break," I whispered.

"Hasn't happened yet," Lucy said, opening the passenger door of her car. "You can come back from this."

"How can you be so cold?" I lashed out. I settled into the seat, and she slammed the door shut behind me. I wanted to hit something.

She walked to her side, got in and started the engine. "How can *you*? You snuck off after Sage fell asleep. How like the Kai-of-old," she taunted.

"I'm a shit—you don't think I know that?"

"Did drinking in a bar help?"

"You know it didn't."

"Then why did you do it? You need to be there for her, and you should let her be there for you."

"I know, God, I know." I rubbed my hand across my eyes. "I hate myself. So much I want to die."

"You don't get to die. Too many of us already have."

It was another reminder that I was unworthy, and that I screwed up every time things got hard. I wondered if my mother was right— I wondered if I'd changed at all.

The sharp anger in Lucy's voice dulled. "This is awful—terrible, but is it any worse than Alice and Keith losing Reece? They *knew* Reece. They watched him grow from boy to man."

I was silent as Lucy drove.

She went on, "Tragedy is tragedy, any way you slice it, but you can let this rip you apart, or you can cling fiercely to everything that matters. There will be more children for you and Sage."

"You sound so sure."

When Lucy dropped me off in the Chelsers' driveway, I didn't wait for her to cut the engine before I was out the door. I stalked into the house and went upstairs. Alice sat by the bed, her gaze accusatory. I didn't pay attention as I crawled in next to Sage and held her while we cried for all we'd lost.

———

"It's not your fault," Tristan says.

"So people keep telling me." I keep my eyes closed. I feel like someone split me open down the middle, the void within me as deep as the Grand Canyon.

"What's it like?"

"What?"

"Feeling your child kick?"

"Dream Tristan is strangely maudlin and soft-hearted. What happened to the guy that raced motorcycles?"

"I change as you change, your hopes are my hopes. I'm a reflection of you."

"I never got to feel it kick," I murmur. So many dreams lost. "Sage felt it though. She described it like a flutter, but not. All wonder and hope."

"Your teenage self would be embarrassed to be seen with you. You know that, right?"

We have a good laugh, and I feel lighter. The darkness around the corners of my vision ebbs a little. I shake my head. "It's weird; you look at yourself every day in the mirror and see the same face. And, then you start to notice the faint wrinkles around your eyes that were never there before, the laugh lines around your mouth don't fade as quickly, your dreams have become different, but you don't remember how you got there."

"Life is kind of like driving on autopilot, hmmm?" Tristan comments.

"Do we wake up at the end of the road and think, 'Is this as far as I can go?'"

"There's not one way, y'know. There are detours, forks, cattle crossings that make you stop, take pause."

"I'm looking around now," I note.

"Do you like who you've become?"

"Very rarely."

"Sounds about right," Tristan remarks with a bland smile.

"I don't think I handle things all that well."

"You come back, though. Every time. It might take you a while, but you do. A fucking boomerang."

"You're not just saying that?"

"You tell me. This is your dream."

Chapter 26

Sage

Sometime the next afternoon, I woke in bed alone. I inhaled, trying to place the smell; it was the scent of comfort, relief—it was chicken soup.

Kai had come home late the previous night—Lucy had seen to it. He'd held me as we fell asleep.

Was he gone already?

I rose, testing my body, feeling sore, used, and battered. Pulling on a pair of slippers and a sweatshirt, I padded downstairs. I was cold.

Alice and Kai were in the kitchen—Alice stirred a large pot of soup, and Kai diced vegetables. I cleared my throat, announcing my presence.

Kai turned, his face ravaged by his own pain, yet he managed to smile for me. Though he had left me for hours the night before, I didn't hold it against him. I'd once blamed Connor for leaving me in my grief, but this didn't feel the same.

"Want some soup?" Alice asked.

"Is it ready?" My voice sounded dry, like the crunching of crisp autumn leaves underfoot.

Alice ladled broth into a bowl and set it on the table. "Chicken soup heals all wounds."

"Even the ones on the inside?" I sank into a chair, not missing the look between Kai and Alice. Kai set down the knife and came to me. Leaning over, he kissed the top of my head and then left the room. I watched him go, wondering how many bowls of soup he'd eaten, and if they had restored him. "Are we going to have a talk?"

"No." Alice pulled out another chair and sat down, and I picked up my spoon. Placing a hand on my arm, she stopped me from taking a bite. "Look at me."

It took a moment, but finally I gazed into Alice's eyes. They were old, battle scarred. They knew things that came from fighting emotional wars she could never win—only temper. Alice knew there was nothing to be said. Some caverns of suffering could not be filled with words.

I was too numb to cry, and I wondered if it would've helped anyway.

———

Alice left me alone on the couch, wrapped in a blanket. Where was Kai? Probably on the mountain, or maybe at the cemetery. Was he praying, hoping for peace, or had he finally given up?

I wanted to comfort him, but I could barely comfort myself.

I heard the back door open, and then Keith was in the living room. "Put on your shoes."

"Why?"

"Trust me."

I sighed, but did as bid and then followed him to the stables and into a stall. "I can't ride yet."

"I know. This is Mabel," Keith said, patting the brown mare's neck. Picking up a currying comb, he dropped it into my hand. "Brush in circles." He gave me a few whole apples and carrots, and then left me alone.

I stared at the mare. What did horses do when they lost their foals? They went on, because nature designed them that way. It was so much harder to be human.

"What have you lived through, Mabel?" Mabel snorted and shook her head, and looked at me with liquid brown eyes. "I wish you had all the answers and you could tell them to me. Do you have infinite wisdom in all things that matter? Of course you don't— you're just a horse. What the hell do you know?" Pulling out an apple, I offered it in the palm of my hand. It disappeared into Mabel's mouth. The horse nudged me with her head, wanting more, and I obliged. I began rubbing Mabel down, losing myself in time and the repetitive motion. It was soothing, calming, like how a mother would feel patting her infant's back. The attention was for both of them. So, I lavished love on the mare because I didn't have a child to hold in my arms—a child I would never know.

It had been a boy.

Kai's son.

Legacy.

Hope.

My tears came like a bubbling geyser; I looped my arms around Mabel's neck and pressed my face against her. And because Mabel was a horse, all she could give was her solid, sturdy presence.

Somehow, it was enough.

———

I reached for Kai but found his side of the bed empty and cold— he'd been gone a while. I trudged to the back porch, knowing he would be staring at the night sky. Looking for answers or forgiveness, I didn't know which.

I pressed a kiss to his shoulder and then sat next to him and asked, "You ever feel like you're trying to break through a wall, hoping to find out what's past the grief?"

"Are you on the other side yet?"

"I don't know. It's only been a week. Are you?"

He took my hand and skimmed my knuckles with his thumb, but did not reply.

"Come back to me, Kai."

We were quiet, and a contentment I never thought I'd feel again embraced me. It made me drowsy, and I cuddled into his arms. We were in the thick of autumn. It would be winter soon. Seasons changed, so did people.

"Still want that house?" he asked.

"Yes."

"Forgive me?"

"There's nothing to forgive."

"Still love me?"

"Always."

———

"Where are you going?" Kai demanded.

I put on a jacket and slipped on my shoes, tugging my hair into a ponytail. "To see your father."

"Sage…"

"Someone has to pull him out of this."

"And you think you're the one for the job?" His eyes were full of concern, unsure.

"I do."

"Haven't you done enough fighting? Do you have the strength to take on his burdens, too?"

"It's been over a month since we lost Memaw, and it's time for him to rejoin us."

Kai hugged me. What could he say? He knew I was right.

"Jules wants to come down."

I shook my head. "No, I can't have another person watching over me." The giraffe Jules had bought as a gift for our child was now mashed underneath our mattress, along with my journal, and everything else I didn't want to contend with.

"Okay," Kai agreed, "but call her and tell her yourself—she

doesn't believe me. Call Celia while you're at it. She wants to hear your voice."

"I will," I promised.

I drove to the Ferris' house and used Kai's keys to let myself in. Knowing Claire was not there made it easier, but I still sighed in respite. She'd come to the hospital when I lost the baby, but had stayed in the waiting room. I didn't know if it had been because she hated me, or because she thought her presence would make my pain worse. I knew she would return eventually, but for the time being I could focus on George.

Alice had given me a casserole to bring with me, hoping that might entice George to eat—I brought a bottle of bourbon. I knew what he needed.

"George?" I called out, but he didn't answer. Following a hunch, I went to the library. He sat on the couch, a newspaper that he wasn't reading spread across his lap. He looked at me, his face not registering surprise.

"Are you taking anything to help you sleep?" I asked without preamble.

"Just bourbon." His voice was rusty, like an old, clogged copper pipe. He held up his glass of melting ice cubes and potent liquor. "What are you doing here, Sage?"

"Thought you could use a drinking buddy." I set the casserole down on the table before opening the bottle of bourbon and taking a swig. It was only eleven in the morning, but there was nothing like death to make a person forget the time.

"Not even going to bother with a glass?"

I shot him a look. "Careful, you sound very much like your wife, who already disapproves of me. Besides, there's no one here to witness my crassness except you."

I poured him a double and then settled onto the couch.

"You shouldn't be here."

"Why not?"

"Because." It was a flimsy excuse.

"Because I'm supposed to be sitting at home in the dark mourning my child?"

He flinched. "I'm sorry for your loss."

"I'm sorry for yours."

"Don't."

"Listen, George, we can do this the hard way or the easy way. Hard way is for you to deny me. Easy way is for you to let me sit here, drink until we're hammered, and I'll listen to you talk."

"I don't want to talk."

"That's fine, then I will. I lost my mother, too, remember?"

"And your father. You were a lot younger than me."

"I don't remember my dad," I admitted. "There's no shame in how you're behaving. We all handle loss in different ways."

"You're pretty transparent. There's no guile in you, no manipulation."

"Your wife doesn't agree."

"Claire doesn't know what to think."

"She's irrational."

"Undoubtedly." He paused. "I'm ashamed."

"Of what? Claire? Kai?"

"Myself—for letting Kai go."

"He was here one minute and gone the next—you didn't have a chance to stop him."

"Didn't even leave a note. Can you imagine?" George looked at me; his eyes held wonder, confusion, hope.

"Not one of his best moments."

"Is my son a coward? I used to think he was, but I'm not sure anymore."

"He left, George, but he did come back."

"Claire told me Kai was supposed to be in the plane."

"Yes."

"God, it's been awful for him, hasn't it? I had no idea."

"Some of us are meant to go on, no matter what life throws at us. Kai is no coward. You know, it was his idea to stay and mend the family after your mother died—it was his idea to build a house on your mother's land. I had nothing to do with that."

He took a long swallow of his drink and rubbed a hand over his mouth as though he tasted bitterness. "It's nice having him home. I've missed him."

"He's missed you, too."

"Really?"

I nodded.

He sighed. "I would really like a chance to get to know my son."

"You will," I promised, "but he is not going to be the person you expect him to be."

George looked thoughtful. "I think he may be someone better."

————

We drank and talked for hours, and I even managed to make George laugh. His face was ruddy with color and bourbon, and half the casserole was eaten right out of the dish by the time Claire returned home.

She popped into the library, her countenance disapproving. "What's this?"

"I came over to cheer George up." I hiccoughed.

Claire looked at her husband as he smiled, his lips curving like the bow of a boat. "It's not even cocktail hour. How long have you been drinking?"

"When did you leave?" George slurred.

"Ten-thirty."

"Then about five minutes after that," George explained, and I couldn't stop a giggle from escaping my mouth. Claire glared at us.

I rolled my eyes, but said nothing. Drinking with my father-in-law seemed to be doing some sort of trick—for both of us.

"Sage?" Kai called out, the front door opening and closing.

"Library," I called back, then grinned at Kai when he came to stand in the doorway next to his mother. "Your dad and I were chewing the fat about life and stuff. Right, George?" I glanced at my father-in-law, whose eyes were closed, and he was on the verge of snoring.

"You outdrank my dad? I'm impressed."

"I'm sleepy," I admitted. "Take me home?"

Claire's watchful gaze followed us, but she said nothing. It was out of character, but I would take any reprieve I could get. Maybe Claire felt bad for all that I had lost. I had no idea.

When we were settled in Kai's car, I said, "Don't take me to Alice and Keith's."

"You said to take you home."

"That's not home. We have a home for the time being—your grandmother's cabin."

"But—"

"I want my own space, and I want to make love to you as loud as I want." I missed our intimacy, our physical connection.

His breath hitched. "The doctor?"

"Cleared me a few days ago."

"How drunk are you?"

"Very."

"Sage…"

"I always want you. Please, Kai, I need you to hold me, so I can feel your heart beating against mine."

We barely made it into the foyer before we fell together onto the floor. It was not making love—it was primal, needy, desperate. And when it was over and he cradled my face in his hands, I felt a deep well open. My breath became shallow and tears seeped out of the corners of my eyes.

"What is it, darlin'?"

"My love for you sometimes overwhelms me."

He pulled me close and rested his lips on my shoulder. "It's nice."

"What?"

"Knowing I'm not alone."

"I'll love you forever."

He sighed. "I'm counting on it."

———

I was on the front porch of Memaw's cabin, a notebook open on my lap, doodling in the corner of a page. The door opened and closed, and Kai came next to me, holding his mandolin. He pulled up a chair and sat down, his fingers strumming the strings a few times before stopping.

"Do you think death is organized or just completely random?" he asked.

"What do you mean?"

"Like, do you think God, or the universe or whatever just picks people off, or is there a method or something?"

"Are you really asking me if there is an algorithm to death?"

He paused in thought before nodding. "Yeah, I think that's what I'm asking." He played a quick song; it sounded familiar but wasn't. It was probably one he had written.

"I don't know."

Kai laughed though it wasn't a joyful sound. "Neither do I."

Somewhere in the distance, a bird cawed. "Play me something."

"What do you want to hear?"

"I don't know. Transport me. Take me someplace else."

"Climb aboard this magic carpet ride." He dipped his head and closed his eyes. His hands moved over the wooden body of the instrument that defined him. Kai was a mandolin player. He'd been other things, too; wanderer, dreamer, survivor.

Experiences shaped us. Some we clung to, others we threw to the wind. I wondered if we ever had a choice in how the song of our lives played, or if we were notes written in permanent ink, our paths already defined.

Chapter 27

Kai

By the time the trees were completely bare, the plans for our house had been completed. I'd wait until spring to begin building it.

It was one of those rare stretches of life when there seemed to be nothing but possibilities in front of us, and everything was calm.

It felt like hope.

One mild afternoon, Sage and I took a picnic basket to a small clearing on our land. We spread out the blanket and watched the clouds roll by. Sage's eyes were closed, her body warm next to me.

"Do you know that sometimes I watch you sleep?" I asked. Her eyes popped open. I was propped up on an elbow gazing down at her. Her features were soft, but she was stronger than steel. My true match. "Sometimes, I can't believe you're really next to me, so I put my hand on your belly and wait for the rise and fall of your breath."

She smiled, reaching up to stroke my face.

I turned my head and kissed her palm. "Lucy and Wyatt set a date for their wedding, and my brother asked me to be his best man."

"What did you say?"

"I said *yes*." I stared across the clearing, neither seeing the trees nor hearing the birds. "But how can I watch him marry my best friend's wife?"

"Wyatt is your brother," Sage said, "and Tristan is gone."

"I know." In anger, I stood.

"Don't you walk away from me," Sage commanded, scrambling up from the blanket.

I stopped my retreat and spun to face her. "You're right, okay? I know she deserves to be happy, and I know he loves her. I know Dakota should have a father, but I just—can't."

She came to me and tugged on the zipper of my jacket. "Are you mad because Lucy found love again, or because she found love again with your brother?"

"Don't know. I'm trying to sort everything out, and Wyatt is wrapped up in all of that. Sometimes I wish life really was either black or white."

"You don't think I know how that feels? It's what I'm going through with my writing and my mother's death."

"It's not the same."

She shrugged. "Trees bend; you know why? If they didn't, they'd snap."

"Adapt or die," I said into her hair.

She paused. "Do you know the dandelion is both yellow and white?"

I was thrown by the change in conversation. "There aren't two types?"

She shook her head. "The dandelion is yellow before the bees pollinate it. Then it turns white, when it's ready to spread its seeds. There's a time for everything."

"When is it our time? To flourish?"

"When we stop fighting what we can't change. Lucy and Wyatt are going to get married, and you will stand next to your brother. And when the time comes and Lucy tells you she's having Wyatt's baby, you can either be happy you're going to be an uncle, or you can destroy any shot of ending this estrangement with your family. You have to stop looking at Wyatt like he's an outsider. You may never be as close to him as you were to Tristan and Reece, but Wyatt is still here. You really want to push him away?"

"You're not supposed to be this rational."

"Someone has to be," she grinned, "because it's clearly not you."

"Ouch." I took her hand and placed it on my heart.

"Call your brother. Tell him you want to take him out for a drink, and try talking to him. Don't yell, don't throw punches —talk."

"Talk," I repeated.

"He asked you to be his best man. He made the overture; you owe him this."

———

I sat with my brother in a low-lit dive bar, taking a swig from my pony neck beer. Wyatt's gaze was wary, like he didn't know what to make of me. I didn't blame him. I had been an ass to him most of our lives.

"I'm sorry," I said.

"For what?"

"For a lot, but for starters, not being supportive of you and Lucy."

"I always thought my bachelor party would include a trip to Vegas. Instead, it's taking place in a shitty bar, and my brother and I are having a heart to heart."

"I didn't have a bachelor party. There wasn't time since Sage and I got married a week after I proposed. I never really believed in them anyway."

"And yet you threw Tristan a party."

"Yeah," I sighed the word. "I did."

Tristan's bachelor party would live forever; the parts I could recall, anyway. Lots of alcohol, cigars, and poker. At one point, I bet my argyle socks because I didn't have any money left. I'd thrown those socks into Tristan's casket, an eternal reminder of an inside joke that would last long after both of us turned to dust.

"He was your best friend. And what am I? Just your brother." His tone could've been snide—it wasn't. It was full of understanding. "You don't think I know how this looks? Everyone knew Tristan, everyone loved him—everyone loved Tristan and Lucy together. I'll be the second husband, always second best."

"Is that how you see yourself?" I asked in surprise. My brother always seemed so sure of himself. Solid, but never cocky. Did we have something in common—were we both sinking under the bulk of our own inadequacies?

Wyatt grinned in wry humor. "No, but I know that's what others will think. I don't want to replace anyone; I just want to make her happy."

"A worthy mission," I said. "I'm sorry I never tried to know you, not the way you deserved."

"It's okay, Kai."

"It's not okay," I insisted. "All these years...I don't expect you to forgive me overnight."

"You're my brother," Wyatt said. "You've had your own share of hardships."

Wasn't that the truth?

"Things are going to be different—I want them to be different."

Wyatt tapped his beer bottle against mine, letting years of tension between us clink away as if it had never existed. It was gracious and more than I deserved. Wyatt was a true gentleman. To think I'd spent years of my life taking my brother for granted, never wanting to be close to him because I had Tristan and Reece. Who did Wyatt have? Lucy, and now he'd have me, the way it should've always been.

"Let me buy you a shot," I said, rising. I had a lot to make up for, but it was a new beginning for Wyatt and me. A new beginning for all of us, maybe.

"Bring a few." Wyatt grinned. "It's not a bachelor party if the groom doesn't get hammered."

I laughed. "If there's one thing I'm good at, it's drinking."

"You're good at a lot of things, Kai. That was always your problem."

"You think so? I always thought I wasn't good at anything that mattered." I sighed. "I'll get those shots."

"Make 'em Jack."

———

I stood in the bedroom doorway, watching Sage turn the page of a book. She was snuggled up in bed, and if I knew her like I thought I did, she'd been there for hours. "I love coming home to you."

Glancing up, she quirked her lips into a smile. "I'm glad. How was your night?"

"Mellow." I plopped onto the bed and kissed her. I'd gotten Wyatt thoroughly plastered before carting him home. I stayed sober. Best man duties. Had to make sure he didn't wind up in an alley somewhere lying in a pile of his own puke. "I have a brother."

"Just now noticing that fact?"

"Yes." My expression sobered. "I can be a real ass."

"It's called being human."

She closed her book, set it aside and pulled me closer to her. I rested my head against her body as she plowed her fingers through my hair, and I sighed in contentment.

"Alice called me with some interesting news."

She toyed with my ear. I couldn't think when she did that. "Yeah?"

"Tristan's parents have reconciled, and they're donating a library to your old high school in his honor."

"Reconciled? Miracles do happen." I lifted my head and looked into her eyes.

"They do. Speaking of miracles—I'm ready."

"Ready?"

"For a baby—give me a baby, Kai."

"You sure?"

She nodded and leaned in to kiss me. I took her into my arms, and it was a long time before I let go.

———

"You look beautiful," I said.

Lucy turned and smiled, running a hand down her yellow dress. "Shouldn't you be out there making sure Wyatt doesn't pull a disappearing act?"

"What man has ever wanted to leave you, Lucy?"

"Good point." She grinned.

"What does it feel like?" I asked. "Getting married for the second time? Are you just as sure?"

Lucy tilted her head to the side, lost in thought. "Yes, but it's incomparable. Tristan was the eye of the storm, and I'd loved him ever since we were kids. I didn't fall in love with Wyatt until I was an adult, a mother. It's just as strong, just as real, but different." She gazed at me. "I knew I was going to marry Tristan since I was a child."

"What do you mean?"

"I just knew he was going to be the boy I would marry."

"You were eight. How could you know something like that?"

She shrugged. "Just knew."

I sighed. "He'd be glad you're happy."

"Maybe. Last night, I dreamed we talked and he threw things and ranted, but in the end he wished me happiness."

"Do you dream about him a lot?"

"Every now and again."

I wondered if I should tell her I had dreamed about them every night until very recently. Maybe I was finding peace. Maybe Tristan and Reece were finding it, too. Smiling, I held out my hand. "Come on. I think it's time I walk you down the aisle."

I wished I could stand in the middle, between Wyatt and Lucy, to let them know I was there for both of them.

"It's okay to be happy, Kai," Lucy said, taking my arm.

"Are you telling me, or yourself?"

"Both."

"Let's go. And try not to trip."

———

"It was a beautiful wedding," Sage said, sliding out of bed. She cracked open the window, letting in the sound of rain, the brisk autumn air and the moonlight. She shivered in her skin. I missed her for a brief moment until she climbed back in next to me, seeking my warmth.

I pressed a kiss to her collarbone, and her fingers trailed down the length of my spine. "I didn't see most of it."

"You didn't?"

"I was too busy watching you until Dakota started throwing a tantrum."

Sage laughed. "Wyatt handled it nicely."

He'd picked up Dakota, who sat in Evelyn Evanston's lap, before returning to the altar. He had promised to protect and love Lucy, and it only made sense to include her son.

"They're going to have a long, wonderful life together."

Tugging her beneath me, I trapped her with my heat. "Do you want to continue talking about the wedding?"

"Nope."

We melded together, one body, one heart, beating the same tattoo of homage to each other. I lost myself, and when I came back I felt as though we were knotted together—our tragedies and hopes intertwined like tree saplings.

We awoke late the next day, ate breakfast for lunch, and then went back to bed.

"I'm going to be sad when we move out of this cabin," Sage said.

"Why?"

She shrugged. "I don't know. It feels like Memaw's home knows you from when you were a kid, and I wish I did, too."

"You and I will make new memories in a new home—with a skylight so we can see the stars from our bed; with a kitchen where we can dance to Tom Petty, and with four extra bedrooms..." I trailed off.

I didn't say what those rooms would be for, but we both knew—

we wouldn't talk about it until there was something to hope for. She snuggled close to me and put her head to my heart; her soft breathing was a lullaby, and it sang me to sleep.

———

From the front porch of a familiar cabin, I watch the autumn rain come down in twisted sheets. Reece sits on a stool, a beer in his hands.

"You gonna share that?" I ask.

Reece passes it to me. "What's on your mind, Kai?"

"Is it always hard? I mean, always?"

"Harder at some points than others. Life is what you make it."

I find my smile. "Sage wants another baby."

"And you want to make her happy, don't you?"

"It's the only way I have a chance at finding it for myself."

"That's deep," Reece jokes, but then turns thoughtful. "You never think you're good enough, deserving enough, but you are."

"You sure about that?"

"Yep. Things happen; people make mistakes. Happiness can grow in even the darkest of places."

The rain lightens, and I breathe in the smell of fresh greenery. I don't feel relief yet, though the calm of the mountains surround me.

"Stop looking back, Kai. Look forward. You'll find your answers there."

Chapter 28

Sage

I sat on the couch with a blanket spread over my legs, a roaring fire chasing away the afternoon chill. Kai walked into the living room, beaming like a loon.

"You're never going to guess who called me."

"Howard Stern."

Kai grinned. "Nope."

"Well, I'm out of ideas."

"It was Béla Fleck."

"Béla Fleck. As in the famous banjo player you got to come to our reception?"

"How many Béla Flecks are there?" He laughed.

"He called you himself?"

"Yeah. He's in New York giving a few concerts. He asked me to fly up there."

"Why?"

"He loved the song I wrote, and he wants to hear more."

"You're kidding?"

He shook his head. "Even I can't believe it."

"Do you have any other songs?"

"Maybe."

"There's a bit of mystery to you, Kai Ferris," I said with a grin.

"I was going to play them for you."

"Hmmm." I pretended not to believe him. This was hardly a surprising turn. I knew what the mandolin meant to him.

"Should I pursue this?" He sat next to me, his leg bouncing in agitation. He took my hand and studied it. "What if something comes of it? It could take me away from you."

"It wouldn't be forever."

"What happens if you get pregnant?"

"Then we have a baby. Do I really need to explain the birds and the bees to you?"

He laughed.

"It's just a meeting, Kai. See where it leads before you worry about all the reasons why you're scared to do it. We have to stop being scared." My eyes poured into him before unveiling something I was holding close to me. "I've been writing—and not just in journals."

"Ah, someone else is being mysterious."

I grinned. "We have to find the things that make us happy."

"So, writing makes you happy now?"

"Denying it has made me unhappy. See this through, Kai. For you. Let this be all for you."

"You make it easy." He pulled me into his arms.

"It is. Our possibilities are endless—like the stars in the sky."

"Endless, huh?"

I smiled and kissed him. "Like my love for you."

———

"We're going to be eating leftover hot dogs and hamburgers for two weeks," I said with a laugh, opening another pack of buns and placing them on a plate. Kai fished through the refrigerator and pulled out every condiment known to man.

"What? You don't want hamburgers for breakfast?" he teased.

"I guess I could crumble them up and add them to scramble eggs," I joked. I put the pan of sliced potatoes into the oven and turned on the timer. "Will you set the patio table?" I handed him a stack of napkins and paper plates.

"Sure. I'll get the grill going. And light the bonfire, too. It's going to be a cold night."

"Want a beer while you do manly things?"

He laughed. "Please."

I opened a bottle and handed it to him.

"Thank you, darlin'," he drawled, placing a kiss in the curve of my neck, making me shiver. "Do we have time before—"

The doorbell rang, and we both laughed. "Would you get that?" I asked. "I want to start the mac and cheese."

"How much food are you making?"

"Enough for a going away party."

"I'll only be in New York for a few days." Shaking his head, he went to answer the door and came back holding Dakota, who shrieked in delight when Kai pretended to drop him.

Lucy stuck a bottle of white wine in the refrigerator and then hugged me. "Can I help?"

"Nah, just sit there and keep me company," I said, gesturing to the kitchen chair. Kai grabbed Wyatt a beer and they went outside, taking Dakota with them.

"Wyatt is really happy," Lucy said.

"Well, he just got married. I hope he's happy."

Lucy laughed. "I'm talking about him and Kai. They're finally acting like brothers."

I shook my head as I put the noodles on to boil and checked the potatoes. "Who knew? Are you guys going to go on a honeymoon?"

"I don't know. Is it a honeymoon if you bring your kid?"

"We'll watch him for you."

"That's a nice offer, but I can't ask you to do that."

"Forget about it, we'd be happy to do it. At least for a few days." I winked.

Lucy smiled. "All right, I'll talk it over with Wyatt. Thanks, Sage."

By dusk, everyone had arrived and we were outside enjoying more food than we could possibly eat. The heat of the bonfire stretched around us, pocketing us in warmth while the crisp autumn air nipped at our cheeks.

"Sit down," Alice commanded.

"I can't," I protested. "I'm the hostess." Alice pushed me into a chair and handed me a glass of lemonade. "Don't you dare clean up," I warned her.

"Paper plates, remember? They just go in the trash," Alice said as she picked up a stack and dumped them into the waiting garbage.

I sighed, realizing Alice would have her way. I caught Kai staring at me, the promise of our future written in the smile lines around his eyes. My love for him swelled like a water balloon ready to burst. He wanted to give me everything, but he didn't realize he already had. His heart was more than enough.

I love you, he mouthed across the backyard before turning his attention back to Wyatt and Keith.

"Who's ready for pie?" I asked, standing up. "I've got banana cream, coconut cream, and chocolate cream."

"Bring them all!" Wyatt shouted.

"Yeah, why choose?" Keith demanded.

I laughed and went into the house. I grabbed a knife and pulled out the pies, slicing them and putting slivers onto small paper plates. The sliding door opened, and I looked up into the hesitant face of my mother-in-law.

"Need some help?" Claire asked.

"Sure," I said, wondering if this was Claire's version of an olive branch. It wasn't as though the woman screamed domesticity.

"Is he looking forward to his meeting in New York?"

"Yes. He's still in shock though. Trying not to get carried away."

"Where will it lead?"

"Not sure; it might not lead anywhere. We don't know."

Claire sighed. "I really do want him to be happy. You too, Sage."

"You have a funny way of showing it," I said lightly. I knew I could have been more gracious, but she'd made Kai's homecoming unnecessarily difficult. The way she had treated her son made me furious.

"I know," she said. "It's hard to let go of the vision you have for your children."

I nodded in understanding. My mother had never let go. There hadn't been enough time. If she had lived, I wondered if I would've found my place—to stand proud and eventually embrace my gift, or if I would have continued to push it away. I would never know.

"I'm sorry—about the baby. I never told you," Claire said, jarring me back to the present.

I looked at my mother-in-law, weighing her sincerity. "Thank you."

"My son can have us both; he doesn't have to choose, does he?"

I smiled and touched Claire's arm. "No, he doesn't." She squeezed my hand, and we didn't need any more words.

After distributing dessert, I settled into a chair. Kai came to sit next to me, and I fed him bites of pie, smearing whipped cream on his lips and kissing it off of him. I didn't care that people could see us. I wanted all his sweetness.

"The banana cream is the best," he said.

"No, the chocolate." I smiled. "What do you think? Is this a good sendoff?"

"Decent," he said and then grinned, "but it won't compare to our reunion."

———

"What are you doing?" I asked from the doorway of the kitchen. Kai was sitting at the table; tools, fishing line, and an assortment of other things were in front of him.

"Did I wake you?" His eyes were tired and his cowlick was in fine form.

"No. What's on your mind?" I took a seat and placed my hand on his thigh. He looked conflicted.

"Am I doing the right thing? Going to New York?"

Definitely conflicted.

"I thought we got past all this," I said.

"Just because we talk about it doesn't mean I stop thinking about it." His fingers fiddled with a fly he was tying. I set my hand on his to still his movements and forced him to look at me. I brushed hair off his forehead and caressed his stubbly jaw. His vulnerability was a layer he didn't show everyone, but he showed it to me. Or maybe he couldn't hide it from me.

God, I loved him.

"What would Tristan and Reece say?"

He smiled slightly. "Tristan would tell me to stop being such a baby. Reece...Reece would want to find out why I feel the way I do."

"Any thoughts on that?" I stood and went to get a glass of water. His eyes tracked up my bare legs before resting on my face. I was in one of his shirts; it was old and threadbare. It was the next best thing to wearing Kai.

He shrugged.

"Everything is going to be okay. You know that right? If this works out and you're away for a time, it will all be fine. Your mother and I are learning to co-exist. You're building a relationship with your brother. And you're not alone. You have me."

Kai sighed. "How is it you know exactly what to say to make me feel better?"

"I don't," I teased. "Half the time I don't even know what I'm saying."

"Liar. You're one of the most thoughtful people I know. Why am I so afraid?"

"Because you're human."

"What are you afraid of, Sage?"

I leaned in to kiss his lips. "It's two in the morning. Do we have to have this conversation now? Come back to bed."

"In a bit," he said.

"Okay, Kai." I wondered if his insecurities and doubts would become too much for him, and whether or not his shoulders would start to droop like an old man's. He needed to remember that I was there to share the load. "Just remember one thing."

He looked up from his project to stare at me. "What's that?"

"Remember that I love you."

His mouth formed a crooked smile. "If there's one thing I never forget, it's that." He rose from his chair. "I'm ready for bed now."

Chapter 29

Sage

The sun hadn't yet made an appearance when Kai kissed me on the lips. "I'll be back before you know it," he whispered.

My eyes fluttered open as I rolled over and grabbed his pillow, hugging it to my chest. "Promise?"

"Promise. Go back to sleep. I'll text you when I land."

When I awoke next, it was late morning. I sat up, a wave of nausea moving through my belly. Just when I thought my stomach had settled, I threw up all over the wood floor. I went to the bedroom window and threw it open, closing my eyes in dreamy relief, breathing in a gust of cool mountain air.

This is how it started last time...

I tended to the mess, went into the bathroom and pulled out a box of pregnancy tests I'd bought a few weeks prior. My pulse drummed in my ears as I waited for the answer I already knew.

I was pregnant.

My first feelings were of elation, followed by a moment of

sadness for the baby I'd lost. But it was not the time to dwell on the past. There was so much good to live for, and that realization hit me with the force of a tidal wave. I felt exhilaration and hope blast to the far corners of my heart. I was a goblet full of happiness ready to spill over.

My stomach groaned in hunger, and I laughed, placing a hand on my belly and giving it a little pat. I went into the kitchen, turned the iPod dock onto shuffle and got down to making breakfast. While I flipped a pancake, Hall and Oats blared through the speakers. I danced around the kitchen, singing into a spatula. The music was so loud I almost didn't hear my phone ring.

"I was just calling to see how you were doing," Jules said.

"Kai and I can be separated for a few days," I teased. "We won't wither and die."

"Glad to hear it, but I really think you should've come to the city. We could've had a few days of girliness."

"School is in session. You have to teach, remember? Besides, I'd rather have you visit here."

I wanted to share the news with my oldest friend, but Kai deserved to know first. Shoveling food onto my plate, I ate as we talked. I let her babble about Luc, and Jules didn't realize I wasn't my usual chatty self. I was too consumed with thoughts of my own future. We hung up, and I went upstairs to get dressed.

Reaching under the mattress, I pulled out the stuffed giraffe Jules had bought me. After I'd lost the baby, I hadn't been able to look at it, but I couldn't fathom the idea of throwing it away. Now, I couldn't take my eyes off of it. It was a symbol of the life Kai and I would have together. Setting it on my side of the bed, I swiped happy tears from my face and went to visit the plot of land where we would build our home. It was only ten minutes up the path from Memaw's cabin, and when it was completed we'd have a panoramic view of the mountains. I coveted winter with Kai here, nestled on the couch, a roaring fire, snowfall outside our window, and his hand on my belly while we made plans. So many plans…

I returned home early in the afternoon and checked my phone. I had a missed call from Kai, but when I called him back, he didn't answer.

Probably in a meeting.

I changed into overalls and a large, floppy straw hat before going outside. I pulled on gardening gloves, found a spade and lost myself in the smell of dirt and the sounds of nature.

It was late afternoon when my phone buzzed. I was in the middle of digging a hole, but I managed to fish my cell out of the front pocket of my overalls. I pressed talk and put Kai on speaker.

"Hello?"

"Hello, my gorgeous wife."

I laughed and then bit my tongue. I wanted to announce our good fortune, but I held it in. "What are you doing?" I asked.

"I'm having a cocktail at the hotel bar, waiting for Béla Fleck to join me for dinner."

"Shut up," I said. "You live such a glamorous life."

"Are you okay with being arm candy?"

"You know it," I teased.

"What are you doing?"

"Guess."

"Walking around naked."

I chuckled. "You really think I'd do that?"

"A guy can dream, can't he?"

"Guess again."

"I don't know—cleaning?"

"I'd be more inclined to walk around naked."

He laughed. "I know. You're a terrible housekeeper. You spill things."

"That I do," I admitted. "So are you ready to know what I'm doing?"

"Enlighten me."

"I'm gardening."

There was a pause on the other end of the phone. "Can you repeat that? It sounded like you said you were gardening?"

"Yep. I'm wearing overalls and a big straw hat."

"Yeah, I'm going to need physical confirmation of that."

"I'll send you a picture."

"Since when do you garden?"

"Since today."

"What are you planting?"

"Nothing. I'm turning the soil and burying eggshells. Getting it ready for spring."

"I don't even know what to say right now. When did you learn how to keep a garden?"

"I bought a book. *Gardening for Dummies*."

"Really?"

I grinned even though he couldn't see. "No."

"You're adorable."

"Right back at you."

There was a muffled voice in the background and Kai responded to it before saying to me, "Sage? My dinner meeting is about to start. Call you later?"

"You better."

"Love you," he said.

"More than your mandolin?" I asked.

"Maybe," he teased.

I was still chuckling when we hung up. I took a photo of my outfit and sent it to him, hoping it made him laugh. I spent another hour outside until my stomach began to rumble. I cooked dinner, had an uneventful night of watching TV, and went to bed early.

———

"Whatcha doin'?" Kai asked.

"Attempting to get up," I said, phone in hand.

"I thought it would be relatively easy since I'm not in bed next to you."

"You would think, but I'm *really* comfortable," I said. "When are you coming home? I can't get a good night's sleep without you."

"I have a few more meetings this afternoon, but I think I can change my flight to this evening instead of waiting until tomorrow morning. What do you think?"

Excitement welled inside of me. "I think you should get your butt home."

He laughed.

"How are the meetings going?" I asked.

"Very positive, but I don't want to tell you anything over the phone. Let's wait until tonight to celebrate."

"Celebrate. So you must have good news?" I had some of my own, but I would wait until he was sitting in front me, and I could see his face when I told him about the baby.

"We've got a lot of celebrating to do," he said, his voice turning low. "We're going to be up all night."

A hum of desire pulsed through my veins and settled in my belly. "I look forward to it."

"Love you," he said. "I'll call when I land."

I decided to go for a drive. An hour later, I was in Nashville. I parked outside an expensive, custom-design baby boutique. As I entered, I was welcomed by cream walls, soothing tones, and quiet classical music. I stopped in front of a dark wooden crib and touched the bumblebee themed mobile.

"May I help you find something?" the young sales assistant asked.

"Just looking, thanks."

"Let me know if you need anything," she said, before moving away.

I drifted around the store, flipping through children's books and studying the bright, happy illustrations. I'd never thought about writing a children's book until that moment, but ideas began to come to me—freely and without reserve, like a heart in love. They had been waiting, ensnared in the web of my mind, and now I was ready to pluck them from their resting places. I was excited to return home and begin writing.

On my way out, a set of stencils caught my eye.

Dandelions.

It reminded me of a conversation I'd had with Kai. He had

asked me when it would be our time to flourish, and I had told him it would be when we stopped fighting what we couldn't change.

We had accepted our losses, and now we were in the springtime of our lives.

I would paint the nursery with yellow dreams.

Chapter 30

Sage

The exhaustion of the first trimester caught up with me while I waited for Kai to return, and I fell asleep on the couch. I didn't awaken until my husband was kissing my forehead. I opened my eyes, staring into Kai's strong face.

"Hi, darlin'," he said in a husky voice that never failed to elicit shivers up and down my spine.

I reached up to stroke his stubbly jaw. "What time is it?" He sat down next to me, and I hauled myself up, leaning into him. Sleep addled my mind and body. I wanted nothing more than to close my eyes and fall back asleep in Kai's arms.

"A little after eight."

"Eight? Oh, man! I had plans to make you a special welcome home dinner."

"That's okay."

"No, it's not! I went to the store, and I bought gourmet cheese and a rabbit."

"Rabbit? You know how to cook rabbit?"

"Celia gave me a recipe. I was going to try it out tonight."

Kai frowned. "Don't worry about it. We'll order Chinese or something."

I buried my face in my hands and started to cry. "There's nothing special about Chinese!"

Kai pulled me against his chest and stroked my hair while I wept against him. "Hey," he said. "Why are you crying? You love Chinese."

I wiped my nose and sniffed. "I was going to make you a home cooked meal and then tell you I was pregnant. You can't tell your husband you're pregnant over Chinese food!"

"Pregnant?" he whispered. "You're pregnant?"

I nodded and turned watery eyes to his. "I wanted to tell you in a special way, Kai. Not like this."

He laughed softly and kissed my tearstained cheeks before settling on my lips. "Best welcome home gift I could've ever asked for."

I clutched his shirt in my hands and sobbed all over him.

"Do you want me to order you beef Lo Mein?" he asked, completely unperturbed by my show of irrational emotion.

"That would be really nice," I blubbered.

He grinned and handed me the box of tissues that were on the coffee table. He took out his cell from his jeans pocket and ordered our takeout.

"Come here," he said, after he hung up. He leaned back against the couch. I draped myself across him while he stroked my hair, his lips caressing my forehead. "I was just wondering if I could be any happier, and then you tell me we're having a baby."

I nuzzled against him, and we lounged in companionable silence. I listened to the drumming of Kai's heart, imagining the tiny heartbeat that would soon live inside me.

"What happened in New York?" I asked, wanting to continue the joy.

"Béla Fleck wants to lay down tracks in the spring. He's asked me to be a guest artist on his new album."

"Oh. Oh, *wow*."

"You know what that means?"

"What?"

"I get to write songs and practice them this winter. It means I get to stay home with you." His hand touched my stomach. "Both of you."

I breathed a sigh of utter contentment. "Life is rarely perfect, but this moment, here with you…"

"I know."

The doorbell rang. Kai rose to answer it and then came back with a bag of Chinese food. We pulled the coffee table close to the couch and didn't bother with plates. We laughed and talked as we devoured egg rolls and hot and sour soup. He fed me a steamed wanton, and I ate the entire container of beef Lo Mein.

After we finished, we headed upstairs to bed. We didn't bother cleaning up, knowing it could wait.

———

"I'm not ready to tell anyone," I said. We'd dozed for a few hours and then awakened, sleepily turning to one another again. I was cradled in his arms, tracing zigzags across his chest.

"Why not?" he asked.

"I just—want to make sure."

"Make sure?"

"Make sure nothing goes wrong this time."

His arms tightened around me, and I hoisted myself up to stare in the direction of his eyes. I brushed my lips across his chin.

"We're having dinner with my family tomorrow. They'll know something when you ask for club soda instead of bourbon."

I shrugged. "Let them guess. It's bad luck to tell anyone before the third month anyway."

"You don't really believe that, do you?" he asked.

"We told people before the third month last time. Look how that turned out."

He threaded his hands through my tangled hair. His thumbs

gently rubbed behind my ears before he scratched my scalp with his strong fingers. I curled into him like a cat.

"I was so happy," I whispered. "I *am* so happy, but what if—"

"No."

"But—"

"No, Sage," he said more forcefully. "No more fear. Do you want the baby to feel that? Feel that kind of fear?"

I was quiet for a moment before I asked, "What happened to us? I thought you were the one that was afraid, and I was the one that had to talk *you* down?"

He kissed my lips, his mouth warm and beautiful, and full of comfort. "Are we going to plan for the worst or hope for the best?"

"We've already experienced the worst, haven't we?" I placed my head against his heart; it pulsed in my ear, solid and steady with hope.

"We've got nothing but happiness. And anything that comes our way, we can deal with—even your fear."

"You sure about that?"

"Yeah, I am. You taught me that."

"Show me what I've taught you," I commanded. "I don't remember." His hand stroked the knobs of my spine and I said, "There's a good chance this might all just be my hormones going insane."

He laughed, and I felt the rumble under my hand. "I thought about that, but even if it is, I'll still find a way to reassure you."

I breathed him in and closed my eyes, warm relief rushing through my limbs. "It will be winter soon."

"Can we build a snowman? We haven't done that together."

"There's a lot we haven't done together yet. Snow angels, for instance," I said. "There's nothing like lying in the snow, closing your eyes and catching snowflakes on your eyelashes and tongue."

"Is that something you and your mother used to do?"

"One of the many things. I still can't believe she's not here to make snow angels with us."

I rolled onto my side, and Kai pressed himself against my back.

His hands splayed across my belly, reminding me that I sheltered the center of our world in my body, reminding me to be grateful for the joy.

Chapter 31

Sage

I clambered out of the car and slammed the passenger door shut. I stared at my in-laws' large and imposing house, but for some reason I no longer found it intimidating.

There was a nip to the air, and I anticipated the first snow of the season soon. Kai came around to grasp my hand. He brought it to his lips and smiled, the corners of his eyes crinkling. I shivered and not just from the cold.

"We agreed, remember? Not to tell anyone until the third month," I reminded him.

"I know," Kai said.

"Wipe that grin off your face," I commanded. "You look way too happy."

"I'm about to tell my family that I'm going to be a guest musician on Béla Fleck's newest album. I could be smiling for that reason."

"You could be, but you're not," I teased. "You look like an actor from a chewing gum commercial. Tone it down."

"Yes, ma'am."

We walked into the house, the smell of dinner wafting from the kitchen.

Meat.

I hoped it was lamb. We headed to the library, knowing the family was partaking in cocktail hour.

"About time y'all arrived," George grumbled, standing up from the couch and setting down his bourbon. He hugged me before turning to his son and shaking his hand.

Wyatt slapped Kai on the back, and Lucy embraced me quickly. I turned to Claire, wondering what to expect from her. At Kai's going away BBQ we had seemed to come to an understanding.

She smiled at me, looking as nervous as I felt. My mother-in-law was beautiful when she smiled. Without thought, I enfolded her in my arms, refusing to let distance continue to rule our relationship. I heard her sigh of relief in my ear, and I pulled back.

"I'm glad you're home," she said to Kai.

He kissed her cheek and squeezed her hand. "It's good to be back."

Without asking, George poured two bourbons and handed them to us. "To homecomings," George said, holding up his glass. We clinked glasses and smiled, and Kai took a healthy sip. I faked a swallow, but caught Lucy scrutinizing me with a narrowed gaze, and I turned away.

"Dinner is ready," Claire said. "Let's go into the dining room."

We settled around the table and I asked, "Where's Dakota?"

"Spending the night with Tristan's parents," Lucy said. "We'll pick him up in the morning. We promised him a trip to the zoo."

I looked at Kai. "Why haven't you taken me to the zoo?"

He grinned. "You want to go to the zoo? We'll go to the zoo."

"You're welcome to come with us," Wyatt said, his gaze darting between his brother and me.

"Sounds fun," Kai said without pause. I glanced at Lucy, and we smiled in mutual understanding. Fences were mending.

As we were served our soup, a split pea and ham, George piped up, "I want to hear about your meetings in New York."

Kai leaned back in his chair, his foot touching mine underneath the table. He looked peaceful and happy as he explained what would occur in the spring.

"This calls for champagne," Claire said.

Kai groaned. "No champagne, Mom. That stuff is terrible."

"Bourbon," Wyatt and George said at the same time.

Kai laughed and shot me a look. "Nah, I'm good. Let's just enjoy the food."

I breathed a sigh of relief. Kai was trying to spare me from having to refuse liquor. I tried the soup, pepper and ham gliding over my tongue. Everything tasted better. I was almost finished when my stomach rolled. Apparently my morning sickness didn't know the time of day. I set my spoon in the bowl and took a deep breath, pressing a hand to my lips.

"Sage?" Claire asked. "Are you feeling all right?"

"Sage?" Kai whispered.

I shoved back from the table and ran from the room. I found the nearest bathroom and threw up the creamy, delectable soup. I gripped the edge of the sink and groaned. I was washing out my mouth when there was a knock.

"Sage? It's me."

I opened the door and let Kai inside. There was a slight smile on his lips. "I thought morning sickness only happened in the morning."

"Not this time, I guess." I frowned. "What did you tell them?"

"Nothing."

"*Nothing?*"

"You won't let me."

"I just threw up in the middle of dinner. I can't lie my way out of this." I glared at him. "Stop looking smug."

He took my hand and led me back to the dining room. Four faces stared at us, waiting for an explanation. I sighed. "I'm pregnant."

Lucy cracked a smile and shot a look at Wyatt. "Told you! Wyatt thought it was the flu."

"She was pale and shaky," Wyatt defended.

"Pregnant?" Claire stood and came to us, her eyes never leaving my face.

I nodded.

She reached out to grasp our hands, her voice quivering when she said, "This *definitely* calls for champagne."

"Absolutely," George said. He left the dining room and returned a few moments later with a chilled bottle.

"Want me to open that?" Lucy asked. George thrust the bottle at her. "I was a waitress once upon a time," she explained to me.

I raised an eyebrow. Claire set down flutes, even one in front of me. "Just to cheers," she said, patting me on the shoulder. Lucy moved around the table serving the bubbly liquid. We raised our glasses, and Kai stared at me, his grin wide.

He gripped my hand and said, "To a perfect moment."

———

"If you want ice cream," Lucy said to Dakota, "then you have to get down off of Uncle Kai's shoulders."

Kai winked at me, but said to Dakota, "You can get back up there when you're done."

"Promise?" Dakota asked.

"Promise." Kai lifted Dakota to the ground, and the little boy latched onto Wyatt's hand. Lucy took her son's other hand, and they approached the snack stand that served ice cream, pretzels, and cotton candy. Half the fun of the zoo was the food.

"Dakota loves his Uncle Kai," I said, kissing Kai's cheek.

He wrapped an arm around my shoulder and kept me close to him. "It's because I buy his affections."

"You're not the one getting him his ice cream."

"No, but I did promise to take him to a baseball game and buy him a hot dog."

He tightened the plaid scarf around my neck. It was chilly and we wore gloves, but it wasn't quite cold enough for hats yet.

"What kind of ice cream did you get?" I asked Dakota when he came running back to us, Wyatt and Lucy trailing behind him.

"Chocolate."

"Is chocolate your favorite?" He nodded. "Mine, too."

He held out his cone and grinned. "Wanna share?"

I crouched down and took a small lick. "Hmmm, delicious. Thank you. Thank you for sharing."

"I like to share." He looked at his mother.

"Did you teach him that?" I asked Lucy.

She shook her head and gestured with her chin to Wyatt. Wyatt ruffled his adopted son's hair. "You ready to see the monkeys, bud?"

"Yeah!" Dakota shrieked. His mouth was stained with chocolate, but like all prepared mothers Lucy held a stack of napkins and wiped Dakota's face. He squirmed, trying to get away, smearing the chocolate even more in the process.

"Almost done," she said. She threw the soiled napkins into the trash and grinned. "Let's go."

I watched the three of them trek towards the primate building. They were a family.

"God, he looks just like Tristan," Kai said.

I squeezed Kai's hand gently as we walked.

"If I bought you an ice cream, would you share it with me?" Kai asked.

I looked up at him and smiled. "Not a chance."

He laughed. "It's because I'm not as cute as Dakota, right?"

"Definitely."

"This is nice," he said.

"It is," I agreed.

"I've become a family man."

"So you have."

"I know they want to see the monkeys, but can we sneak away to see the penguins?"

"I'm good with that. Penguins are cute. They mate for life, you know."

His eyes found mine. They were vast, a pool of flinty blue. He swallowed, emotion catching in the back of his throat. "Yeah, I know."

———

The soft sounds of Kai's mandolin teased me awake. Before I even opened my eyes, I knew it was the middle of the night. It was happening with greater occurrence—Kai and I would fall asleep together, but inevitably, he'd stir, slip out of bed and spend a few hours writing music. Come dawn, he'd collapse next to me, sinking into a deep, rhythmic sleep.

I got out of bed and went downstairs. Kai sat on the couch, his mandolin across his lap. A pad of paper rested on the coffee table, and he scribbled something before looking up. The fire cast him in demonic shadows and hid the tiredness in his eyes.

"Did I wake you?" he asked, setting the instrument aside. I sat down next to him and curled into his side.

"Not really. I was coming out of a dream."

"What did you dream about?"

"Dragonflies."

"Dragonflies?"

I nodded. "I was on the bank of the lake, the one behind the farmhouse. The dragonflies were all different colors, and I felt the beat of their wings against my cheeks. A fish shot out of the water, parting it like a seam. It looked like a trout, but it was gold. Its scales caught the sun and shot prisms of light across the lake. I thought it was beautiful. Then it suddenly opened its mouth and devoured the dragonflies—and me, in one bite."

"Where was I?" he asked.

I shook my head. "I didn't even think of you. Not in the dream."

"Your heart is racing," he said, his hand at my neck.

"Play me a song." I pulled away from him. His brown hair had grown past his chin. It fell into his eyes, and he brushed it back. The scruff along his jaw made me sigh in longing. But none of that compared to the look on his face when he picked up his mandolin and played me a song from the depths of his heart.

There weren't lyrics.

The song didn't need any.

When he stopped, I could barely make out his shape through my tears. "How do you do that to me?" I whispered.

He placed his mandolin in its case. I pulled him to me, my back hitting cushions, his body looming over mine. Kai traced the arches of my brows, the curve of my mouth, the apples of my cheeks with his thumbs.

"We are so lucky," I said into his lips.

"You and me?" he asked, brushing away emotion that had escaped the corners of my eyes.

I smiled. "Yes, but I meant the baby and me. We're lucky to have you, Kai Ferris. We're lucky we get to love you."

Chapter 32

Sage

The Ferris library was overrun with family. George and Claire had invited the Chelsers to spend Christmas with us. The tree had been trimmed for weeks, long before the first snowfall. At the moment, we were waiting for a blizzard, but none of us cared. We were inside, warm and happy.

Alice handed me another glass of her homemade Eggnog and I took a sip, enjoying the sugary creaminess. I sighed. Though it was good, it would've been better with rum.

"It's too bad the Germains couldn't come for Christmas," Keith said, his arm around his wife. "I would've liked to have met them."

"Celia said Christmas is their busiest time of year. And Jules wanted to spend the holiday with Luc. Can't say I blame her."

"You guys ready to open presents?" Wyatt asked.

"But Christmas isn't until tomorrow morning," I said.

"We're a present-on-Christmas-Eve kind of family," Kai explained. "What was Christmas like with your Mom?"

I laughed with fond remembrance. "No real celebration.

Chinese food and a movie. Then we'd hit Max Brenner and have hot chocolate and fondue. It was great. The city was deserted and quiet. Almost magical."

"Did you have a Christmas tree?" Wyatt asked.

"We had a shrub of sorts."

"You don't miss New York at all, do you?" George asked.

"Not even for a second."

"Okay, presents," Claire said. Dakota sat in her lap, and she brushed his hair off his face.

I stood, but everyone waved me back down. "What's going on?"

"You'll see," Kai said.

I peered at him. "What do you know?"

He smiled. "Nothing."

"Here," Lucy said, setting a green wrapped box on my lap.

"This is from Jules and Luc," I said, reading the note.

"They're sending gifts as a unit? That's serious," Kai said.

I unwrapped the present and held up a pair of baby tennis shoes. "These are so cute I want to punch someone," I said.

Everyone laughed and then Wyatt handed me a shiny red box. "This is from us."

"And me!" Dakota said.

I looked at him and grinned. "Will you help me?"

He slipped off of Claire's lap and bounded over to me. He ripped off the wrapping paper, and I pulled out a knitted green baby blanket. I was starting to see a theme for the gifts. "This is beautiful," I said, running my hand across it. "Thank you."

"Momma made it," Dakota explained.

I looked at Lucy. "Really?"

She nodded. "I knit now."

"What did you do, Wyatt?" I demanded.

"It was my idea," he said with a grin.

"Ah, the idea man," I said. "Team effort, I like it." Kai took the blanket from me and set it aside. I glanced at him. "Did you plan this?"

"Plan what?"

"Did you tell everyone to get us baby gifts?"

"Maybe." He smiled.

I leaned against him. "This is Christmas, not a baby shower."

"They all agreed with me," he said. "We wanted to celebrate."

"Ready for the next gift?" Keith asked.

I nodded.

Alice handed me an envelope, and I took out a photo. "What——?"

"Keith made you a crib," she said.

"Made?" I squeaked. "You *made* this?"

"Totally upstaging our gift," Wyatt said with a smug grin.

Keith beamed. "It's at the ranch," he explained, his bright blue eyes searching mine. "I can bring it over to the cabin whenever you're ready for it."

I shook my head, tears falling down my cheeks like snowflakes from the sky. I was up off the couch, lunging for Keith and Alice's arms. They held me while I cried, even after Kai came over and joined in the hug.

I pulled back and smiled. "Thank you," I said, my voice hoarse. I turned to George and Claire who were holding hands and smiling.

"Please tell me your gift won't make me cry again. Please tell me your gift sucks."

George laughed and then gestured to the mantle. My eyes traveled over the ornate stockings, reading each of the names, every member of the family until I came to the last two. One had my name sewn in thick green thread—the other was unmarked, for the child I carried.

"Son of a…" I whispered, overwhelmed with love.

Alice handed me a tissue, and I dabbed at my cheeks.

"Also, Celia and Armand are flying in from France for New Year's. That's their gift."

"You know what would make this night even more perfect?" I asked.

"What?" Kai stroked my cheek without a care that we weren't alone.

I grinned. "Alice's apple tarts."

"Finally!" George said.

———

"Are you sure you can't stay longer?" I asked, pulling back from Celia's embrace. "It feels like you just got here."

She shook her head with regret. "Believe me, I wish I could, but we left Luc in charge of the bed and breakfast. Who knows what state of disarray it will be in when we get back?"

Kai unloaded the Germains' suitcases from the car and set them on the curb. He shook Armand's hand and then hugged Celia goodbye.

"Love you," Armand whispered in my ear as we embraced. "We'll see you soon."

Kai and I got back into the car and watched as Celia and Armand ambled inside with their luggage. Sadness invaded my heart as I watched my surrogate parents leave. When we drove towards downtown Nashville, Kai reached over and touched my knee in silent understanding.

"I miss France," I said.

"You do?"

I nodded. "I like it here, of course I do. It's beautiful, and we have family here, but we have family there too. *Tours* is home to me, I think. It's where we fell in love. You bought us a farmhouse. I breathe differently there, I *feel* different there. I don't know how to describe it."

"I do. It's how I feel when I'm in the mountains." Kai paused and then said, "I think we should move back to France."

"What?"

"After I'm done recording in New York, we should move back to France."

"You just admitted to feeling at peace in the mountains. I can't you ask you to give that up. What about the house you want to build us? What do we do?"

"We do whatever we want," he said. "We won't start building the house until the spring anyway. Wyatt can oversee things for me. It will be done by next fall. We can come back to Monteagle, Sage —whenever we want. Every summer or winter. I don't care."

I fisted my hands in my lap, wondering how I had managed to find a man who wanted me as the center of his world, who let our lives revolve around my happiness.

Kai was selfless.

"I used to think it was mountains. Now, it's about making you happy because it makes me happy. I don't need much else."

"What about your parents and your brother? I don't want them to think I'm choosing the Germains. That I'm making *you* choose the Germains."

"Dad is semi-retired anyway. Mom doesn't work. The Germains run two businesses. My family can travel. The door is always open to them. But we can live in two places. We have choices."

"Choices."

"You don't have to worry. About anything."

"No, I guess I don't. I didn't realize…"

"Realize what? That I'd give you everything you ever wanted?" he teased.

"You gave me yourself, Kai. No better gift than that."

"You should be happy today. Today is the day we find out the sex of our baby."

"I am happy."

He parked the car in the lot of Nashville OBGYN Associates and cut the engine. "We should make a bet. I think it's a boy."

I smirked. "What do you want to bet?"

"A kiss."

"So either way we both win?"

He smiled. "I've already won."

Chapter 33

Sage

I rolled over and kissed Kai's shoulder. He scooted closer, throwing a leg over mine and made a startled noise when I put my cold foot in the crook of his knee.

"Ahhhhh!" he gasped. "What are you doing to me!"

I wheezed with laughter. "My feet are cold and you promised to take care of me forever, remember?"

"Yeah, but *come on!* Warn a guy first, huh?" He crawled out of bed, opened a dresser drawer and pulled out a pair of his wool socks. He came back, removed the comforter, and searched for my feet. He tucked me back into bed before slipping in next to me. He wormed his way under my t-shirt and rested a hand on the elegant swell of my stomach.

"You feeling okay?" he asked.

"Hmmm. Better now. Warmer." My eyes closed, the feeling of Kai next to me making me drowsy.

"Should we talk about names?" he asked.

"Do we want to honor those we've lost?"

"There are so many of them," he said.

"How do we decide?"

He was quiet for a long time, but I knew he hadn't fallen asleep. Then he spoke, "Maybe we should name her in her own right then."

"Are you sad we're having a girl?" I asked. I knew what it meant for a man to yearn for a son. Or at least I could imagine it. I was a woman; I carried and brought forth life, I would know my child before the world did. It wasn't the same for Kai. He was a man's man—I couldn't wait to see him cradle our daughter in his hands; hands that gutted fish, hands that stroked a stringed instrument and played the most beautiful songs that had ever been created, hands that made me cry out in longing.

"Sad?" He shook his head. "She'll be like you."

"You think?"

"Yeah, except I'm going to teaching her how to fish when she's young," he warned as he kissed my belly.

I'd felt her kick a few days ago, but she was quiet now. Maybe dreaming of eddies and rivers. Maybe dreaming of mornings with her father when it would just be the two of them. Even if she was like me, I had no doubt she would be a daddy's girl. I had never known my own father, and with that thought I wondered how he would've shaped my life.

My chest rose as I breathed for myself, for my daughter—Kai's daughter.

"A tiny you," he whispered as he drifted off to sleep.

———

The snow fell steadily, and Kai continued to write music. He wouldn't play for anyone except me and the baby. Each night, I received a private show in front of the fire. He was stunning in his talent. The baby swam circles in my belly while we listened to Kai's musical poetry.

Happiness was a greater inspiration than tragedy.

One late winter evening, Kai set down his mandolin and said, "Damn, you're beautiful."

I snorted with laughter. I rested on the couch, feeling bloated and fat. "I think you may be a bit biased," I teased and then sang, "'I know an old lady who swallowed a horse…'"

Kai laughed. His skin was streaked gold in firelight. I wanted to nibble him like a decadent caramel.

"I know that look," he said, leaning in to me.

"Not my fault," I joked. "Pregnancy hormones make me randy."

"Who's Randy?"

"You dork!" We laughed until we could hardly breathe.

"You were like this before the baby, don't lie. You can't get enough of me." He stood and pulled me up like the twenty extra pounds I had gained were nothing.

"Well, that's true." We headed for the stairs.

"I can't get enough of you, either," he pointed out.

I removed my shirt, pushed down my sweats and stepped out of them, leaving a trail of clothing to the bedroom. His hands reached around to cup my roundness. I wanted him to seep into me like watercolors on a canvas. His fingers traced the seams of my stretch marks. They existed no matter how much he attended to them, no matter what lotion he rubbed onto my body. I didn't like them, but Kai kissed each one in reverence.

"Some of us wear our battles on our skin, others on our hearts," he said.

I touched his brand, a T&R for the friends he had lost. "Some of us have both." I held out my arms to him and he hugged me tight, despite my belly between us.

"It doesn't matter," he said into my neck, "because you're my salve."

———

"I swear to God, this baby is part fish!" I complained. "You're the fish whisperer, do something!"

Kai grinned, like I'd given him a compliment, his teeth white against his handsome new beard.

"*Your* child is making me miserable!" My feet hurt, my clothes chafed my skin, and I was annoyed—all the time. Usually at my husband. The moments when rationality did make an appearance, I remembered how much I loved him, how much I loved our life together, how much I already loved his child.

I picked up my mug of ginger tea. The fresh flowers Kai had brought home from the grocery store were losing their potency. Maybe I was sick of winter, sick of being stuck inside. The weather was about to break, I could feel it, but it hadn't come yet. Soon, I hoped.

"I have a surprise for you."

"Me? Or the baby?"

Kai didn't reply as he got up and went to the front closet. He came back with a large cardboard shoebox. I opened it and withdrew a pair of brown UGGS.

"Try them on," he urged.

I managed to pull on the boots, sinking my feet into soft wool. "Oh. My. God." I sighed. "These are the most comfortable things I've ever put on my feet."

He laughed. "Glad to hear that."

"It makes winter almost worth it."

"I can't remember a winter this brutal or this long," Kai said.

I gazed out the window; I was bombarded with beauty. It was all around me. Not just in my view of snow-capped peaks, but also in the man I had married, in the child I carried. There were so many blessings; I wondered how I'd become so fortunate.

"She still giving you trouble?" he asked.

I winced, trying to dislodge her foot from underneath my ribs. My insides felt like they were black and blue.

Kai pulled up my shirt and muttered nonsense syllables against my belly. The baby shifted, and he placed a cheek against my body. We were skin to skin.

Skin.

Nothing more than a thin veneer that held our child safe and warm.

———

I buried my head in my hands and sobbed uncontrollably. The more I thought about it, the harder I cried.

"Sage? Darlin'? What's the matter?" Kai asked as he shut the front door. He carried a hot pepper sandwich on a baguette, and the smell made me forget my sorrow.

"Is that my sandwich?" I reached for a tissue and blew my nose before crumbling it up in my fist. Kai sat down next to me and handed it over. I took a bite and moaned in pleasure. Nothing, I mean, nothing compared to satisfying a pregnancy food craving. I finished the sandwich, sipped on a ginger ale, and glanced at my husband.

He peered at me like I was an alien. "You okay?"

I put my hand on his leg, trying to reassure him that I wasn't going to throw a vase at his head. I'd only done that once, a few weeks earlier. It hadn't even hit him. He wasn't one to hold grudges.

"There was a really sad commercial on television," I explained.

Bless his heart, he didn't even flinch. There was crazy, and then there was *pregnancy* crazy.

"I love you," he said with a charming grin. I stroked his beard and leaned into his body. His arm came around me, and I sighed.

"How much do you love me?"

"You want ice cream, don't you?"

I nodded into his chest. "With extra sprinkles. *Please?*"

He brushed his lips across my forehead, then trailed down my nose and settled on my mouth. Before he could pull away, I reached for his belt and kissed him back, smelling of spicy peppers and desire.

"God, you're perfect," he said.

I cried again, only this time it wasn't in sadness.

Chapter 34

Sage

Spring came, and it was wet with gloomy skies. A bout of massive hailstorms littered the countryside, laying waste to all that tried to bloom. But the mountains were green, and my body was round and ripe.

"I look big, don't I? I mean, really big."

Kai bit his lip, like he was debating on smiling. "Why do women do that?"

"Do what?"

"Ask questions they already know the answers to."

I glared at him. "You could be a little more sensitive. I know I'm almost six months pregnant, but come on…people think I'm carrying *twins*. I'm huge!"

"That was one person, and she was a twenty-year-old cashier at the grocery store. She smacked her bubble gum for Christ's sake. Who cares what she thought?"

"I don't care what she thought," I yelled. "I care that she said it out loud! Whatever happened to having a filter and not saying *every single thing* that comes to your mind?"

He rubbed a finger across his mouth. I knew he was smiling, the bastard. "It's a generational thing."

I arched an eyebrow. "Generational, huh? Okay, Grandpa."

Kai sighed in mock defeat. "I miss my wife. She used to be so nice…"

I gnashed my teeth at him. "You're lucky you're cute, Ferris. That's the only way I'd allow you to get away with teasing me."

"Can I hug you? Or do you have a weapon I need to know about?"

Before I could answer, he came to me and I collapsed my bulk against him. He held me for a moment and said, "I think I have something that will cheer you up. Put on your shoes."

"Why?" I asked. We walked to the front door, and I used his arm to steady myself while I slipped on the UGGS he had bought me. He grabbed my light jacket and helped me shrug into it.

We stepped outside, and I breathed in the fresh air. It was in the mid sixties, but the sky was clear. Perhaps it wouldn't storm today. "Where are we going?" I asked as Kai took my hand and led me up the path.

He didn't reply, and ten minutes later he stopped when we came to a cement spot surrounded by a small clearing with a panoramic view of the mountainside. "It's not much to look at yet," he said. "It's just the foundation, but it's solid enough to build the home of our dreams."

I gripped his hand, letting my tears fall in the silent morning.

————

"You have your wallet?" I asked Kai.

"Yep."

"Got your ticket?"

He nodded.

"Lyrics?"

He pulled them out of his shirt pocket. They were hardly legible, and the papers were wrinkled.

"You ready?"

He grinned and kissed me. Dropping to his knees, he stroked my belly and kissed it. "I'll see you soon," he said to my stomach.

"I'm up here, buddy," I said with a smile, my fingers toying with his beard.

He kissed me again, slower, almost endlessly. I sank into him. "Love you," I whispered, pulling back.

Kai tugged on a strand of my hair. "Love you, too. I'll call when I land." He picked up his small travel bag and mandolin case. I opened the front door and stood on the porch, watching him depart.

I traipsed back into the house and settled myself on the couch.

A few hours later, my buzzing phone jarred me awake. It made a loud rattle across the coffee table.

"Just wanted to tell you that I landed, and I'm about to get into a cab and head to the hotel," Kai said.

"That's nice," I mumbled.

"You were asleep, weren't you?"

"No..."

He laughed. "Liar. Go back to bed you little incubator. I'll talk to you later."

I made myself a sandwich and went upstairs to the nursery. Keith had come over a few weeks ago and dropped off the crib. It was pushed against the far green wall. Kai hadn't let me climb the ladder to stencil the dandelions, so he'd asked Alice to do it. They dotted the trim in pale yellow. I sat in the comfortable rocking chair and ate my meal, content that our daughter would grow up in a room full of dreams.

After taking some time in the nursery, I headed out to the front porch, wanting to catch the last of the afternoon sun, and maybe the sunset. George's car pulled into the driveway, and even though he hadn't called, I wasn't surprised by his appearance.

"Hi," he greeted, trudging up the porch steps.

I stood and hugged him. "Hi."

"I'm on my way to the country club, but thought I'd swing by and check in on you."

"Can I get you something to drink? I have some freshly brewed iced tea in the fridge."

He smiled. "Thanks."

We walked inside and into the kitchen. "Ice?"

"Please."

I dropped some cubes into a glass, added a slice of lemon and the tea.

He took a sip. "Peach?"

I nodded.

"It's good."

"Thanks."

"Sorry I didn't call first."

"It's okay. I kind of like you showing up unannounced. It has a very intrusive family feel," I teased.

He laughed. "There's a purpose to my visit, not just to surprise you. I was wondering if you'd like to spend a few days with us? You know, while Kai is gone?"

I opened my mouth to refuse, not wanting to be a burden, but I found myself saying, "That sounds really nice."

He looked pleased. "Really?"

"Yeah, it can get kind of lonely up here. Thanks for the offer, George. It was very thoughtful of you."

"It was Claire's idea," he admitted.

"Was it? Well, that's a bit of a surprise."

He nodded. "For you and me both. I can swing by and pick you up on my way home from the club. Give you a chance to pack a few days worth of clothes."

"Perfect."

———

"You're never going to guess where I am," I said to Kai over the phone.

"I love guessing games. What are you wearing?"

"Don't make this dirty," I teased. "I'm in your parents' house—in your childhood bed."

"I don't understand."

"Your father invited me to stay over for a few days, but it was your mother's idea."

"I'll be damned."

"I think she's finally coming around to the idea of me."

"You're my wife and the mother of my child. It's about time."

I laughed. "Hey, she's trying to make peace. Anger is exhausting."

"Damn straight."

A patch of silence fell between us, and then I asked, "How's New York?"

"Loud, dirty and expensive. I don't know how you ever lived here. On the upside, though, Jules is driving down tomorrow and we're having lunch. I'll show her the studio."

"Not fair."

He sighed. "It's not too late you know, for you to join me up here."

"I—can't." I hadn't been back since my mother had died. I'd never seen her headstone. I wasn't ready.

We were silent again before he said, "Listen, I should get some sleep. I've got an early morning. And the sooner I go, the sooner this is done, and I can get back to my girls."

I patted my stomach. "We'll be waiting."

I attempted to fall asleep, but I was restless. I got out of bed and quietly crept downstairs to the kitchen. I was rummaging through the freezer for the carton of vanilla bean ice cream when the kitchen light turned on.

"Gotcha," George said with a grin.

I smiled back. "Sorry, did I wake you?"

He shook his head. "Nah, just had a hankering for something sweet."

"Me too."

"You were going to take that last piece of strawberry rhubarb pie, weren't you?"

"Maybe."

"I'll fight you for it."

"I'm carrying your granddaughter."

He laughed. "Trump card. You win."

"Let's share it."

"Better idea. That way Claire can't yell at me about my cholesterol."

"She loves you. Wants you to be around for a while." I opened the drawer and pulled out two spoons and the ice cream scooper. The last piece of pie was on the cake stand underneath a glass lid. George went to the cupboard and withdrew a plate. I placed two huge scoops on top of the pie and stuck the tub back in the freezer. We settled at the informal kitchen table, but before I took a bite I snapped a photo on my cell phone and sent it to Kai saying, "Wish you were here".

"Trying to make him jealous?" George teased.

"Alice will bake him a welcome home cobbler. He's got nothing to be jealous about."

"Hmm. Hopefully it'll be peach. Alice makes a damn good peach cobbler." He licked his spoon before diving back into the ice cream. "So why are you awake?"

"Late night call with Kai," I explained. "Plus I'm pregnant. I'm asleep and awake at the oddest hours."

He chuckled.

"Why are *you* awake?" I demanded.

"Age. Can't sleep through the night."

I snorted with humor. "I don't buy that excuse."

"No?" He looked thoughtful. He pushed the plate towards me and set his spoon down. "I've been doing a lot of thinking."

"About what?"

"Retiring."

"You're semi-retired already," I pointed out.

"I know, but I don't think I want to work anymore. At all. I want to play more golf, have more time with my family. Be able to travel."

"Have you told Claire?"

"Yeah, she knows I'm thinking about it. I'd been thinking about it before Kai came home and now…"

"Now there are more important things than work?"

"Exactly."

We smiled at one another until Claire's voice interrupted our moment. "What's going on in here?" she demanded. She wore a silk white robe and house slippers.

"Busted," I stage whispered.

"We're sharing dessert," George said with a boyish smile. I saw Claire's lips twitch in amusement, but she feigned anger. She stalked to the cupboard and pulled out a bag of marshmallows and a tin of gourmet hot chocolate.

"If you're going to do this, you're going to do this right," she commanded. "George, get me the mugs."

———

"You're so going to think I'm the bestest best friend that has ever lived," Jules said over the phone.

I laughed as I threw my dirty clothes into the washer. George had dropped me off at the cabin earlier in the day. I'd enjoyed my time with my in-laws, but I was ready for Kai to come home. It had only been four days, but it was still too long to be apart.

"Oh, really? Why is that?" I asked.

"I'm coming to France this summer. After you move back."

"For how long?"

"The entire summer. Before the baby's born. After the baby's born. And if I can get things in order…"

"Order?"

"I'll be a permanent resident. I'm shackin' up with Luc."

I nearly dropped my phone. "*Shut. Up.*"

"Told you. I'm awesome."

"You better not be lying to me. I will kill you."

"Not a lie. I better start practicing my French now."

"Yeah, and kissing doesn't count." My phone beeped, and I looked at the screen. "Jules, I gotta go. It's Kai on the other line."

"Okay, call me later."

I switched over to call waiting and said, "Hello?"

"It's me."

"Hi, Me."

He laughed. "I'm coming home early."

"Really? You're not teasing me, right?"

"Not teasing. Did Jules tell you her news?"

"How did you know about it before I did?"

"I had lunch with her, remember?"

"You both are sneaky sneaks." I was beaming. "So when are you coming home? Tomorrow? The day after?"

"Tonight."

"Tonight? Too good to be true," I said.

"Try and stay awake."

"I make no promises."

"See you soon, darlin'."

We hung up, and I finished loading the washer. I heard a rumble of thunder in the distance. Spring storms seemed to come out of nowhere. I went out onto the porch and watched the rain. It came down hard and fast in sheets, but it abated quickly, like it had an explosive temper.

Even after the rain had stopped, dark clouds continued to loom, and I knew there was a good chance the squall hadn't yet run its course.

Chapter 35

Kai

I paid for my cup of coffee from the airport Starbucks, took my change and shoved it into my pocket. I had some time before my flight boarded, so I wandered into a gift store that had everything from snacks to magazines. As I scanned the tacky shot glasses and t-shirts, my eyes landed on the wall of books. One name, in big black letters, stood out from all the rest.

Penny Harper.

I picked up the book, flipped it over, and quickly read the blurb. My mouth quirked into a smile as I gently placed the book Sage's mother had written back in its spot.

"It's a good read. If you were on the fence about buying it," a man said. He looked like he had popped out of a GQ ad. He was tall, blond haired, and blue-eyed and wore an expensive suit; the silver Rolex at his wrist caught the light.

"Thanks," I replied. "I'll think about it."

"I'm a fan of Penny Harper," he went on. "Read all her stuff, but that is her best work. By far."

"Doesn't seem like your genre."

"Not usually," the man agreed.

"Why did you read it, then?"

A sad smile flitted across his face. "I was trying to impress a girl. She wouldn't let me take her out on a date until I'd read it. Anyway… Gotta catch my plane."

I decided against buying Penny's book. After all, I could just borrow a copy from Sage. I left the store and headed to my gate. I sat down, tapping my hand against my leg, my thoughts turning from Penny Harper to her daughter.

Would I ever see Sage's name on a book? Would it become a *New York Times* bestseller and grace the shelves of bookstores around the world? Sage had a gift, one she had only started to embrace, but I would be there when she accepted it.

I couldn't wait to get home to her.

———

"Told ya," Tristan says.

"Told me what?" I demand.

"Told ya you'd find your way," he grins.

Reece laughs. "Took you long enough to listen."

"I'm a stubborn ass," I say.

"We know," Tristan and Reece say at the same time.

I sigh. "It looks different here." I glance around. The lake isn't silver, but golden and it looks like it's covered in ice.

"Think we can walk across it?" Reece asks.

"Maybe, try it out," Tristan urges.

"Okay." Reece steps onto the lake. When its clear he won't fall through, he looks at us and grins. After he reaches the middle, he drops to his knees. "You guys have to see this!"

"What is it?" Tristan asks, even as we go to join him.

Reece doesn't reply, he just points. Tristan and I crouch. I touch the surface of the golden ice, but it's not cold and I wonder if it's ice at all. Underneath, the water ripples and I can barely make out the floating shape. But soon, I can see what it is. There is a goldfish, bright as the sun, swimming in circles.

I stare at it for what seems like an eternity, and finally, before my eyes, the goldfish breaks through the ice.

It begins to transform; fins turn to arms, its tail turns to legs. Scales melt into glowing, golden skin. It has become a woman—a beautiful, naked woman with chestnut colored hair and gray eyes that carry many secrets.

I don't know where my friends have gone. I am alone with the goldfish woman. She smiles and holds out her arms to me. Unable to stop myself, I go to her. She wraps me in a tight embrace.

I see nothing but golden light.

Chapter 36

Sage

I awakened in the middle of the night to the sound of thunder and a banshee wind whipping tree limbs against the glass windows of the cabin. Somehow, I managed to tumble back into dreamland before I could think about moving upstairs.

I woke just as the sun was climbing over the mountains. I sat up, stretched my neck, and rubbed the crick in my lower back. I checked my phone; I had received a text from Kai at 1:00 AM saying he'd landed.

I called his cell, but it went straight to voicemail. I frowned. He'd gotten in late. Maybe he had decided to rent a hotel room by the airport to catch a few hours of sleep before driving home in the morning.

I was in the middle of making breakfast when I heard a car pull up in the gravel driveway.

Kai.

I turned off the burner, dumped my scrambled eggs onto a plate, and went to open the door, excitement blooming inside me.

"Mrs. Ferris?"

I stared in confusion at a young police officer, and my smile slipped from my face. I nodded slightly.

"I'm sorry to bother you this early, but we found your husband's car off of…"

My vision went blurry, and I dug my nails into the palm of my hand to keep from fainting.

Words had lost all meaning in the wake of true destruction.

I collapsed like a matchstick dollhouse, broken, defeated in the new day's light.

———

"She hasn't moved in hours," whispered a voice. It might've been Alice, or maybe Lucy. It all sounded the same. Nothing penetrated the grayness of grief.

Kai is dead. Kai is dead. Kai is dead.

The chant played over and over in my mind, a wail on repeat. My lungs felt like iron spikes had punctured them.

My tears had long since dried, and my cheek was stuck to the wood floor.

"Sage?"

I opened my eyes and stared into the concerned face of my best friend. Jules lay next to me, her body mirroring mine. I watched her mouth speak; yet I didn't hear words. I blinked.

"Sage?" Jules said again. "Would you like to move to the couch?"

"Maybe we should call Keith. He can come over and lift her," Alice suggested from somewhere above me.

"He's with George, Claire, and Wyatt," Lucy replied.

"Sage will get up when she's ready," Jules said.

Ready? How will I ever be ready?

Standing up would mean that Kai was really gone. It would mean he had lost control of his car in the middle of a storm, and that he had hit a tree and died in his beloved mountains.

It would mean we would never have a life together.

On the floor, which was encrusted with my dried, salty tears, I could pretend for one more moment that Kai was coming back.

Sometime later I fell asleep, but woke again not long after—screaming. Jules' arms surrounded me while sobs wracked my body. When they subsided, I croaked out, "Water." I touched my head. It throbbed in pain. Someone gave me a glass.

Lucy.

Alice went into the kitchen, and when she returned she set a sandwich in front me, but I didn't touch it. I drank more water.

I didn't know how long I sat on the floor, but eventually I stood. Alice and Lucy helped me to the couch. I felt like someone had pulled a plug in my heart, and all my joy had drained out of me.

"Sage, you have to eat something," Jules coaxed.

I dutifully shoved food into my mouth, but almost choked on it. I dozed off again.

I dreamed of Kai. I traced the smile lines at the corners of his eyes, and he held me against his chest. We swayed to the song he had played for me when we first met.

When I awoke, my cheeks were wet again. I'd been crying in my sleep.

I looked out the window. The sky was inky purple; it would be dawn soon.

———

It was night.

I touched his side of the bed, curled my fist around smooth sheets and then flattened my palm. Staring at the ceiling, I debated looking at the clock. Time no longer mattered. With each pulse of my heart, I was unable to forget.

Not even in sleep.

Not even in the dark.

I felt like a starfish with one of its limbs ripped off. Would I be able to grow it back?

I sat up and shoved hair out of my face. I padded downstairs and went into the kitchen.

Kai's flies and the contents of his tackle box were spilled across the kitchen table like child's toys on the living room floor. His fishing pole rested in the corner by the back door, like it was waiting for him to come home.

I picked it up. It felt wrong in my hands, so I set it down.

I filled a glass of water and took it to the couch. I sat in the blackness and the silence until the sun soared over the mountains. It had been cloudy for days, yet bright beams managed to paint through the gray.

For others, it would be a beautiful day, a welcome change from the gloomy weather. For me, it would be the day of my husband's funeral.

———

"Have you eaten today?" Alice asked.

I clasped a pearl earring to my lobe and shook my head.

"Can I make you something?"

I swiped my hair back into a bun as I met Alice's eyes in the mirror.

She needed to be needed. She was a mother without a child. I was a child without a mother. And a wife without a husband.

"Toast would be nice."

"How about something more substantial?" She looked at my swollen belly.

"Toast."

Resigned, she nodded. Before she left the room, she pulled me into her arms. I felt like a moldy old tower with most of its bricks missing. I was teetering, ready to fall. Alice left me, and I could hear muffled conversation downstairs.

I stared at my reflection. My eyes didn't look haunted—they looked empty. I lifted my chin, but my lip quivered. I bit it hard, giving myself pain to distract me from my emotions. I gripped the edge of the dresser, my knuckles white.

"You will not fall apart, you will not fall apart," I whispered.

I took the stairs slowly, my heels clacking on wood. The swell of conversation dimmed. I found Celia's eyes first. Armand stood next to her.

Jules was tucked away in the crook of Luc's arm, her face pale and her eyes watery. It hurt my heart—seeing them together. Knowing they were happy. Knowing they'd found each other.

Knowing what I'd lost.

Keith stood tall and somber. He'd removed his cowboy hat, showing neatly combed hair liberally streaked with gray. His black cowboy boots were shined with polish, and I focused on them. Alice came out of the kitchen with a plate. She handed it to me. I picked up a piece of toast and stuck it into my mouth, forcing myself to chew. My stomach rebelled, and I thrust the plate at her before I ran for the front door. I barely made it outside before I threw up in the green bushes.

I coughed and choked, and I spent a moment bent over at the waist. I heard footsteps on the porch and rose. Celia held out a glass of water. I walked to her and took it. I swished it around my mouth and spit it out.

"You ready?"

"Loaded question, isn't it?" My voice was a croak. I set the glass down on the porch. She came to my side, then took my hand and squeezed it.

I closed my eyes as we drove towards the cemetery, towards the moment when I would have to bury Kai.

———

Wyatt stood by his brother's grave, his eyes downcast. I could see the tears on his cheeks. Lucy stood next to him. Her red hair was a bright flag of color in a sea of black.

I went to Claire. I took her hand, and she clasped onto mine. We had become family by marriage; now we were a family in sorrow.

Where is George?

White, elegant roses covered the casket that housed my husband.

I felt my legs about to give way. I didn't want to take Claire down with me. I tried to drop her hand, but she held on.

"Breathe," she whispered in my ear. "Just breathe."

I sucked in air and choked on a sob as they lowered Kai into the ground. It started to rain and someone opened an umbrella to shield me.

I lived my life under an umbrella of death.

Mud stained the living grass, and still they shoveled the wet earth onto him. They were smothering him. Kai was drowning in dirt and rainwater—drowning in spring.

I wished to place my body on top of his, feel his lips on mine.

I didn't want him to be alone.

I pushed the umbrella out of the way and turned my face to the storm. The sky cried with me.

I was not broken—I was annihilated.

I wanted to collapse and never get up again.

But I had to.

For the baby.

Kai's baby.

———

I lay on Kai's childhood bed, dozing as the sun set. I felt a body sink down next to me and for one moment I believed it was Kai. But there was no smell of mountains, no scent of sunshine.

Kai was gone.

"Are you awake?" Wyatt asked.

I rolled over and looked into Wyatt's golden brown eyes. The Ferris brothers did not physically resemble one another. I was eternally grateful for that fact.

"Did I dream it?"

Wyatt paused before shaking his head *no*.

"It's not fair," I whispered.

"I know."

I turned my head away. "George didn't go to the funeral, did he?"

"No. He couldn't face it. I think—I think this might kill him, Sage." We lapsed into silence before he said, "Are you still planning to return to France?"

"Yes." I sat up and rubbed a hand across my face.

"I wish you'd stay," he murmured before rising.

I took a deep, shaky breath. "To stay would kill *me.*"

———

I awoke before the rest of the house. Grabbing my belongings, I went out onto the front porch to call a cab. It arrived fifteen minutes later, and I climbed into it, sliding across the ripped black leather seat. I gave the driver the address to Memaw's cabin and then directed him when he almost lost his way.

The house was quiet.

I journeyed upstairs and paused outside the bedroom I had shared with the love of my life. I made myself cross the threshold and swallowed the lump of emotion in my throat.

I changed out of my funeral dress and threw on a pair of jeans and one of Kai's t-shirts.

It smelled like him.

I went to my side of the bed, lifted up the mattress, and pulled out a stack of papers. If it hadn't been for Kai, I never would've found the strength to write. He'd become my foundation, my support beams, my lean-to out of the rain. He'd been the reason I claimed my gift.

He'd been my inspiration.

I set the manuscript down on the bed, and slipped on my shoes. I walked the familiar path to the foundation of our unfinished home.

I wanted to burn it to the ground, but it was cement.

Something caught my attention out of the corner of my eye. Crouching down, I plucked a dandelion from its resting place. I made a wish, took a deep breath and blew. The seeds swirled around me before being carried away by the spring breeze.

Who knew where they'd fall or if they'd take root?

The wind changed, and a seed I thought long gone floated back and caressed my cheek.

I closed my eyes.

I felt Kai at my back, solid and sturdy as his arms came around me, settling low on my round belly, sheltering us.

The baby kicked.

Kai's lips grazed my hair, and I smelled the sunshine on his skin. My hands covered his, and I sighed, lost in a moment of contentment.

There's powerful magic in a dandelion wish.

To dream is beautiful.

To love is a blessing.

To hope is human.

Part II

Prologue

Sitting on the bank of the lake, I stare at the sun-speckled water. I hear movement behind me, but I don't turn. Kai plops down next to me and sticks his bare feet in the lake. He's wearing his favorite pair of ratty jeans.

"I love it here," he sighs.

"I know."

"I meant being here with you—not the lake."

"Oh." I smile, deliriously happy to be here with this man.

He wraps an arm around me, and I press my face into the crook of his neck and breathe him in. I can smell the sun on his skin—it's been baked into him.

"I dream of you often," I reply.

"I know."

Kai pulls back and pushes a piece of hair away from my face. It's endless summer in the place where Kai and I meet—a place of in-between—where hopes are as plentiful as dandelion seeds. In this place, the sun always shines. I stare directly into the glowing orb in the sky, and it doesn't hurt my eyes, reminding me that this is only a dream.

"I think I'm making it harder for you, Sage."

Awake, I know only loneliness. But here, in this place, I am never lonely.

"Stay with me," I whisper.

"I can't," he says, his voice full of anguish, his face crowded with pain. "I have to go."

The salmon-roe colored sun sinks slowly behind the mountains.

Soon, I am in darkness.

And I am alone.

Even in the in-between.

Chapter 1

I heard their voices in the hallway. They wanted to help me, be with me, care for me. I closed my eyes, my hand gliding across my bulging belly. She moved—hesitantly, peacefully.

The door opened, but my eyes did not. I began to sing again.

"What's she singing this time?" a hushed voice asked.

"Simon and Garfunkel," came the reply.

Someone called my name, but I continued to sing.

"Celia…" Jules said.

"I know," Celia answered.

"I'm worried about the baby. Sage won't eat."

My eyes drifted open. They felt heavy. Two faces stared at me until Jules, my best friend, crouched down next to the bed and ran a hand across my lank, greasy hair.

"She's been this way since we came back to France a few days ago." Jules looked at Celia, who bit her lip in indecision before it was replaced by firm resolve.

"She needs a bath," Celia commanded.

Jules shot up. "I'll start the water." Relief painted her face, knowing she could at least complete that task.

Celia reached her hands out to mine, and I took them. She was thin and willowy, but managed to hoist me up despite my bulk. Jules had set a green towel on the sink in the bathroom.

"I've got this. Call and order food," Celia dictated to Jules.

"You sure?" Jules asked. Celia nodded. "But I don't speak Fren —never mind. I'll figure it out."

The bathroom door shut.

Celia tugged on my shirt, and I lifted my arms like a child. I felt no shame. I sat in the tub of hot water while Celia washed my hair. A torrent of tears fell across my cheeks, lost in the bathwater, with no need to try and wipe them away.

"Love is pain," I murmured.

Celia tilted my chin upward, so I was forced to meet her steady, somber gaze. Her mouth opened and she said, "I know."

———

Bold sunlight splattered through the glass windows of the bedroom. My swollen eyes refused to open, abused from days of crying.

I smelled coffee and bacon.

The little fish lurched inside me, and I gave a startled laugh. The sound resonated in the silence. I pressed a hand to my stomach. "*Okay*. Okay."

The scene in the kitchen wasn't a unique one. Celia stood at the stove, the sound of grease sizzling in a pan. Jules and Luc sat at the table, cups of coffee in their hands, speaking in hushed tones. Armand hovered near the bacon, filching a piece from the waiting plate. Celia smacked her husband's rough, brown knuckles and grinned at him in affection. The sight before me almost made me smile as I stood in the doorway, feeling like a stranger in my own home.

"Sage!" Jules exclaimed when she noticed me hovering.

I shuffled into the room like a dying hospice patient.

"How did you sleep?" Luc asked. His gaze scanned my face, searching for the answer he already knew.

Evading the question, I asked, "Shouldn't you be at the vine-yard? Gotta get ready for the harvest in a few months."

"We have help," Armand interjected. "Don't worry about us."

I nodded absently as I took a seat at the table. My head buzzed from their presence. Celia set a plate of food in front of me and touched my shoulder before leaving the kitchen. I ate, but didn't taste. Armand, Jules and Luc spoke softly to each other so as not to drive me back to my room. After just a few minutes at the table, the little strength I had found waned and I was tired again.

"I'm going back to bed," I announced.

I walked upstairs and into my bedroom as Celia was finishing making the bed with freshly laundered sheets. She straightened and peered at me before touching my arm and commanding, "Get some rest." She left, and moments later, I heard people shuffling towards the door, and my house was quiet once again.

I went over to the chest of drawers and pulled out one of Kai's flannel shirts. It was red and black, faded from many washings. Raising it to my nose, I inhaled deeply.

I shrugged into the shirt and drew the collar up around my chin. I settled into bed and tugged the covers up over me, including my head. Shrouded in darkness, I exhaled under the comforter.

———

As I gripped the edges of the porcelain sink, I stared into the mirror. "Say it," I commanded my reflection. "Come on, say it."

Taking a deep breath, I said the words I had trouble forming. "Again." My knuckles were white with stress, my mouth taut with rage. "Widow. I am a widow—widow, widow, widow."

Tears of anger glistened in my eyes. "Widow!" I shouted as I punched the mirror. The glass shattered, but I didn't feel my knuckle slice open.

"Widow," I moaned, sinking down onto the floor, clutching my bleeding hand. I breathed heavily, trying to control my sadness, my tears, but it all came at me with the force of a mountain squall.

"Sage!" Jules cried from the doorway of the bathroom. "I heard —" She crouched down next to me. "What the hell did you do?"

"The mirror..."

She looked around, as though she didn't know what to do. Settling on a course of action, she grabbed my uninjured hand and helped me up. "Go to the bed and wait for me. I'll clean all this up after I tend to you."

"My very own nursemaid. Perfect."

She shot me a look that spoke volumes, and then gently pushed me towards the bedroom and out of the destruction. In resignation, I sank onto the bed and examined my right hand. Bloody mess.

Minutes later, Jules came into the bedroom, carrying first aid items and putting them on the bed. "Why?" she asked, swabbing my knuckles with hydrogen peroxide. I winced at the sting.

"I'm a widow." I waited while she cleaned my hand, picking out a few shards of glass. "You going to tell on me?"

"So they can commit you to a psych ward?" she joked, despite the fear in her blue eyes.

"You think they'll go that far?"

"If you keep hurting yourself. You're pregnant."

"I know."

"Are you *trying* to hurt yourself?" she asked, deeply concerned.

"Blunt New Yorker, party of one."

"Sage, that's not funny. You have a *baby* to think about." She sighed and continued wrapping my hand in a bandage.

———

"What happened?" Armand demanded as he clutched my hand to examine my wound.

"Glass," I said.

"How?" Celia's gaze slid to Jules, but I answered before she could say anything for me.

"I broke a mirror."

They glanced at my bandaged hand.

"Jules already gave me a lecture," I informed them, wanting to spare him wasting his breath on a needless scolding.

"I don't care what you two have talked about. I know you're

hurting—but this? This *cannot* happen again," Armand stated. "Do you understand what I'm saying?"

Jules nodded in silent agreement as he spoke, seemingly glad that he was reprimanding me.

Armand continued, "Sage? Answer me."

"Okay, I hear you," I replied.

Armand's look softened, and he moved slowly to take me into his arms. "We're worried about you, Sage."

Celia cut the tension by asking, "Are you sleeping well?"

"Okay," I said.

We walked into the kitchen and Celia took a casserole dish out of the oven and placed it onto the counter. Jules and Luc set the table, and Armand poured a couple glasses of wine. I pulled up a chair and made myself comfortable.

"I'm not singing to myself anymore," I said to break the silence.

Luc stifled a chuckle, smiled, and patted me on the shoulder. Everyone else glanced at me to see if I was joking.

"I'm fine, seriously."

The meal was relatively quiet. My makeshift surrogate family observed me closely, watching to see how I behaved. I felt like a monkey in a zoo. I wondered what they would do if I climbed onto the table and started to make chimp noises. The idea had me laughing hysterically.

"What's so funny?" Jules asked.

"Nothing."

"Seriously, what is it?"

I began to sing, "'*And all the monkeys aren't in the zoo, every day you meet quite a few*'."

Luc cringed. "I thought you were done singing?"

"It comes and goes," I replied. I stood. "Thanks for dinner."

"I made a cake," Celia said. "Would you like a slice?"

"Thanks, but maybe later. Dinner was great." I kissed her cheek and left the kitchen.

"She's manic," I heard Luc say as I walked away.

"She's grieving," Celia corrected.

I wasn't ready for bed, so I headed to the turret. I hadn't been up there since I'd returned to France, but it was as welcoming as an old friend. Taking a seat near the window, I stared out at the darkening sky. "*'Would you like to swing on a star…'*"

———

"You're awake," Jules greeted in surprise as she came into the kitchen.

"Yep." I continued to whisk a bowl of eggs with my uninjured hand.

"Did you sleep?"

"Yeah, crashed hard."

"Good."

I heard the relief in her voice.

"You're cooking."

"Trying to," I said. "The bandaged hand makes it difficult."

She paused and bit her lip before asking, "Are you feeling any better?"

I didn't look at her when I answered, "Nope."

"I'm still worried about you. We all are."

I nodded. "Yeah." I dumped the eggs into a heated skillet; they crackled and the smell wafted up to my nose. There was hunger behind the pain. The baby was determined to keep me alive, no matter how much I wanted to give up. She needed me, depended on me. I had to pull it together—if not for myself, then for my daughter.

"I'm not suicidal," I promised. "I'm just—"

"I know." Jules's blue eyes raked over me, taking me all in.

My hand went to my stomach. She was my lifeline, yet I felt completely disconnected from her. "I can't give up," I said. "No matter how much I want to."

Jules poured herself a cup of coffee, the smoky steam rising up to curl around her face. She smelled it and sighed.

"I'm glad you're here," I said when I had finished eating.

"Really? I'm not unwanted?"

"No. I'm not sure I've said thank you for living with me."

"That's what friends are for."

"Yeah, but you're more than a friend," I stated. "You're family. Anyway, I hope I never have to return the favor. I hope life treats you better than it's treated me."

She swallowed and looked like she wanted to say something, but she didn't. So unlike Jules.

"Your presence pushes out the silence. Thank you for that." I stood and stretched my arms over my head. My lower back was habitually tight. I winced.

"Where are you going?"

"I think I'll walk around the lake," I said. "Get some fresh air."

"Want some company?" she offered.

I shook my head. "Do me a favor?"

"Anything."

"Don't turn on the *Mama Mia!* soundtrack and sing to me."

Jules gave a small smile. "I thought you were the one who liked to sing."

Chapter 2

I walk along a dirt path littered with summer leaves. In the distance, I hear the call of birds and the chant of the wind. I turn my face up to the sky and smile.

An old grandfather of a tree rests in the middle of a small clearing. Through its bending and twisting branches, I see a jean-clad leg hanging out of the canopy. I hurry over to the tree and, without thought, climb it. I swing up and settle myself next to the owner of the leg.

Kai holds a box of Cracker Jacks and pops a handful of caramel deliciousness into his mouth. I hear the crunch, crunch, crunch of popcorn, caramel and peanuts.

"Want some?" he asks. "I'll share."

"You'd share your Cracker Jacks with me?"

He grins and pushes the brim of his baseball cap higher on his head. "Does that prove how much I love you?"

I laugh. "Without a doubt." I reach for the Cracker Jacks, and after I swallow a bite, I inform him, "I wrote a book."

"Did you?"

"Impressed?"

"Very. You are a woman of many talents."

"Not so many," I murmur.

"No?"

"What do you do with too many gifts?" I ask.

"Use them."

"Or lose them?" My smile turns into a grimace. "If you had asked me what I wanted a few years ago, I would've given you an entirely different answer than the one I'd give now."

"What did you want a few years ago?" he asks.

"I'm not sure I remember anymore. I don't think it's important."

We fall silent. I wait for the wind, but no breeze strokes the leaves or teases my hair. Things feel stagnant in a way I can't describe.

"I'm proud of you," he says finally.

"Why? Because I wrote a book?"

"Because you're no longer hiding who you are. It takes courage to be who you really are."

"Or it takes too much effort to bury who we truly are. Maybe I just got tired."

He snorts. "You don't really believe that, do you?"

"No, I don't think I do." I lean my head back against the tree and close my eyes. I can't look at him when I admit, "I don't tell people about you."

"What do you mean?"

"Here. This place. Wherever we are. I don't tell them we meet and talk."

"You think they wouldn't understand."

I open my eyes and glance at him. "I don't want to share you. Not even your memory."

———

Scattered pages of the manuscript surrounded me like a blanket of fallen leaves. I rubbed my face with ink-stained fingers, leaving smudges on my cheeks.

Now, as the pinkness of dawn crept through the drapes, I set the papers aside and sat up. There was a small foot underneath one of my ribs. I winced and gently pressed against my belly. She moved her foot, and I took in a deep breath.

I got out of bed, careful not to disturb the papers. The chaotic mess was something only I understood. Taking the stairs slowly, I went into the kitchen and put on water for tea. Just as it started boiling, I heard a sharp mewl coming from outside. It was grating and whiny, but the neediness went straight to my heart. At the sound of it, shivers danced up and down my spine. Opening the back door, I stared out at the lake, seeing nothing. The warm air of early summer clung to my skin. It was the kind of morning that only made my longing worse.

I felt something rub up against my leg and almost let out a shriek.

The culprit of the noise was an emaciated black cat staring up at me with slanted green eyes. It sauntered into the farmhouse with a swish of its tail and a cock of its head.

"What are you doing here?" The cat waltzed in as if it owned the place. "I'm not going to lie, I'm not one for cats." I closed the back door, and the cat purred as it wrapped itself around my legs.

It sat down on the kitchen floor and licked a paw and then looked at me and *meowed*. I went to the cabinet and pulled out a can of tuna fish. "You're going to have to settle for this. I don't have cat food."

Jules padded into the kitchen, covering her yawning mouth. She gave a startled yelp when she saw the cat voraciously attacking the tuna.

"What is that?" she asked, slinking around the ragamuffin animal. She filled the coffee pot and pressed brew.

"A cat."

"I know that. But where did it come from?"

"Outside."

"It could have fleas," Jules said in disgust. "*Or worms*."

"Yeah."

"I'm calling Luc. They have cats on the vineyard that catch mice. He'll know what to do." She looked at me. "You have of smear of something on your cheek."

I nodded. "Ink, probably."

"I would say I'm surprised, but I know you." She picked up the phone and dialed Luc. Thirty minutes later, the cat was napping when Luc walked through the front door.

He crouched down and examined the animal. "Well, it's a 'he' for one. Two, I see no hopping fleas, so that's a good sign, but I brought some flea shampoo anyway."

"What about worms?" Jules demanded.

He shot her a grin. "We won't know that until he poops."

"Ew." She wrinkled her nose.

Luc rolled up his shirtsleeves and glanced at me. "Have you ever given a cat a bath?"

"Can't say that I have."

He sighed in resignation at the anticipated battle to come. "I'll help you. The first time is a bit tricky."

———

The little bugger protested, loudly and angrily, but I grabbed him by his meager scruff and said, "Listen, you. You're a guest in my house. You want to stay, you need a bath." Surprisingly, he quieted, and Luc laughed in surprise.

"What are you going to name him?" Jules asked.

"*Chat.*"

Luc raised an eyebrow. "You're naming him the French word for 'cat'?"

Chat meowed and I smiled in triumph. "He approves."

Jules stood up from the kitchen table. "You guys got this?" she asked rhetorically. Without waiting for an answer she announced, "I'm going to shower."

I waited until I was sure she was gone before saying, "You've got to get her out of here."

"Has she finally gotten on your nerves?"

"No. Not at all. That's why you've got to get her out of here."

"I don't understand."

My hair was falling out of its ponytail. I shoved loose strands behind my ears and rested my hands across my expanded middle. "If she doesn't leave now, I'm afraid I'll never know how to live without her, live alone in this house."

He was quiet and then, "Are you sure you're ready for that?"

I pretended to study my cuticles. "You both need to start living your lives. It's not her job to take care of me. You all have keys, so you can come and go as you please. I doubt I'll be left alone for long periods of time. Besides, I don't have any Jack Daniels or a straight razor."

Luc's lips did not quirk into a smile at my dark jest.

"I'm sleeping regularly. I'm eating regularly. I'm okay." I didn't think there was a need to mention the dreams.

He looked at me for a long moment. "I want to propose to her, Sage."

"I guessed as much."

"I mean, soon." Worry pervaded his eyes.

"You've been waiting, haven't you? Because of me?"

He gave a noncommittal shrug of his shoulders.

"Don't wait anymore, okay? Not on my account." The idea that my best friend would soon be planning a wedding filled me with warring emotions. Duality lived inside me. But when Luc proposed and Jules said yes, because she would say yes, I'd slap a smile on my face. I'd be happy for them, even though it would remind me of all I'd lost.

Chat, looking sleepy and motley, settled down in the corner of the kitchen. Before I knew it, he was asleep.

"Should I pick you up some cat food?" Luc asked, as if he was grateful to change the conversation.

I made a face. "I refuse to have that stuff in my house."

"You going to keep feeding him tuna?"

"He likes it okay, I think."

I looked at *Chat*, whose tiny belly rose and fell. I envied his calm sleep, and I wondered if it was the first peaceful night of his young life. He was mangy and thin, on the brink of starvation, but his cry had been powerful. His pain had literally called to me.

We were linked, this cat and I.

———

I pulled up the collar of Kai's old flannel shirt, feeling comforted by the familiarity of wearing his clothes. My belly felt stretched and thin, like a layer of jam spread over too much toast. "Are you on 'Sage watch' today?" I asked, leaning against the doorway of the nursery.

Armand spread out a blue tarp across the floor before he looked at me and smiled. "You all but kicked Jules out."

"I did no such thing."

"That's not the story she's telling." His grin grew wider.

I sighed. "She knows me. I tried to spin it so it sounded like it was about her and Luc instead of her and me. Frankly, I would've been happy if she stayed forever."

"She feels guilty—for leaving you."

"She shouldn't. She's here. Just not *here*." I gestured to the empty house. Empty except for one very strange cat, Kai's clothes, and me. "How are Jules and Luc settling into the cottage?"

"They're nesting. Jules has a thousand things going at once."

"Yeah, she's a force."

He paused. "I'm worried about her."

"What do you mean?"

"She doesn't know how to sit still, does she?"

"No. She's a doer."

"She's having a hard time adjusting, Sage."

"She doesn't speak French very well. It will take her longer to feel at home here."

"She doesn't speak French at *all*."

"Maybe she should enroll in French classes at the university. She needs other people besides us to interact with," I said.

"You should tell her that. She'll accept it from you."

"Maybe. She hasn't been here for very long. I think we're all just —adjusting."

Chat lurked in the doorway, a thin black shadow. I patted my leg and he came to me. I leaned down and scooped him up into my arms, running my fingers down his knobby back. He was eating constantly, he'd put on some weight, and his fur had started to grow back. His alien green eyes stared into me, through me. He under- stood me in the instinctive way animals seemed to understand people. Maybe we had found each other, maybe we were meant to save each other.

I watched Armand open a can of paint and prep it for the pan and roller. "It's not your job to paint the nursery. I can hire someone."

He shot me a 'don't be ridiculous' look. "Pull up a chair, hang out with me. Green, right?"

I nodded. "Can I at least offer you a beer? When you're finished. Consider it payment for services rendered."

He grinned. "Sure, thanks. You guys seem to be getting along."

"Who? Me and *Chat*? I think he tolerates me. I have become a guest in my own home." I continued to stroke *Chat* until he'd had enough and jumped down from my lap.

Armand laughed. "Yeah, that's the way of cats."

"He sleeps on Kai's side of the bed," I blurted out.

Armand didn't take his eyes off the wall he was painting. "Does he?"

"Yeah."

He sighed, set down the roller, and came to me. "Stand up."

"Why?" I asked even as I did as commanded.

"You need a hug." He put his arms around me, and I settled myself against the firmness of his chest.

I closed my eyes and rested my head on his shoulder. He pulled back so he could look at me. His face was weathered and brown, but his eyes saw more than the lines of pain and exhaustion around my mouth. He saw more than my huge belly that sheltered Kai's daughter from the world.

He saw more than I wanted him to see.

So I let him hold me—the man I had come to consider a father. I clung to him, hoping it was enough to see me through the moment.

Chapter 3

"What do you do when you're not here—with me?"

"I fish," Kai answers.

"All the time?"

"Pretty much."

"I never understood how you could be so patient. You tried to teach me, once." I remembered that day clearly. Time had not diminished its sharpness. It was the day we'd lost a child.

"Fishing is not just about being patient," he explains. "You have to learn how to listen."

"Listen? To what? The fish? You really are a fish whisperer."

"I am, indeed." He grins arrogantly. "Want me to teach you how to listen?"

"Yes."

"Okay. Close your eyes."

I do as he says and shut my eyes.

"Take a deep breath. Let it out. Do it again. Good. Now, what do you hear?"

"Nothing."

"Wrong. Try again."

After a moment, I speak. "My heart. I hear my heartbeat." I open my eyes and stare into his. I brush the silky dark hair from his face and kiss his lips.

He smiles. "What does your heart say?"
I smile back. "I think you know."

———

Jules held out her hand and showed me the vintage engagement ring. Her smile was brighter than the diamond in the center of the band. I hugged her to me, despite my uncomfortable bulk.

"It's beautiful. Family heirloom?"

She nodded. "His grandmother gave it to him on his last visit."

"When did it happen?"

"Last night." She sat down at the kitchen table, and I opened a bottle of wine and poured her a glass. I settled for iced tea. It was the height of summer, and the heat and my body were making me miserable.

"Tell me about it."

She smiled. It was soft and dreamy. "Sunset, walking through the vineyard."

"Poetic," I observed.

"Very. Sweet. Simple. It was perfect."

It made me think about Kai's proposal. In a car. Ending in us half clothed and breathing each other's air.

"What?" Jules asked.

"Nothing."

"No, tell me."

"This is about you and your moment. Not me."

"Thinking about Kai?"

I ran a finger over my own wedding band. "I'm always thinking about Kai," I said. My mind struggled to hold onto the threads of reality. When I closed my eyes, he came to me in my dreams. I was safe there. Loved. Awake, I was bereft.

She nodded and took a sip of wine. *Chat* came into the kitchen and, without missing a step, jumped into my lap.

"He's getting bigger, isn't he?"

"The boy loves his tuna. He's a lawless rogue." *Chat* purred and pushed his head against my stomach. The little fish moved. "When is the wedding?"

Jules blew out a breath of air. "Next fall. September."

"Good. A year should be enough time to get my figure back."

She laughed, but then sobered. "Will you be my Matron of Honor?"

I blinked. "Matron of—"

"Honor, yeah."

"Even after—"

"Even after. You're Sage, and I'm Jules. Will you be my Matron of Honor?" She reached for my hand, grasped it and we sat in silence, my best friend and I.

———

Chat perched on my desk and peered at me with slanted green eyes. He cocked his head to one side, lifted a paw, and licked it.

I sighed. "You think I'm ready to do this?"

He *meowed*.

"You're right. I know you're right. Why am I scared?"

He swatted his paw at me.

"You're telling me to stop being a baby?"

I was asking a cat for advice—and thinking about taking it.

Picking up the manuscript, I put it into a padded manila envelope, dashed off a note in an almost unreadable scrawl, and sealed it shut. "I should do this before I lose my nerve. You want to ride shotgun to the post office?"

Chat stood up as if signaling he was ready, and I hauled him into my arms. He rested his head against my body as I carted him—and the envelope—out to the car. It was a European model, small and compact, easy to navigate on the narrow, uneven cobblestone streets of *Tours*.

I parked outside the post office, looked at *Chat* and said, "Stay here." Then I snorted in laughter. I was unraveling like a spool of yarn.

I wasn't ready to return home after my trip to the post office. It was nice being out of the farmhouse, in the fresh air and away from the sadness of my loss. I drove around the countryside, passing different chateaux in the area and cursing the fact I couldn't drink wine. Everything was ripe and green, and with the window rolled down, I breathed in the clean, sweet smell of flowers and trees. I inhaled life.

I didn't get home until sunset and when I walked into the farmhouse, I saw Celia sitting on my couch, absentmindedly flipping through a magazine. I set *Chat* down and he immediately scuttled from the room.

"Hello," I greeted. "What are you doing here? Did we have plans that I forgot about?"

"You didn't answer your house phone."

"I was out."

"You didn't answer your cell, either."

"I didn't take it with me."

Her brow furrowed. "I was worried. We were all worried."

Celia's tone made me instantly defensive. Jules had moved out, leaving me to myself. I was a grown woman, a widow, and a soon to be a mother. I didn't have to check in with anyone. "I'm not a teenager, you know? You can't just barge in here and demand to know where I've been or what I was doing and why I didn't answer my phone."

She stood up slowly, her eyes blazing with something I didn't understand. "I didn't know if you were dead or alive."

"You're not my mother." My voice was soft, but she flinched like I'd hit her. "It's not your job to make sure I'm okay."

"Then whose job is it?" she demanded. Tears leaked out of the corners of her eyes. "Or have you forgotten I was the one who sat you in a tub and washed your hair for you because you couldn't— wouldn't—do it?"

I dropped my eyes, shame flooding my cheeks. I wanted to reach out and touch her, to apologize, to tell her I'd needed her then. I knew I wouldn't have gotten through those first few weeks after Kai died without her.

I was slowly regaining my strength and I didn't need to be

reminded of my fragility. I needed courage; I needed fortitude. Falling apart had not changed the fact that Kai was gone and I was alone. And in the end, it was up to me to put the broken pieces back together.

No one could do it for me.

"Fine, Sage. I'll stop hovering."

"Good. I don't need a keeper."

Her eyes bore into mine, glittering with tears and pain. Her hand dropped down by her side and she turned and walked out of my home. Guilt gnawed at me, but I shoved it down, burying it as deep as it would go.

I had other things to worry about.

———

Shifting my position on the couch, I pressed a hand to my back, trying to ease the cramp that had taken up residence. Unable to get relief, I stood, massaging my lower spine. I was walking around the living room when the front door burst open.

"You've got a lot of nerve!" Luc yelled.

"What is it with you people? Ever hear of knocking?" I snarled.

He held up his key.

"Give it back! It's given you far too much power. It's given *all* of you too much power."

Disregarding what I'd said, Luc shoved the key into his pocket. I was tired of people not listening to me.

"I mean it, Sage." Luc stalked towards me, looking like he wanted to do me bodily harm. "My mother hasn't stopped crying."

I saw *Chat* leap onto the couch. He swished his tail, watching Luc with predatory eyes. I wouldn't put it past him to go for the jugular.

"Why are you pushing people away?" he asked, his voice softer.

"I'm not trying to push people away."

"Like hell you're not."

"I went for a drive, Luc. And I didn't check in or answer my phone. I'm an adult, or have all of you forgotten?"

"We haven't forgotten," he said. "We just care about you. We're still worried. Can't you cut us a little slack? Do you hear me, at all?"

"I hear you," I murmured. "But maybe you need to listen to *me*. I'm doing this the only way I know how, and ultimately, it's up to me to find a way to... live... without Kai." Was I finding a way to live without Kai? Sometimes, I felt like I was nothing more than a delusional mess. Where were my moments of clarity?

He gaze softened in understanding. "I'm sorry I barged in here."

"Does that mean you'll give me back my key?"

He smiled. "No."

The cramp in my lower back intensified, and I groaned in pain. There was a gush between my legs. "And I think my water just broke."

"You're not due for another month."

"Baby has other plans."

"Blood," Luc whispered.

"What?"

"It's blood."

It was all so familiar. My first child—the one I had lost in a haze of blood and pain.

It was happening again.

Terror seized me.

Luc rushed me to the car.

And as he sped towards the hospital, I waited, wondering if the last piece I had of Kai would be taken from me, too.

———

Faces swam in and out of my vision. I attempted to speak but couldn't. There was the sound of rushing water in my ears, crashing waves inside my head. My back was on fire; so was my arm. Someone's voice. Deep, resonant. I looked towards it. Saw nothing but blackness.

Eventually, I came to, feeling like a burlap sack of bones. A middle-aged nurse changed my IV bag. She had a warm smile, but tired eyes.

"What happened?" I asked. My lips were dry, chapped, and my throat parched, like I'd drunk a glass of sand.

"Your placenta ruptured."

I tried to sit up, but the nurse put a gentle hand on my shoulder and forced me back. "My—my daughter—is she—"

"She's healthy. The doctor did a caesarean and she came out screaming."

Tears gurgled from deep within. They were tears of feeling everything I had ever felt all at once.

"Would you like to hold her?"

I nodded and sniffed, rubbing my nose with the back of my hand. I expected the nurse to leave my room, but I was surprised when she went to a bassinet on wheels in the corner. She came back with a swaddled little package. I reached out, and she set the baby into the cradle of my arms.

My daughter was pink—ethereal—with ears the color of coral. I counted her fingers and toes, and I brought my lips to her head, which was covered in light blonde fuzz. Her eyelashes brushed her cheeks in soft fans. She was asleep and the corner of her mouth curled upward.

I finally knew what my mother had been trying to tell me. My daughter was my greatest masterpiece, and I loved her instantly. It was swift and constant, like a river bursting through a dam. All the gray leaked out of me; my heart grew, swelling to make room for the tiny thing who had become my light.

"Have you thought of a name?" the nurse, whose presence I'd momentarily forgotten, asked.

Unable to tear my eyes away from my daughter, Kai's daughter, I nodded. Her name came to me like a whispered dream. And it was perfect. Just like she was.

There was a hand on my shoulder. I turned my head and looked into Celia's eyes.

"She's okay. You both are," Celia whispered.

I swallowed, emotion clogging my throat. I stared into my child's face—the face of unique perfection.

The nurse left us alone and we sat in silence, two women, two mothers, who understood this moment without the need for words.

———

Get *Season of the Sun* Here!

Don't forget to sign up for my newsletter and get the scoop before anyone else!

Chapter 4

The midwife had placed the baby back in her bassinet, but my daughter stayed with me during the night. Babies were kept with their mothers at all times in France. I decidedly liked French health care.

"I've got a present for you," Jules said the next afternoon as she sat by my hospital bed. She peered towards the door, and after making sure the coast was clear, she pulled out two beers from her bag.

"You're insane," I said.

"And you deserve it, at least a sip." She popped open the bottles and handed me one.

"This is so *Fried Green Tomatoes*," I quipped.

"A tale of friendship." Jules clinked her bottle against mine and took a sip. "Are you going to introduce me?" She looked down at the baby in my arms.

I grinned. "Georgia Katherine Ferris, may I present your godmother."

"Georgia?" Jules repeated. "*Georgia*? What kind of name is that? No daughter of yours is going to go by something that formal, right?"

"We'll call her Gigi. That okay with you?" All levity left me. "George Kai Ferris. I had to name her for Kai. Just had to."

"Gigi is a good name. And so is Georgia. I was just teasing."

"I know."

"I hate the movie *Sleeping Beauty*."

I laughed. "What? Why?"

"You know the three good fairies? What the hell were they thinking? The gifts they gave Aurora were ridiculous. The gift of song? The gift of beauty? Stupid, useless, worthless. I wondered what Merryweather's gift would've been if Maleficent hadn't cursed Aurora."

"You've thought about this a lot, haven't you?"

She nodded. "It's going to be my job to make sure Gigi grows up with a good head on her shoulders. *I am the godmother.*" She said it like she was Brando.

"Okay, tell me what gifts you want to give her." I stared down at Gigi, her mouth slackened, every part of her soft and delicious.

"Compassion. Gigi, I give you the gift of compassion."

"That's one."

"Courage. Your mom has that in spades, Gigi, so you better live up to it."

I smiled, tears brimming in the corners of my eyes.

"And last, I give you the gift of hope. Because without it, the other two are impossible."

"You're better than Flora and Fauna." I took another sip of beer, loving the coldness moving down my throat.

"What about Merryweather? Am I better than her?"

"Until you turn an annoying bird into stone, I'll withhold my judgment."

———

Five days later, Gigi and I were released from the hospital. I was ready to be home, and after a nap on the road I came awake with a start when Celia parked the car.

"Do you want me to carry her inside?" Celia asked.

"No, I can do it. Thanks." I unstrapped Gigi from her car seat and carefully lifted her into my arms. I wasn't ready to share Gigi, even though I was exhausted. Exhausted but euphoric.

Celia pushed opened the front door of the farmhouse.

"Surprise!" my mother-in-law said, strolling out of the kitchen.

"What are you—"

"Celia called us from the hospital a few days ago," Claire explained, smoothing her hand down her pressed black slacks.

I blinked. Joy I didn't anticipate flooded through me. My smile was wide and to my consternation, I felt tears come to my eyes. Again. I wondered if my hormones would ever return to normal. Rollercoaster from hell.

"Where's George?" I asked.

Claire grinned. "Napping on the couch."

"That sounds nice."

"I'll let you guys settle in," Celia said, heading for the front door. "I'll come by later with a casserole."

"You don't have to do that," I protested.

"I know," she agreed. Her smile was nothing but forgiveness, nothing but a mother's smile.

The front door closed and I adjusted Gigi in my arms. "Would you like to hold her?" I asked, hesitant to hand over my daughter, but knowing it meant the world to Claire.

Claire's eyes misted and she nodded. "Let me wash my hands."

When she came back from the bathroom, we went into the living room, and she settled herself into a chair. I gave her Gigi and all but collapsed into a vacant seat. George continued to slumber, his mouth agape. His blond hair was grayer than the last time I'd seen him. It was to be expected.

"She's beautiful," Claire whispered. "Did you decide on a name?"

"Celia didn't tell you?" I asked in surprise.

Claire shook her head.

"I named her after Kai. Georgia Katherine. I'm calling her Gigi."

Claire slowly pulled her gaze away from her granddaughter and peered at me. Her eyes were glassy with tears.

Emotion constricted my throat.

Gigi started crying. Claire shot me a slight smile and reluctantly gave her back to me. George woke suddenly.

"Afternoon, George," I quipped.

"Damn jet lag." He wiped a hand across his face as he got up. He came over and pressed a kiss to my head before staring down at his granddaughter, his brown eyes warm and golden. "Good set of lungs on that one."

"I'll let you get acquainted with her—right after I feed her." I stood up and gingerly took the stairs. I closed the door to the master bedroom, but I was sure Gigi's howl could still be heard downstairs. It was reassuring—her strength was reassuring.

Fumbling with my shirt and nursing bra, I put Gigi to my breast and gave a startled grunt of pain as she began to suckle. I was back in my body and all too aware of the discomfort as my newborn daughter intended to drain me dry. And yet in spite of the pain, I wanted to give her everything, the way it would always be.

———

"She looks like Kai," George whispered as we leaned over the crib. Gigi was fast asleep.

"How can you tell?" I asked back. "She's pink and squishy. She doesn't resemble much of anything. And she's blonde. Kai was dark."

"Not when he was born." He glanced at me and smiled. "Trust me." He wrapped an arm around my shoulder. We stared at Gigi a little while longer before venturing out of the nursery. She'd awaken soon enough.

"How are you, George?" I asked when we were sitting at the kitchen table. A glass of bourbon was in front of him, untouched, and I gripped my tea mug and blew on the contents.

"What's Claire been telling you?"

"Wyatt," I corrected.

"My son has no loyalty, huh?" He finally picked up his glass and took a long swallow.

"Said you're retired now."

"Yep."

"Said you're drinking—a lot."

"Yep." He drew the word out, but kept his eyes on mine.

I nodded. "Is it helping?"

"I wish it was. What about you, Sage?"

"I'm okay, I guess. Hanging in." I cleared my throat. "I'm not supposed to expend a lot of energy while my incision heals. I need help."

"You need help?"

"Yes. Would you and Claire stay and help me?"

George looked surprised and delighted. "Really? We wouldn't be an intrusion?"

"The best kind of intrusion," I joked. "I'll need you both for a few weeks. Is that okay?"

His smile was wide. It reminded me of Kai. What didn't?

———

I didn't know the time. Up was down and down was up with a newborn. Hours, minutes, and seconds were broken into tears, feedings, and diapers. I had a blissful moment of silence to tend to myself, so I went into the bathroom to change my dressing, grimacing when I saw the scar. Add it to the list of things I needed to make peace with. I was too tired to care about it. I'd feel it later, after more than a few catnaps.

I was on my way to the kitchen when I heard Celia and Claire's voices sweep towards me in hushed tones of concern. I paused, wanting to listen.

"His shoes are still by the front door, like she's waiting for him to come home," I heard Claire say. "His clothes are still in the closets."

There was a pause before Celia slowly said, "When she first got back, she used to lay his clothes out on his side of the bed as though he was there next to her."

Claire sucked in a breath. "Should I talk to her? Or do you think it will do more harm than good? She and I don't—I mean, things are different now, but still—"

"We've all tried talking to her. She doesn't want to hear it any more. Can't say that I blame her."

"George was having a hard time—still is, but I think he's past most of it." Claire didn't say more, and I knew it was because of pride. No wife wanted to admit she'd been losing her husband to grief—and bourbon. "I think seeing Gigi has helped. Do you think having the baby has helped Sage? You know her better than I do."

"I'm not sure. If I had to guess, though, I'd say she's not through it."

I didn't think I could enter the kitchen, slap a smile on my face and pretend I hadn't eavesdropped on their conversation. Not that I blamed them, but I didn't want them to worry I was a bomb in danger of detonating. I doubted I could prove to them I was stronger than I used to be, but I had to try.

I climbed the stairs and closed the bedroom door. I sank down onto the bed and reached for the bedside table. Opening the drawer, I pulled out Kai's wedding band. I held it in the palm of my hand; it was scratched and no longer shiny. In the short time he had worn it, life had left its mark on the metal.

It hadn't taken Kai long at all to leave his mark on me.

———

"I feel disgusting," I commented.

Claire grinned. An old dishtowel covered her shoulder as she walked around, patting Gigi's back. Gigi let out a milky burp and we both smiled. "Why don't you take a shower?"

"That bad, huh?"

"Your hair is pretty greasy," Claire admitted.

"That's putting it kindly." I looked at *Chat,* who sat on the arm of the couch, watching Claire with a strangely humane gaze. "You want to come with me?"

"Good luck," Claire said. "*Chat* hasn't left Gigi's side this entire week."

"Little beast," I said, heading out of the living room.

"If you want to take a nap, go ahead. I've got her."

I smiled in relief at the thought of a few minutes of rest. Exhaustion tugged at my limbs, but I forced myself into the shower. I made the water blistering hot and let it beat down on me. My eyes closed and I swayed. I put my hand to the wall to steady myself, but I lost my balance and tumbled out of the tub, ripping down the shower curtain as I went.

My knee collided with porcelain, and I let out a stream of curses. What if I'd still been pregnant with Gigi? I breathed a sigh of relief that I wasn't. I'd take all the pain life could dish out if it meant protecting her.

Wrapping the shower curtain around me, I began to cry. The water had turned cold and splattered the walls and floor, dousing me in cool drops. I buried my head in my hands and sobbed, feeling stupid and needy, exhausted and overwhelmed. There was only one cure for this, but he wasn't here. He couldn't take me in his arms, no matter how long I sat on the tile of the bathroom floor, wishing. I cried harder, gasping for air, reaching for someone who was gone. I lay down on the bathroom rug, pressing my cheek to the fuzzy mat. I closed my eyes, the sound of running water in my ears. A hand touched my shoulder, jarring me awake. I squinted, looking up into the concerned face of my mother-in-law.

"What happened?" She went to shut off the shower, and I slowly sat up.

"I fell." My tongue was heavy in my mouth, as if speaking was some great ordeal. "And then I fell asleep."

"Did you hit your head? Are you hurt?"

"My knee, but I'm okay."

"Come on," Claire said, helping me stand. "Gigi's asleep for now. Why don't we get you into some pajamas and you can sleep in a bed."

I took a step and winced, my knee aching. Claire led me to the bedroom and began opening and closing drawers while I stood by, blinking my eyes in bleary fatigue. She handed me a t-shirt and sweatpants. I put them on and then climbed into bed. Just as I was settling down, Gigi's shriek came through the baby monitor. I sighed and threw back the covers.

"I'll get her and bring her to you," Claire said, leaving the room. She came back almost immediately and handed Gigi over. Her tiny fists were clenched, and she didn't quiet until I put her to my breast.

"I feel like I just did this."

"You'll feel that way for the first few months," she told me. "Plus, she's a preemie. Harder in the beginning. Kai was a preemie."

"Why doesn't that surprise me?" I shook my head. "I feel like a cow." I grinned, not at all upset by it. My emotions were not my own.

She laughed. "Yep, sounds about right."

I heard the front door open. "George?" I asked.

"Probably. I'll go see."

She left me alone and I took a moment to study Gigi. She had blue eyes that were turning grayer, framed by faint blonde eyelashes. The bow of her mouth was a pretty pink. I kissed her minuscule fingers, breathing her in. Closing my eyes, I rocked Gigi against me. When she finished nursing, I put her to my shoulder and burped her. She let out a little sigh as she fell asleep. After placing her in her crib, I went downstairs and into the kitchen. Claire was turning off the oven and removing a heated casserole Celia had dropped off. My freezer was full of them, but I wasn't complaining.

I greeted my father-in-law with a kiss to his whiskered cheek. He sat at the kitchen table with a glass of bourbon in front of him.

"Thought you were going to try and sleep?" Claire asked me, standing at the counter.

"I'll try later, the window for sleep has closed. Is it cocktail hour already?" I asked with a glance at George.

"Never too early to celebrate," he replied.

I raised an eyebrow. "Celebrate? Celebrate what?" My gaze darted between George and Claire.

"We bought a house," George announced.

I shook my head, trying to understand. "Don't you already have a house?"

"In Monteagle we have a house. We bought a house. *Here.* In *Tours.*" George grinned.

"Really?"

Claire nodded, looking nervous. "We've been talking about it, and we just thought, since you're here—and Gigi. It made the most sense to have a place of our own. When we visit."

"We want to come back for Christmas. Lucy and Wyatt, Keith and Alice want to come, too. They can stay with us."

"I think," I said through a tear-filled throat, "that sounds like a wonderful idea."

————

I focused the phone's screen on Gigi for one more moment before turning the camera back to me. "Well?" I said once I'd closed the nursery door and padded down the hallway.

"She's beautiful," Lucy said.

"I think so." I grinned. I was proud in a way I couldn't describe. Proud in a way that was basic, human and maternal. I had created something with Kai—created the center of my new universe.

"People warn you," I said suddenly. "They warn you about the exhaustion, but it's all consuming. I never could've imagined it."

"Yeah, I remember. It's worth it though." Lucy returned my grin, blue eyes twinkling. I lost sight of her for a moment as she wrapped her red hair into a messy bun and pulled it back.

"You say that now looking back, but Dakota sleeps through the night, and you and Wyatt have moments alone."

"That's true. Is it nice having George and Claire there?"

I nodded. "I honestly don't know how I'd do it without them. They tell you they bought a house?"

"They did."

"That's where they are now," I said. "I think Claire is looking at fabric swatches."

"I can't wait to see it. Christmas in France. Sounds pretty good."

"It will be nice to have you here. Have you all here."

"I'm going to let you go," Lucy said. "If she's asleep then you should be asleep."

"Sleep when they sleep?"

"Yep. And just remember, if you ever get to eat hot food again, count your blessings."

"What about my boobs? Can I expect them to go back to their original state?"

"I plead the fifth."

"Damn it."

Lucy laughed and we hung up. I was just sinking into oblivion when my cell phone buzzed. I'd forgotten to put in on silent. I debated sending it to voicemail, but I saw a New York number.

The conversation was brief, but after it ended, I sat in stunned silence for a good five minutes. It wasn't until Jules pushed the bedroom door open and peeked in that I finally looked up from my cell resting in my hand.

"I came to see if you were awake. You okay?"

I nodded.

"You hungry?"

"Yeah."

"George and Claire are back. Come on."

I followed Jules, who continued to look at me like some oddity. Everyone was in the kitchen. Luc and Armand were opening bottles of wine while George sipped on bourbon. Celia was at the stove and Claire was next to her, though she wasn't helping. She was a novice in the kitchen. Gigi was asleep upstairs, but the baby monitor rested on the counter. At her smallest cry, she would have a flock of people who'd come to her rescue.

They had all come to my rescue as well, I realized.

Their attention turned towards me and I shrank away, needing a moment to compose myself. "If you'll excuse me, just for a minute?" I said and headed to the back door. I felt *Chat* at my heels, wrapping himself around me. A bunch of startled gazes followed me, but they let me go. *Chat* trailed after me and then sat down when I stopped at the lake.

I looked at him and grinned. Glowing cat eyes stared back at me. "Happy dance, *Chat*. It's finally time for a happy dance."

———

George and Claire were asleep in the guest room. Armand, Celia, and Luc had gone home, but Jules had stayed. We were on the couch, lights dimmed, Gigi asleep at my breast.

"What was that about?" Jules asked me over her glass of wine.

"What was what?"

"I saw your happy dance out by the lake."

I grinned at her observation. "Spying on me?"

"Curious," she said. "I know you. Something happened before dinner. You barely ate, barely spoke, and the corners of your mouth twitched like you were trying not to smile."

I bit my lip, but couldn't stop myself from beaming. "If I tell you something, you have to promise me you'll keep it to yourself."

She raised an eyebrow and then crossed a finger over her heart in a sign of swearing to silence.

"I, kind of, wrote a book while I was in Monteagle," I said hesitant to share my secret. "I sent it off to my mother's agent about a month ago. She called to tell me she's already gotten some interest, and she's hopeful I'll be getting an offer soon."

Jules's eyes widened. "You're shitting me."

"Nope."

"Holy shit. What does this mean? Are you going to be a famous author?"

"I don't know, maybe."

"Oh my God, I want to yell, this is so exciting."

"Don't yell. Gigi's asleep."

Jules grinned, set her glass of wine on the table, and jumped up. "Happy dance indeed! God, we need to toast."

"Breastfeeding."

Jules made a face. "You had a beer right after you had Gigi."

"I had two sips."

"Celia told me a beer is good for breast milk."

"She did not."

"Did too. I remember being horrified by the knowledge. You could use the calories anyway. You're looking thin."

"Yeah, right."

"Come on," she pleaded.

"Fine."

Jules nearly ran to the kitchen. She came back holding a bottle of Peroni and handed it to me. "Cheers," she said, raising her glass of wine. "To you. To your awesomeness."

Chapter 5

We sit in the tree, shoeless. Our toes dangle out of the canopy, high above the rest of the world. Kai has adorable toes. They twitch; he is unable to remain still.

I cradle the fishing pole in my hand, wondering why I'm sitting in a tree and fishing, when there is no water below me. There are some things I'll never understand—even in dreams.

"You've got that mom smell," he says quietly.

"And what's that smell?"

"It's hard to explain." He leans over and sniffs me like a dog, and I giggle. "You... smell like... old wishes."

"Old wishes? As opposed to new ones?"

He nods.

"And what do old wishes smell like?" I wonder aloud.

"Can't describe it. But when you smell it, you just know."

I shake my head at his whimsical side. "You want to explain to me why we're fishing without water?"

He grasps the end of my pole and doesn't answer. "You have a bite."

"How can I have a bite?"

"Just reel it in."

With a sigh, I reel in my line. At the end is a flopping fish. Kai reaches for it and grasps it in his hands. Its mouth gapes open as it fights for air, and Kai looks at me.

"This is the thing about dreams," he says. "They're kind of like wishes. There's an endless amount of them and things you never thought could happen, happen." He throws the fish into the air, and I watch in amazement as the fish curls in on itself and explodes in a cloud of gold dust. In place of the fish, a great loon appears from the golden air, flaps its wings and soars away.

———

Dr. Andrews, a middle-aged woman with graying hair, pulled down my shirt. "Your incision looks good. I can clear you to drive. Among other things."

"Other things?"

"Moderate exercise. Sex."

I clamped my mouth shut, not wishing to explain to the doctor that I no longer had a husband. Absently, I fingered my wedding ring. Dr. Andrews scribbled something on my chart and closed it.

"How is she doing?"

"Gigi? She's fine. Never would have thought she was a preemie. Growing like a weed. She's got her two month checkup next week."

After a few more minutes of chitchat, I walked into the waiting room. Claire and George were at home with Gigi, so Jules had driven me.

"Well?" she asked as we walked into the parking lot. Fall had arrived, though I'd barely noticed. It was crisp, tangy, like hard apple cider.

"I can have sex."

She looked at me sharply. "Is that an offer? I love you, but not like that."

I laughed as we climbed into the car. I rested my head against the cool glass of the window.

"She didn't know, Sage."

"And if she had known, I would've had to see the pity in her eyes when I mentioned the word 'widow'. *Widow.* Hateful word."

Jules kept her eyes on the road and her mouth closed. There was nothing to say. She pulled up to the farmhouse and looked at me. "Want me to come in with you?"

I shook my head. "Nah. Thanks. I'll see you later." I headed inside, trying to shake off the sadness.

George was on the couch, flipping through TV channels and Claire was next to him, reading a book—one of my mother's, I noticed. George settled on some sporting event, but muted the sound and then they both looked at me.

"Everything is good," I said, suddenly feeling very tired. "I'm healed enough that I can take care of myself." I tried to joke, but it came out forced. I pressed a few fingers to my third eye and rubbed.

"That's good to hear," George said.

Claire smiled at her husband. "That's Sage's polite way of telling us she doesn't need us anymore. It's probably time we went back to Monteagle anyway," Claire said gently.

"You're coming back in a few months for Christmas. It'll be here before you know it," I said.

George's face fell. "I know, but I just—"

Claire placed a hand on George's arm. "Don't make it harder on her than it already is."

"Okay," George grumbled.

"I'll send you photos. Every day," I promised.

"She'll get big so fast. We'll miss stuff."

Kai would miss everything, I thought, but I didn't say. Instead, I wrapped my father-in-law in a hug and tried to shut out the ache.

———

Luc and I were walking around the lake with Gigi, who was bundled in a fleecy onesie and wearing a lavender hat that Alice and Keith had sent. Though it was just the beginning of autumn, I made sure Gigi was well insulated from even the slightest chill.

She was pressed up against me in one of those weird baby carriers that was strangely convenient for lugging around a child while being able to keep my hands free. I felt like a kangaroo.

The air felt good in my lungs. I'd been cooped up for so long, I had forgotten what the outside world looked like, felt like. It was a nice reintroduction. Claire and George had left a few days prior, and I was on my own again.

"Can I talk to you about something?" Luc asked.

"As long as it's not about me," I said, taking a deep breath.

"It's not about you—it's about Jules."

"Ah. Then, yes."

"The first few months she was here, she had something…"

I smiled and threw him a wry look. "She was babysitting me, but now she no longer has a project."

"She misses teaching, I think, but she denies it. She started her French classes at the local university, but it's slow learning."

I frowned in thought.

"I worry she's always going to feel like a foreigner. Like even if she manages to learn French, she's never going to feel completely at home here. Not like *Maman*, not like you. Did Kai feel like that, like he didn't belong?"

I shrugged. "I'm not sure. Kai didn't speak French, but it never seemed to bother him. He knew *Tours* was home for me and he was willing to live here—even after he admitted to missing Monteagle."

"Do you think he would have ever thought of this place as home?"

Emotion thickened my throat and I swallowed, trying to force words past it. "Home for him wasn't *a place*."

"*You* were home," Luc said slowly.

I nodded.

"Could you have lived in Monteagle? Made a life there?"

"Yes. I would've been happy there. With him." I looked at Luc. "Are you thinking of moving to the States?"

He shook his head. "My family owns a vineyard. I'm the only son, and more importantly, I want to be here. I love the family business. I never saw myself living somewhere else, but if Jules is unhappy… I don't think she knew what it would be like moving here, not speaking the language. She has you, and that's great, but—"

"I'm not enough." I nodded. "And you're worried you're not either."

We continued to walk around the lake, the smell of fallen leaves surrounding us. Gigi made noises in her sleep, but didn't wake up. I stared down at her, wondering what it would be like when she was old enough to fall in love.

I stopped and looked at Luc. "Listen, I'm going to give it to you straight, okay?" He nodded and I went on, "There are some people who lose their way and need others to help them find it. And then there are others, like Jules, who need to find it themselves. What would you do if she came to you and said, 'Luc, I love you, but I can't make a life here'? What would you do?"

His eyes grew sad. "I worry she's going to leave me. I worry she'll never find her way here."

"That's not what I asked. Would you sacrifice your home, your family, your livelihood for her?"

He took a deep breath. "No. No, I wouldn't."

"Then how can you ask her for the same when you won't do it for her? You're getting married in a year, Luc," I said quietly. "It's harder to end a marriage than a relationship."

"Are you saying I should end it?" he asked, his mouth tight with pain.

I shook my head emphatically. "I'm not saying that at all. What I *am* saying is that there's nothing wrong with time. Giving yourself some time. The both of you—to figure out what you really want."

He scratched his jaw, stubbly with the sprouting of dark blond whiskers. "Has she mentioned anything to you—about this?"

I hesitated before carefully choosing my words. "She hasn't, which means she's trying to deny there's even an issue. This is going to fall to you, Luc. You're going to have to be the one to talk to her about it."

He sighed. "Yeah, I thought you were going to say that."

We turned back towards the house. I pushed open the back door and looked down at Gigi. She was awake, her blue eyes open and alert. They had changed from newborn blue to a blue I was achingly familiar with. Gigi would want to nurse soon. Her mouth was making that motion I recognized, letting me know what she wanted.

We were greeted by *Chat* as he wrapped himself around Luc's legs. Luc reached down and scooped him up. *Chat* let himself be carried to the living room before struggling out of Luc's embrace. I removed Gigi from the baby contraption, took the nursing blanket resting on the back of the couch, and threw it over me. I managed to nurse with a bit of modesty. To give Luc credit, he didn't appear at all taken aback by my actions. The French were not as uptight about nudity as Americans, I thought.

"What do I do?" Luc asked. "What do I do if she—and I can't —what do I do?"

"You do what the rest of us do. You find a way to go on living."

———

I watched the alarm clock turn to 3:00 AM. I'd been awake for hours. My body no longer felt weary. I'd pushed past the point of tiredness. I was awake.

Taking the baby monitor, I crept down the hall and peeked in on Gigi, but she was sleeping with no signs of stirring. I'd won the baby lottery. She wasn't colicky or fussy, and she was already sleeping through the night. She was a blessing.

I went downstairs into the kitchen, pulling out ingredients to make a yellow cake with chocolate icing. I shoved it into the oven, set the timer, and picked up the phone. Alice answered on the first ring.

"I was wondering when I'd hear from you," she said. Her voice was warm and soft, reminding me of the first time I'd met her at the Chelser ranch. Kai and I had returned to Monteagle, and before we'd gone to see his parents, we'd stopped off to see Alice and Keith. They were his surrogate parents, and I'd been worried about how they were going to accept me. I shouldn't have been concerned; she'd embraced me like I was family.

I sighed. "I'm baking a cake. And then I plan on eating the entire thing because I can't drink. What are you doing?"

"Keith and I just got home from having dinner with Claire and George."

"Did Keith wear his cowboy boots?"

"Yes."

"His clean ones?"

She laughed. "What do you think?"

"How's George?" I asked.

Alice paused.

"He's still drinking, isn't he?" I asked. "He seemed to have cut back when they visited."

She sighed. "He did, but, well… I don't think retiring was a good idea."

"He needs to be busy. He needs to occupy his mind."

"Don't we all?"

The oven beeped and I went to check on the rising cake. It needed a few more minutes, so I left it in.

"Tell me something that makes you happy," she demanded. "We need a shot of happiness."

"Gigi smiled for the first time the other day." I wished I could bottle that feeling and keep it with me always.

"Ah, milestones. One minute, she'll need everything from you, and then one day she'll stop listening to you. She'll stop taking your advice when she can pick out her own clothes. And because she's Kai's daughter, I wouldn't put it past her to start even before that. Wait until she throws her mashed peas on the floor and refuses to eat anything you've made for her."

"Mashed peas? Gross. What's the grossest thing Reece ever ate?"

"A goldfish."

"Excuse me?"

Alice laughed. "Kai and Tristan dared Reece to put a goldfish in his mouth. He accidentally swallowed it."

I snorted with laughter and, before I knew it, tears of genuine amusement were streaming out of the corners of my eyes. Alice laughed along with me. It felt good to laugh, really laugh, from the belly. I laughed until it hurt. It was the best kind of hurt.

Gigi's squawk came through the monitor.

"I've got to go," I said. "Gigi's awake."

"Happy Kai's birthday, Sage."

"Happy Kai's birthday, Alice."

———

I never found writing to be the daunting part. I never had a problem with words coming to me, assaulting me with their desire to be put on paper. It was the *editing* that was demoralizing, when the manuscript needed so much work it never felt like it would be a completed entity. My mother always said writing a book was like watching a dress rehearsal of a play. It was nothing but actors forgetting lines, unfinished costumes, and incomplete sets. And then, on opening night, it all magically came together.

A book was like that.

I scribbled notes in the margins of my printed manuscript before setting down the pen. I forced myself out of the chair and did some stretches. There was a light knock on the door of the turret.

"Come in," I said.

The door creaked open. "I brought you some tea—and a sandwich."

"Mastering the art of cooking," I said, lifting my arms above my head.

Jules laughed. "Come on, eat something. You're thinner than you were before you got pregnant."

"You wouldn't be trying to build up my ego, would you?" I reached for the sandwich. "Thanks." I took a bite of the baguette and nearly hummed in delight. "How long have I been up here?"

"About four hours—since I came in to grab Gigi from her bassinet."

"Four hours!"

"She's fine. You know that little contraption called a breast pump? It does wonders by allowing you to store milk so other people can feed the beasty."

I settled back down in my chair, my heart calming. "You fed her."

"And burped her. And changed her. It's a good thing she's cute and you're her mother; otherwise, you couldn't pay me enough for this." She peered at me. "Did you really forget for a moment that you had a kid?"

I took a deep breath and nodded, my cheeks heating in shame. "Longer than a moment. Four hours, apparently."

"I'm not judging. Remember when you'd lose Penny for weeks? She'd get caught up in something she was writing and just forget the world around her."

"I remember. I was one of things she had forgotten." I smiled at the memory of my mother, and there was no bitterness to it. Not anymore. I hadn't understood it, not until now. It gave me a sense of peace knowing that I hadn't been the center of her life, at least not all of the time. She'd been my mother, but she'd had her own passion, her own existence outside of me.

Scarfing down the rest of my sandwich, I walked with my best friend down the hall to the nursery. I stole a hand down Gigi's back, checking to make sure all was well.

"I feel like I should pay you," I said as we headed to the living room downstairs.

"Don't even think about it. I was joking earlier. It gives me something to do and it sure beats trying to memorize French verbs." She took a seat in a chair and crossed her legs.

"Jules Barrister, super nanny."

"Shut up."

I grinned.

"How are the edits going?"

"Mind numbing. My brain hurts."

"I envy you," she said quietly.

"Me? Why? Should I remind you of all the stuff I've been through?"

She quirked her lips into a sad smile. "The writing—you've embraced it. You have something that is just for you. You're going to

307

be a published author, Sage. Your mom would be proud. So would Kai. You found your way."

My breath hitched and I tore my eyes away from her. It hurt to look at her face.

"We're all lost in different ways, Jules."

"Did you like being pregnant?" she asked.

"That's a switch in conversation."

Jules didn't smile. "Did you?"

I shrugged. "It was—unique. My situation wasn't like other people's. I was so sad. It ruined what it was supposed to be. I know what it feels to share my body with another life, but I don't know… Nothing compares to looking at Gigi now and seeing her, watching her grow. Why do you ask?"

"Don't know. Just thinking about stuff."

"Baby stuff?" I wondered.

Jules stood up. "You want another cup of tea?"

There was something she wasn't telling me—something she didn't want to talk about. I'd wait. Jules would tell me when she was ready.

Chapter 6

I looked around at the many piles of dirty laundry. It was a never-ending battle. I glanced down at the shirt I was wearing; I couldn't remember the last time I had changed it. Grimacing, I pulled it over my head and threw it in with the pile of grays. The dryer beeped and I opened the door, fished around for a new shirt, and put it on. *Chat* sat on a pile of black dirty clothes and stared at me.

"You're weird," I told him. "You like dirty laundry. Well, as long as it's not clean laundry, I guess."

I started a new load, took the clean basket of laundry to the couch, and began to fold. Gigi was in her bassinet in the corner of the living room, but she was awake. She was learning the sound of her own noises. I smiled.

I got up when there was a knock on the door and peeked through the peephole Kai had installed. I opened the door and signed for the package. Taking the manila envelope to the couch, I ripped it open.

My breath caught in the back of my throat as my fingers reached for the contents. I held the CD in my hands and shook my head. Béla Fleck's signature streaked across the liner in bold black sharpie. Accompanying the CD was a note. After I read it, I folded it along the creases and shoved it back into the envelope. I stared at the CD for the longest time, turning it over and skimming the back. My eyes slid to the last song. It was written by Kai.

With great trepidation, I stuck it into the sound system and shuffled to the end of the CD. I closed my eyes when the sounds of Kai's mandolin, captured forever, warbled through the speakers. Emotion gripped me in a powerful embrace and I began to shake. I reached towards the music, reached for the love ballad he played for me. I grasped air, wishing I was in Kai's arms, knowing I'd never feel them around me again.

Immortalized in death.

I sank to the floor and let myself be haunted.

———

The CD ended, yet I couldn't move off the floor. Not even when my tailbone started to hurt and my legs went numb. Not until *Chat* came over and bumped his head into my side, nudging me, as if saying, "Get your ass up. There have been worse knocks to your heart."

"You're right," I whispered to him, burying my face into his fur. I wiped the tears from my eyes and made myself stand up. I went to Gigi. She was on her back, kicking her legs. She had no idea what I'd just been through.

"Okay," I said, picking her up. I needed something—something I could sing to, something to dance to.

I put on The Beatles. "Here's the thing about The Beatles, Gigi," I explained. "They changed the sound of rock 'n' roll, but it was even more than that. When you're older, I'll show you the old Ed Sullivan Show—the girls screamed for The Beatles. And when they broke up and when John Lennon was shot… those were moments when the earth stopped moving, the sun stopped shining and the whole of humanity cried as one."

I moved around the living room, one song playing to the next. I breathed in the smell of Gigi's hair, her warmth a comfort against me.

"We all live in a yellow jelly bean, yellow jelly bean, a yellow jelly bean." I

laughed. "Those aren't the real lyrics, but my mom used to sing them to me, and now I'm singing them to you."

I went upstairs, the sound of Ringo's voice calling to me from the living room. I nursed Gigi and put her to bed, feeling drained, but a bit lighter.

And then I looked at my bed. My big, empty bed.

I went to the dresser and pulled out a pair of Kai's old, ripped khakis and one of his t-shirts. I placed them on his side of the bed and got in on mine. I pulled the covers up to my chin and put a hand to his shirt.

"I miss you," I said. "All the time, I miss you." I closed my eyes, sinking into sleep.

———

We aren't in the tree this time, instead we're lying on the grass, staring up at the sky, watching cloud pictures.

"Oh, look over there!"

"Where?" he asks.

I point to the right. "See that cloud? That looks like a frog wearing a top hat."

He laughs and it's belly deep. "I see it."

"Have you ever seen that cartoon about the singing and dancing frog?" I ask.

"No."

"No? Really? It's a classic!"

"Doesn't change the fact I've never seen it."

"'Hello, my baby, hello, my honey, hello, my ragtime gal'," I sing and Kai laughs again. "I really wish I had a top hat and cane. Makes it better."

"What are those over there?" Kai gestures behind us. I turn around and sure enough, there is a top hat and cane resting on the grass.

"Will you sing the song again?"

I'd do anything to see that smile on his face.

———

I dashed to the couch and haphazardly threw the cushions onto the floor. I overturned blankets and pulled out drawers, spilling their contents. My breaths came in short little pants as I moved from room to room, coming up empty handed. It was gone. I had lost it.

My wedding ring.

I hadn't noticed its absence. When had it disappeared? It was gone—and I'd never get it back. Closing my eyes, I climbed onto my unmade bed, pressed my face into a pillow and screamed. Screamed until my throat was raw.

I heard the front door open and braced myself for having to face someone. Not just someone. My best friend.

"What the hell happened to your house?" she demanded from the doorway of my bedroom. Her voice softened when she saw my devastated expression. Jules came to the bed and crawled onto it, her face resting on the pillow next to me. I stared into her blue eyes.

"I lost my wedding ring," I whispered.

She closed her eyes briefly before opening them, and then she sat up. She took a deep breath and then said, "No. You're not doing this. If it's gone, it's gone. It's just a *thing*, but Kai will always be with you." She began to sing, *"Chiquitita, tell me what's wrong."*

"Jules," I said. "Stop."

She didn't listen as she sang on.

"This isn't going to work," I said in frustration.

Still, she didn't listen.

"Mama Mia! is not going to help," I growled, but I sat up. "This is serious."

Jules stood up on the bed, and reached a hand down to me. I sighed and grasped it and she hauled me up so we were both standing.

"I'm going to skip most of this and get to the really poignant part, okay?"

I nodded.

"And you're going to sing with me."

"No."

She picked up a pillow and hit me with it. "You will sing."

I grabbed the other pillow and battered her arm. She raised an eyebrow and said, "Come on, Sage."

"Fine." I gripped the pillow in my arms and I began to sing. Jules joined and my voice grew stronger, the words hitting plaster and paint of the room I'd once shared with Kai.

The room fell silent as the words came to an end. I wanted to collapse, and I was in danger of doing so—until Jules hit me with a pillow.

Too shocked to cry, I glared at her and hit her back. She grinned and swatted me. Jumping up and down like a monkey on the bed, she continued to assault me. I retaliated.

Feathers rained down on us as we battered the pillows into submission. I laughed. I laughed and didn't feel like crying.

————

I bundled Gigi up and stuck her in the carrier close to my body. I locked up the house and began to walk. All the leaves had fallen off the trees, leaving them bereft. They looked pathetic, naked; their branches exposed for everyone to see their flaws, their insides. I meandered around the Old Square, taking a side cobblestone street. I opened the door to the jewelry store, my heart lurching.

My ring finger felt as naked as the bare autumn trees.

I strolled to the counter. A stooped old man with a jeweler's loop around his neck and dirty fingernails looked at me as I approached. Pulling out the small pouch from my purse, I handed it over to him and explained what I wanted. He muttered something under his breath but nodded and told me when I could pick it up. I headed out onto the street, taking a deep, shaky breath. I ran a hand across Gigi's back and looked down. She was awake, her eyes taking in everything. I gave her my finger and she wrapped her hand around it. It eased my suffering.

Jules was right. My wedding ring was just a piece of jewelry. It was a symbol to the world that I had once had a partner. But that's all it was, a universal sign that so many people willingly threw away. No one knew what Kai and I had shared. A wedding ring wasn't a true expression of our love.

It was poetic, really. Losing my love, losing the ring he had given me. But we were still bound—by memory, by joy, by the daughter I carried in my arms.

I'd go on. I'd put one foot in front of the other. I'd watch Gigi grow. I'd hold her hand and tie her shoes. I'd braid her hair and tell her how much her daddy had loved her. I would tell her stories of him that would make her laugh, and when she was old enough, I'd tell her not to settle for anything less than a man who loved her with everything he was. I'd tell her to find a man who made her laugh until she couldn't breathe. I'd tell her to find a man who would dry her tears or even cry with her. I would tell her to find a man she wasn't afraid to share everything with—not just her body, not just her heart, but her soul, the true essence of her.

I had to believe she'd find a man like that, because if she didn't, she'd find herself surrounded by many people, but somehow always alone. I had once known the warmth of true love. My world was darker and bleaker without it. But I'd had it—once. And that was more than most people ever had in their lifetime.

———

"Where do you want it?" Luc demanded, his face tensed and strained.

"Uh…" I looked around the room.

"Quickly, quickly," Luc stated. "This tree is a bit heavy."

"Corner, by the fireplace."

Armand and Luc hauled the large, green pine to the other side of the room and turned it upright. The top of the tree nearly grazed the ceiling.

"Job well done with that tree," I commented. *Chat* hissed. I had no idea if he was in agreement or not.

"Maybe he can be the tree topper," Luc commented.

"If he'll let you hold him long enough to put him up there."

"He likes me," Luc said.

Celia came out of the kitchen, drying her hands on a dishtowel. "That tree is better than the one at the bed and breakfast!"

Armand grinned. "I know. It's Gigi's first Christmas. She needed a really good tree."

The front door opened and Jules walked in carting a handful of shopping bags. "Nice tree."

"That seems to be the general consensus." Luc kissed her hello.

"Is Gigi asleep?" Jules asked me, coming to sit down on the couch.

"Yes. We had a rough night," I explained.

"So, it would be a bad idea to wake her up just so I can see how she looks in this?" Jules reached into one of her bags and pulled out a bright pink onesie with the word *Diva* written across it.

"You've got to be kidding me," I said with a laugh.

"What? What's wrong with it? I couldn't decide between 'diva' and 'princess'."

"I'm not letting Gigi wear that. She'll grow up spoiled."

"Uh, Sage, she *is* spoiled," Luc lamented.

"Hush," I growled.

"It's true," Armand said.

"No, she isn't."

"Hate to break it to you, but, yeah, she is," Jules went on.

"How can a four-month-old be spoiled? All she does is eat, sleep, poop, and smile."

"You want me to give you a list?" Luc asked.

"She's got more clothes than a teenage girl," Jules teased.

"She's got three sets of grandparents!"

"Keith wants to buy her a horse, George has already set up a trust fund for her to go to college, and my parents?" Luc looked at Armand and Celia with a grin. "My parents want to name the next batch of wine 'Gigi'."

"He's kidding, right?" I looked at Celia.

"Sort of." Celia laughed. "If Gigi is spoiled it's because she has a lot of people who want to spoil her."

"That's my point." I held up the *Diva* onesie. "I'm putting my foot down. No."

"Okay, then what about this?" Jules dug around in one of the other bags and came up with a t-shirt that said *Pop Tart*.

"Yes. Absolutely," I said with excitement. "Where did you

find this?"

"Amazon."

"God, they have everything, don't they? Why don't they make this in my size?"

Jules grinned and then held up an adult-sized shirt with the same writing.

"I am so spoiled." I grabbed the shirt and put it on over my white thermal top.

"Is the brood on their way?" Jules asked.

I glanced at the clock. "Their flight is about to land. I expect a massive influx of text messages any moment."

"In the meantime, who's ready for lunch?" Celia asked.

As if on cue, Gigi's cry came through the baby monitor. We all laughed and I stood up. "Now, if you'll excuse me, Her Majesty is hungry."

I put Gigi to bed and returned to the kitchen. The farmhouse was full of people who loved me, and I marveled at the patchwork family that had become my life. The men had moved to the living room, sitting around, talking about Keith's ranch and Armand's vineyard. Dakota, Lucy's son, had fallen asleep in the corner, curled up with *Chat*.

The women had congregated in the kitchen, but I didn't hear their buzz of chatter as I studied Lucy. She looked a little pale, her mouth strained. Alice handed her a glass of eggnog, but Lucy didn't take a sip. She smelled it, grimaced, and set it aside. I didn't put it together until I saw her place a gentle hand to her belly. Her eyes caught mine and widened. I gestured with my chin and she nodded. No one noticed when we slipped away. I led her up to the turret and shut the door. I turned to face her and waited.

"I'm pregnant," she admitted, sounding defeated, dazed.

I pulled out my office chair and gently pushed her into it. Sensing she needed reassurance, I took her hand and squeezed it. "Wyatt doesn't know, does he?"

She shook her head. "I just found out. I went to the doctor before we left, and I..." Her blue eyes were bright with a sheen of tears she wasn't trying to hide. "It's going to change everything."

"Babies do that," I said softly.

"I mean with Wyatt and Dakota."

"I don't understand."

Lucy sighed and stood. She went to the window and looked out. "Dakota isn't his. This baby is. What if—what if Wyatt loves the baby differently? Treats the baby differently."

"Wyatt? Or you?"

Her head snapped around, her eyes widening. She covered her face and began to cry. I went to her and put my arms around her. She was taller than me by a good five inches, but I held on.

"You know what's amazing?" I whispered, when Lucy's tears abated.

"What?" She sniffed pathetically, pulling back and swiping at her wet cheeks.

"The heart. It changes. It makes room. Love isn't finite. If that were the case, we wouldn't be able to love more than one person at a time."

"I'm afraid."

"I know, but you've got Wyatt. Lean on him."

———

Dakota sat on my lap a few days later, playing with the pendant around my neck. It was a flat metal disk, the size of a nickel. He took a small finger and ran it across the engraving.

"What's it say?" he asked.

"They're letters," I explained.

"Daddy is teaching me to read."

"Yeah?" I asked, looking at Lucy. Her eyes were soft, her face glowing. She sat in the crook of Wyatt's arm, and they both appeared happy and content. I was glad she had told him so soon about the baby.

"Can you read them?" I asked Dakota.

"Maybe. This one is a G," Dakota said.

"Yes."

"K?"

"Uh huh. And the last letter?"

"F."

"You got it." I grinned.

"What's it for?"

"Those are Uncle Kai's initials," I explained. "And they're also Gigi's initials."

"Really?"

"Yep. And one day, when Gigi is old enough, I'll give her this necklace."

I smoothed the curls off his forehead and hugged him to me. Dakota let me hold him for a moment longer, but then he scrambled off my lap and went to sit next to Gigi on the carpet. He got down on her level and looked her in the eyes. It made my breath hitch, it made me wonder...

"I've got a present for you, Dakota," I said.

He shot up, looking excited. "But it's not Christmas yet!"

"Few more days," I agreed. "But this is too special to wait." I got up and went to the foyer. I picked up the baseball hat off of the front table and came back into the living room. I adjusted the hat, making it the smallest it could be and stuck it on his head. It was still too big, but he'd grow into it. The hat had once belonged to Tristan, Dakota's father. Kai had taken it from Tristan's things after he passed away in a plane crash.

"This hat belonged to Uncle Kai. Now it belongs to you." It wasn't my place to mention Tristan—that would fall to Lucy and Wyatt when they thought Dakota was old enough.

Dakota pulled it off his head and looked at it. "Thanks!" He traced the frayed lettering on the cap before putting it back on his head. I looked at Wyatt and Lucy. Both of their eyes were misty.

"You ready to play Go-Fish?" I challenged, clearing my throat, trying to move past the moment. "I think you'll lose this time."

Dakota gave me a toothy smile. "Wanna bet?"

Chapter 7

It was cold in the days after Christmas. The family spent most of
their time at the farmhouse, their lives momentarily revolving
around food, Gigi, and me. The snow began to fall two days before
New Year's and the temperatures dropped even more. The
roads iced.

I refused to let anyone drive.

After losing Kai, I wasn't going to take any chances with family,
weather or cars. Jules and Luc hunkered down in their cute little
cottage and Armand and Celia were at the bed and breakfast. I
made them all promise me they'd stay put until the weather
cleared up.

I gave George and Claire my bedroom. Alice and Keith were in
the guest room and Lucy and Wyatt were on the pull out couch.
Dakota slept on a pallet by the fireplace, like a warm, snuggled up
little puppy. I was supposed to be asleep on an air mattress in Gigi's
nursery, but I was restless.

Quietly, so not as to disturb the sleeping house, I wrapped a
thick wool blanket around me, stuck my feet into UGGs, and
slipped outside onto the back porch. I sat in a chair, listening to the
silence as snow bathed the trees and ground.

The back door opened, drawing my attention. Wyatt.

"Couldn't sleep?" he asked.

I shook my head. "You?"

He shrugged. "Mind if I join you?"

"Please, sit."

He sat down near me, shoving his hands into his winter coat. He was more prepared for the outside than I was, but I tugged the blanket closer around me, burrowing into it.

"Beautiful, isn't it," he said.

"Very." Flakes hit the dark glassy water of the lake, melting, joining the frigid water.

"He chose this place because of the lake, didn't he?" Wyatt asked.

"Yes." I touched a finger to my lips. They were cold, but not just from winter. It had been too long since I had felt Kai's mouth on mine. Sometimes, I didn't believe it—that he was really gone. There were moments when I expected him to walk through the back door, pole in hand, fish on a string, and a smile on his face.

"I never really knew my brother," Wyatt observed, startling the quiet. "Not in the way brothers should have known each other."

"You would've. Eventually. We would've stayed in Monteagle, and you guys would've had time."

He nodded. "Yeah, that's true. But I don't think I would've ever *known* him, understood him. Not like you. You got him in a way no one else did. You got through all the noise."

"I ache for him," I whispered.

"I know you do."

"I wish for so many things, Wyatt. I wonder if Gigi will mourn the father she never knew. Do I want her to?" The frigid air caressed my cheeks, freezing the tears of pain on my skin. I shook my head. "This wasn't supposed to be my life. I wasn't supposed to be alone. We weren't supposed to be alone."

Wyatt took a hand out of his pocket and reached for mine. I gripped it, needing something to bring me back to reality. "I keep hoping I'll find a tucked away letter somewhere, waiting for me. Like there was something incredibly special he wanted to say to me. But there isn't one. And the last real moment we have together was Kai kissing me goodbye, kissing my belly goodbye. And then he was gone." I looked at him. "You never think it will be the last time."

I pulled my hand from Wyatt's. My body was stiff with cold and memories that always lingered just below the surface of my mind. Memories of the wreckage I was forced to live through.

"Do you believe in Heaven?" I asked.

"I don't know," he said. "I like the idea of Heaven and the comfort it brings people. I think the comfort part is more important than anything else."

"What if," I said, my voice breaking. "What if this is it? This is the only chance we get—to love, to live. It's not enough, Wyatt. It's not enough. I need Kai. I need to know I'll see him again, love him again."

I put a finger to my mouth to signal being quiet. Dakota nodded in understanding and scrambled up from his pallet on the floor and nearly ran towards me. He wrapped his arms around my legs and hugged me. I ran my fingers through his mess of dark curls, loving the little boy's affection. I wondered when he would stop wanting to give hugs and blow kisses.

I took his hand and led him into the kitchen. "Do you like hot chocolate?" I whispered.

He nodded, his green eyes bright with excitement.

"You want to help me?"

"Okay," he said.

I pulled a chair to the stove, got the fixings ready, and turned the burner on low. "Your job is to stir it," I said. "We want little bubbles, but not big ones. Okay?"

"Okay." He concentrated fiercely, taking his job very seriously.

"Was your pallet on the floor comfortable?"

He nodded. "Like a slumber party," he said. "Why didn't we sleep at Grandma and Grandpa's?"

"Because the roads were icy and it would've been dangerous to drive. I didn't want Grandma and Grandpa to get into an accident."

"Like Uncle Kai?" he asked.

"What do you know about Uncle Kai?"

"That he died."

I breathed in a sharp breath, stabbing pain shooting through my stomach. I forced my voice to remain strong and unaffected. Dakota had no idea how his words disturbed me. He was a child, both innocent and knowing at the same time.

Lucy and Wyatt padded into the kitchen, looking sleepy. Wyatt's hair was a wild mess. Lucy kissed her son's head good morning and then went to the coffee maker. "No coffee," she said.

"We're making hot chocolate," I explained. "And I forgot to put on the coffee."

"No worries, I'll do it." Lucy filled the pot with water and then dumped the coffee grounds into the filter. She paused.

"Luce?" Wyatt asked. "You okay?"

She dropped the coffee bag onto the floor and covered her mouth with a hand as she ran from the room. Wyatt gave a gentle laugh and shook his head.

"What's wrong with Mommy?" Dakota asked.

"Kids see everything," I said to Wyatt.

"Tell ya what, sport," Wyatt said, coming to stand next to Dakota. "Let's go check on her and see if she's okay." Wyatt hoisted Dakota over his shoulder like a sack of chicken feed and carried him out of the room.

I manned the hot chocolate alone. The rest of the house was waking up just as I was getting the bacon ready. Alice came downstairs holding Gigi.

"Someone was awake," she said, placing Gigi in her high chair.

"Thanks for grabbing her," I said.

"Where's Lucy?" she asked.

"Throwing up," I said with a smile.

"Ah, impending motherhood. And Wyatt and Dakota?"

"Probably having the facts of life talk as we speak."

"Mornin', Sage," Keith greeted, hugging me. He went to the coffee maker and pulled out the empty pot. "What, no coffee?"

Ten minutes later, the kitchen was overrun with food, family, and laughter. Dakota ran around, telling everyone he was going to be a big brother. I smiled, comfort washing through me.

———

Chat rested next to me on the couch, letting me pet him. He purred, his eyes closed. I was hoping to take a nap soon; I forgot the craziness that came with hosting. Everyone else was back at George and Claire's house, and Lucy and I were able to have some time to talk.

"Finally, a moment alone," Lucy said, sipping her tea. "It's a new year. What are you going to do with it?"

"Damn fine question," I replied.

"I wish you'd come to Monteagle. It would be nice… to have you close to home."

"I can't," I said softly. "I'm not ready."

"Will you ever be ready?" she asked. "Change of scenery might help."

"I can't live in that house, on that mountain. It would be like living in the shadow of his ghost."

"This house doesn't do that to you? Make you feel that way?" she wondered.

"Different. I don't know. Back there, in Monteagle, it's Kai and his past—his history. Here, I don't know. We had dreams here, a future. It's different," I said again, not understanding it any more when I said it aloud.

I reached for my own mug of tea on the coffee table, just to have something to do. "Why did you stay? In Monteagle. After Tristan. Was it the promise of Wyatt? What?"

"I never thought of going some place else." She shrugged. "You and Kai leaving—that was your way, not mine."

"Yes," I agreed.

"So you're never going to come back to Monteagle. To live, I mean."

"I don't think so. I love it here. I feel peace here."

"You don't give up your peace. Not for anything."

"Sometimes I wish I could leave it all behind," I said slowly. "There are days when I feel swamped by it all and I just want to run. Run far away—by myself."

"What about Gigi?"

"I would never abandon her," I stated. "But sometimes, I wish it was only me." I knew deep down that without Gigi I would've died of a broken heart. Did that make me weak? Did that mean I had truly loved with abandon, with no thought for myself? I hadn't held anything back, not with Kai. I had given him everything, every piece of me, and he had left me Gigi in return. And she was enough to keep me alive through the pain.

"I write Tristan letters," Lucy admitted. She stared at me with deep, knowing blue eyes.

"Do you," I said.

She nodded. "Sometimes it's just a few silly sentences. Other times I wake in the middle of the night, swearing I can feel his lips on my cheek. Writing to him makes me feel like he isn't really gone."

"You ever tell Wyatt?"

"He knows."

"Isn't he jealous?"

She smiled, but it was tragic. "Jealous? Tristan was the one who died. Tristan didn't get to see his son being born. Tristan didn't get to grow old. Jealous? Wyatt is the one who gets to live."

"Life is hard. Isn't it?"

Lucy's hand settled on her still flat belly. "Hard. But so worth it."

———

"Claire, we have to go or we'll miss our flight," George said as he stood by the door of the farmhouse.

Gigi was curled against her grandmother, sound asleep. Gazing down at Gigi, Claire's reluctance was evident. "One more minute."

I smiled. "Take all the time you want."

Everyone else had already flown back to the States, but George and Claire had stayed an extra few days. It was nice being able to spend time with them alone, and they enjoyed the extra time with Gigi.

"I'm getting in the car. I'm leaving in five minutes with or without you," George warned. With one last hug goodbye, George left.

"He won't really leave you. Will he?"

"Not if he knows what's good for him." With great reluctance, Claire handed Gigi to me. My daughter didn't wake upon transference. Secure in her world, she slept hard and sure.

I kissed Claire on the cheek and said, "My door is always open to visit. You know that, right?"

"I do. Thanks, Sage. Thanks for putting up with us."

"What are you talking about?" I demanded.

"Us, being in your space. I know it can't be easy."

"What would I do without you?" I asked, my eyes staring into hers, needing her to know how much I loved, valued, and appreciated her. I loved all of them. I needed them. My family, who would be there for me no matter what.

I stood on the front porch and waved to them as they drove towards the airport, to head back to their home and their lives.

I needed to get back to mine.

Chapter 8

Shrieks ripped through my eardrums, jolting me awake. I bounded out of bed and ran towards the nursery. I flipped on the light and went to the crib. Tears streaked down Gigi's chubby cheeks. She howled in abandon, her fists clenched.

It was a sound I'd never heard from her. I picked her up, pressing my lips to her head. She was hot to the touch. She'd been teething and fussy for a few days with a slight fever, but this felt like someone had put an electric blanket under her skin and cranked it up to high.

I went cold with fear, the acrid stench of it hitting my nose.

Gigi attempted to lunge from my arms. I paced the hallway with her, but it only seemed to enrage her more.

I dialed Celia. Her voice was confused, and I hated knowing I'd woken her up out of a sound sleep. She rose early in the mornings to run the bed and breakfast.

"What's that noise?" she asked. I could hear her stifling a yawn.

"Gigi," I said, panic creeping into my voice. "I don't know what's wrong with her."

"Take a breath," she said calmly.

I inhaled deeply.

"Does she have a fever?" Celia asked.

"Yes, but I think it's higher than it's been the last few days."

"Did you give her the infant's acetaminophen?"

"I forgot—I didn't think—I can't think—"

"Sage, give her the acetaminophen. I'll be right over."

"You don't have—"

"Twenty minutes, okay?"

I hung up with Celia and went into the bathroom. My own tears were falling. I made a garbled noise and choked on a sob. I juggled Gigi in one arm and the bottle of liquid in the other, spilling some of the medicine as I tried to get Gigi to swallow the dosage. Her cry abated, turning into a whimper, right before light pink vomit spewed from her mouth, covering both of us. Some it of went into my hair, but I hardly noticed.

The front door opened and Celia called, "Sage?" Her quick footsteps came up the stairs and she entered the bedroom. She was still in pajamas and her hair was a tangled mess. She took in the scene quickly.

"Come on," she said. "We'll take her to the hospital."

"Hospital?" It felt as though I had shouted the word, but it came out in a pathetic whisper.

"Yes. Let's get her there so they can find out what's going on."

I dressed Gigi quickly, her wails piercing my ears and hurting my heart. In my haste to prep her for the hospital I forgot my own coat, but I didn't feel the coldness of the February night as we walked to the car. Nothing mattered.

Nothing except Gigi.

We pulled up to the hospital and parked. I removed the car seat from its base and nearly ran into the lobby, heading directly to the admissions desk. A young blonde nurse with a pinched expression handed me some forms to fill out before she would see Gigi. I didn't want to fill out forms; I wanted her to take care of my daughter. I yelled at the nurse in French, but she appeared unconcerned. Celia joined me at the desk and guided me over to a chair.

"Sit," she commanded.

I sat.

"The sooner we get these forms filled out the sooner they'll see Gigi." She picked up a pen and started to ask me questions. She wrote quickly, filling everything out before returning them to the nurse.

We didn't have to wait long before we were ushered to a bed, but Gigi managed to throw up twice more. "Where the hell is the damn doctor?" I hissed.

Celia moved to put a hand to my shoulder, saw that it was covered in baby vomit, and retracted it. "I think that's him." She gestured with her chin to an approaching grandfatherly figure with bushy salt and pepper eyebrows. His voice was calm as he asked questions and checked Gigi, not at all fazed by the sight of both of us covered in pink goo. A nurse took Gigi's temperature and a urine sample.

I held my daughter close to me. I was beyond scared, past the point of fear—I was numb. I thought about the day she'd been born, about how she could've died. I thought about her death being another loss I'd have to live with. She was the one piece of Kai I had left. I wouldn't survive her death.

I was forced to shove all those thoughts away when the nurse handed the doctor the results of the urine test.

He nodded. "As I suspected. She's got a kidney infection. We'll start her on antibiotics and give her something for the pain. Her temperature is quite high, so we'll keep her here to monitor her. Try not to worry."

"She'll be okay?" I asked, my voice gravelly.

He smiled and nodded. "It's good that you brought her in, but she's healthy. In a day or two the antibiotics will kick in and we'll send her home with you to rest once the fever goes down."

I took a deep, shaky breath before throwing up all over the doctor's shoes.

———

After two long days and nights at the hospital, Gigi and I returned home. Celia had wanted to stay with us, but I urged her home to her own bed. Gigi went to sleep sometime around dawn, and by that time I was incoherent. I sank into my bed, clutching the baby monitor to me.

I awoke in early afternoon to the faint sound of pots and pans clinking together in the kitchen. I got up, checked on Gigi who still slept, and padded downstairs. Armand fiddled with the oven knob and set the timer. He looked over his shoulder at me.

"Are you okay?" Armand asked.

I paused, thinking about it. "No," I replied.

"Kids are resilient. When Luc was a toddler, he fell and hit his forehead on the coffee table. There was blood everywhere. Of course we were not okay with that. But six stiches fixed it and life went on."

I nodded absently. I wished I had known that once I became a mother I would never stop worrying about my daughter. There was joy in motherhood, but fear, too. So much fear. "For one moment, I wished she had never been born, so she wouldn't have had to go through the pain."

"You can't protect them from the world."

"If I don't do it, who will?" I demanded.

"You do the best you can. And you're doing a great job."

I'm doing it alone, I didn't say. I had people, of course I did. But it always came back to this: Kai wasn't here. I thought about the day Gigi would get married. Would she be devastated she didn't have a father to walk her down the aisle, or would she settle for me? There were certain things I couldn't give her, no matter how much I wanted to.

I wasn't going to be enough for her. I didn't know how I knew that, but I did.

"Sage, stop it."

"Stop what?"

"I can see the look on your face."

I smiled, but I wanted to cry. I wouldn't, not this time. I couldn't break down every time things got hard because they were hard all the time. I was sick of myself and my wallowing, but I felt like a whale of fear had swallowed me whole. I was trapped in the belly of it without a light and there was no way out.

"I thought it would get easier," I admitted quietly when Armand was checking on the heating food. "Well, maybe not easier, but I thought I would find a way to live without Kai. I found a way to go on after Mom died. But with Kai… I think I might be one of *those* women…"

"What women?"

"I've had the love of my life—and lost him. I'm living through it, but I don't think I'll find happiness again."

"Doesn't Gigi make you happy?"

I nodded. "I love my daughter, but it's not the same."

"Follow me," he said, heading towards the stairs. We went into the nursery and stood by the crib. "Look at her. And I mean really look at her."

I glanced down at Gigi's sleeping face. A wash of peace came over me, despite the undercurrent of fear and sadness.

"She doesn't just need you—you need her. It's okay to admit that, Sage. Rome wasn't built in a day and the heart doesn't heal in one, either."

———

"Why are you looking at me like that?" I asked.

"Like what?" Jules's eyes widened with sham innocence.

"Out with it," I demanded. Gigi pounded her hands on her high chair and made a hungry noise. I scooped out a spoonful of applesauce and put it into her waiting, open mouth. She made a happy, content sound at the back of her throat before demanding another bite.

"I want to have a girls' night out. You and me, outside the house. Where you put on real pants and actually style your hair."

"Ouch," I said, not at all offended. I set the empty bowl aside and removed Gigi's bib, a blue little thing with a patchwork airplane across it. Celia's handiwork.

"Seriously. Please? It's been so long since we've gone out. Gigi is fine. She had a kidney infection, Sage, but she's fine."

I looked at her in amusement. "You done?"

"Yes."

"Good, because I agree."

"I—really?"

I unstrapped Gigi from her highchair and picked her up. Her small hands found their way to my cheeks. She was always so warm, a little bundle of heat.

"Yeah." I glanced at my best friend and she watched me carefully.

"Friday? I already asked Armand and Celia if they'd be available to babysit."

"Did you."

"Just in case."

I grinned. "Pick me up at seven. And wear something hot."

———

"Thanks for doing this," I said.

Armand reached for Gigi, who squealed in happiness and eagerly went to him. "Are you kidding me?"

"You're going to be okay without Celia?"

Armand nodded. "She'll be over later, but she had to finish up some things at the bed and breakfast."

I sighed. I wasn't sure I was ready to leave Gigi—not after what we'd both been through. I already felt the tugging on my heart, but I couldn't give in. I needed to go out. I'd have a glass of wine, maybe two. I'd talk with my best friend, remember that I could interact with adults and that there was a world outside my daughter.

It was going to be damn near impossible to remember.

"There's breast milk in the refrigerator and mashed bananas—"

"Don't worry. I got it," Armand said. "You look nice."

I smiled. "Thanks." I'd pulled my hair back into a bun since I hadn't had it cut in months. I was wearing a pair of dark jeans, a velvet blazer, and black boots. I heard Jules honk the car horn, so I grabbed my purse, and with one last look at my daughter and her surrogate grandpa, I left.

"You look hot," Jules proclaimed as I climbed into her car.

"Thanks. I feel pretty good, actually, despite being in real pants."

Jules laughed. "Do your jeans have a little spandex in them? We're going to be eating a lot."

"I'll survive. So where are you talking me?"

"There's a new Vietnamese restaurant in the heart of downtown."

"I haven't had Vietnamese food since I left New York."

"I had a feeling." Twenty minutes later, she parked the car and we climbed out. We went inside, walking past the hostess.

"Where are you going? Don't we need to ask for a table?"

Jules grabbed me by the wrist and turned her eyes to mine. "Just remember, we did this because we love you."

"What are you talking about?"

She tugged me forward and then we stopped. We didn't need to ask for a table because Luc was already sitting at one, but he wasn't alone. A man sat next to him. They rose from the table when they saw us.

"Don't be mad, please?" Jules whispered.

I shot a glare in Luc's direction. To his credit, he kept eye contact. "Do I look completely horrified?" I demanded.

"More like betrayed," Jules said, trying for levity and failing.

I glared at her before turning to leave. "Why did you blindside me? Why not ask me if I was ready for this?"

She followed me. "You would've said no."

"Damn right." I stalked outside and took a deep breath, trying to see past the anger.

"Will you stop?" Jules demanded.

I faced her, wondering how ugly it was about to get. "You had no right."

"Okay, I admit this wasn't the best way to go about this, but I… can't stand to see you like this. Shut away in the house, surrounded by Kai's things you refuse to get rid of."

"Stop."

"No. You listen to his CD on repeat. You wear his clothes."

"So?"

Jules reached out and touched the necklace around my neck. "You had his wedding ring made into a pendent."

"I'm doing the best I know how," I gritted.

She didn't react to my anger. Her eyes were sad when she said, "You might be alive, but you're not living."

I wished my hair wasn't pulled back from my face because I suddenly wanted to thread my fingers through it and scream like crazy Ophelia. "Did it ever occur to you that all I want to do is raise my daughter and write?"

"It's not enough for you."

"I don't want anyone else. I'll *never* want anyone else."

"How do you know?"

"There are two types of people in this world, Jules. There are those who remarry after the death of their spouse, and those who don't. I found the love of my life, and he's gone. No one can compare to Kai. You setting me up with that guy in there—," I pointed to the restaurant, "—was a shitty move. Not just for me, but for him, too. What did you even tell him? You know what? It doesn't matter. I'm out of here."

———

My blood felt like it was boiling, rolling through my veins like lava. I didn't care where I was going, only that I needed to be somewhere, anywhere else.

My legs carried me across familiar cobblestone until I was outside McCool's. I walked inside, the faint sounds of an Irish band playing. I prayed it wasn't Dorian and Finn, the two men who had once played on stage with Kai. I quickly realized it was some other band and I breathed a sigh of relief.

As I slid onto an empty stool in the corner of the bar, I let down my hair. My scalp felt tight. The bartender approached me and I ordered fish and chips and a glass of Bushmills. I downed half of it almost immediately and then thought about pacing myself.

When my food arrived, I finished my drink and asked for another one. I ate quickly, not caring that it was so hot it burned the roof of my mouth. The band finished their break and geared up for another set. Taking my drink, I headed to the middle of the dance floor. I was alone. No one liked to be the first one to dance, but I'd had just enough whiskey not to give a flying fuck.

The band played a jig and I began to move with abandon, closing my eyes, not wanting to see anything. The whiskey swirled in my head and in my arms. I felt bodies close to me. I opened my eyes. Others had finally joined me on the dance floor.

I got another drink.

I got drunk.

And still, I felt everything.

———

I closed the door to the cab and stumbled up the front steps of the farmhouse. Most of the alcohol had burned off, but just enough remained that I swayed, still feeling like I was dancing. I crept into the living room; the main lights were off, but one lone lamp was turned on. Armand was asleep in the chair, his mouth hanging open, the TV on low. Celia sat on the couch, flipping through a magazine. She glanced up. I stood in the foyer, feeling like a teenager who had come home after curfew.

"Did you know?" I asked quietly.

Celia stood up and came to me. She led me to the kitchen and gestured for me to sit down. She put on water for tea and set a piece of cake in front of me. Lemon. She couldn't come over to my house and not bake.

"I didn't know," she said after a stretch of silence. She turned to face me and leaned against the counter. "If I had, I never would've supported it."

I breathed a sigh of relief I hadn't been aware I'd been holding.

"But they have a point."

Something caught in the back of my throat. Surprise. Anger at realizing it was the truth.

"You can't keep doing this to yourself, Sage."

"Doing what?" I murmured, though I knew.

She heaved a sigh. The teakettle whistled and she poured me a cup and brought it to me. I blew on it before setting it aside. I picked at the cake with my finger. I scooped off a glob of buttercream frosting and stuck it into my mouth, crystal granules lingering.

"You think I should date?" I asked.

"I think you shouldn't be afraid to put yourself out there. Not date. Just be *open*," she said. "Sometimes we need a little push before we're truly ready."

"I miss him. Every day I miss him. It doesn't wane; it doesn't stop. I can't breathe without pain."

She didn't placate me by telling me she understood. No one could understand. Well, maybe Lucy.

Lucy.

She'd found love again after Tristan. Maybe she'd have some words of wisdom.

But did I want wisdom?

Anger wasn't getting me very far.

———

Jules stood on my front porch steps, holding a sweet-smelling baked good. I leaned against the doorframe and tried to look upset. "Did you make that?"

She shook her head. "I enlisted Celia's aid. It's good, I promise."

I let her inside. Gigi was sitting in her Pack-N-Play, engaged with a ring of plastic keys, but she made a garbled sound when she saw Jules. *Chat* watched from the arm of the couch. He looked more like a jungle cat now than anything else. I liked that he was protective.

"Your cat is judging me," Jules accused with a grimace.

"No doubt."

We sat down.

"I'm sorry. So, so, so sorry."

I smiled slightly. "One 'so' would've been enough."

But Jules didn't smile. "I feel guilty."

"About what?"

"Luc."

"I don't get it."

She finally looked at me. In the eyes. "I know how much you loved—love—Kai. I know how happy you were together. Every time I hug or kiss Luc and I see you out of the corner of my eye, it's like I'm watching you relive losing Kai. Does that make any sense?"

I swallowed the egg of pain in my throat and tried to speak past it. "I relive losing him every day I wake up. I relive losing him every time Gigi smiles and I recognize the pull of her lips. Don't you get it? I'm still mourning, Jules, and I wonder if I'll always be in mourning. My heart wears black. Dating anyone—trying, making an effort—I don't have the strength to do it. I don't even have the *want* to do it."

Somehow, we found ourselves crying in each other's arms. I wondered if there would ever be a time when I didn't feel like crying when I thought of Kai. I wanted to smile when I thought of him. Smile through the tears.

We pulled back and reached for the box of tissues on the coffee table at the same time. We both laughed.

I looked at my daughter. Kai's daughter. She gave me a toothy smile and my heart broke all over again when I thought of her growing up without Kai. I had to grow up without him, too.

Chapter 9

I entered the *fromagerie*, sighing when I saw there were six people ahead of me. I juggled my other shopping bags, my annoyance level creeping up. Errands always took far longer than I ever expected them to—and I hated them.

I'd left Gigi at the farmhouse with Celia and it felt like a part of me was missing, but it was nice not having to drop everything in order to see to an infant's needs.

"Sage?"

I turned at the voice calling my name. The man looked vaguely familiar. "Yes?"

"We were supposed to meet the other night," he said, a rueful grin spreading across his face. "I'm friends with Luc."

"Oh, you're... sorry, I never got your name," I said, feeling sheepish.

"Sébastien," he introduced, holding out his hand. I adjusted my shopping bags so I could shake his hand. "Nice to meet you."

"You, too." The line moved and I took a step closer to the counter. Just a few more customers to go. "Sorry about the other night."

"Don't apologize. I gave Luc an earful when I found out you had no idea it was a blind date."

"We have crappy friends," I said with a wry grin.

He laughed. "Don't we? Still, they thought we'd get along."

"Hmmm," I said noncommittally.

"Would you be interested in grabbing a cup of coffee sometime?"

"Listen, you seem like a really good sport," I said, "but I'm just not in a dating place."

"Date? I'm talking about a cup of coffee. Maybe even a croissant. I'll even let you buy so you don't have to worry about me misconstruing things."

I smiled but didn't answer. The man at the counter called out, "Next!" I quickly placed my order.

"If you change your mind..." Sébastien said with a shrug as he turned to walk away.

"Wait. Do you have any plans after you order your cheese?" I asked.

———

"What are you doing?" Luc asked from the doorway of the turret.

I was leaning back in my chair, a book open across my face. "Having a moment."

"Will I understand this?"

I pulled the book down. "Probably not." I looked at him. "Has Jules told you?"

"Told me what?"

I took a deep breath and handed him the book. He took it, his eyes widening. "Your name is on this."

"Yes."

"You wrote a book?"

"That's a proof," I explained. "But yes, I wrote a book. It comes out in few weeks, I think. I've lost track of time with all the things going on."

Part II

After my initial phone call with my agent, things had come together quickly. I had waited less than three weeks before the phone rang again and it was confirmed. I had an offer. A good one. My mother's career had paved the way for me.

"Are you fucking kidding me? How could you have kept this a secret?" he exclaimed, shock permeating his voice.

"Jules didn't tell you?" I asked in amazement.

He shook his head.

"Damn, I never expected her to *actually* keep it to herself. Impressive."

"We have to celebrate!"

I didn't reply as I got up and we walked down the hallway to the nursery. Gigi was awake in her crib, but she didn't look like she was about to cry. She giggled as Luc scooped her up into his arms. We went downstairs into the living room and settled onto the couch. Luc put Gigi on his lap, propping her up. *Chat* was nowhere to be found, which meant there was a good chance he was outside hunting something to leave on my doormat.

"Do you want to talk about your book?"

"No."

"Why not? This is amazing."

"Yes."

"Then why—"

"I just… take the proof and read it, okay? Then we'll talk about it."

"Really?"

"No. Actually, let's just pretend I didn't write anything at all and just move on."

"Why?"

"Because," I tried to explain, "it's like a movie actor watching his performance. He'll find all the things he did wrong and want to change it, but can't."

"You should be proud of yourself."

"I am. But I'm also embarrassed. Like, really? I wrote something people actually want to publish? This isn't me fishing, I swear. I don't want you to puff me up. I wrote a book, but it almost feels like I didn't. I don't know. Forget it."

"Okay." He paused. "Sébastien called me."

I sucked in a breath of air.

"You didn't tell me you had coffee with him."

"I ran into him when I was running errands."

"And?"

"And what? We had coffee. That's all."

"He liked you."

"He was very likable, too," I said.

"That's Sage speak for 'nice guy, never going to happen'. Am I right?"

I shrugged. "He was nice. You have great taste in men."

Luc rolled his eyes. "*But…*"

"Just wasn't—couldn't see—I don't know, it just felt… off. And made me realize I'm not ready for anything."

"I'm sorry."

"For what?"

"I push a lot. We all do."

I nodded. "I agree with that assessment."

"You pissed?"

"Pissed? Why would I be pissed? You can't be pissed at family for loving you too much."

———

Gigi kicked her feet excitedly, making happy baby noises. I poked her soft belly, my heart warming when she began to laugh.

"Hah, Luc has the same reaction when I poke him in the stomach," Jules stated.

"Too much information," I said with a smile. I grasped one of Gigi's feet and kissed it. "She turned over onto her stomach the other day."

"Yeah?"

"Yeah." I shook my head in apology. "Sorry. Mom moment."

"It's cool."

"It's hard sometimes. My brain gets overcrowded with things. She takes up a lot of my headspace."

"Make sense," Jules said. "Hard though, right? I mean, having to always put her first?"

"Yeah, but it's worth it."

"You don't ever get frustrated? Like when all you want to do is write, but you have to take care of her?"

"I guess I get frustrated," I admitted. "I'm human. But I don't resent her, if that's what you're getting at."

"That's what I'm getting at."

"I did," I admitted. "After Kai died, all I wanted to do was lie down and never get up. If it hadn't been for her, I might have. I resented her for keeping me alive, but once she came into the world I was grateful."

"You really think you would've given up?" Jules wondered. "I just don't believe that."

I shrugged. "It was bad, Jules. I look back and it's all sort of hazy. Like I know I lived it, but I can hardly remember." I looked down at Gigi and pressed my lips to her belly and blew. "Kai isn't here to see all this, experience all this. But I am. I know it's hard for you to understand since you're not a mother, but I could spend hours watching her. Marking the changes. I don't know. Having a baby has done something to me. It's opened up my mind and heart."

"You have to be completely selfless to be a mother," Jules said.

"Yep. And at this age, she needs me to be selfless. She won't live without me. It will change, the older she gets, but for now…"

"You like it, don't you? Having someone needing you to live?"

"I don't like it—I love it. My life is richer because of Gigi. But Jules," I said, looking at her, "when you become a mother, your life is no longer your own. And you're never really ready for that."

———

I leaned against the cement block of the Francois Rabelais statue out front of the university in *Tours* where Jules was taking her French classes. I waited with two cups of coffee as students with annoyed looks traipsed sluggishly through the melting snow puddles, bundled in scarfs and coats. The end of winter clung to the city; it was relentless, and I wondered if spring would ever arrive.

The door to the building opened and Jules came out, wearing a black beret, blending in perfectly with her classmates. She walked among a few other students who appeared to be much younger than she. One of them was a guy who couldn't have been more than twenty-two. He was gazing at Jules with a bemused look on his face. Jules saw me and waved. Turning to her friends, she said her good-byes and schlepped towards me, reaching for her coffee with gloved fingers.

"This is so romantic of you, Sage. Waiting for me with a cup of steaming coffee." She closed her eyes in delirium as she cupped the hot beverage. "Are you avoiding going home?"

"Maybe."

She sighed. "Wouldn't it be better just to answer your agent's phone calls and hear about how well the book is doing?"

I shook my head. "No. I don't want to know a thing. I want to pretend like I don't have a book out there."

The phone had been ringing off the hook for days, and I couldn't handle it anymore. I had turned off my cell phone and silenced the ringer on the house phone, but I still felt bombarded by the contact and wanted to leave. I'd dropped off Gigi at Celia's and decided to meet up with Jules at the university.

"How's the acting class?" I asked, changing the subject.

"Pretty good," she admitted. "It's helping my French a lot more than sitting in a class memorizing verbs and stuff."

"Well, you're really using it, not just learning the words for 'curtain' and 'table'."

Jules grinned. "*Le rideau, la table.*"

"Nice."

"Is it too early for dinner?"

"No. I'm starving," I said.

"What are you in the mood for?"

"A burger. I want a burger," I said.

"I know just the place, come on."

Ten minutes later, we were seated at a table in the French version of a sports bar. It was crowded with college students drinking beer and eating fries by the basketful. There were six screens around the room, all varying in size. The largest one took up almost an entire wall and showed a rugby game.

"I'm so out of my element here," I said, slipping out of my coat and setting it aside.

Jules sipped on her draft beer. "I come here at least once a week. Usually with kids from my acting class. I think I miss being in school full time."

"Really?"

She shrugged. "I miss the excitement. I miss that feeling…"

"What feeling?"

"That feeling of openness. Where it's nothing but excitement and learning and you can do anything. You can pick your path in life."

"You can still pick your path," I said. "It doesn't stop just because we get older, just because we're on one road. There's nothing stopping you from changing your direction."

She looked away. "I'm really unhappy, Sage."

Our food was set in front of us, but I didn't touch mine. "I know it's hard adjusting to a new place where you don't speak the language."

"It's more than that. I don't know if I can explain it."

"Try."

"I love Luc, but I feel trapped."

I took a breath. "Did you know that every morning I woke up next to Kai, I was happy? It didn't matter what else was happening, it didn't matter what fell apart, nothing mattered because we had each other."

"Oh," she said in bemusement, like she didn't understand what I had just told her. She reached for her beer and downed it, setting the near empty glass aside.

We ate in silence, leaving me to my thoughts about what was going on with my best friend. Jules's cell phone buzzed.

"It's Celia asking if I can work the desk tonight. She wants to take Armand out for a date. I told her I could be there in a few hours."

"You should relieve her now," I said. "Give her time to primp."

"You don't mind if I leave you alone?"

"Not at all. In fact, I'd like some time to myself."

She looked at me for a long moment. "You sure?"

"Yes. You were there when I needed you most, Jules. I never forget that. I'm here for you, too."

Jules opened her mouth to answer but then snapped it shut. Her eyes clouded with tears and she nodded, then grabbed her coat and left.

As I drank the rest of my beer I thought about the choices people made in life, and realized I was starting to go into that place of darkness I had worked so hard to get out of. Maybe time by myself wasn't what I needed. I forced heavy thoughts away and finished my fries, my eyes perusing the room, taking in pockets of people as they laughed and drank with each other.

My eyes came to rest on a man at the corner of the bar reading a book. He had disheveled dark-blond hair, but I couldn't make out the rest of his face since he was staring down at a novel. *Who reads a book in a sports bar?* The room erupted into cheers as one of the rugby teams scored. The man didn't even register that something had occurred. He finished his beer and set his book down to hail the bartender.

I watched in fascination as a young, determined woman stalked towards him and tried to engage him in conversation. It was as though she had intuitively sensed the opening she had been waiting for. She couldn't have been more than twenty years old, and it was obvious by her confidence she knew she was attractive. She tossed hair over her shoulder as she approached him.

They exchanged a few moments of chitchat, but the man clearly wanted to get back to his book. The woman continued to flirt as he tried to gain the bartender's attention. I saw resignation settle across his face as he realized the woman wasn't going to give up her pursuit.

I was intrigued by what I was seeing, and I wanted to get closer to watch them. Scooting out of the booth, I headed for the bar, standing close enough to hear their conversation while I waited to order a beer.

"I'm not a big reader," the woman said.

"Oh yeah?" the man asked lightly.

"Why read when you can experience life?"

"And how do you experience life?" he wondered.

"I go to bars and stuff. You have to go out to experience the world."

I held in a groan, but couldn't help an eye roll. Turning to look at him, I met his eyes. "Antoine?"

He frowned. "I'm sorry, but I think you have the wrong—"

"Antoine! It's been so long!" I spoke in French and prayed the guy would recognize a good rescue attempt.

A look of relief washed across his face as he put the puzzle pieces together. "Hi! Yeah, it's been forever. Sit. Grab a beer with me and lets catch up."

"I'd love to," I said.

He turned to the woman. "It was nice talking to you."

Her eyes flickered to mine. She tried not to appear put out, but I could tell by the clenched jaw she was angry that I'd foiled her plans. There was no way she could stick around now. With one final glance, she walked away.

"Thanks," the man breathed.

I smiled. "You're welcome. You looked a bit… cornered."

"I should remember never to set down my book." He shook his head. "Can I buy you a drink? As a token of my appreciation?"

"Don't worry about it. It's not often that I get to play superhero."

"She's still looking," he commented. "Will you sit down? Just for a moment?"

"Sure, why not," I said. "I left my stuff in a booth. Let me grab it." When I returned, I took the vacant stool next to him.

I was finally close enough to notice the color of his eyes. Hazel. And framed by the tiniest of wrinkles, hinting at his age.

Glancing at the book he was reading, I laughed. "Really? You're *that* guy?"

"What guy?"

"The guy that reads Hemmingway in a sports bar."

"You don't like Hemmingway?"

"I *love* Hemmingway. So, do you have a real name or should I just call you Antoine?"

He smiled. "I'm Henry," he said, reaching his hand out. "Henry Gerard."

"Sage Ferris," I said, shaking his offered hand. It was warm and he had long aristocratic fingers. He wore a tweed jacket with elbow patches and underneath he had on a Kooks t-shirt. The whole picture was a bit of a mismatch.

"The Kooks are good," I noted.

"Better than good," he stated. "My brother and I once camped out all night in the dead of Chicago winter just to make sure we got tickets to their concert."

I blinked. "Chicago?"

He nodded. "That's where I'm from. And you?"

"New York."

"Ah. That explains the courage to save an unknown man from a terrible fate," he said, switching to English.

I laughed. "So, you're from Chicago? What are you doing here?"

"Here? As in this sports bar being *that* guy reading Hemmingway, or here, as in France?"

"France."

"I'm a history professor; I was offered a position as a guest lecturer for the spring semester."

"History professor?" I asked. It explained the tweed but not much else. "I never would've guessed that."

"It's the t-shirt, right?"

"Among other things," I murmured before I could stop myself.

His gaze turned appreciative. "You sure I can't buy you a drink? I like to pay my debts."

Henry was smiling, the grooves around his mouth deep and obvious. They were smile lines, and I was sure each one had a story. I wasn't surprised that women found him attractive, and I was unnerved by my own reaction to him.

I pushed back from the bar. "I actually have to get home. I'm glad I could save you from some unwanted attention."

"Can I walk you out at least?" he asked, standing up. "You see, if you leave me alone, she'll just come back. She might even bring a friend."

"Wait, isn't that every guy's dream?"

"I plead the fifth."

I laughed. "I really do need to get home, but you can walk me to my car if you want."

We walked out into the cold and I sank my hands into my pockets. Henry wore a black pea coat over his tweed jacket. His scarred, brown leather messenger bag was slung over his shoulder.

When we got to my car I said, "Good bye, Henry. It was nice meeting you."

"Wait," he said. I turned back to look at him. His smile lines were doing things to my insides. I was a sucker for smile lines.

"Can I call you?"

I paused. "I don't think so."

He looked confused, but not hurt. "You don't actually like The Kooks, do you?"

I bit my lip so I wouldn't smile. A late winter wind snapped through the street, ruffling the hair at Henry's ears. I noticed things about him. Things I wasn't sure I should be noticing.

His glance went to the back window and I knew he had seen Gigi's car seat. Instantly contrite, he said, "I'm sorry. I didn't realize you were married."

"I'm not." I shifted my weight, fumbling with my keys. "I'm a widow," I blurted out, not wanting to tiptoe around the issue.

"I'm sorry," he said again. "I didn't mean to make it—"

"It's fine," I said, interrupting him. "There's not really a good way to—it's fine." It wasn't, though, not really.

He shoved his hands into his coat pockets and sighed. Almost like he understood the futility of our conversation. "Bye, Sage. It was nice meeting you."

"Good bye, Henry." I climbed into the car and drove away, watching him disappear in my rearview mirror.

Chapter 10

Jules carried a garment bag over her arm, and I instantly shrank away. "That better be your wedding dress you're showing me," I said.

Chat purred when Jules reached down to stroke his back. "Why would I come to *your* house to show you *my* wedding dress?"

The accurate assessment increased my wariness. Not to mention the fact that my thoughts were still on Henry Gerard and his ridiculously warm smile.

"You're gonna love this, trust me," she said, snapping me out of my reverie.

"Just show it to me," I commanded.

She unzipped the bag, pulling out a knee-length emerald green dress. I touched the fabric and breathed a sigh of relief. It was made of material that would allow movement.

"Try it on."

It was comfortable and beautiful, not too form-fitting. I looked in the full-length mirror in the bedroom and nodded. "Gorgeous."

"You can thank Celia for that."

"That woman can do anything," I said. "Sew, knit, run a bed and breakfast, and plan your wedding. Can she fly, you think?"

"I wouldn't put it past her abilities."

"You do realize you have another five months before you get married, right? Any reason my dress is already finished?"

She tucked a lock of hair behind her ear. "Weddings are stressful."

"Yes."

"I'm trying to limit the stress. Have to get things done early so they don't sneak up on me."

"Good luck with that." I hung the dress up on the hanger and put it in the garment bag. We walked downstairs and into the kitchen. I filled the teakettle and turned on a burner as Jules took a seat at the kitchen table.

"Do you remember what it was like trying to find a place in Kai's family," Jules asked.

"Yeah. Why do you ask?"

"Just thinking about Luc's family and my place in it."

"Family dynamics can be challenging."

"I feel like Celia and Armand are just tolerating me."

"What makes you say that?"

She shrugged. "Just a feeling I get. Luc's an only child. I feel like there's a lot of pressure on me to make their only child happy."

"I felt that way with Kai's mother," I admitted. "You have two choices. You either ignore it or you have a conversation with your future in-laws and clear the air."

She made a face. "You and Kai's mother are okay now, though, right?"

I nodded. "Yes, but I think if he had lived it would've taken her longer to warm up to me."

"She would've though," Jules stated adamantly. "Everyone loves you."

"Have you talked to Luc? About your concerns?"

"A bit."

"Did you tell him *Tours* doesn't feel like home?"

She glanced away. Jules was still living in the ignore-what-she-didn't-want-to-deal-with phase. It would be messy when it all came to a head. I knew that from personal experience, but I knew my advice would fall on deaf ears, so I remained quiet.

The phone rang, distracting the both of us.

"Answer it, already," Jules grumbled after I let it ring four times.

With a sigh, I realized I could no longer shut out the world. I reached for the phone and answered it. Jules got up and went to tend to Gigi who was crying in her Pack-N-Play. She returned with my daughter as I hung up the phone, setting it down on the table.

"Was it your agent?" Jules asked as she bounced Gigi on her hip.

"Yeah," I said.

"Good news? Bad news?"

"My book—" I said, my voice coming out mangled, "—made *The New York Times* Best Sellers list."

―――――

Luc, Celia, and Armand came over bringing food and wine for the celebration. The wine was rich and decadent as it slid over my tongue. We toasted my success. I smiled and laughed, but it felt hollow without Kai.

The phone continued to ring off the hook. Most of the calls were from those in Monteagle who had learned the news, courtesy of Celia's mass email.

"It's your agent," Jules said, trying to hand me the phone. "Again."

"Take a message!" I stage whispered.

"She knows you're here," Jules hissed, all but flinging the phone at me.

I rolled my eyes. "Hello?"

"Don't 'hello' me," Lulu growled. "You know who this is."

"What can I do for you?" I asked. I looked around the kitchen and then retreated upstairs, wanting privacy.

"You *know* what you can do for me."

"I can't do a book tour," I said.

"Sage—"

"I have a child, Lulu. I can't leave her for weeks on end. She's not even a year old."

Lulu paused. "I know that. But I've already thought about it and it's not a problem. You have family in *Tours*, yes?"

"Yes—"

"Excellent. You'll do three days at a time, with a week back at home in between stops. It's settled then."

"Three days—"

"It's not that long, we're covering all your flights, hotels, food, everything. You'll do a reading, come home, rest and do a few more. In a couple of months you'll have hit all the big cities and you're off the hook."

I was silent for a moment, and thought about the conversation I'd had with Jules. I didn't want my life to remain stagnant and this had been my dream when Kai was alive. I had to embrace it.

"Okay, Lulu. I'm in. Where's the first stop?"

"*Tours*. I've already set it up with the university. They're really excited to have you."

"Thanks, Lulu."

"You're welcome. Now check your email. I sent you the details days ago."

I clicked off and fell back on the bed, pulling a pillow over my face.

There was a knock on the door. "Sage?" Celia asked.

"Come in," I said, still not removing the pillow from my face. I felt the bed dip when she sat.

"What is it, honey?"

I sniffed. "It's stupid."

"I doubt that."

"I'm supposed to be happy, right? This is incredible; this is what authors dream of. This is an achievement, a milestone. And yet…" I flung the pillow off my face and stared at the ceiling. "It doesn't even feel like it's happening to me. It doesn't feel like it means what it should mean."

Celia patted her thigh and I moved to rest my head in her lap. She ran her fingers through my hair as she let me talk.

"I'm insane, aren't I? This isn't enough. Gigi... she's not enough. I love her and I don't know how I would've gotten through those first few months after Kai died without her, but... she's not enough."

———

"What the fuck am I going to wear?" I demanded as I went into my closet.

"*Language*," Jules admonished. She was holding Gigi in her arms, but Gigi looked unperturbed by my cursing.

"Who are you kidding? Her first word is going to be the f-bomb."

Jules shook her head. "Nervous?"

"No," I lied.

"Don't worry, Gigi, I'll teach you how to lie since your mom sucks at it."

"We're terrible influences. What about this?" I held up a black dress with long sleeves for Jules to see.

"No, not that one. Wear something with color."

"I've got a red scarf to go with it. Does that work?"

"Yeah, you can make it work if you wear the scarf. What earrings are you going to wear?"

I paused. "Pearls. In honor of my southern character."

"Well played."

I slipped into the dress and then went to my closet for the scarf. Standing in front of my full-length mirror I wrapped the scarf around my neck and twirled my hair into a messy bun. Jules handed me my pearl earrings and I put them in as I surveyed my appearance. I turned to Jules and asked, "Do I pass?"

"You look great."

I wasn't expecting a large turnout for the reading. I lived in a small town tucked away in the Loire Valley. It would be mostly students, maybe some professors, and a few expats, but that was it. And yet, it was still as daunting as thinking about a reading in some New York setting.

My mom used to love this part. I had no idea why. The nerves were already getting to me, climbing up my throat.

"I'm not sure when I'll be home. There's breast milk in the——"

"You act like I've never babysat before. I've got this," Jules urged. "Still wish you'd let me come—let any of us come."

"I don't want to know anyone in the audience."

We walked down the stairs, and I put on my jacket, grabbed my keys and headed to the car. I hopped into the driver's side and waited for it to heat up. I drove slowly towards the university, my heart speeding up the closer I came.

I forced myself to continue on, in spite of wanting to turn around and head home. After I pulled into the parking lot and had a very heated, vocal debate with myself, I managed to get out of the car. I found my way to the school bookstore, grimacing when I saw the signage for my book and photo plastered in the windows.

I'd arrived a bit early, and after finding the woman who was in charge, I had some time to kill. I wandered around the bookstore, pulling out copies of Balzac and Flaubert. Before I knew it, the coordinator was back, tugging my arm and leading me to a stool. I hadn't fully realized how many people there were going to be until I sat down and looked out at the crowd. All the chairs in front of me were filled, and those that couldn't find seats stood at the sides and in the rear of the room.

I smiled and thanked the woman who introduced me. "Hi, everyone," I greeted. "Thank you so much for being here. I'm a little nervous, so please bear with me."

I grabbed a copy of my book on the table behind me and flipped to the scene I wanted to read, turning back to the audience. I stared at my words for a moment, feeling like I hadn't been the one to write them. It was as if they belonged to someone else. I blinked, bringing the words into focus, reading from my favorite chapter, my voice strong and unwavering.

Ten minutes later, I closed the book and looked into the faces of the audience. No one moved, no one breathed for one collective moment. *This*, I realized, was why my mother wrote. Emotions silently swelled, feeding off one another. There were slight smiles on the lips of people who found meaning, a connection to the book I'd written—made more real by my voice.

No one seemed inclined to say anything, and it was up to me to break the spell. I smiled and said, "This is the part where you get to ask questions."

There was laughter, splintering the emotional tension blanketing the room. It only took one person to raise her hand before the questions began. *What was I working on? How did I get my ideas? Are any of your characters like you?* And then there was a question I hadn't been prepared for. *Why did you dedicate your book to winter? What's the significance?*

I recognized the voice. My breath hitched as I met Henry's eyes. I wasn't going explain my dedication. I smiled and said, "I'll leave that open to interpretation."

Chapter 11

"You're a writer," Henry said, setting his copy of my book in front of me. "Seems like you would've mentioned that the other day."

"It seemed more important to talk about The Kooks." I held a pen in my hand and smiled. "Anything you'd like me to write—aside from my signature?"

"Still waiting on your phone number."

"You're shameless, professor," I teased.

"And I'll stay shameless until I'm successful."

"Have you read my book?"

"No, just the dedication. I'll read it, though. Promise. Scout's honor." He held up his hand in the classic Boy Scout honor pledge.

"You're holding up the line," I said, gesturing to the people behind him.

"Phone number," he whispered.

"This is harassment," I whispered back. Despite myself, I smiled and before I could think about it, I wrote my number down for him and handed back the book.

"You didn't sign it," he complained.

"Good bye, Henry," I said pointedly.

He gave me another cheeky grin and then stepped aside. I

engaged and smiled with the rest of the readers who had come to support me. I thanked them for their time and for choosing to read my book. There were so many stories out there, and they had chosen to read mine. It was humbling. I felt undeserving—I owed it to them to get back to the turret and write my next book.

I gathered up my belongings, shook the hand of the coordinator one last time, and walked out into the cold air. I looked for Henry, hoping he'd stuck around, but he was gone.

When I got home, Jules was feeding Gigi. My heart swelled as I saw my child. I'd missed her. She smiled when she saw me, letting out a noise of excitement.

"How'd it go?" Jules asked.

"Good."

"Good? That's it? That's all I get? I'm still upset you wouldn't let me come."

"I know. But I wasn't sure what to expect, ya know? Like, what if you and the family had been the only people there? I would've felt worse than if no one had showed up."

"And how many people showed up?"

I shrugged. "A good amount." I turned away, not wanting her to see my cheeks flooding with color.

Henry. Henry. Henry.

His named echoed in my head, lingering in my smile. What was it about him? Was it that he hadn't taken 'no' for an answer? I never thought I'd see him again after telling him I was a widow. That was a lot of baggage, and most men wouldn't even think of carrying it. I wondered if he realized I was the sum of all the things I'd lost.

My smile died, and I began thinking about Kai.

"You okay?" Jules asked me.

I nodded. "Yeah." I took Gigi into my arms, pressing a kiss to her nose. She giggled and snuggled her head under my chin. I saw Jules out and waved to her as she drove away. I went back inside, turned on some music, and danced until I was out of breath.

———

357

A few days later Gigi was in her Pack-N-Play, hitting plastic toys together while I was in the kitchen trying to open a sticky window. It remained steadfastly shut. My cell phone buzzed, moving across the counter. I answered the call, even though I didn't recognize the number.

"Hello?" I asked.

"I'm in need of a superhero. Do you know any for hire?"

I laughed. "How long did it take you to come up with that line?"

"Just winging it," Henry explained. "Is this a bad time?"

"Not at all," I said. "Just interrupting my dispute with a stubborn window. It's winning. Know any brawn-for-hire?"

"I'll do it for free."

"Really?"

"Yeah."

"How soon can you be here?"

"Depends on where you live."

I gave him the address.

"That's a ten minute walk from me. I'll be right there."

Ten minutes later, there was a knock on the door.

"Nice outfit," he said with a large grin.

I forgot that I was in overalls and had my hair done up in braids. "Superhero disguise," I said. I waved him inside and he stepped into the living room. His gaze landed on Gigi.

I went to her, picking her up. "This is Gigi. Gigi, Henry. Henry, Gigi."

"Now that is a munchkin if I've ever seen one." He offered Gigi his finger. She gave him a toothy, drooly smile and he laughed. "She could give my nephew a run for his money."

"You're an uncle?"

"My older brother and sister have six children between them. Davey, my sister's youngest, is two. Thief of hearts. Now, where is this problematic window?" He gently disentangled Gigi's finger from around his and looked at me.

I pointed in the direction of the kitchen. Henry smiled and strolled past me. He was wearing a pair of old jeans and a black pea coat. He took it off, revealing a faded, vintage Pac Man t-shirt. It made me laugh.

"What?" he demanded, looking at me, a wry grin across his lips.

"Your shirt. I like your shirt."

"This one?" he asked, gesturing to the window over the sink.

"Yeah."

"And why do you want to open a window in winter?"

"Just a crack," I explained. "So when spring comes I can open the window for fresh air. It has to warm up soon, right?"

He smiled at me for a moment, nodding. "Do you have a tool-box? I have an idea."

"Front hall closet I think. I'll grab it." I put Gigi back in her Pack-N-Play and then went to the closet, my gaze momentarily resting on some of Kai's jackets. I pulled out the toolbox and then shut the door.

"Here you go," I said, a little too loudly when I walked back into the kitchen.

"Thanks. That window is really stuck." He opened the toolbox and pulled out screwdriver and a hammer before leaning over the sink towards the window.

"So, you're a college professor."

"Yep. I have a PhD in history. Ancient Gaul."

"Ah, explains why you're a guest lecturer in France, huh?"

"Exactly." He wedged the screwdriver head under the sill and gently tapped the handle with the hammer to lever the window up. Setting down the tools on the counter, he reached for the window and opened it easily.

I smiled in relief. "Thank you."

He grinned, running a hand through his already disheveled hair. "Glad to be of service. I haven't read your book yet."

"Oh," I said in confusion at the change in conversation. "Okay?"

"It's not that I haven't had the time. I have had the time, but I want to… sink into it, ya know? Like really give it what it deserves."

I smiled, running a hand across my mouth. "That might be the best reason I've ever heard for someone *not* reading a book."

"You only read a book for the first time once," he said as we went into the living room. "You have to savor it."

I couldn't have agreed with him more.

"Want me to build a fire? It's cold out there."

"Really? I mean there's hitting on someone, and then there *hitting on someone*, you know?" I teased. "Yes, please."

He laughed and went to crouch in front of the fireplace. After a few minutes the hearth raged and warmth spilled through the living room. The late afternoon light was dying, slinking away, and Henry looked incredible in firelight. Soft lips, hair the color of caramel, eyes flecked with gold.

Suddenly nervous, I was aware of Henry in a way I hadn't been aware of a man in a long time. The yearning surprised me and caught me off guard, hitting me low in my belly.

He slowly stood up as he stared at me. "Can I ask you a question? Before I go…"

The stab of disappointment shot through me when he announced he was leaving. I'd enjoyed his company. It was easy and fun. Light for the first time since I could remember.

"Sure."

"What's your favorite Pink Floyd song?"

"That's the question you want to ask me?"

He grinned. "Favorite Pink Floyd song."

"How do you even know I like Pink Floyd?"

"Don't you?"

I shook my head and shot him a wry grin. "I *love* Pink Floyd."

He laughed.

"*Wish You Were Here.*"

"Two lost souls swimming in a fish bowl," he recited. "Wise choice. I had fun today, Sage."

I blinked stupidly.

"See you soon."

Before I knew it, Henry had left and I was standing in the middle of the living room completely dumfounded.

It was a few days after I'd seen Henry, and Jules and Luc were over for dinner. I was trapped in my thoughts about the man who'd helped me out with my stubborn window—and I didn't want to be.

"Sage? Sage!" Luc waved his hand in front of my face. "Everything okay?"

I nodded.

Jules and Luc exchanged a look.

"What's going on with you?" Jules asked.

"What do you mean?" I evaded.

"You've been quiet, and you've barely touched your food. And… you put on pants. *Real pants.* Not pajamas." Jules studied me, wondering what the hell was going on.

"Do you think—do you think men and women can be friends and nothing else?" I asked.

They exchanged another look.

"Have you been watching *When Harry Met Sally* again?" Jules wondered.

"You're annoying," I said, shooting Jules a glare.

She grinned impishly.

"Out with it," Luc demanded.

"Can men and women just be friends?" I repeated.

"Nope," Luc said immediately.

"Why do you say that?" Jules demanded as she looked at Luc.

"When we first met, did you think we'd just be friends, or was it something more?"

"Well we both wanted to sleep together…"

"Right," he went on, "wanting to have sex with your supposed friends always gets in the way of true friendship. It just doesn't work."

I was silent for a moment and Jules and I exchanged glances.

"Is this where I excuse myself and let you guys talk alone?" Luc asked.

I smiled. "That would be really nice of you."

Luc stood. "I'll go hang out with Gigi in the living room. She likes sports, right?" He touched my shoulder and left us alone.

I picked up my wine glass, swirling around its contents. I stared at it as I slowly admitted, "I met someone. Someone… different. I think."

"Go on," Jules said, reaching for her own glass of wine.

"After you left me at that sports bar a couple of weeks ago I met a man." I went on to explain our exchange, and Henry randomly showing up at my book reading. "He came over the other day."

"Did he now? This just got interesting."

I reiterated what happened. Or what didn't happen, actually.

Jules raised her eyebrows. "He didn't try to kiss you?"

I shook my head.

"Did he ask you on a date?"

"No. I mean, when we first met he seemed interested. But when he came over to help me with the window…" I shrugged.

"Hmmm."

"It's weird, right?"

"Yeah, it's weird. Especially when he made such an effort to get your number."

"I know, right? God, I feel like those idiot girls in high school who have no idea what to expect from guys."

"And you haven't heard from him in how many days?"

"Three. No, four."

"Do you think, maybe, he's just trying to be respectful—letting you come to him? He knows you're a widow. Do you even want to go to him?"

I took a small sip of wine as I thought about it. I felt uncomfortable and guilty at the same time. As if I were somehow betraying the memory of Kai by wanting another man.

She stared at me. "What's he like? Henry?"

"Blunt. Quick wit. Wears fun t-shirts."

"The darkness—losing your mother and Kai, those things don't have to be what defines you."

"And yet, they are the only things I seem to think about. It's not fair to invite him in and dump all that on him."

"You clearly like him," Jules stated.

I looked away from her, not ready to admit that she was right.

"Why else would you be asking if you thought men and women

could be friends, analyzing why he didn't kiss you, and doing the turtle in the shell thing?"

"What the hell is that supposed to mean?" I snapped.

Jules stood up and raised her glass of wine. "It means, dear friend, you've been hiding. But apparently, this guy, this *Henry*, makes you want to put on jeans, do your hair, and ask why he didn't kiss you." She grinned and sauntered out of the room, leaving me alone.

———

I sat with my back against the headboard, my hair spilling over my shoulders. The moon was nonexistent and blackness covered me. I had tried to go to sleep hours ago, but it eluded me. I'd tossed and turned, churning Jules's words over in my mind.

A spurt of courage ran through my veins and I took advantage of it. I picked up my cell phone, hitting the number I hadn't yet found the grit to save.

He picked up on the third ring. "Sage?" His voice was husky with sleep.

It was devastating—I remembered Kai's raspy voice when he'd turn to me in the night, but it was Henry I pictured in my bed.

"Why didn't you ask me out?" I demanded.

He yawned, not even bothering to try and hide it.

"You were asleep. Sorry," I said.

"I'm awake now. It's good to hear from you," he said pleasantly.

"I—why didn't you ask me out?" I asked again.

"Why didn't *you* ask me out?" he fired back.

"I asked you first."

"I asked you second," he said, childishly.

"No. You don't get to—you fixed my window."

"Yes, I did."

"You wear Pac Man t-shirts and you knew I liked Pink Floyd even though I never said so."

"Ok, now I'm confused."

"You make me laugh," I whispered. "You make me feel... like me. At the beginning... of something."

He said nothing.

"Henry? Are you still there?"

"Yeah, I'm here."

"Say something. Please."

He sighed. "Reverse psychology, you've heard of it?"

"Of course." Clarity came to me. "Is that what this is? You don't pursue me and then all of a sudden I want to kiss you?"

There was another pause. "You want to kiss me?"

I heard the smile in his voice and said, "Shut up, Henry."

"You do! You think I'm cute. You want to kiss me!"

"Not anymore," I stated.

"Liar."

I sighed.

"Sage?"

"Yeah?"

"I want to kiss you, too."

I was unable to stop the grin from spreading across my face. "Good night, Henry."

"Good night, Sage."

Chapter 12

"You're brilliant, did you know that?" Henry asked.

One thing I already knew about Henry: his greetings always started as though we were already in the middle of a conversation. *In medias res*. I liked it, the familiarity of this one little quirk that was part of him. It was an intimate detail.

"Do you want to come in?" I smiled. "It's cold out there."

He grinned, looking light and boyish. He crossed the threshold of the farmhouse. "You have a cat," he said in shock. "Did you have a cat the other day?"

I closed the door and looked behind me. *Chat* and Henry were studying one another. "Yeah, I thought you knew?"

He shook his head. "I didn't see him."

"Oh, well *Chat* is somewhat of a skulker. And also Gigi's protector, so you might want to lie on your back and show him your belly."

"That only works for dogs."

"*Chat* is more dog than cat, so it might work." I scooped up the big black monster and brought him close to Henry.

"Hello, fellow," he said. *Chat* blinked. "Do you mind if I pet you?" *Chat* cocked his head, like he was giving permission. Henry reached out and *Chat* leaned into his touch.

"So are you going to tell me why I'm brilliant?" I asked as I let *Chat* down. He immediately ran up the stairs. I knew he was headed for Gigi, who was taking a nap in the nursery.

"I read your book," Henry said. "It's why you haven't heard from me for a little while."

I froze.

"I think it was one of the most brilliant works I have ever read."

My heart thudded in my ears. "You're just saying—"

"If I had read your book and hated it, I never would've mentioned it. And then I would've disappeared from your life forever because I can't lie."

"Honest to a fault, huh?"

"Exactly." He plopped down onto the couch and I sat next to him. "It was incredible, Sage. Really."

I smiled. "Really, really?"

He reached out to take my hand. "Really."

My breath hitched at the spark of his touch.

"I've never read anything like it. It was beautiful."

"Thank you," I said, humbled. I glanced at him, wanting him to see how much his words meant to me.

He smiled. When he did, I noticed the slight crookedness of his teeth, but the perfection of his lips. I wondered how they'd feel over mine. Would we fit together? Would our kiss be effortless? First kisses had the potential to be a disaster. I never thought I'd have another first kiss after Kai.

Kai, whose touch I missed. But he wasn't here—and Henry stirred something inside of me that I thought had died with my husband, the father of my child.

"What are you thinking about?" he asked.

I bit my lip and my gaze dropped to my lap. "I'm not supposed to want you, Henry."

"You're thinking about your husband, aren't you?"

"Kai. His name was Kai."

"Kai." He nodded. "How long has he been gone?"

"Nine months."

It felt strange to bring up Kai with Henry, but he had to be discussed. Kai's daughter was asleep upstairs. It wasn't just me anymore. Kai's memory would live on through Gigi, the living reminder of the husband I had lost.

Panic began to settle in my stomach when I thought of all the reasons why I shouldn't be sitting on the couch with Henry, yearning for his lips on mine.

Henry's grip tightened as if he knew I was about to flee. "Sage, look at me."

I shook my head.

"Sage," he pleaded quietly. "Please."

Taking a breath, I forced myself to have some courage—and met Henry's eyes.

"I won't pretend to know what you're going through. But I'm here and I'll wait. I really want to kiss you, Sage, but only when you let me. This has to be your choice. I won't take that away from you."

"You don't even know me. Why would you want to get involved in all this?"

"That's exactly why, Sage. I want to get to know you if you'll let me." He sounded so sincere, so heartfelt.

Terror and curiosity warred within me.

I wet my suddenly dry lips, my gaze dropping to his mouth. "Kiss me."

"Are you sure?"

"Yes."

He paused just for a moment and then his lips covered mine. He felt foreign but familiar, comfortable but exciting. It was easy and I wanted it to continue, but before I was able to sink into Henry, he pulled back.

"Are you okay?" he asked, touching his nose to mine, his hands reaching up to cradle my face.

"Yes," I whispered.

———

"You *what?*" Jules asked, her lips forming into a smile.

"Kissed him," I said, digging into the bowl of ice cream. "Yeah."

Her spoon fought with mine. "You always take all the chocolate," she complained.

"There's a solution to this problem."

"Another scoop of chocolate?" Jules asked hopefully.

"Your own bowl," I stated.

"It tastes better out of yours."

Sighing, I got up and went to the freezer. I pulled out the tub, scooped out some more chocolate, and plopped it into our shared bowl. "Happy?"

"Immensely. Now tell me about this kiss."

It was a good thing my back was to Jules because I was sure I was grinning like an idiot and my cheeks were hot and red.

"It went on for several hours," I said, striving for casual and failing miserably.

"What? You mean you had an old-fashioned high school make out session?"

I bit my lip, but smiled through it. "Maybe."

"What base did he get to?"

"Jules!" I laughed.

"What, didn't you sleep with Kai the first night you met?" She shut her mouth quickly after realizing what she'd said. "Disregard that. Please. I'm a jackass. A big one. An insensitive one."

"It's okay," I said quietly. I stirred the melting puddle of ice cream with my spoon, not meeting my best friend's gaze.

"No, it's not. Look what I did. You were so happy and I—"

"I don't want to talk about Kai," I said with force, finally meeting her gaze. "I want to talk about Henry."

"Yeah?"

I nodded.

"Tell me more about him."

"History professor. He's here for the semester teaching a few classes, and then he'll go back to Northwestern."

"You can do that?"

"Do what?"

"Date him knowing there's an end in sight?"

I shrugged. "Guess we'll find out. I'm not looking for an attachment."

"Then what are you doing? Trying to get laid?"

"You're crass, you know that?"

"Yep. So is that what this is about? Scratching an itch?"

"You're an impossible person."

"And you love me for it. You're not going to answer the question, are you?"

"Nope. I don't have the answer to your question, anyway."

"Didn't think so."

"He read my book," I said, changing the subject.

"And?"

"He thinks I'm brilliant."

"He's smart." She smiled. "Because you *are* brilliant."

"It's fun, ya know? I've never had just—enjoyment for the sake of enjoyment. Kai was… everything, all at once. But Henry… I don't know. He's here, and he's light and warm and I'm enjoying him. He makes me feel—safe—in my own scarred skin."

"That sounds good. Really good." Jules licked the melting ice cream off her spoon.

"It is."

"When do I get to meet him?"

"You mean, when do I introduce the two of you so you can scare the shit of out him and put him through the ringer?"

"Yeah, that."

"Not for a while."

"What?" she exclaimed. "Why?"

"Why?" I raised my eyebrows. "Because I would like—"

"A few more hours of uninterrupted kissing first?"

"That," I agreed. "But this is the very beginning. I don't need to clobber him with my protective family. Not yet."

"Fair enough, but I won't stop bugging you about it."

"I'd expect nothing less from you."

———

"You have the most incredible lips," Henry said against my mouth.

"I bet you say that to all the girls."

"No, I don't. Yours have the perfect blend of firmness and softness. And sweet. They're like—saltwater taffy. Yep, that's what they remind me of. Saltwater taffy."

I chuckled and dropped my head, letting it rest against his shoulder. "That's a weird comparison."

"It works in my mind. And there are no other girls."

"Huh?" I stared into his eyes—his warm, beautiful, laughter-filled eyes.

"I'm not complimenting any other girls." His hands cradled my cheeks.

"What about Gigi? I heard you telling her she's smart for rejecting the pureed peas."

"Have you ever tried them? They're disgusting."

"You're a man child," I teased.

He laughed as he kissed me again. We'd lost hours to the meshing of our lips, but for some reason, it felt like a great accomplishment. The melding, the feeling, the joy.

"Are you complimenting any other fellows?" he asked, pulling back. He settled against the couch, his arm coming around me. I rested my cheek against the steady thudding of his heart.

"No," I murmured. "No other fellows. Except for *Chat*."

"He's an acceptable fellow. That makes me very happy." I could hear the smile in his voice.

"Who do you think I am?" I asked, pretending to be affronted. "A woman with many callers?"

"You'd have them if you wanted them."

"Good thing I came down with an extreme case of hermititis."

He laughed, trailing a hand up and down my arm. I shivered. "How do you feel about dinner parties?"

"Giving them or attending them?"

"Attending."

"Show up with flowers and wine and then eat and drink for a few hours? Can it be that bad?" I asked.

"I was hoping you'd say that."

"Why?"

"The head of the history department at the university is having a dinner party next weekend. Would you like to go with me? As my date?"

"You do realize we haven't gone out on a first date yet?"

"Every time we attempt to leave your house we get distracted." He grinned. "It's true, we haven't gone on a first date, or even… ya know…"

"Ya know?" I raised my eyebrows.

"We haven't hugged each other naked yet."

"Henry!" I shouted, my face flaming.

"What? You don't seem the shy type." He peered at me. "Does that make you nervous? Do *I* make you nervous?"

"No," I lied.

"Tell me what it is, Sage."

I looked down at my hands. "I haven't been with anyone since Kai. I have a daughter. I'm just…"

"Hey," he said, making me look at him. "There's no rush."

"Yeah?"

"Yeah." He nodded. "I'm not going to lie, I'm very excited to get to that part. But I do have some willpower, some self-control."

"Really?" I drawled.

"Really. Do you honestly think I'd pressure you to do anything before you were ready?"

I sighed. "No, I didn't think that." The truth was, it was all I could think about. Having Henry in my bed, next to me. I wanted to feel the heat of his skin. I wanted…

But being intimate with another man meant Kai was really gone. It meant I was living my life. It meant I was open to something new.

"Your brow is furrowed again, which means you're analyzing, which means I should distract you."

I smiled. "Okay, go ahead."

371

He leaned in to kiss me and I let him.

"Hmmm. Sweet like taffy," he mumbled.

———

I passed Luc the mashed potatoes and kept my eyes trained on my plate. They were scrutinizing me. I'd been absent from family dinners, and my phone calls had been sparse. They knew. They knew about Henry. Jules had told them. And now I was waiting for the questions. The only sound in the bed and breakfast kitchen was Gigi's happy noises as she grasped the cereal scattered in front of her and shoved it into her mouth.

I felt like a teenager, waiting for my parents to ask about my new boyfriend. Only Henry wasn't my boyfriend.

Was he?

"How's the writing going?" Celia asked.

I looked up and met her eyes. I breathed a sigh of relief. Maybe I'd get through this unscathed. Maybe I'd get through this without having to explain anything.

"I don't want to hear about the writing," Luc said, speaking before I could. "I want to hear about the professor."

Jules kicked him under the table and glared at him.

"Ow." He winced. "I refuse to retract my statement."

"We're getting to know one another," I said slowly, feeling the heat climb up into my cheeks.

Luc raised an eyebrow and smirked.

"You're an insensitive jackass," I snapped at him.

"Maybe," he agreed. "But you look happy. Are you happy?"

Four pairs of eyes rested on me, waiting for an answer. I nodded once. I picked up my fork and took a bite of the now cold mashed potatoes.

"The writing's going well," I said, steering the conversation away from Henry. I tried to find at least an hour a day to spend in the turret. It was getting harder and harder. Henry's presence lent quite the distraction. It was easy to focus on him.

"What are you working on?" Armand asked.

I shook my head. "That I won't talk about."

"She's always like this," Jules stated. "Never tells anyone she's writing until it's done."

"For me, telling someone what I'm writing is like parading around in my underwear," I explained.

"You're weird," Luc teased.

I grinned. "Hope so."

The conversation drifted away from me onto other things. We discussed the vineyard. Everyone was eager for spring and thankfully it was just around the corner. I was ready for warmth, ready for sunlight. I thought about taking Gigi on a trip to the coast. Maybe Henry would want to go with us. Inviting him was a big step; a boyfriend-girlfriend step. Was I ready for that kind of label?

I caught Jules staring at me from across the table. She knew. It was written across my face. She nodded, and we both stood up from the table, excused ourselves, and went to find a private place to talk. We headed to the small cottage behind the bed and breakfast, the cottage Kai and I had lived in when we'd first met. Now Jules and Luc lived there. It was a place for lovers.

"What is it?" Jules asked, closing the front door of the cottage.

I sank onto the new blue couch and sighed. "Bourbon."

"I don't drink bourbon," she said.

"Tequila, then."

She poured us two shots and we downed them easily. It burned in the very best way. "I think I have to end things with Henry. Whatever it is, I need to end it."

"Why?" Jules wondered.

"Because you're right. I don't do casual. I can't do it. I'm not built that way. And he's going to leave when the semester is over…"

"You're already becoming attached."

"It's stupid," I grumbled. "We haven't even slept together yet. We haven't had any of the hard conversations. We haven't…"

"Henry is not Kai," she said softly.

"I know that."

"Do you?" She peered at me. "Because you keep acting like you expect things to unfold the same way. They don't; they won't. So stop comparing what you had with Kai to what you could have with Henry."

"I can't have anything with Henry! The semester will end, he'll go back to his life, and what will I do, Jules? Go back to how things were? Living in a house that feels like a tomb—surrounded by Kai's clothes and memories? Raising Gigi alone? I don't want to be alone!"

I began to cry, putting my face in my hands. Jules wrapped me in her arms and I cried against her.

"Can I ask you a question?" she asked, when my sobs had muted.

"Yeah."

"Is it that you don't want to be alone? Because, being with the wrong person is worse than being alone."

"Are you talking about Luc?"

She shook her head. "Connor. Remember?"

My fiancé from my life before Kai.

"They aren't the same," she reiterated. "Kai and Henry."

I nodded.

"So why do you expect things to be the same? You're not the same, either. Not after what you've been through."

"I forget that sometimes. I don't want anyone but Kai and then… Henry smiles at me or makes me laugh, and I feel guilty for wanting to go on living."

"Life is complicated," she stated. "Kai would want you to be happy. The question is, are you ready for happiness?"

Chapter 13

It was the night of the faculty dinner party and my nerves were a jumbled mess. I was conflicted about my growing feelings for Henry, but when he laced his fingers through mine and guided me inside the house and smiled at me, I knew I wouldn't be able to let him go.

Three hours later we were getting into the car as Henry said, "I can't thank you enough."

I laughed. "Henry, you've thanked me at least a hundred times."

"God, I had no idea how boring history professors are."

"You're a history professor."

"I'm changing careers. We're like the accountants of the academic world." He made a noise like he had fallen asleep.

"You're so full of crap. Don't lie, you loved every minute of it," I teased. "You got to talk about your work, their work, work you want to do in the future…"

"Yeah, I had fun," he admitted sheepishly. "But seriously, I'm glad you came as my date. If you hadn't, they would've tried to hook me up with Sheila, the single linguist professor. Linguists. Nerd alert!"

I laughed. "She was nice, but she was totally making eyes at you. Woman on the prowl."

"That's what I'm saying!" He chuckled. "They all really liked you."

"They were nice. Focused on their own passions, but I completely get that. They made me feel comfortable."

He grinned. "Am I driving you home yet?"

"I don't know about you, but I could use a real meal. Why do they serve food in such tiny proportions?"

"They're French, therefore obsessed with their weight." His stomach growled. "Want to split a steak or something?"

"There's a café in the Old Square that has great food."

"On it, Chief."

Fifteen minutes later, we were parked and walking hand in hand to the café I had in mind. As we were seated and menus placed in front of us, Henry asked, "So, as far as first dates go, how do you think this is going?"

"I think it's going very well." I removed my gray shawl, revealing my bare shoulders in a strapless black dress. I felt young, vibrant.

"You impressed me with your intellectual prowess," I remarked.

"You dig the nerds?"

"I dig you," I said softly.

His smile was wide and perfect. "You're a nerd in your own right, you know."

"I know."

"But you're a hot nerd."

"Glad you think so."

"And… I'm cute, too?" he fished.

"You're cute, too," I agreed.

"You having fun?"

"Yes."

"Promise?"

"Promise."

We held hands over dinner, our feet colliding with one another's under the table. I got lost in Henry's face and his smile lines. Those damn smile lines.

"What's the worst thing that's ever happened to you?" I asked.

He frowned. "I don't know. Why the question?"

I shrugged. "You're just so—happy. All the time. You laugh all the time."

"Does that bother you?" His eyes twinkled with jesting good humor.

"No. I just—wonder what darkness you're covering."

"Are you asking as a writer or as my girlfriend?"

My breath hitched. "Girlfriend?"

"No other girls, no other fellows, remember? Just makes sense I'd call you my girlfriend."

I looked away from him, trying to summon up the courage to put into words what I was feeling. Before Henry, I felt like I had been crouched in the corner of a cold dark room, and now, I was standing in a beam of sunlight.

"We should celebrate," he said.

"Why?"

"Because the university extended my teaching contract."

A knot around my heart unfurled. "Did you do that because of... me?"

He scoffed. "Are you insane? I've known you for a month. We haven't even—and you think—without talking about it with you first? What am I, a stage three clinger?"

Suddenly, I grinned. Henry's own smile was slow and bright. His eyes. *Damn.* His eyes in candlelight.

"Darkness, Henry. Any darkness in your past?" I pushed.

"Back to that, huh? Let's see. I wasn't picked to play basketball even though I was tall."

"That's the worst thing that's ever happened to you?"

"It was devastating," Henry said. "To learn that no one wanted me on their team. Terrible. Then again if I'd played basketball, I never would've gone out for track and never placed first at State three years in a row. Never would've gotten that athletic scholarship for college."

I rolled my eyes. "Let me guess, you had really good luck with girls in high school."

He shrugged. "I was just odd enough to be really popular."

"Instead of a social pariah?"

"Exactly."

"Did you wear vintage t-shirts then, too?" I teased.

"Maybe."

"So this athletic scholarship. What school?"

"Vanderbilt," he said.

My gaze snapped up from my plate. "Vanderbilt. Really?"

"Yeah." He studied me. "Sage?"

I reached for my water, taking a sip and trying to recover from the shock. I set it down, my hand shaking.

"What is it?"

"Kai," I said through a tight throat. I cleared it and tried to speak again, "Kai went to Vanderbilt."

"Oh," he said, surprise tingeing his voice.

"What are the odds?" I murmured.

At that moment I felt as though Kai's ghost had risen from the earth and taken a seat at the dinner table between us. All the laughter and lightness of the evening fled. I was no longer hungry, so I pushed my plate away. Henry signaled for the check, and then we walked out into the night.

We were silent the entire drive back to the farmhouse. He escorted me to the front porch and asked, "Sage?"

"I don't want to talk about it. Not right now."

"Will you ever want to talk about it?"

"I don't know. This is—I didn't anticipate this." I thought about fate and coincidence.

"I want you to know that I was having a lovely time with you," I said, trying to steady my voice. "I wasn't thinking about Kai at all. Not until you said Vanderbilt." I looked away, unable to meet his eyes. They were fierce and strong, and because they were, they'd give me a reason to collapse. I couldn't let him pick me up. That wasn't his responsibility.

I was so conflicted. "Maybe we shouldn't—maybe this was a bad idea."

"What?"

"Us. Trying to date. Pretending we can do that—that I'm ready. I'm not ready."

"None of us are. I like you. We have pasts, they affect us."

"I'm trying to wrap my head around all of this."

"Don't…"

"Don't what?"

"Don't shut me out. Please."

I took a deep breath and nodded. "I want you to come in, I do, but you shouldn't. Because if you do, then I'll—"

"I know," he said. "I respect your decision, Sage. I respect you."

"Thank you," I whispered. I leaned in and kissed him on the cheek. As I closed the front door, I waved to him with my finger. His smile was small, but it was there.

Nothing wrong with a little bit of time—for both of us. I sighed, setting my purse down in the foyer.

"Hey," Jules called from the living room.

"Hey," I said.

"Where's Henry? Thought he would've come in so I could grill him," she joked.

"Things didn't go according to plan," I said. "Gigi?"

"Asleep. You okay?"

"I don't know," I answered truthfully.

"Want to talk about it?"

I shook my head. "I just need to sleep."

"Okay," Jules said, rising to leave. "I'll call you tomorrow."

"Thanks." I hugged her, knowing she'd always lend an ear if I needed to talk. There was no replacement for a true best friend.

———

I was still awake at two AM.

My mind was a swirling mess.

So what? They'd both gone to Vanderbilt. It was odd, but I was tired of trying to find answers when there were none.

No longer wanting to be alone, I got up out of bed and went to the nursery. Gigi was asleep and I wasn't about to wake her. Still, I derived a measure of comfort from her presence.

"Hey, tater-tot," I whispered, stroking her corn silk hair. "I'm a mess. A frightful mess. And I'm trying to get it together, and just when I think I might have it all figured out, something else wallops me."

I sighed. "I think I found a good man. A really good one. I'm terrified of him, though. Your daddy was a good man and he died. I can't go through that again. I just can't."

With one last gentle caress of her tiny ear, I left the nursery and then made my way back to my empty bed. My large reminder that life was better when you shared it—the pain, the triumphs.

Not caring that it was going on three AM, I reached for my cell phone and called Henry. He answered on the first ring, like he'd been waiting for me to call. "Hi," I said softly.

"Hi."

Quiet breathing.

"You busy?" I asked.

He chuckled. "Very. I'm building a canoe."

"Oh, sure." I bit my lip. "If it's not too much trouble, would you mind, possibly, coming over?"

"Are we drinking or talking?"

"How about both?"

"I'll take it. See you in a bit. Sage?"

"Yeah?"

"Thanks for calling."

I smiled as we hung up and then went downstairs. I got two glasses ready, along with my favorite scotch, and then I waited for him. Fifteen minutes later, there was a light rap at the door.

Before I could say anything, I was crushed against his chest. I burrowed my nose into him. He smelled of bedtime and sleep; he smelled of promises we hadn't yet made to each other.

"I left because you asked me to, but I didn't want to," he mumbled into my hair.

"I didn't want you to either," I admitted. "But thanks for giving me what I thought I wanted."

"Thought you wanted?"

"Space."

"I think space is overrated."

"Me too. Come on. Let's have a drink." I moved out of his arms but stayed close to him as we sat on the couch. I handed him a glass.

"You have good taste in scotch."

"My mother's favorite. Every time she sent off a new book to her editor, she cracked open a bottle and had a few."

"And when did you start celebrating with her?" he asked.

"I think I had my first glass of real scotch—single malt, you understand—when I was about sixteen."

"And did the boys think you were an incredible bad ass? Or should I say 'bad lass'?"

"You're good." I laughed. "No. Unlike you, I was oddball weird. Jules and I were left alone."

"Jules? Your best friend?"

"Yes. More like a sister, really. She moved here with me after he…"

"Tell me about him."

"You sure?"

"Yes. He's part of who you are."

"So is my mother. She's gone, too."

He sighed. "We'll get there. I promise. But first, I want to know about Kai."

"Is this really how it's done? Talking about my late husband with scotch and moonlight?"

"I don't know. Can't we make up the rules as we go along?"

"I suppose so." I stood up, grabbed the bottle and baby monitor.

"Where are you going?"

"Follow me." We headed upstairs to the turret, my safe place.

"Sage?"

"Wait," I said. I poured us more scotch, even though I didn't think I needed any more. My head was already buzzy. I turned on the Bose speaker and a moment later the sounds of the banjo and mandolin crowded the room. It didn't shove out the heightened feeling of emotion, only added to it. It was as though Kai was between Henry and me, watching us with a solemn blue-gray gaze.

"What is this?" he asked softly.

I handed him the CD case, watching his face as his eyes scanned it, watching as he learned what it was.

"Sometimes, I'm supposed to be good with words. But right now I can hardly... I've got baggage, Henry."

"I know."

"I can't ask you to carry it."

He stared at me for a long moment. "Being a baggage handler isn't the worst job. They get to wear cool looking hats..."

"Stop making jokes."

He smiled. "What I feel for you... what I think I can feel for you, that's serious enough. So all the other times, I just want to be silly with you."

"I don't have that luxury. I've got a daughter. Don't you want someone less complicated?"

Henry took another sip of his scotch. "Complicated? You mean flat, boring, one dimensional?"

"No, just someone who's not a widow, a mother. Someone brighter, younger—"

"Faster? When did we start talking about sports cars?"

Despite myself, laughter escaped me.

"We do that a lot," he noted.

"Do what a lot?"

"Laugh."

"Yeah. I guess we do."

"Natural, right? Feels natural?"

I nodded.

"We don't have to have it all figured out. One day at a time. One glass of scotch at a time."

"It's not fair."

"What's not?"

I looked at him. "You know my past, my secrets."

We had sunk down onto the floor. Henry scooted closer to me, reaching for my hand. He skimmed his thumb across my knuckles.

Another man had once done the same and told me I had elegant knuckles.

"Are you afraid you won't find happiness again, or are you afraid that you will?"

I paused. "Both, I think."

Chapter 14

I didn't know the time, but I knew dawn was creeping towards us. We were on the floor, lying on our backs, the room was almost spinning, but not quite.

"Sage?" he whispered.

"Hmmm?"

"You asked me about the worst thing that's ever happened to me."

"You didn't answer."

He paused so long I felt my eyes closing.

"I've never been in love."

"I don't believe you," I said, suddenly awake.

"Puppy love. But no life-lasting love."

I turned my head, peering at him. Moonlight painted his cheekbones sharp, his mouth soft. A mouth I wanted to know as my own.

"How can that be?" I demanded.

"I don't know," he said.

I put a hand on his chest and he covered my hand with his.

He took a deep breath. "Is that enough? For now?"

"It's a good start," I said. "Do you think a woman is a slut if she sleeps with a man on a first date?"

He let out a huff of a laugh. "Scotch and truth go hand in hand, huh? No, I don't think a woman's a slut if she sleeps with a man on a first date. Sex on a first date doesn't change whether or not a guy's going to call you. He either likes you enough to call or he doesn't. Sex won't change how he sees you."

"People don't date anymore, do they?" I asked. "That was a generational thing, and we don't do it."

"Don't do it—I don't even think we know *how* to do it."

"People confuse lust and love. That's the problem when you sleep with someone too fast."

"What's the right amount of time?" he asked. "It's different for everyone, isn't it? What was right for you and Kai isn't what's right for you and me."

I took a deep breath. "Everything with Kai… it was all so fast. From how we met, to how we fell in love. Even his death. I still feel like I'm spinning. And you—" I looked at him, "—are bringing me to a stop." I moaned, collapsing against him. "I'm drunk."

"Me too."

"I'm going to be so hungover tomorrow. I'm going to look like crap. You're going to see me looking like crap."

"If it makes you feel any better, I'm going to be hungover looking like crap, too."

"I guess that's okay. That's real life, right?"

"Real life. Yeah," he said. "Sage?"

"Hmmm?"

"Do you think we can sleep in a bed tonight? I've got back problems."

I lifted my head, resting my chin on him. "Is this a ploy? A ploy to get into my bed."

"Alright fine, I don't really have back problems, but I promise I won't grope you."

I didn't know if I was happy or sad at his pronouncement. "No groping?" I asked, pulling back to right myself.

"Just spooning. You do like to spoon, don't you?"

"People who don't like to spoon have issues."

"Major issues," he agreed. We got to our feet and staggered to

385

the bedroom. I flipped on the light and winced at the brightness. Henry stripped down to his undershirt and boxers. He left on his black dress socks.

"My feet get cold," he explained.

I found his confession so endearing I nearly cried—overcome with scotch and emotion.

Through my haze, I wondered if he could love me in spite of my fractured past. Could he put me back together with his laughter and his humor, his general Henry-ness?

"Which side should I take?" he asked.

"Right side," I said.

He'd be sleeping on my side. I wouldn't let him sleep on Kai's. Not because I thought it was sacred, but because Henry deserved more. It wasn't his job to fill Kai's void. I wanted Henry to be Henry, and no one else.

I flipped off the light as he climbed into bed. I stripped down and put on pajamas. For a moment, I just stared at Henry. He'd rolled over, his back to me. I scooted under the covers, coming into contact with his warm body. I shivered in delight and comfort. And something else. Relief. Tonight, I wouldn't be sleeping with a ghost. I had next to me a flesh-and-blood man; a heart that beat, a mind that dreamed.

"What are you doing?" I asked, when Henry made no move to take me into his arms. "Why aren't you spooning me?"

He looked at me over his shoulder. "I like to be the bitty spoon," he explained, giving me a lopsided grin and blinking in the darkness.

"You can't be this cute," I said.

"Yeah, I can. Come here." He pulled my arm to move me close to him, so I was pressed against his back. "Isn't it better this way?"

I snuggled against him, breathing in the smell of washed cotton and the hint of what was beneath. Orange and cinnamon, I thought.

"Jet pack," he sighed. "You're my jet pack."

I closed my eyes, wrapped an arm around him, and fell asleep.

Part II

———

"You are a terrible influence," I said with a squint.

"Me? You were the scotch pusher." Henry put a hand to his head. "Do I look like crap? I feel like crap." His complexion was gray and his eyes were dull. He should never have dull eyes. But even pale, with dark shadows under his eyes, he looked calm and happy. Perhaps it was the smile lines around his mouth. I wanted to live in them.

"You've looked better," I said with a small grin. "I need to change Gigi. Meet you downstairs?"

"I'll start the coffee."

"Thank you."

The coffee was brewing when I came into the kitchen holding Gigi. As we waited, Henry came up behind me and enfolded his arms around both of us. I inhaled a sharp breath, but then leaned my head against his chest. He was tall and I could feel him hunch so that his chin rested on the top of my head. We stayed that way even after the coffee was done brewing.

"How do you take it?" I asked, reluctantly trying to leave the comfort of his arms.

His arms tightened. "No, don't move. I like you here."

I smiled. "Okay."

"Cream and three sugars," he said.

"Really?"

"The coffee is just a vehicle for the sugar."

"Ah."

"How do you take yours?" he asked, finally letting me go. I moved to the cabinet and pulled out two mugs.

"Black. Like my soul."

We laughed. Henry took our coffees into the living room and I placed Gigi in her playpen. Henry and I curled up on the couch, and I dragged a blanket over us. I heard the key in the front lock.

"Who is that?" Henry wondered.

"It could be any number of people," I said.

My guess was Jules, coming over to check in on me. She'd seen the state I was in the previous evening. Keys hit the front table before Jules popped into the living room.

"Hello," she said with a wide smile, not looking at all surprised to find Henry in my house. "You must be Henry."

"And you must be Jules." He rose, reaching out to shake her hand. "It's all true."

"What is?" Jules wondered.

"All the good stuff Sage has been saying about me."

"I could've been saying bad stuff," I teased.

"Please," Henry scoffed. "You mentioned my t-shirts, right? I'm super cool."

Jules laughed and shot me a glance. There'd be a conversation later, and there would be no getting out of it.

Gigi was a little bit fussy, but before I could get to her, Henry was already picking her up. She calmed down immediately.

"He's got the magic touch," Jules noted.

"It will come in handy when she's a teenager," Henry joked. Jules and I sobered instantly, but Henry was too busy paying attention to Gigi to realize what he'd said.

Jules glanced at Henry. "Henry, are you free Wednesday night?"

Gigi's hands were flailing around, landing on Henry's lips. He made bold kissing noises, causing Gigi to smile. "I'm free."

"Would you like to come to dinner?"

Henry finally turned his attention away from Gigi, but he didn't look at Jules, he looked at me—for permission, for acceptance. An unspoken conversation passed between us while Jules waited for Henry's answer.

"Yes, we'd like to come to dinner," I said.

Jules's smile was wide and knowing. "Good." Her mission completed, she left and Henry and I were alone.

"I'm meeting your family," he said.

"Yep. Seems inevitable. They all have keys anyway. You might as well get a really good meal out of it. Celia's an amazing cook."

Henry placed Gigi in her Pack-N-Play. "How about this? I'll go home, shower, change, maybe grab a nap. I'll come over tonight and bring dinner. We'll have a low key night."

I grinned. "Sounds pretty good."

He pecked me, leaning back with a delightful grin across his lips. "See you soon?"

"Henry?"

"Yeah, Sage?"

"You can nap here," I blurted out. "You know, after you shower and change, feel free to come back sooner rather than later." I felt my cheeks heating. Henry looked at me for a long moment. His dark-blond hair was marvelously disheveled, his hazel eyes warm and bright like stars in the sky. And that smile. So hopeful. So pure. So full of joy.

I smiled back and Henry left with a nod and a jaunt in his step.

———

"Is this okay? I really wasn't up to cooking," Henry said.

I grinned, taking another bite of pepperoni pizza. "Are you kidding? This is perfect."

"I can't drink like a twenty-year-old anymore," he lamented.

"I know. My body hates me."

"Mine, too. I'm sorry I didn't come over earlier, but I fell asleep. Sitting up."

"Liar."

"Seriously!" he said. "You're a rager, Sage. And I can't keep up with you."

"New name for you: Old Man Gerard."

"I need a wooden walking stick and a pipe."

"And a beard of bees."

"This could work for me—if the professor thing should fail."

I laughed. "It's good to have options."

Henry cocked his head to one side before leaning across the table and placing his lips on mine.

"Spicy," I said.

"Thanks."

"I meant the pepperoni."

He grinned and took another bite of pizza. "Is it weird that I want a beer?"

"Oh, thank God!" I exclaimed. "I've been dying for one, but I didn't want you to think I was a lush." I got up and grabbed us two pilsners and cracked them open.

After we had all the pizza we could handle, I wrapped up the leftovers and stuck them in the fridge. "Ready for popcorn?"

He nodded. I took out the old-fashioned popcorn popper. The sound of sizzling oil and popping kernels hit my ears.

"Movie?" I asked.

"How about *Terminator 2*," Henry answered with a boyish grin.

I smiled back. "I've seen that movie about a billion times. And you know what? It's awesome. Every. Time."

"Exactly," he laughed. "You've got that bag of peanut M&M's?"

"Yes. Should I get a bowl or are we eating them right out the bag?"

He looked at me with a raised eyebrow, opened the bag of M&M's, and dumped them into the bowl of popcorn. "Try it."

I reached in and took a handful of popcorn with some candy. "Holy crap that's great. Salty and sweet."

"Right?" he said knowingly.

"How did I live this long without experiencing this?" I asked, taking the bowl and heading to the living room.

"No idea. Should I bring your beer?"

"Please."

Henry joined me and sat down on the couch. "Ready?"

"Play it," I said.

The glare from the TV was the only light in the room. I sipped on my beer, enjoying the comfort of Henry next to me, the familiarity of the movie in front of me. I didn't remember falling asleep, but I came awake slowly. A blanket covered me and my head rested against a warm chest.

I pulled back, realizing his arms were around me. I was close enough to see the stubble along his jaw. His skin glowed from the light of the television. But his eyes weren't on the movie—they were on me.

"Did I miss it?" I asked, my voice raspy.

"Most of it," he said.

I smelled the crisp pilsner on his breath and wondered if I kissed him, would I taste it. Would I taste anything but him?

"Sorry."

"For what?"

"For falling asleep, for falling asleep on you."

"I'm not complaining."

"You're not, are you?"

"Feel free to fall asleep on top of me any time you want."

I started to laugh, but I was stopped by his lips covering mine. He tasted like beer and peanut M&M's. This kiss was different. It was urgent and needy. And it felt like I had never been kissed before, not in my entire life. The way his mouth moved over mine made me feel like I was in love for the first time. His kiss was like a balloon in my head being blown full of helium. I was in danger of floating out of my body, away from the world, nothing but a string tethering me to a little girl's wrist.

His kiss was everything I hadn't been looking for and wasn't expecting to find.

Saying his name against his lips made me ache for things I thought I no longer believed in.

He gently pulled away from me to stare into my eyes. The movie still played on in the background, but I heard nothing.

"Will you stay?" I whispered. I cleared my throat. "Will you stay the night with me? Again?"

Henry pressed a kiss to the end of my nose. "What about the morning? Can I stay the morning with you, too?"

"I don't want to think about the morning because that would mean our first night together—our first real night together—will be over. And I want to savor it."

I reached for the remote and turned off the TV and DVD

player, and then I held out my hand. Henry stood up slowly and grasped it. He held my hand tightly, like he was afraid if he let go, I'd disappear. I led him up the stairs. Aware of sleeping Gigi, we stepped quietly.

When we were in my bedroom, I flipped on the lamp, soft warm light washing over us. I turned to him, my mouth open, wanting to say things and spill emotion.

He kissed me, making words obsolete.

Henry hesitated only a moment before reaching for his shirt and taking it off. My breath hitched. Henry was long and lean. Taut and athletic with skin the color of orange blossom honey.

There was a dull pink scar running down the center of his chest. I trailed a finger down it and he shivered. "What happened?"

"Open heart surgery. When I was a baby."

"And you never thought to mention it?"

He shrugged. "It never came up."

"No? I asked about the worst thing that had ever happened to you."

He smiled. "This scar is a big part of who I am. I was born with a hole in my heart. I was supposed to die. Instead, I got to live. How can that be the worst thing?"

"I didn't realize…"

"Realize what?"

I met his eyes. They seemed to glow. "Realize there were still optimists."

A smattering of dark blond hair covered the rest of his chest. Placing a hand on him, I touched it. I ran my finger down the contours of his body as I walked around him, wanting to sketch the knobs of his spine. The back of his neck beckoned me, like the sweetness of a ripe cantaloupe. I pressed my lips there.

Henry sucked in a breath. I lay my cheek in the space below his shoulder blades. He muttered something under his breath.

"Are you counting?" I asked.

"Maybe."

"Why?"

He let out a strangled laugh. "Really? Do I really have to break it down for you?"

I smiled even though he couldn't see. "You don't want to rush."

"I swear I can hear your heart beat. It's going a mile a minute."

"I'm nervous," I admitted.

"Sage? Can I turn around and hold you?"

I nodded, my chin bumping his spine. He turned in my embrace and suddenly I was against his chest, my cheek against his scar. His warm, solid chest smelled like oranges. It made me laugh.

"What?" His hand stroked my hair.

"Nothing."

"Tell me. Please?"

"Will you kiss me again?" I looked up at him, imploring him to stop my brain from thinking. His strong fingers outlined my jaw and moved to my eyebrows.

"I've wanted to kiss you since the first moment I saw you," he said softly. "It took everything in me not to lean across the bar and put my lips on yours. You've been worth the wait."

To my consternation, I felt tears behind my eyes.

He saw them and his mouth softened, making me want him more. "We don't have to do anything tonight. There's no—"

This time, it was my mouth covering his, stopping the words.

And then I took Henry to my bed.

———

My eyes were wide open. Henry's face filled my vision, and I smiled. I reached up and plowed my fingers through his hair. The window drapes were pulled back, the moon's silvery glow caressing the stretch marks on my body. Henry worshipped them. With his tongue. His hands. His heart.

He moved my hands over my head and we linked our fingers. We were like a delicate chain, bound and wound together, and with the slightest tug...

He filled me.

I cried out, and then I cried.

His face went to the crook of my neck and I felt his breath bathing my skin. I felt complete, the lock clicking open at last. Henry had become my key and I was forged around him.

I needed him to breathe. I needed him to fly. I was complete in a way I never thought to be again.

"Henry," I said, a chant, a call home.

He answered.

Chapter 15

Henry cracked the windows of the bedroom, the fresh country air filling the room. It was still a bit chilly, but it was warm enough to give a hint of what was beneath. I closed my eyes, letting the scents come to me. Carried on the breeze, I smelled the pungent perfume of new flowers—tender young buds escaping the grip of winter, coming to life in spring.

The weather had changed overnight. One day it had been cold, the next, there was the promise of warmth. I felt it in my cheeks, in my limbs. I felt it all the way down to my cells. Henry climbed back in bed and I slid into his arms. We entwined our legs like the roots of trees in a river.

"What's this?" Henry asked, his finger gliding over a divot on the top of my left arm.

"Chickenpox scar," I said. "My mom had to tape oven mitts to my hands to keep me from scratching."

"Oh man, please tell me there's a picture of that somewhere." Henry laughed at the thought.

"I'm sure there is. My whole face was pink from Calamine Lotion and crusted oatmeal. I was a mess."

"How old were you?"

"Five, I think."

"Bet you were the cutest kid in the world."

I snuggled closer into his arms, pressing myself into the strong wall of him. His scar was rough to the touch. I was familiar with men who bore their brands on their chests. "So, you had open heart surgery."

"I did." He paused, skipping a finger over the curve of my shoulder. "Even when I was a kid, I grew up knowing I was lucky— that I could've—that I should have died. I climbed the highest trees. I tried out for sports. I pushed myself because I refused to ever be 'the sick kid'."

I laced my fingers through his, bringing them to my lips. What little guard I'd had around my heart washed away with Henry's confession.

Gigi's cry echoed through the baby monitor, but before I could get up, Henry was on his feet, pulling on a pair of boxers. "I'll go." A moment later, I heard him talking to her through the monitor, and I smiled when I listened to him speaking to Gigi in French. After he changed her, he returned and brought her to me.

"I don't think you want to stay for this," I said, putting Gigi to my bare breast.

"Why not?" he asked.

"Because you might not find it beautiful."

Henry came to the bed and crawled in next to me. "Do you think that when we started this, I didn't know you came with a daughter? I know I played no part in her creation, but my heart doesn't know that." He kissed me softly on the lips. "She's a part of you."

I winced in pain as Gigi suckled with her teeth. I glanced at her for a moment before returning my gaze to Henry. "I'm a mother, but I want you to know me as more."

He leaned back against the headboard, looking thoughtful. "Are Kai and I at all alike?"

I peered down at the face of my child. Kai's blood flowed through her veins. Her features were stamped with familiarity. "You are, in the ways that matter, I think. I laughed with him—the way I laugh with you. But you're… light. You don't live your life like you've ever been touched by darkness. Even though you have the heart thing."

"And Kai?"

"His two best friends died in a plane crash. Kai was supposed to be with them, and he never forgot that. He had a lot of guilt—for living, for loving, for moving on. I don't want to compare you two. It's not fair to either of you. But it's like you both fit me perfectly, yet in different ways."

Gigi had fallen asleep at my breast.

Henry kissed my cheek before settling in next to me. We fell silent, the rise and fall of our chests like the hands of a clock, our breaths a measurement of time.

———

Henry curved around me as dawn broke through the night. There was no stirring from the nursery yet, but we were on borrowed time. Gigi would awaken soon and our time would no longer be our own.

"Are you awake?" he whispered.

I bit his wrist in answer. "You smell like oranges."

There was a rumble against my back. "I do not."

"You do."

"Just oranges?" he asked, his voice still laced with disbelief. "Or are there any spices thrown in there?"

I turned over in his embrace, resting my chin on his chest, meeting his eyes. They were lit with contentment, but there were shadows attesting to his lack of sleep. I sniffed. "Cinnamon and cloves. And oranges."

"I smell like a scented candle. What a lovely comparison."

I grinned. "Should we get up?"

"In a minute." He stroked the bare skin of my lower back as I settled myself in the nook of his body.

"How was sharing a bed with me?" I asked. "Did I give you enough space?"

He laughed. "I hate to break this to you, Sage, but not only are you a bed hog, but a cover hog, too."

"Am not," I argued, sitting up, hair falling over my shoulders in a tangled mess.

Henry reached for me and I let myself collapse into his arms. He kissed me all over my face.

"Did you win the cover war?" I asked, a bit breathless.

He caressed my cheek. "I did."

My insides felt as warm as melted butter. I turned my head, listening to the baby monitor. "She's awake."

"How can you tell?"

I smiled. "Breathing is different."

He shook his head in amazement.

I kissed him. "You get the coffee going. I'll get Gigi." Gigi was standing up in her crib, clutching the edge, smiling and noisy.

"Look at you!" I said, reaching in and picking her up. *Chat* was resting on the rocking chair, his long sleek tail swishing. "Did you know about this? Of course you did, you secret keeper."

Gigi, *Chat,* and I went downstairs into the kitchen. Henry was bare-chested—I was wearing his shirt. His red scar was bright in the morning light. There was a man in my kitchen who wasn't my husband.

I settled Gigi into her high chair before going to Henry. Running a hand across his taut back to gently coerce him out of the way of the refrigerator, I grabbed a jar of baby food. I dumped it into a saucepan and turned it on low.

After a few minutes I assessed that her food was hot enough and poured it into a bowl. I took a bite to make sure it wouldn't burn her and then sat in front of Gigi, fastened a bib around her neck, and gave her a bite. Her face screwed up into a picture of euphoria.

"Sage? You okay?" Henry asked as he watched me.

I nodded, my throat constricting. I fed another spoonful into Gigi's bird-like mouth. Her blue-gray eyes followed my every move-ment, tracking me as she waited for more.

Henry came over to the table and set down two cups of coffee. He placed a hand on my shoulder. "Come on, what is it?"

Tears pooled behind my eyes and emotion I hadn't wanted to feel, or expected to feel, burst out of me.

"I really have no idea." I sniffed. Gigi plowed through the cauliflower and still looked hungry, so I sprinkled some cereal in front of her. She made a grab for it, dive bombing like a war plane.

Henry wrapped his arms around me. He was warm and perfect and he didn't say anything. He just let me cry for things I didn't understand.

———

"We should let them in," Henry said as we stood in the foyer of the farmhouse. Gigi was in his arms, fiddling with the buttons on his blue shirt.

"They have keys."

"They're respecting boundaries."

"We can hear you!" Luc called through the door.

"Let us in! We'll be nice!" came Jules's voice.

"Do you promise?" I yelled back.

Jules snorted. "No."

Sighing, I opened the door. Celia, Armand, Luc, and Jules crowded the steps and spilled into the hallway. We were surrounded by hugs and introductions as Celia plucked Gigi from Henry's arms.

"You look so beautiful in your pink dress," Armand said to Gigi.

"She kept tugging at everything I put her in until that dress." I grinned.

"Told ya, princess in the making," Jules said with a roll of her eyes.

"Can I offer anyone a drink?" I asked.

Armand held up bags. "I brought wine."

We made our way to the kitchen and Luc went to the cabinet to pull out wine glasses. I tossed Armand the wine opener. As Armand poured wine all around, Celia set Gigi in her high chair.

"Can I help with anything?" Celia asked. "I feel awful, I really wanted to be the one to cook dinner."

"It's all taken care of," I said, "but thank you for offering."

"Did you do the cooking?" Jules asked me.

I shook my head and gestured to Henry. "I baked," I said.

"He cooks?" Luc asked in shock.

I grinned. "He cooks."

Jules tugged on my arm and we took our wine to the corner of the kitchen. Luc and Armand engaged Henry in conversation and I watched him out of the corner of my eye.

"So are you going to tell me? Or are you going to make me ask?" she teased.

My cheeks heated.

"Ha. I knew it. I'm happy for you."

I took a sip of wine, trying to be inconspicuous while studying Henry. All of sudden, he turned to look at me, gave me a goofy grin, and then went back to conversing.

"Well, he's obviously in love with you."

Her words gave me pause. Could she see it in his eyes? In his gestures? "I think Henry is in extreme like," I said in answer. "Not love."

She made a noise of disbelief. "He seems to be fitting in okay."

"I think so."

Celia had set lukewarm, plain noodles in front of Gigi, who was jabbing them into her mouth. The timer dinged. When we were all settled around the table and the bread had been passed, Luc said to Henry, "Sage said you're a history professor?"

Henry nodded. "At Northwestern. And now, at the Université Francois Rabelais. For another semester, at least." He smiled at me.

As dinner progressed, I noticed the subtle tension between Jules and Luc. Though they sat next to one another, they hardly interacted. I wondered if Armand and Celia noticed it. I tried to catch Jules's eyes across the table, but she evaded me.

At one point during the meal, Henry grabbed my chair and pulled me to him, not caring that we were on display. Neither did I as I ran my hand across his cheek. Celia and Armand weren't subtle at all when they exchanged a glance, obviously taking in our affection. Henry had everyone in stitches with his blunt good humor.

"Want to help me clean up Gigi?" I pointedly asked Jules, who was staring morosely into her glass of wine. Her eyes were bleary, but she nodded. I took Gigi out of her high chair and carted her upstairs. She went down quickly and I dragged Jules to the turret.

"Don't turn on Kai's album, please," she said when I moved towards Bose speaker. "I can't hear it any more. It's fucking depressing."

I frowned. Jules was honest, I'd give her that.

"I'm sorry," she said as she collapsed into a chair. She looked tired, but not from lack of sleep. I knew that look. Exhausted from life. Beaten, down in the mud, wondering if you'd ever be able to get up again.

"What's going on, Jules?"

She stared out the window and wouldn't answer me.

"Come on. You can tell me."

"I don't think I can."

"Hey," I said, kneeling in front of her. "We don't have secrets."

She stared at me, her eyes sad. "What about when you married Kai and didn't tell me?"

"Moment of insanity," I stated. "Won't happen again."

"Yeah, right," she said but gave a small smile.

I wrapped my hand around her ankle, placed my chin on her knee, and waited.

"I don't think I can marry Luc." She said it slowly, like she was just coming to the realization in the moment.

"Why not?" I asked, trying to hear over the thudding of my heart. "Don't you love him?"

"Of course I love him. I never would've stayed if I didn't love him." She closed her eyes.

"Then what's this about?" I pulled on her jeans until she joined me on the floor. She placed her head in my lap. I ran my fingers through her dark hair, letting her talk.

"How long have I been here?"

"Almost a year."

"I don't feel any more comfortable now than I did when I first got here."

"Your French is better," I said.

"Yeah, but it never feels right on my tongue. The culture eludes me, so do the nuances. I miss New York, I miss teaching, I miss... my life. I just thought…"

"What?"

"I thought love was enough." Her voice was small and thin. "Pretty stupid, huh?"

"No. Not stupid."

"Sage."

"What?"

"No lies."

"Not stupid," I reiterated. "Naïve, maybe."

"I didn't realize how hard it was going to be. Adapting to a new life, a new language, new people. I think I fell in love with the idea of it. I miss theater, I miss—me."

"You're in an acting class. Have you even tried to find a way to teach a theater class?"

"Acting class isn't—it's not—there's more, Sage."

"More what?"

"I don't want kids." She said it like it was an evil confession. I heard the shame and confusion in her voice. I also heard resoluteness.

"Ah."

"Ah, what?"

"I knew something was going on with you. When you kept asking me about Gigi and motherhood."

She shrugged her shoulders, which was awkward as she was still lying down in my lap. "I've been having these thoughts for a while."

"So it's not a cold feet thing.

"Doesn't feel like cold feet. I was finally able to vocalize what I want. Or don't want, actually."

"You told Luc, didn't you? That's why you guys are acting so weird at dinner. Did you have this talk right before you got here?"

"No. We had the talk a few days ago," she said. "It all came out —in a bad way. He says—he says that I lied to him—about wanting kids."

"Did you?"

"No. Maybe. I don't know. I think I was always ambivalent and he took that to mean I'd eventually come around. I'm so over-whelmed." She gave a lamenting sigh.

"You have to talk to him, Jules. Really talk. Hash it out."

"He wants kids, Sage, and I don't. There's no hashing. It's inevitable. We're over." She began to sob.

I didn't know what to say. I'd only had one glass of wine, but my brain felt like it was swimming around in a river of grapes. I had no words of comfort, so I just let her cry.

Luc found us on the floor of the turret, Jules weeping across my lap. I sent him a pleading look. Sighing, he crouched down to Jules and whispered something soft in her ear. She reached for him and he picked her up into his arms and carried her out of the room.

I was still on the floor when Henry came to stand in the door-way. "Luc and Jules just left. Is everything okay?"

"No. No, it's not."

———

Henry and I sat on the couch, a few lamps casting their glow around the room. Aware that something brewed like a storm between their son and his fiancée, Armand and Celia had left soon after Jules and Luc. The air crackled with tension and energy, waiting for the tempest to blow through. Destruction was coming, we just had to brace for it.

"What do you think will happen between them?" Henry asked.

I sighed. "They don't agree on a fundamental part of sharing a life together. I think we know how this will play out."

"Just so you're aware, I like kids. I want kids."

"You like kids? I had no idea."

He grinned. "I just want you to have all the information. No surprises about the important things."

I leaned my head back against the couch. "You know what's weird? Before Gigi, before Kai, I was sort of ambivalent to the whole kid thing. I mean, I always thought I'd have them, but I was never really gung-ho about it. I never planned my life around it.

And then, somewhere down the road, it all sort of changed for me. I wanted them. I wanted them desperately. A whole gaggle of them."

"Yeah?" he asked with a slow, hope-filled smile. I recognized that smile. It was the smile of a man who thought we had a future together.

"Yeah. I wanted five. Too many? Too crazy?"

"Just crazy enough."

"I wanted to pack lunches and draw pictures on their hard boiled eggs. I wanted to climb trees and play in their tree house. I wanted them to come home dirty with skinned knees and happy smiles. I wanted them to swim in mountain lakes and learn how to fish. I wanted them to grow up in a home with two parents whose love was Shakespearean sonnet-worthy. That guy knew how to write love."

"Come here," he said.

I crawled into his arms and pressed my head against his chest. There was a time I'd lain against a different heart and wished for things I thought were a given.

Two different men, two hearts, but the beat was the same.

Henry's hand toyed with my hair. I sank into him and closed my eyes, wanting to sleep as soundly as Gigi. Gigi, who didn't yet know what she'd lost.

"Will you stay? With me? With us?"

He smiled. "I'll stay. If you want me to."

I didn't yet pull away from his body. I wanted the security. I wanted to breathe him in. I wanted him to vanquish my past and give me a future.

Chapter 16

I woke up the next morning, bleary-eyed and confused. I'd slept hard. I didn't even remember dreaming. Henry wasn't in bed; I assumed he was downstairs having a cup of coffee and reading the paper. He was so steadfastly archaic about some things. He liked the tangible feeling and smell of newspaper and ink. He was so delightfully odd.

Sounds of laughter hit my ears as I came down the stairs. Henry was lying on the floor, lifting Gigi in his arms and playing the airplane game. He made ridiculous motor noises as he maneuvered her around.

"Good morning," I said, dropping to the carpeted floor and kissing Henry's cheek.

"Good morning," Henry said.

"You guys been at this a while?" I asked, rolling over onto my back.

"About twenty minutes."

Gigi peered down at me, smiling and reaching out her arms. I took her from Henry and she cuddled against my chest. I held her against me as I awkwardly sat up.

I yawned. "I need coffee."

"On it," Henry said. We got up and padded into the kitchen. He filled the pot with water and I took a moment to study him. Henry's hair had shades of light brown to dark blond. It was a bit long, brushing his neck. His skin was like dusted gold. He turned, his eyes catching mine—more green than hazel today.

"What?" he asked.

"If I had you as a college professor, I doubt I would've been able to pay attention in class."

He grinned.

"Have you ever slept with one of your students?"

His face screwed up in a figure of disgust. "And be *that* guy? No way! I know some professors who sleep with their students, though. Mostly in the theater department. Would you like to come to one of my lectures today?"

"I'd love to, but I can't. I'm expecting Jules to drop by. Deep talking will happen."

Henry fixed our coffees and sat down at the kitchen table. I fed Gigi as I sucked down coffee like I needed it to live. Henry was chipper. I envied morning people.

"I could get used to this," he said.

"Hmm?"

"Mornings with you—and Gigi."

I ran a hand across his dark blond stubble. I stood and wrapped myself around him from the back. "Do you want breakfast before you have to go?"

"What did you have in mind?"

"An omelet with goat cheese, chives, and spinach."

"Really?"

I grinned. "Nope. How about cereal?"

He laughed. "Cereal sounds great."

———

As I put Gigi down for her nap, I heard the front door open. I came down the stairs, surprised to see Luc. I'd been expecting Jules. "What are we drinking?" I asked without preamble. "Wine? Beer?"

He looked heartbroken and crushed. Lost. "Got any tequila?"

I raised my eyebrows. "Are you serious?"

He nodded.

When I managed to recover my voice, I asked, "Margaritas okay? It's the perfect day for it." The kitchen windows were open and *Chat* was sitting on the windowsill, soaking up the warmth.

I pulled out the ingredients, including margarita salt. I juiced the limes, stirred in the agave, and made Luc a double. For me, it was limeade.

After Luc had a few sips he said, "She told you—about not wanting kids?"

I nodded.

He ran a hand through his hair, sighing in defeat. "We'd sort of been dancing around it, but last night it all just… it was ugly, Sage. I accused her of lying to me."

"Did she?"

"I don't know. I feel like she was trying to work through her stuff alone. Like she didn't even think to confide in me." He fished out a melting ice cube and put it into his mouth. "How did you do it?"

"Do what?" I asked in confusion.

"How did you figure out yourself while being with Kai?"

"Oh." I ran a finger around the edge of my glass. "I don't know how to tell you this, but I have absolutely no idea. We just—worked. Things change between people because individuals change, but Kai and I—we wanted the same things and we changed together. And we wanted each other more than we wanted anything else in the world."

"Does that mean what Jules and I have isn't special?" he wondered. "Does it mean we love each other less?"

"You can't compare what I had with Kai to what you have with Jules. No one understands what you two have better than you and Jules."

He didn't say anything as he finished off his drink. I got up to make him another. "What does Celia say?" I asked when I sat back down.

"I refuse to talk about this with my mother and father."

"Why?"

"Because they're my parents and they're biased."

"And I'm not? Jules is my best friend."

"I know, but it's different." He played with the squeezed lime in his glass. "I drove her to the airport last night."

"What?" I asked in shock.

"I drove her to Paris and dropped her off at the airport. I told her she needed to figure out her life and she had my blessing. I don't want her resenting me, and I don't want to resent her. I know what I want, Sage. I want to live here, work the family business, and have kids. That might not be enough for Jules."

I couldn't believe it. Jules was gone. And she hadn't called to tell me. But I knew what it was like to need to get away, to sever yourself from everything—at least for a little while.

"You don't think she'll come back, do you?" he asked.

"Do you?"

He took another swallow of his drink and shook his head.

"If she did come back," I began with caution, "would you trust her? Believe her? That she wanted what you wanted?"

"I don't know."

I stood. "You know what I think?"

"What?"

"I think we should forget about margaritas and go straight for the shots."

———

Luc passed out on the couch after three margaritas and two shots of Patron Silver. The French weren't built for heavy tequila drinking. I put a pillow under his head and, as an afterthought, a trashcan next to him. I was still sober.

The house was quiet as I made my way up to the turret. Gigi and *Chat* were hanging out in the nursery and I wondered if anyone had ever had a child who liked to be alone as much as Gigi did. She was fairly independent, a self-contained entity.

I sat down at my desk and started to write, but stopped just as quickly, my mind occupied by the thought of more children. The idea had been buzzing around the back of my head for days; ever since Henry told me he liked kids.

I wanted Gigi to have siblings. I wanted a house full of laughter and disaster. And for the first time since Kai died, I thought about a real future—a future with someone else. I wanted to share my life with someone. I wanted Gigi to grow up with a father.

A stab of betrayal ricocheted through my heart.

It hadn't been that long since Kai had died. Was my heart already open? Had it ever been truly closed?

If Kai had lived, I had no doubt we would've lived together until the day we died. We would have been old and happy, with grandchildren and great-grandchildren. We would've sat on the porch of the house we started building in Monteagle, and we'd close our eyes and collectively remember our lives. We would've wanted for nothing, we would've had each other.

But Kai was gone, and I was not.

He would want me to be happy. He would want me to love again. He would want a father for Gigi, someone to dry her tears, someone to kiss her scraped elbows.

And I could see it being Henry. I could wake up every morning next to his goofy smile and his ears that stuck out just a little. I envisioned us together, surrounded by family, surrounded by happiness. But I knew that those things could only happen if Henry felt the same way.

Did Henry love me?

Jules had said he did. But he'd never been in love before, and I wasn't arrogant enough to believe I was the woman who had changed that for him. I believed he cared for me—and for Gigi. That much was clear.

But was it enough?

———

I glanced at Henry who looked adorably confused as he attempted to separate the endless amounts of laundry. "You don't have to help me do this, you know."

"Why would you turn down laundry help," he asked. "Besides, I want to learn how to sort clothes."

"You don't sort your laundry?"

"I just toss it all in together on cold and hit wash. That's all I know."

"Well," I teased. "It's a good thing I came along."

He smiled. "It sure is. Want me to take out the garbage?"

"You're amazing. Statues will be erected in your honor."

"I put the toilet seat down, too, ya know?"

I grinned. "Pure gold statue." I threw another sock into a pile. "This is what happens when you have a baby. Nothing is ever clean."

Henry pulled up his white undershirt, revealing his taut stomach. He sniffed his shirt and grimaced. "Yeah, you might be right." He took off his shirt and threw it in the whites section. *Chat* let out a call and then poked his head through the hole of an arm.

I laughed. "Did you know he was there?"

"Nope."

"Strange animal," I mused. "Are you going to put on another shirt?"

"Wasn't planning on it."

"No?"

He danced towards me, forced me to put down the dirty clothes, and grabbed my hands. "Come on, let's dance." He took me into his arms and dipped me, but instead of holding me up, we both sank down onto the mounds of clothes, his body covering mine. He kissed me.

I pulled my mouth away. "What are you doing?"

"I thought it was fairly obvious," he said, trying to get me out of my own dirty shirt.

"But we're doing laundry."

"Laundry is romantic."

"No, it's not."

"Sage," he said, taking my head in his hands and forcing me to look into his eyes. They were lit with humor. "Life is about these moments. Roll with it. I'm giving you some of my best work, okay? Can you at least try and be a bit amenable to it?"

I laughed, wrapped my legs around him, and dragged him closer. We got lost in a tangle of limbs, kisses, and laughter.

After, when I was snuggled against his chest with his arms curled around me, I said, "You're right, I don't think people appreciate these moments enough. The everyday moments. The little moments that make up a lifetime." Henry's arms tightened and I pressed a kiss to his bare chest, loving the feel of his skin beneath my hands. I traced the scar on his heart.

"One day, I'll be old and I don't want to have missed these moments." I buried my face into the crook of him, wondering why I was suddenly overcome with emotion.

"Is that why you write?" he asked. "So you can put little pieces of yourself in characters, so you'll never really forget yourself or be forgotten?"

I looked up at him, and he brushed a tear from my cheek. He didn't seem at all concerned when I lost myself to my feelings. "I think you're quite wonderful," I said. "There aren't many men who'd…"

"Who'd what?"

"Hold me the way you do, make me laugh the way you do. Understand me the way you do."

"So there's more to me than my mad laundry skills, huh?"

———

A shaft of afternoon sunlight streaked through the bedroom window. *Chat* lazed on the floor, sleeping in the warmth and I was grateful for his presence. I sat on the bed with a mug of hot tea, staring at my clothes. Next to them hung Kai's. There had been so many times I'd pulled out a shirt, putting the fabric to my nose, longing for the scent of him. When had I stopped needing that small piece of comfort?

His belongings had once been a great consolation, but now they felt like chains holding me back, rooting me too firmly in the past. I grabbed Kai's clothes and began to shove them into waiting garbage bags. I moved from drawer to drawer, closet to closet in a mindless frenzy until there were six bags of clothes bundled up by the front door, waiting to be removed. I picked up Kai's mandolin and brought the body of the instrument to my cheek. I closed my eyes and sifted through my memories until I found a happy one. Kai, playing the mandolin on stage, his smile bright and easy as he looked at me.

Opening my eyes, I set the mandolin aside and reached for the fishing rod. Kai had loved to fish more than anything. My fish whisperer, I thought with a smile. I put the pole aside, too. One day, when Gigi was old enough, I'd give her the mandolin and the rod and tell her about her father.

Trapped in a current of longing for my deceased husband, I wondered if it was possible to love two men at the same time. I touched the pendant at my neck and closed my eyes. When I pictured Kai, I felt the things he'd made me feel when he was alive, more than I could remember the exact details of him. I remembered parts of his face, the overall feeling he gave me, but his subtleties were disappearing.

I knew that I would never forget Kai; our love was eternal. But I was beginning to realize that part of healing was holding onto memories while still finding a way to move forward. The realization didn't stop a new layer of grief and guilt from bubbling up inside me.

As the sun set, I fed and bathed Gigi before putting her to bed. Not ready for my own bed, I went to the turret and sat in a comfortable chair by the window, gazing at the night sky.

I didn't remember falling asleep.

———

I stare at a lake surrounded by a bed of green. Water lilies float atop the blue-silver water. A gentle swell of mist seeps over rocks and land. In the distance, I see a house. White washed stone. Familiar. Warm. A place I belong. I hear laughter and voices. Family. I long to be there.

But I blink and the mirage disappears, replaced by mossy ground, brown earth, and headstones as far as my eyes can see. I stand alone, reminded of things that used to be.

Kai appears in front of me.

"What is this place?" I ask him.

"It was once a place of dreams," he says softly.

"A graveyard of dreams?"

"Yes," he says.

"I want the white house back." My voice is shrill in the still air.

"No, you don't. You've made that much clear," he answers.

He turns to look at me and pushes the brim of his cap away from his face so I can see him, really see him. Blue-gray eyes. Dark hair. A mouth with a hint of mischief, which lacks all cruelty but shows me pain.

I follow Kai through row upon row of nameless headstones until I see two names I recognize.

Penelope Harper, beloved mother.

George Kai Ferris, loving husband.

"I haven't dreamt of you in a while," I admit as he stops and turns to look at me.

He watches me with solemn intensity. "I know. Do you still love me?"

"Forever," I say, and the moment I do, Kai vanishes like an apparition.

Chapter 17

I sat at the back of the room, watching Henry pace as he lectured. I was reminded of the scene in *Indiana Jones and the Last Crusade*, where Dr. Jones spoke and all his female students gazed at him with worshipful eyes.

It was like being put under a spell. Henry—thoughtful, funny Henry wearing a Rolling Stones t-shirt and black horn rimmed glasses—had captured the attention of every student in the lecture hall. It was clear that he was a dynamic, enthusiastic teacher. People responded to him and his excitement. He was good.

The end of class arrived and the students packed up and stood to leave. I had to hold in my laughter when I saw a few bold female students attempt to speak to him. He answered their questions while packing up the stacks of papers on his desk. He looked up and caught my eye, winking brashly. To my idiotic consternation, I blushed like a college girl.

"Dr. Gerard," I greeted as I approached him.

He smiled and shot a look between the two young women vying for his attention. "See you both next class." He picked up his messenger bag and reached out to take my hand. I heard their lamenting sighs and curses as we left.

"Can I buy you a cup of coffee?" I asked as we walked outside.

"Absolutely. Wait a second," he said, forcing me to stop. "Hello."

"Hello."

He leaned in to kiss me, his mouth warm and comforting. When he pulled away, I gently tapped his Clark Kent style glasses. "I like these."

His grin was lopsided and adorable.

"You look like a hipster—cool t-shirts and hip, nerdy glasses."

"That was an insult if I've ever heard one. Besides, I was dressing like this before it was cool."

"You're old."

We laughed and continued walking towards a café, his hand enclosing mine. I took a deep breath, glad the last of winter had finally disappeared. It was officially spring, and I was strolling arm-in-arm along cobblestone streets with a man who made me laugh.

"How's Luc?" he asked as we sat down at an outdoor table at a café.

I munched on a cherry pastry and sipped my espresso. "Not good."

"You hear from Jules yet?"

I shook my head. "Let's talk about you. You're incredible, did you know that?"

He grinned. "Liked my class, huh?"

"I loved seeing you in action. Have to say, you're wicked hot. And smart. And funny. And all the girls love you."

Henry leaned across the table, his eyes going soft and melty. "I don't care if the other girls love me."

I caught my breath, wondering if this was the moment when I'd learn how he really felt about me, but his eyes slipped away from mine and I let it go. After coffee, I invited him back to the farmhouse.

When we arrived, Henry set his bag down in the foyer and looked around.

"Something's different. Kai's shoes—"

"Yes," I said.

Henry walked to the front closet and opened the door. He stared at the empty hangers. "Where are his coats?"

"With the rest of his clothes," I said, my voice small.

"And those are where?"

"I donated them. It was… it was time."

He opened his mouth to say something but then closed his lips.

"Got a little speaker's block?"

Henry's smile spread across the entire countenance of his face. "Speaker's block?"

"You know, like writer's block, but for the voice."

He laughed. "Come here, Sage," he commanded softly. I went to him and nestled myself into his chest. He took my hand and placed it on his heart. "Are you sure you're ready for this —for me?"

I nodded my head against his chest. The dream I'd had of Kai and the graveyard still lingered, and though it left me with a strange feeling of bereavement, I felt lighter, too.

"Thank you." His voice was heavy with emotion.

"I should be the one thanking you," I whispered. My throat was tight, overwhelmed with emotion that ran through me like an electric current.

"For what?"

"For finding me."

Did I have to choose between my past and my future? Between Kai and Henry? I shoved those thoughts away and focused on the moment. I led Henry upstairs to my bedroom. He slowly unbuttoned his shirt, revealing the scar marking the transformation of his life. He could've let it be something dark; instead, it showed him the beauty of life.

In one quick motion, I pulled off my shirt. When I stood naked before him, he pulled me to him and traced my cesarean scar with his lips.

He thought I was beautiful, and he told me with the brushes of his mouth, the shortness of his breaths, the heat of his body when he came to me. He kissed away the tears that rolled down my temples into my hair, and he held me against him in the after.

I pressed myself to his neck and his hand stroked the curve of my shoulder.

"Do you know what I felt when I read your book?" he asked.

I shook my head.

"It was like having poetry stitched onto my heart. I carry your words inside me. Forever."

The tears he'd kissed away came again, but this time they fell onto his golden skin. I sketched his scar, wondering how he'd managed to piece my own heart back together.

"Want to see something?" he asked.

I nodded again and he moved to sit up. He stuck out his right leg, and pointed to three freckles in a perfect diagonal. He looked at me and grinned. "I've got Orion's belt on my ankle."

I laughed. "Part stardust, are you?"

"Straight from the heavens," he agreed.

I leaned down and kissed the little brown dots on his skin. Then I scrubbed the drying tears from my face, knowing they were tears of joy, knowing it didn't matter if he was in love with me, because I was in love with him.

I was in love with Henry Gerard.

———

I stood in the living room, crouched over Gigi, who was standing on wobbly legs, gripping my fingers and attempting to take a step forward. "How's Luc?"

Celia sighed. "Still hungover, I think."

"It's been a week."

"Hangover of the heart."

"Poetic."

"I've been around you long enough." She smiled in humor, but her smile turned sad. "I think I should cancel the wedding."

Gigi bounced on chubby legs, smiling and happy, before plopping down on her bottom. I sighed and gave up. She'd walk when she was ready. *Chat* ran into the room, curled around Gigi, and bumped her with his head.

"I think that would be wise."

Celia pinched the bridge of her nose. "There's nothing like watching your child go through a heartbreak. He's thirty years old, and it hurts me the same way it did when he'd fall as a kid."

"I don't think Jules did this on purpose."

"He's still hurting."

"So is she."

"How do you know? Has she called you? She hasn't called him."

I bit my lip in thought. "Somewhere along the way, Jules got lost. She just needs some time to find herself."

"Find herself." Celia shook her head. "She had to do it at the cost of hurting Luc? She didn't have to move here, she didn't have to accept his proposal. It was selfish."

"Yes," I agreed.

Celia met my eyes; they were cloudy with a mother's pain. "I never thought they were a good fit."

"You made her a wedding dress."

"What was I supposed to do? Tell Luc how I really felt, tell him I didn't think she wanted the same things? Did you listen to *your* mother when she talked to you about what's his name? Connor?"

I pursed my lips. "Point taken."

We both fell silent, the strain of Jules's absence between us.

"What is Jules running from?" Celia wondered.

"Herself," I answered. "I hate that she hurt Luc. I hate that he's a causality in her quest to find out who she is, but we have no idea what she's been carrying around, what she's been keeping close to her."

"You're more empathetic than I am, I think."

"Maybe." I shrugged. "Then again, no one's hurt Gigi yet. God help the man who breaks her heart. I'll murder him."

"Oh, I don't think you'll have to worry about Gigi. If she's anything like her mother, she'll do the heart breaking."

I looked at Gigi, with her slowly darkening mop of hair and eyes the color of Kai's. I wasn't ready to think about her being old enough to break hearts, old enough to charm men with a mysterious smile.

"She'll be okay," Celia said. "You both will be okay."

"What?" I asked, turning my attention to Celia.

"I'm glad you're happy, Sage."

"So am I."

———

"You got me a gift?" I asked in surprise.

"Just something small," Henry replied.

I reached for it, took off the silver wrapping paper and laughed when I saw what it was.

"It's stupid, I know—"

"It's not." I pulled out the plastic figurine and held it up. It came equipped with a cape, but he looked like no superhero I'd ever seen.

"I got it at one of those one-stop shops. The French version."

I laughed again and went to put it on the mantle. "This is better than a bouquet of flowers."

"Thought so."

"Sage?"

"Yeah, Henry."

"Can I say something without you freaking out?"

I turned slowly, trying to stall the running of my heart, and nodded.

"I've never had this—this language, this shorthand—with someone. But I think—I think it's more than just inside jokes and laughing. It's more than intimacy. It's more than love. It's something else; something entirely its own. Like a unique little sun at the center of the universe. You're the sun at the center of my universe, Sage. I know I love you. It wasn't even a question I had to ask, I just knew. I love you."

His speech should've made me smile. I'd been hoping for it, his declaration, wanting to know I wasn't out in the void all alone. But through his words, through his truth, I'd become afraid.

"Sage? Say something. Please." He pulled back so he could look at me.

"Suns collapse," I whispered. "Suns die. But before they do, they burn so bright they incinerate anything that comes too close."

His hand sank into my hair. "You think your light will swallow me?"

"Sometimes I think my darkness will. One moment, I feel fine. The next, I'm overwhelmed by... life. My past. You."

Henry pressed his lips to my forehead before letting me go, and I sank onto the couch, staring at my hands.

"I've never met anyone like you, Sage. It's okay to be afraid. I'll let you be afraid." I expected him to leave. Instead, he went into the kitchen and a moment later he returned to the living room. He gently whacked me with a very long implement.

"What the hell?" I demanded, shooting a look at Henry.

He was grinning at me like a fool, holding the sausage like a sword.

"You're kidding, right?"

"What? Don't think you can win? I challenge you to a duel."

"We're supposed to eat that."

He shrugged. "So we'll go out to dinner. I'm not letting you live in the dark."

"You said it was okay to be afraid," I pointed out.

"It is," he agreed. "But you're not alone. You seem to forget that. So I'm reminding you I'm here."

"Challenging me to a duel."

"Challenging you to a duel *with a sausage*," he reminded me with a boyish smile.

I looked around. "What am I supposed to use?"

"There's a baguette in the kitchen, too."

"A baguette won't stand a chance against a sausage."

His grin grew bigger. "Don't worry, there's always tomorrow. Another time for a rematch. Now are you going to stand there, or are you going to go get your weapon?"

———

I scrubbed the hell out of a pot encrusted with oatmeal. I was in a wretched mood. I'd been up all night with Gigi, who'd been gassy and fussy, spitting up constantly. When I finally got her down and trudged back to bed, I'd been alone. Henry had slept at his place.

And I hadn't liked it, not one bit.

I wanted him next to me. I slept better when he was there. I liked rolling over in the middle of the night and curling against his back. I liked waking up with him.

I heard the front door open and close and then, "Sage?"

"Kitchen," I called to Henry.

He removed his messenger bag from his shoulder and haphazardly threw it in the corner. It just added itself to my list of grievances. I was exhausted and definitely not in a rational frame of mind.

"Hi," he said, kissing me on the cheek.

"Hello," I muttered, continuing to scrub the pot.

"What's wrong?"

"Nothing."

He made a noise sounding like a buzzer. "Try again."

"I had a rough night with Gigi... among other things."

"Other things?"

I gestured to the pot I was scouring.

"Stop scrubbing."

I set the scrub brush aside and Henry picked up the pot and threw it into the garbage. "There. Problem solved."

"You can't just—what are you thinking?"

"It was making you upset. I don't want you to be upset."

I fished it out of the trash. "You can't throw things out just because you don't want to deal with them."

"Sure, I can." He sounded amused, and it infuriated me.

"You're such a man-child."

He sighed. "What's going on, Sage? It's not really about the pot, is it?"

I shook my head, drying my hands on a dishtowel. "Gigi had a rough night, so I had a rough night, and then when I got her down, I went back to bed, alone."

"Alone?"

"You weren't there, Henry. I like sleeping next to you."

"That's nice to hear." He wrapped his arms around me and I leaned into him.

"I'm sleep deprived, haven't written anything today and I just… I'm in a funk."

"Funky monkey," he teased.

"I'm sorry I just dumped all of that over you."

"It's okay. That's what I'm here for."

"And what am I here for? To make your life harder?"

"Take a deep breath." I followed his command. "Another one. Better?"

I snuggled against him. "Better."

"You're allowed to have bad days."

"I feel like I've had a bad week. I miss Jules. I miss my best friend. Distract me, tell me about your day."

"College girls are fearless," he began.

———

"Show me the view from the side," I commanded.

"Hold on, this might take me a second," Lucy said. "Face-Timing isn't second nature to me like it is to you. Okay, there we go." Lucy turned her body so I could see her bump. Her stomach filled the iPhone screen.

"How are you feeling?" I asked.

"Really good," she said. "Second trimester energy spike."

"Already? Damn, I forget how fast time goes."

Lucy took her seat in her chair and frowned. "I'm really bummed we're not going to be there for Gigi's first birthday party."

"Yeah, that sucks." I bit my lip.

"Okay, what's up with you?"

"What do you mean?"

"Is it Jules? Have you finally heard from her?"

I shook my head. "It's not Jules. Lucy, I need—can I tell you something? In confidence?"

She nodded, her blue eyes perceptive and open.

"I'm… with someone."

"Yeah?"

I told her about Henry.

"I thought something was different about you," she remarked. "You seem happy in a way I haven't seen since before Kai died. Henry's special, isn't he?"

"Yeah." I sighed. "I think he… that we could be…"

"You don't have to say it, Sage. I get it."

I smiled in relief. "I knew you would understand."

"Just enjoy it. Don't rush into anything—you'll know what's right, whatever it is."

"The thing is… if this felt like a passing something, I wouldn't think about telling George and Claire, but I don't think this is a passing something."

"Real deal?"

I nodded, finally admitting it out loud to someone other than myself. "I'm divided, though."

"About?"

"Part of me worries I don't love him for him, that I love him for the relief he gives me."

"It's allowed to be all wrapped up together. It's complicated—what you and I have lived through—and loving again after that…"

"Did you ever feel guilty?" I wondered. "Like you were betraying Tristan?"

She nodded. "It's hard, ya know? Reconciling all of that. Part of me thinks it would've been easier if it had just been me, not me and Dakota. It's hard to explain…"

"I get it. It's not just that I want a partner—someone to share life with—it's that I want the right father for Gigi. But who would've been a better father to her than Kai?"

"You can't think about it—you just have to feel it. Because if you think about it, it will get the best of you and you'll just be miserable. You love Henry?"

I nodded.

"He loves you?"

I nodded again.

"Right now, that's enough."

"I wish you were here," I said. "Or I wish I could be there."

She smiled. "They have this miraculous invention called an airplane? Maybe you've heard of it?"

"Smart ass." We laughed. "We'll come to Monteagle soon, I promise."

"When you say 'we' does that include Henry?"

I grinned. "Goodbye, Lucy."

"Bye, Sage." We clicked off, her face disappearing before my eyes.

"Sage!" Henry called. "Dinner's ready!"

I stood up, gripping the edge of the desk. There was a man downstairs who made a mess in my kitchen and cooked me dinner. There was a man downstairs who was feeding a child who wasn't his. There was a man downstairs who I'd sleep next to that night, who'd take me into his arms and laugh with me.

There was a man downstairs who loved me.

Chapter 18

Out of the corner of my eye, I saw Henry and held up a hand, signaling for him to give me a moment. There was a small window of time to get down one last thought before it eluded me forever. With one final tap of a key, I pressed save and looked up.

Henry stood in the doorway to the turret, leaning against the doorframe. He was dressed in a pair of dark shorts and an old muted-gray t-shirt that had once been black.

"It's a nice day out," he said.

I glanced at the window, seeing the sharp rays of the sun.

"You didn't notice," he said.

I smiled in apology.

"You were up early," he said.

"I woke up in the middle of the night and haven't gone back to bed." He came into the room and put his arms around me. I snuggled into his chest and hugged him.

"I have an idea."

"Shoot." I pulled back to look at him.

"Why don't we have a picnic under the tree out back?"

I wrinkled my nose. "A picnic involves planning. It involves food and wine and—"

"We already went grocery shopping."

"What? When?"

"Gigi and I just got back. By the way, your daughter is totally a chick magnet. She's better than a puppy."

I laughed. "You dork."

"You are really unaware, you know that? A burglar could come in, take everything you own, and you'd have no knowledge of it."

"I'm dedicated to my craft," I said dryly.

"I'm very much aware of that." He took me by the hand. "But don't your eyes hurt, staring at a computer screen for all those hours?"

"They do."

"Then the sun will do you good. Come on."

We walked to the nursery to get Gigi. She looked up at me and smiled, her nose scrunching up in happiness. She reached for me and I scooped her up.

"If you want to keep writing later I'm sure I can convince Gigi to watch old Bugs Bunny cartoons with me," he said.

"Maybe, we'll see. I'm so tired I can hardly think straight. Besides, I like Bugs Bunny, so I might want to join you guys."

We headed out the back door and I saw there was already a plaid blanket spread out under the tree, a picnic basket near the trunk. I sighed in dreamy enjoyment. Gold rays glinted off the lake and dragonflies glided across the water.

"Henry?" I called as we took a seat on the ground, getting Gigi settled.

"Hmm?"

"Thank you."

"For what?" He set a tub of olives aside and went for the cheese.

"For bringing me down here. I can get lost up there."

"Up where? Your mind?" he teased.

"There, too, but I meant the turret. It's second nature for me to want to be alone. Thanks for dragging me back to real life."

"Anytime."

"You have soft cheese or hard cheese?" I asked.

"Both."

"Will you cut me a little sliver of some soft cheese? I want to give Gigi her first taste."

Gigi's face lit up in surprise or shock; I couldn't tell which. She looked like she was about to spit out the Brie, but she kept it in her mouth and swallowed. A moment later she opened her mouth, demanding more.

"Brie for the win." I grinned, feeding her another small bite.

Henry bit into an apple and looked at me. "What are you thinking about?" Henry asked, handing me a slice of prosciutto.

"Nothing. Just enjoying the moment." I leaned over and kissed him on the lips. They tasted of sweet apples and spicy olives. "So, Gigi's first birthday is coming up." I put my hands under Gigi's arms, helping her stand. She bounced enthusiastically.

"When?"

"August."

"Oh, and does she have grand plans for her birthday? Fly to Manhattan, rent out a penthouse, and invite one thousand of her closest friends?"

"That sounds like a nightmare," I said. "Actually, Kai's parents are planning on flying in for it, along with Alice and Keith."

"Alice and Keith? Remind me who they are again?"

"Reece's parents. One of Kai's best friends who died in the plane crash. Alice and Keith were like Kai's surrogate parents."

"You have a mishmash of family, don't you?"

"Strange, I know."

"Is this your segue into telling me you don't want me at Gigi's birthday party?"

I looked at him, startled. "What? How did you get that idea?"

He shrugged and looked away from me, staring at the lake.

"Henry," I began quietly, "I told you they were coming so you'd know it's going to be weird when I introduce you. I didn't want it to be a surprise."

"Really?" he asked, his tone hopeful.

I smiled and nodded. "Of course. You're in my life, you're in Gigi's life. They should know you and you should know them."

He grinned and touched my cheek. "I'm in your life, huh?"

427

Pretending to frown, I answered, "I think it might be difficult to get rid of you at this point. Easiest thing to do would be to go with it."

"Glad you realize that." He tilted his head to one side. "You haven't told me you loved me yet."

I gasped. "That's not true!"

"Yeah, it is. Think about it. I told you I loved you days ago. I'm still waiting for you to say it back, Sage."

"I must've been distracted by the dueling sausage."

He tapped his wrist where he didn't wear a watch. "I'm waiting. Even though I already know the answer."

I grinned. "If you know the answer, why do you want to hear me say it?"

"Sage," he growled.

"I love you, Henry Marvin Gerard."

"Marvin. I could kill my parents for that middle name."

"I just told you I loved you and you're complaining about your middle name? Come on, man, where are your priorities?"

He shrugged. "I already knew you loved me. That was a nice declaration, though. Thanks."

"You don't have to sound so cavalier about it," I grumbled.

Henry grinned. "Sage? I love you, too."

I shook my head and chuckled. Gigi crawled over to Henry and plopped herself into his lap. His arms went around her immediately —and my heart warmed even more.

"You love her, don't you?"

"Yeah," he said simply. "I do."

"After Kai, I never—" I swallowed, "—I never expected to love again. I didn't *want* to, and then you were there and I just…"

"It's all or nothing with you, isn't it, Sage? I love that about you."

I looked into his hazel eyes. They were lit with sunlight, warm and breathtaking. Filled with love and hope and the promise of a future.

"I was thinking about taking some time off. To write a book," he said.

"A book?" I raised my eyebrows.

He grinned. "Not fiction," he clarified, "historical nonfiction."

"You mean, like a history book?"

"Yes. It will take a lot of time to research, but I'm inspired here, so why not?"

"If I asked you a hypothetical question, would you give me a hypothetical answer or a real one?"

"Depends on the question."

"Hmm. What's the appropriate amount of time to wait before asking your boyfriend to move in with you?"

"I thought you hated the word 'boyfriend'."

"I do. This is hypothetical, remember?"

"Right. Well, in that case, I think if both people enjoy spending time with each other, and the guy's already been leaving his socks and underwear at his girlfriend's place, and they've said the L-word, then I think the next step is moving in together."

"The L-word? What are you, five?"

"Maybe."

"Henry?"

"Yeah, Sage?"

"Do you want to move in?"

Henry looked at Gigi. "What do you think, Gigi? Would you like me to move in?"

Gigi pushed against him, wanting to stand. Henry helped her up and then looked at me. His smile was wide and the lines around his eyes crinkled with excitement.

———

Three pairs of eyes stared at me, blinking in rapid succession. My hesitant smile shifted into a grimace when I saw their stunned reaction.

"It's fast, I know," I said.

"Very fast," Luc agreed.

"But you all like Henry," I said.

429

"We do. A lot." Celia looked at Armand before asking, "Are you sure you're ready for this, Sage? Gigi isn't even a year old."

I pursed my lips in bitterness. "Is this about Gigi, or Kai? I know he hasn't been gone very long."

"Well, there is that," Celia said.

"Say it," I demanded.

"What's the hurry?" Luc asked.

"You and Jules set me up on a blind date. You were the ones who dragged me against my will, and now that I've found someone you want me to slow down?"

Luc's face paled at the mention of his absent fiancée. At least we still assumed she was his fiancée. No one had heard from her since she left.

"There's a difference between getting your feet wet and diving in head first," Celia said.

"I jumped with Kai—are you going to tell me that was a mistake? I didn't plan for Henry anymore than I planned for Kai. I love quickly and deeply. That's who I am and I refuse to fight that." I sat back in my chair, not at all surprised by their response. It gave me a glimmer of how my in-laws were going to take the news. I glanced at Armand. He hadn't said anything. I stared at him, pleading.

"Loving Henry doesn't mean I don't love Kai, or what we had together, or what our life would've been like had he lived," I said. "But there's no timeframe for grief. I'll always remember Kai. I'll always love him."

I stood.

"Sage," Armand started.

"Don't. You don't have to understand. No one has to understand."

"Where are you going?" Celia called after me.

"Outside. I need some time." I went to Gigi, taking her out of her high chair. She cuddled against me as if intuitively knowing I needed the comfort.

"Sage!" Luc yelled.

I slammed the back door and walked to the lake. The day was

bright and warm, but I didn't feel it. Why was life always so hard and complicated? Henry and I, our love should've been simple. It *was* simple. It was everyone else who made it hard. It was my past that made it hard.

My feet hit the path along the lake, my shirt slowly sticking to me in the humid afternoon's dying sunlight. My ponytail swung against my shoulders as I continued to walk around the lake. Round and round I went. I didn't stop. Not even when Gigi grew heavy and my arms began to ache. I welcomed the ache. I embraced the ache —and the pain in my heart. We were twins, pain and I.

As the sun sank I became dimly aware of footsteps next to me. "Sage, what are you doing?" Henry asked.

"Walking," I answered.

"I'm aware of that. Why?"

"I told them you were moving in."

"Yeah, they mentioned that, but I think they're confused about your reaction to their reaction."

"The walking?"

"Sage, stop."

I did as commanded, and let Henry take Gigi from me. She was asleep and didn't awaken upon transfer. Shaking out my arms, I tried to restore blood flow.

"They didn't understand," I said.

"So?"

I blinked. "So—they think it's fast."

"And what do you think?" he asked, tilting his head to one side.

"I think I want you to move in. I asked *you*, didn't I? You and no one else."

"Want to know what I think?"

I nodded, and Henry went on.

"I want to move in. Know what else I think?"

I shook my head.

"I think it doesn't matter what other people think, even if they're the people who love and care about you. Only you and I can determine what we're ready for."

"Did you tell your parents? Your siblings?"

"Yes."

"And?"

"They can't believe that I'm moving in you—and they certainly can't believe I'm going to live in France. That then spurred the conversation about my career." He grinned. "They haven't met you yet. When they meet you, they'll understand—or they won't."

I smiled.

"Don't worry so much about what others have to say," he said. "Let's go back inside."

"They're in there. Their reaction made me nervous for when my in-laws visit."

"You know what they say, right? Plan for the worst, hope for the best."

"That applies not only to my life, but also to George and Claire. Especially George and Claire."

———

I came down the stairs into the living room. The TV was on low, the soft sound of French warbling in the background. Henry was asleep on the couch, Gigi, also asleep, cuddled against his chest. Taking out my phone, I snapped a photo, and then I stared at them for a long time, my heart full and happy.

Henry finally stirred, his eyes opening. He met my gaze and smiled sleepily. Henry looked down and ran a hand across Gigi's back. Her nose wrinkled and she flipped her head to the other cheek.

"Should I wake her?" Henry whispered.

I shook my head. "I'll get up with her later if she doesn't sleep through the night. Stick her in the Pack-N-Play in the turret."

He smiled. "While you write?"

"Maybe. Gigi sometimes respects my muse."

"It's really disconcerting waking up and not having you next to me."

"We should get another set of baby monitors and use them as walkie-talkies," I teased.

"I'd enjoy that."

Henry got up off the couch and went upstairs to lay Gigi in her crib. I went into the kitchen and opened the refrigerator, pulling out leftovers. Henry strolled in with a yawn.

I set down our plates of food with silverware and took my seat. We ate in companionable silence and when we finished, I got up to clear the plates.

"Leave them," he said. "It's a nice night out. Want to sit outside for a little while? Enjoy the moonlight?"

"You're good with the romance thing," I said with a smile. He took my hand and brought it to his lips.

"How do you feel about rose petals?"

I made a face. "Romance and cheesiness are not the same thing."

We sat together on a comfortable padded bench, and I fit myself into the crook of his arm. I watched the moonlight turn the lake silver and navy, stars shining down on us. "Did you ever think you'd fall in love with a widow who had a young child?" I asked out of the blue.

His hand stroked up and down my arm, making goosebumps rise on my skin, though it wasn't cold.

"Did you ever think you'd fall in love with a history professor who dresses like a hipster?"

"I see your point."

"Do you still think I'm a rebound?"

I looked at him. "I never said you were a rebound."

He smiled. "You didn't have to."

"Do you think you're my rebound?"

"A rebound you asked to move in with you? No."

"Are you just saying that, or do you actually believe it?"

He shrugged.

"When my mom died, I was spinning—"

"And Kai reached out to steady you. Did you ever think he was transient?"

"No, but others thought we weren't real, that we weren't going to last." I sighed. "The things we carry and refuse to put down. Kai and I… we lost a baby. A boy."

Henry wrapped himself around me, offering sympathy but never pity. There was a fine line between the two, but Henry navigated it well, like a ship through rocky waters. I hadn't cried for my son in a long time; there'd been other things to cry over.

Henry's fingers wound their way into my hair, urging me to meet his lips. I no longer thought of the people I'd lost, not when Henry's lips were on mine and he was branding me with love so deep I felt it sear me below my skin. His touch became desperate, and so did I. I never thought I'd feel this again. I didn't think I was capable.

So I held him to me, clutched him tightly, wanting to drown in all that he was.

Chapter 19

"Do you like boats?" Henry asked.

I spooned another bite of oatmeal into Gigi's mouth. "I guess. I don't dislike them."

"I was thinking we could go to *La Rochelle* for the weekend."

"Isn't it a seaport? What will we do? Watch people sail?"

"Maybe," he said with a grin. "Or do other things. Botanical gardens, a museum. I've never been. Have you?"

"No, I haven't. Is this your idea of distracting me from thoughts of my in-laws coming into town next week?"

"It might be."

"Then I accept."

He grinned. "Good, because I already made our hotel reservations."

"I like a man who takes charge," I teased.

"How soon can you be packed?"

"It's summer and we're going to a seaport coast town. Swimsuits and wraps. I'll be packed in ten minutes."

Three hours later, with more luggage for a baby than for two adults, we were finally on the road. Gigi was bopping along to The

Beatles and I was breathing in the fresh air. Henry rested his hand on my leg and I soaked up the familiarity, the comfort of his touch.

"Okay, Gigi," Henry said, scrolling through the iPod. "We know you like The Beatles—the psychedelic stuff."

"That's telling," I quipped.

"Let's see if she likes the Stones."

"Were you transported from the 60's?"

"Okay, then what about the Top Gun soundtrack?"

"Kenny Loggins? Oh, please."

"Come on, Goose, what do you say?"

"Okay, Maverick. You win."

Henry smiled as he slid on his aviator sunglasses and then belted out *Danger Zone*. "Sing with me!" he commanded.

I smiled, joining in, loving the feel of the breeze teasing strands of my hair free. After a two-hour scenic drive, we pulled into the small bed and breakfast. We dumped our luggage in the room and then Henry suggested a walk around the *Vieux Port*, the Old Harbor. It was the heart of the city and lined with seafood restaurants. We had our pick. The walls of the town were open and well preserved and Henry rattled off historical facts.

"*La Rochelle* was once a stronghold for the Huguenots. Sorry," he apologized sheepishly. "Sometimes I forget you're not into history as much as I am."

I pushed Gigi's stroller along the promenade and threw Henry a smile. "Don't ever apologize for who you are. And, for the record, I like who you are."

He kissed me briefly. "You ready for dinner?"

"Let's wait," I said. "I just want to sit with you on a bench and watch the sun go down."

He wrapped his arm around me and steered us in the direction of the marina. Gigi had fallen asleep, so she was missing the beautiful splashes of color streaking across the sky—it was probably lost on her anyway. I rested my head on Henry's shoulder, sighing when the last few rays of gold disappeared.

"Are you hungry at all for dinner?" he asked.

"No, Henry. It's not food I want."

———

The next morning, we woke up early to get a start on the day. We had a quick breakfast before taking a ferry to the *Île d'Aix*. We spent the morning exploring the island and walking along the rocky shoreline. We ate ice cream in lieu of lunch, and I couldn't remember the last time I had enjoyed time in the sun with no worries, no cares.

By mid-afternoon, I was ready for fresh seafood and a glass of wine. We took the ferry back to *La Rochelle* and found a café with shade. Sipping white wine while we waited for our food, we talked of nothing consequential, enjoying being with each other.

"Okay," I said, picking up a piece of crabmeat. "Let's see if my daughter has good taste in food."

We watched Gigi chew, her mouth screwing up into a comic picture. I loved watching her discover new things, watching emotions play out across her face.

"We have a winner," I declared when Gigi opened her mouth, ready for more.

A middle-aged woman walked by our table and stopped. She looked at us for a moment and said to me, "You have a beautiful family."

"Thank you," I answered, my eyes finding Henry's.

"How long have you two been married?" she asked.

I let out an uncomfortable laugh. "Oh, we aren't."

Henry reached across the table and grasped my hand. "We're very happy, though."

The woman smiled and continued on her way. The French weren't caught up in legalities and marriage. People were together or they weren't.

Gigi began to fret and cry. Henry scooped her up out of the stroller, but she reached for me and didn't calm down until I put her to my shoulder. Sometimes a baby wanted its mother and no one else.

"She's never going to need me the way she needs you, is she?"

"Oh, she'll need you. When a boy breaks her heart, she's going to need you to tell her she's perfect and smart and lovely and the boy is an idiot. Because she won't hear anything I say."

"That sounds like future talk."

"Too soon?" I asked, quieting Gigi.

"We do cohabitate. That's a salute to the future, isn't it?"

"Yes. Just a lot when I break it down and think about things."

"Then don't think. Just enjoy." He pushed my glass of wine towards me and I took a drink. "You really think Gigi is the one who's going to get her heart broken?" he asked.

"Part of life. Besides, she needs to get her heart broken once or twice. By guys who are completely awful. Then she'll know what it means to be loved by a good man. To want a good man."

"I hate the thought of any guy catching her attention. She's not dating, Sage. She's going to remain single, a spinster. We're going to get her many cats and she'll learn how to knit us afghan blankets."

I laughed. "You don't really mean that, right? You want her to find someone, don't you?"

"Someone or anyone?"

"The right someone."

"Am I your right someone?"

I smiled. And then he smiled.

"Kiss me," I said.

"Gladly."

———

I hugged George, standing in his arms like a daughter who'd been born to him. I smelled the mint on his breath and the aftershave on his cheeks. "I'm so glad you're here."

"Me too," he whispered with a kiss to my cheek. I closed my eyes a moment before moving out of his embrace to greet the other occupants who were standing in my living room.

"She's huge," Claire exclaimed, picking up Gigi from her playpen.

"She's long outgrown the onesie Alice and Keith bought her," I said.

"Is she old enough for a cowboy hat?" Keith teased, hugging me to him. He was tall and broad and his arms swallowed me.

"Can't have the hat without matching boots," Alice said, running a hand down my hair.

I watched Claire holding her granddaughter, having a small inkling of how she once looked holding her own children. The lines of Claire's face softened, like butter that'd been left out on the counter.

"So, Sage, what's new?" Keith asked. It was his turn to hold Gigi, and I was unable to stop the smile from streaking across my face. He was huge, a bear of a man, and my daughter looked like a tiny blonde sunbeam sitting in his lap.

"I'm writing a new book," I blurted out.

"What's it about?" George asked.

I shook my head.

"Oh, right, you don't talk about what you're writing," George amended. "I smell coffee."

"Anyone else need a caffeine boost?" I asked. They all raised their hands. George followed me into the kitchen. I retrieved four mugs and set them on a tray.

"You look good," George said.

"Thanks. So do you."

"You put on some weight."

"You lost some."

"I've cut back on the drinking," he said.

"Ah."

"And Claire has me on a diet."

"Yikes!" I grimaced. "That sounds terrible."

He rolled his eyes. "All we eat is fish and kale."

I pretended to look in the living room to make sure everyone was well occupied before opening the refrigerator and pulling out a wedge of cheese.

"It's always better when it's contraband," I whispered, handing it to George.

He broke off a piece and popped it into his mouth. "You're a life saver."

"You better finish that fast." I winked at George and picked up the tray, carrying it into the living room and setting it on the coffee table.

"Tell me news of Monteagle," I requested, sitting on the carpet. George popped out of the kitchen and came into the living room, taking a seat in a vacant chair.

"Not much to tell," Alice said. "We got a new stallion. Wild thing. Threw Keith a few times. I had to Tiger Balm his bruised back for an entire week."

I looked at Keith. "You ever think of doing something far less dangerous? Like running with the bulls or handling plutonium?" I teased.

"They call me the 'horse whisperer of Monteagle'. What else would I do?" Keith wondered.

"They really call you that?" I raised my eyebrows.

Keith gave a chagrined smile. "No."

"Not a lot has changed," Claire said. "Lucy is a few weeks away from her due date, but you knew that."

"What do you want us to do with the house?" George asked out of the blue.

"House? Memaw's house, you mean?" Kai's grandmother had left me her house and land. It had been a shock and shaken up the Ferris family dynamic.

"And the house you and Kai were building," Claire added.

Silence fell across the room. Gigi squirmed to get down off of Keith's lap, so he set her on the carpet. She crawled towards me, placing her hands on my raised knees. She pulled herself up and my hands went to her bottom to steady her.

"I don't want to continue building the house. As for Memaw's —" I swallowed, "—do you mind just looking after it? Kai is gone, but we are not. We'll be back to Monteagle at some point."

George nodded, his eyes pained.

No one really knew what to say after that, so we all watched Kai's daughter stand on wobbly legs, trying to take her first steps.

———

"I didn't tell them today," I whispered.

"You'll tell them tomorrow," Henry said, his fingers dipping into the divot of my collarbone.

"I don't know how I'm supposed to."

"The longer you wait, the harder it will be."

I sighed. "You're right, I know that."

"Gigi's birthday party is in a few days. Don't you want to give them some time to process before forcing them into merriment?"

"I need some tea," I said, sitting up.

"Do you want company?"

"Actually, I just want some time to myself. That okay?"

"Yes." He kissed my shoulder and then rolled over, taking up more than his side of the bed. I knew I'd have to fight for space when I returned, but it was a fight I'd enjoy. He made fighting fun.

I went to the living room—my phone vibrated once and danced across the coffee table. It was a text from Alice asking if I was awake. I took a deep breath, and texted her, asking if she was up for a late night chat in person. She was.

I grabbed my keys and was out the door. Alice and Keith were staying with George and Claire at the house they'd bought during their last trip to France. It was a ten-minute drive from the farm-house, and as I pulled up, I saw Alice waiting outside. She headed towards the car and opened the door.

"Where to?" Alice asked as she sat down and buckled herself in.

I frowned. "What are you in the mood for?"

"You hungry?"

"Yeah, I could eat. How does fish and chips sound?"

"Delightfully out of place," she said with a smile. "But sounds good to me."

I drove to downtown *Tours* and parked on a side street. We entered McCool's, found a vacant table, and sat down.

"I can't remember the last time I was out this late," Alice said after we'd ordered food and pints.

"It's been a while for me, too." I looked at her and said, "You know, don't you?"

She shrugged. "I have my suspicions. There's no hiding the happiness in your voice, Sage. Not even when we talk on the phone. What's going on?"

"I met someone."

Alice took a sip of her pint and nodded her head. "Go on. Who is he? How did you two meet?"

"Henry Gerard. He's a history professor at the university." I stared at the table when I finally said, "We live together."

"When did that happen?" she asked.

I made myself look at her. "About a month ago."

The waiter brought our food. Heat rose from the fish and chips, the battered smell hitting my nose, but my stomach was in knots.

"Do you think it's too soon? Too soon after Kai?"

Alice reached across the table and took my hand and squeezed it. "There's no timer for grief, Sage."

"I just—I don't know how to tell George and Claire."

"You don't know how to tell them, or you're afraid they won't understand and be happy for you?"

"Gigi is their granddaughter. Will they ever be okay with someone else in her life? Someone filling that fatherly role? Someone who isn't Kai?"

"I don't know," she said. "I don't know how they'll feel about it. And you won't either, not until you tell them."

"I know."

"Okay, good. So that's the short version, now I want details…"

———

I crept quietly into the house, not wanting to disturb the sleeping occupants. Turned out I didn't need to worry. Henry was in the nursery, sitting in the rocking chair. Gigi was curled against his chest, her tiny fists clenched, but she was still awake. I stood in the doorway for a moment, taking them in.

"Hello," he said softly.

"Hi. Did I worry you?"

He shook his head. "Figured you were out and needed to clear your head."

"I was with Alice."

"Ah. Gigi and I are having a late night rock fest."

"Rock fest in the rocking chair, huh?" I grinned. "Aerosmith or AC/DC?"

"Zeppelin."

I laughed. "Should I put her back in her crib?" I asked.

"Just another minute," he said, running a hand down Gigi's back, a look of contentment on his face. "You okay?"

"Think so."

"How was it?"

"Alice was Alice. Accepting, understanding… all the things I could've hoped for."

"That's good, isn't it?"

I let out a breath. "Yeah. It is good. Can I ask you something?"

"I think I've got a few brain cells still awake at this late hour. Shoot."

"What happens when you have children of your own?"

"Children of my own?"

"You want children; you said so."

Henry got up and walked to the crib, gently placing Gigi down and covering her with a blanket. She was asleep before we even left the nursery.

"I do want children. Who am I having these children with, just so I know?"

"Don't patronize me, please," I said.

"What's this about?"

"Parents don't love their children the same."

He rubbed a thumb down his jaw and I heard the scraping of stubble. "Do you love me the same way you loved Kai?"

I flinched. "I… no. It's different. But complete. I don't know how to describe it."

"Then doesn't it make sense that people would love children differently, too?"

"But Gigi isn't yours. One day, you'll have your own and… it might be…"

"When you came home, what did you see?"

"You were rocking Gigi to sleep."

"She was against my heart, Sage." He paused. "Is this really about Gigi? Or is it about you?"

Goose bumps of awareness rose up on my skin. How long was I going to feel pulled by two men, warring with myself and my heart?

"Do you love me?" he asked.

"Yes."

"Do you want a life with me?"

"Yes."

"Do you want children with me? Do you want dreams and milestones and tomorrows with me?"

"Yes," I said through a tight throat.

"Then kiss me and remember you're allowed to live."

———

"Are you okay?" George asked.

"Fine," I murmured distractedly.

"You're bouncing your leg. You sure you're okay?" Claire asked.

I'd invited them over for lunch and had been attempting to get up the nerve to tell them about Henry for the better part of twenty minutes.

"I met someone," I said, playing with the crust of my sandwich. I sighed and pushed the plate away from me. *Chat* jumped up into my lap, as if knowing I needed the emotional support.

"You met someone," Claire repeated slowly.

I nodded, holding air in my lungs. "We've been dating about five months." I closed my eyes, getting ready to rip off the rest of the Band-Aid. "He's moved in. We live together."

Claire's face showed curiosity, but lacked censure. It confused me. I expected her to have an outburst, I expected her to revile me. I expected hatred. "Why did you wait to tell us?"

"I thought it would be better to explain in person." I looked at George. He still hadn't said anything, clutching a glass of bourbon in his hand.

Finally he asked, "So, when are you getting married?"

"Excuse me?"

"Married—you must be getting married soon. Otherwise you never would've let him move in. It was the same with Kai, wasn't it? It happened fast with him, too. Kai wasn't special, was he?"

My head began to reel, his words piercing my heart with their sharpness. It hurt to breathe. For weeks I'd thought of everything I thought George might say, but it still stung. I'd already worried that loving Henry was betraying Kai. Knowing George felt the same way sliced me to the bone.

I'd expected this from Claire. I could take it from Claire. Not from George. Not from the man whom I got drunk with after he lost his mother and I lost a baby.

"George," Claire said softly.

He slammed back the rest of his drink and set his glass on the table. "If you'll excuse me, I'm not very hungry."

He stalked out of the farmhouse, the sound of the front door echoing behind him. I was left alone with my mother-in-law and without something to drink.

I didn't know what I had been hoping for—understanding, forgiveness, an allowance for being human.

"You thought I'd be the one to fly off the deep end, didn't you?" she said. I looked at her in shock and she chuckled, but her face instantly sobered. "No one can doubt the love you had for my son."

"I still love him."

"I know. I don't think that will ever go away. But you're moving forward. You're building a life, for you and Gigi. And all Kai would've wanted is for you to find a good, kind man."

"Henry is the kindest." I felt tears prickle my eyes. "I wanted you and George to meet him—before Gigi's party, but now I don't think—"

445

"Give George some time," Claire said. "He just needs some time."

Somehow, I found myself in the arms of my mother-in-law. I'd once worried we'd never be close, that I'd never feel about her the way I felt about Celia or Alice. But in that moment, Claire became my mother and she was giving me her blessing to find happiness. I cried, but they weren't tears of sadness, they were tears of relief.

Chapter 20

"Do you think we have enough food?" I asked.

"No," Henry said automatically.

"Really?" I looked around the kitchen. There was no counter space due to the large number of casseroles, and the kitchen table was laden with baked goods and desserts. I'd been cooking for hours.

"I was kidding, obviously." Henry held Gigi, who was busy gnawing on a fist.

"What did I tell you?"

He sighed. "You said no humor. You need a dose of humor. Actually, you need a shot of humor. Or just a shot. How about bourbon?"

The doorbell rang and I went from nervous to outright panic. "This was a bad idea."

"This is necessary. I'll get to know them, they'll get to know me. They'll see I'm not an axe murder…"

I answered the door.

Alice came through the door first, wrapping me in a hug. In my ear she whispered, "Relax."

A part of my spine unbent. I hugged Keith and then Claire. "George?" I asked.

Claire shook her head. "I'm sorry. He's not coming."

I tried not to let George's absence steer the mood, so I forced a smile and said, "His loss. Henry's grilling steak."

Three pairs of eyes finally turned to Henry, who stood by watching everything with a calm gaze. He smiled. "Hi, I'm Henry."

Keith reached out with a bear paw to shake Henry's hand. "Good to meet you. Keith Chelser. My wife, Alice."

Alice was less formal and moved in to hug him, which didn't work so well considering Henry still held Gigi. "You don't look like a college professor," Alice said.

"Tried to warn you," I interjected.

Henry grinned and then handed Gigi off to me so he could face Claire, who had been quiet and waiting. Henry's face lost some of its humor, replaced by tempered honesty. "Thank you for being here," he said. "Hopefully, in time, you'll see that I'm… not here to replace anyone—"

Claire held up her hand to stop Henry from speaking. "Sage is a good judge of character. If she thinks you're worthy, then I do too."

My mother-in-law's eyes slid to mine and she smiled. "Let's eat and drink and say no more about it. Okay?"

"Okay," I agreed through a tight throat.

"What are we drinking?" Henry asked.

"Beer," Keith said.

"Wine," Alice said.

Henry looked at me. "Sage? What are you drinking?"

"What are you drinking?" I queried.

He grinned. "Bourbon."

"Atta boy," Keith said, slapping Henry on the back.

"We've got it all. To the kitchen," I said. "And then we'll head outside. Table is set and everything." Everyone went ahead of us, but I put a hand to Henry's arm, holding him back. "You did that on purpose."

"Did what?"

"Said you'd drink bourbon. Are you trying to impress them or something?"

He grinned, the corners of his eyes crinkling. "Why? Do you think it's working?"

———

Gigi sat on my lap as I talked to Dakota through the computer screen. She leaned forward and placed her hand on the screen where Dakota's cheeks were. He eagerly waved to her.

"Why can't she talk?" he demanded.

"She's not old enough," I explained. "She likes you, though. And she wishes you were here to celebrate her birthday tomorrow."

"When do I get to see her?"

"I'm not sure. Soon, I hope." Lucy's face came into focus when she scooped up Dakota and sent him on his way. Her red hair was piled on top of her head and her blue eyes were bright.

"I forgot how miserable the last few weeks are," Lucy griped. "I'm ready for this one to come out already."

"Forgetting is nature's way of telling us to keep procreating," I said with a grin.

Lucy cocked her head to the side. "How are you?"

"I—told them."

"I know."

"You know? How?"

"George called Wyatt," Lucy explained.

"How's Wyatt taking the news?"

"He's okay. He wasn't too happy when he found out I already knew."

"I'm sorry. You shouldn't have to keep my secrets from your husband."

"Wyatt understands, though. After all, he's a second husband."

"Henry isn't a second husband."

She shrugged. "He's as good as one, isn't he? He's the next man who means something to you."

"George won't talk to me. I invited everyone over for dinner last night so Henry could meet them. George didn't come."

"How was it? Everyone meeting him?"

I smiled. "They loved him."

"Never doubted that."

"What do I do, Lucy? Everyone says to give George time, but what if he can't get over this? What if nothing is the same ever again?"

She smiled sadly. "It was never going to be the same. Not after Kai."

———

"You know why George is mad, don't you?" Henry asked that night over dinner.

"Because he thinks I betrayed his son?"

"George doesn't think you betrayed Kai. He thinks you betrayed *him*."

"You don't even know George."

He touched my hand, running a finger down the length of my wrist. "We are the masters of our own emotions, but sometimes people need time. George needs time. This isn't about you right now —not at all. No matter what he says."

"He's not saying anything!" I stood up from the table and went to Gigi's high chair. She was covered in pureed yellow squash and she stared at me with wide blue-gray eyes. Familiar eyes.

"She needs a bath," I muttered, unstrapping her and hoisting her into my arms.

"Sage," Henry said.

I turned to look at him. "It can't ever just *be*, can it? Life, I mean. Why does it always feel like I'm living through an emotional disaster?"

Without waiting for an answer, I walked out of the kitchen, out of our picture of harmony and took my daughter upstairs. *Chat* followed me and ducked into the bathroom. I drew the bath and stripped off Gigi's soiled clothes and set her in the tub. She splashed around, gurgling in delight.

Would things ever run smoothly? Were they designed to be a constant struggle? The older I grew, the more complicated life became, yet it became more meaningful, too. Did I need the hardships to really appreciate the good?

I wasn't sure I'd ever know the answers to the questions I was asking. I wasn't sure I was meant to.

———

Keith and I walked among the vines of Armand's vineyard. It always gave me a feeling of peace. The smell of ripe fruit and dirt hit the back of my throat as the sun peeked out from behind the clouds. I looked at the landscape, breathing in the green and the leaves.

Gigi was strapped to my chest, her face to the world. She was wearing a sunhat, one chubby fist wrapped around my finger while her other hand waved in the air towards Keith.

"Beautiful, isn't it?" I asked.

"Gorgeous. Almost as beautiful as my ranch."

I grinned. "Cowboy."

He pushed back the brim of his hat. "There's something to be said for being able to gallop across a field on the back of a horse. It does something for the mind. Clears it all out."

"They don't make men like you anymore, Keith, do they?"

"I think they do." He looked at me.

"What? You mean Henry?"

"Henry. Kai. They're not so different."

I was startled by his thought. "How do you figure?"

"Both of them saved you in their own way."

Kai had rescued me from drowning in my mother's death. But we'd been each other's life rafts. And Henry. He had rescued me after Kai. I wondered what I gave him in return.

Keith wrapped his arm around my shoulder. "I'm proud of ya."

"For what?"

"For finding a way to live."

"Damn it, Keith, don't make me cry," I sniffed.

"It's good to see you smile again and have it reach your eyes."

There are people you are born to and there are those who come to you. We don't always have a choice and sometimes fate chooses for us. I could claim to be unlucky, but then I'd be lying.

———

I was putting the finishing touches on the second cake, the one for adults, when people began to arrive. The front door opened and with it came the sound of voices.

"Where is the birthday girl?" Alice asked.

"Upstairs. Henry is fighting her into a dress as we speak."

Everyone laughed and Armand called out, "Drink orders. What does everyone want?" Most people settled for beer.

"Gorgeous cakes," Celia said, brushing her cheek against mine.

"No masterpieces like yours, but I think they'll do," I said with a smile.

I glanced around, the warm feeling of my family surrounding me. I missed Wyatt, Lucy, and Dakota. And Jules. I hoped she was safe. I hoped she was figuring out her life.

"Claire and George?" I asked Alice.

Before Alice could answer, I heard the front door open. A moment later, Claire was in the kitchen, sending a look behind her. George filled the doorway and it was as though the swarm of chatter increased to cover the awkwardness of our silent exchange. It was no secret how he had reacted to the news of Henry. We stared at one another and then I gestured with my chin. He nodded and we headed outside, away from the others so we could finally speak unencumbered.

It struck me as odd, in the wake of Kai's death, it had been Claire who'd been the strong one, the one to lean on. She'd been monumental and gracious—she'd been all the things I could've hoped for in a mother-in-law. It was a shame it had happened after

Kai's death. He would have loved to have seen the harmony that enveloped his family.

I didn't say anything as I looked at George. His recent losses had aged him and hardened his heart. He stared at me, but didn't see me. His eyes were glassy, but not with bourbon. They were tears he hadn't yet shed that he tried to hold back.

"Does my loving another man change how you feel about me? Are you casting me out of your family? I can't stand losing another Ferris man. Losing one was hard enough. I can't lose you, too."

"Do you really mean that?" he asked quietly.

"Of course I do. George—I wish we didn't have this strain between us."

"You don't wear your wedding ring," he said.

I felt tears come. "I lost it."

"And if you hadn't lost it, would you still be wearing it?"

How could I answer that? If I still had my wedding ring, not wearing it would've felt disrespectful to Kai's memory. But wearing it would've also felt disrespectful to Henry. I picked up the pendant resting around my neck. "Do you know what this is?"

George shook his head.

"It's Kai's wedding band. I had it melted down and engraved with his initials. Kai was my husband."

"And what is Henry?"

It was strange hearing Henry's name on George's lips. I was uncomfortable with placing a label on what we had. I wasn't sure I could. It wouldn't change what we were, what we meant to each other, what we were starting to mean to each other.

"Do you hate that I found someone?" I asked. "Do you want me to wear black my entire life and wail and bemoan the fact that your son made me a widow before I was thirty? Do you want me to live out the rest of my life like a martyr? Do you want me to raise Kai's daughter *alone*?" My voice wobbled with the emotions I was attempting to hold in. I was afraid if I let myself cry, I'd never stop, and I'd flood the backyard like Alice in my own version of Wonderland, where all the characters were a little mad.

"Everyone is telling me Henry is a good guy," George said.

"He is," I agreed.

"I know I'm supposed to be happy for you. Even more so because you found someone who is good. It would have been so much easier if he was terrible for you, but I don't think he is. He's going to raise my granddaughter, isn't he?"

"He already is, George."

"Stepped in, just like that." He shook his head.

"Do you know that I used to curse Kai? All the time. He loved me so much that it was his downfall."

He frowned in confusion. "What are you talking about?"

My breath was shaky. "Because of me, he wanted to come home early from New York. Because of me, he was on the rain-slicked road. Because of me, he crashed his car."

"Oh, Sage…"

I shrugged. "It's something I live with. Another seed of guilt I carry around." I didn't need to tell him that his own reaction to Henry was like taking a watering can and helping the guilt flourish.

"Well, that's something we have in common, I guess."

"What do you mean?"

"I'm his father. And I didn't protect him. Couldn't."

"It wasn't your fault he left after Tristan and Reece's funeral. It wasn't your fault he was on the road. It's no one's fault." I said the words, but I wasn't sure I believed them. That was the problem with guilt. The mind was rational, but the heart wasn't. You couldn't reason with the heart. And once the guilt took hold, it was almost impossible to remove, like a field of weeds that sprung up without your permission.

"How did you feel when Gigi was in the hospital?" he asked.

I remembered nothing but fear. It had burned in me like wildfire and I was sure George could see the memory on my face.

"The world is a dark and dangerous place," I said. "What are we supposed to do? Keep them locked away? They might be safe, but they'd never experience all the beauty that's possible. They'd never find love, they'd never find themselves."

"How do you find what is lost?" George looked me in the eyes, and I knew he wasn't asking about Kai.

"When a hand appears in the mist, it's your choice to take it," I said softly. "Do you want to be found?"

"I—" His face flashed in pain.

I took a step towards him. "George?"

His hand went to his heart, clawing at his shirt. He gasped in short pants and then he reached out for me. He sank to his knees, like a man in prayer.

"Sage," he whispered, his face gruesome. "Don't let me die."

Chapter 21

We all sat in the waiting room in silence. Numb disbelief painted the faces of those around me. Henry clutched one of my hands and I held Claire's with the other. Alice sat in the crook of Keith's arm. Gigi was with the Germains. Time passed with each beat of my heart.

I had caused this, I was sure of it. I was cursed. I was the plague upon the Ferris house. I destroyed everything. And it was destroying me. I was the theme of this never-ending saga. Life was asking me to endure, but I couldn't do it. I felt myself falling into black, no light as far as the eye could see. So many losses. They had carved out pieces of my heart—I didn't know how it was still beating.

I couldn't do it. I couldn't sit in the hospital waiting for news that George had died in surgery, and I'd been the one to kill him.

"Sage?" Henry asked. I'd pulled my hand from his. Though he was sitting next to me, his voice sounded very far away. I looked at him. He didn't look like Henry. He had become unrecognizable.

Addressing everyone and no one, I said, "I can't be here." I headed for the exit. No one tried to stop me except Henry.

"Where are you going?" Henry asked, catching up to me. I

walked down the long white hallway, the smell of sterilization in
my nose.

"I don't know."

"You're in no position to drive. Let me drive you."

I didn't disagree with him. I relinquished my keys as we walked
out into the sunshine. The irony didn't escape me—the sun shone
while my heart continued to shrink and curl up in fear. Shock was a
heavy cloak.

"Where are we going?" he asked.

"Home."

Twenty minutes later, I was inside the house. The cakes had
been covered, but the balloons and decorations still remained. My
life. From celebrations to death. It was all too familiar. There was a
bottle of bourbon on the counter and I swiped it before heading out
the back door.

Henry finally spoke as he followed me. "Where are you going
with that?" His eyes were rich with unfathomable emotion. Just
when I thought I was escaping grief, it came back and caught me in
an undertow. I was gasping, wondering how I was supposed to swim
when I wanted to drown.

"A life with me won't be much of a life at all," I said.

"Why do you say that?" He looked curious, but not at all upset.

"Should we go back over the track record of those I've lost?"
My tone was acerbic and sharp, like a bitter grapefruit.

"You think you're cursed or something?"

"Aren't I?"

"I refuse to believe that."

"Then you'd be the only one." I wanted to open the bottle of
bourbon and chug it, but it wasn't time. I had to get this out first.
"George is having heart surgery. He could die."

"Yes."

I loved that about Henry. He never offered me empty, cold
platitudes.

"But you didn't cause the heart attack."

"Maybe not directly, but indirectly."

"You think you shouldn't have told him about me? Would that

have changed the outcome?" I shrugged as he went on, "Or maybe, you were meant to be there when he started having pain."

"I caused the pain!" I shouted, tears coming to my eyes.

"You brought a family together," Henry said. "I know what you've done for the Ferris family. I've talked to Wyatt."

"What? When?" I demanded.

"After you told George and Claire. I called him, wanting him to know me a little bit. He told me Kai was estranged after the deaths of his friends, but because of you, he came back. Because of *you* they have something left of him."

"You should leave."

"What? What are you talking about?"

"I'll ruin your life, too. I'll bring you nothing but death and misery." I unscrewed the lid of the bottle and took a swig.

"Sage," he pleaded. For the first time since I had met him, Henry sounded desperate, wanting.

My eyes searched his handsome face, the face I'd grown to love. "You're a good man, Henry, but you can't barter with fate. If you stay with me, this won't end well. I know it."

Henry's hazel eyes were deep. I wondered if they had a bottom. I wondered if I fell into them, would he be able to catch me. I was nothing more than a barely beating heart.

"No," he said quietly but resolutely.

"No, what?"

"No, you don't get to do this. You don't get to push me away. I won't let you."

"It's not your choice."

"Like hell it's not," he nearly yelled. Henry wasn't a yeller.

"Don't you get it? I'm afraid *all the time*! I won't survive losing you, too. I just won't."

"So you're going to create your own misery before it finds you first? It might not ever find you, Sage, and then what happens? You go back to being alone? You raise Gigi without a father? She deserves a father! She deserves siblings. And you deserve to have me love you. So why the hell won't you let me?"

We stared at each other, taking each other in.

"This is bullshit," he stated. "And you know it."

"It's not," I whispered. "Please go. I want time—alone."

"Space?"

"Yeah."

He looked at me for a long moment, weighing my words. Finally he nodded and left.

I was alone again.

———

"Sage? Sage, open your eyes. Open your eyes or I'm going to get the hose."

My eyes flew open and I groaned. My head hurt and my throat was parched. The sun was setting, the sky awash with shades of orange and purple. I stared into Keith's weathered face, twilight caressing his strong jaw.

"You're a damn fool. You know that, right?" he asked even as he reached a hand down to help me. He hoisted me up and steadied me. My left hand was still clutching the almost empty bottle of bourbon like a lifeline.

"I've been called worse by New York cabbies," I said.

"Are you still drunk?"

"I think so, yeah." He held my arm while we walked the path to the farmhouse. "How did you know I was out here?"

"Henry. He's with Alice and Gigi at the Germains'. He's a fucking wreck. What did you say to him?"

Henry. I couldn't think about him and what I'd done. "George? Is he—"

"Out of surgery. He made it through the surgery, Sage."

I stumbled over a stone and Keith caught me, but I lost the bottle of bourbon in the struggle. It hit the ground, spilling what was left of its amber contents. It was a shame. It had been an expensive bottle. I picked it up and sighed. We made it into the farmhouse, and I was thinking about collapsing onto the couch, but Keith steered me towards the front door.

I stopped and shook my head. "Nope."

"What do you mean 'nope'?" he demanded.

"You want to take me to the hospital, don't you?" I took the last sip of bourbon.

He took the bottle from me, his voice angry. "What the hell is wrong with you?"

I sighed. "So much."

"This martyrdom crap needs to stop."

I looked at him. "I'm not being a martyr."

"Aren't you? You have a chance at being happy. Why are you trying to piss it away?" Keith's eyes were trained on me.

"How do you know that's what I'm doing?"

"Henry was fairly open about what transpired between the both of you. You really think hiding is going to spare you from life's pain?"

"I was happy and then I lost it."

"So what? You don't think I know that life can hand you so much shit that you're nothing but anger and resentment. You've got a choice to make, Sage. You can be that brittle, irate person, or you can choose happiness. Choose happiness. It's not too late."

I inhaled a shaky breath. "Take me to the hospital."

———

I peered at George's sleeping form, barely able to make him out in the dark. Visiting hours had been over long ago, but it was the night shift and the nurses had other things to contend with.

There were a lot of wires attached to George. I'd seen this man in the different stages of grief. I'd watched him live there. We'd spoken of life and of love. We drank, we shared, we cried.

I cried now. Silently—so as not to wake him.

"I'm not dead yet," came a sleepy, groggy voice.

"George?" I whispered, coming to the side of the bed. I crouched next to him. "I'm sorry." I was sorry for words that had hurt him and heartache. I was sorry I'd left, and hadn't been there when he woke up. I was sorry for so many things I couldn't control, but felt like I owned them anyway.

"Nothing to forgive," he said, his voice a muddied murmur. "Would've died if you hadn't been there."

The tears came again. He didn't blame me, not for his heart attack. Maybe not for other things, too.

———

"Where to, Sage?" Keith asked when we were back in the car.

"The farmhouse," I said.

"You don't want to go get Gigi?"

"It's late. I'll let her sleep at the Germains'."

We drove in silence until I finally broke it. "What was it like between you and Alice? After Reece…"

I saw his jaw clench, his hands tighten on the wheel. "Bad. Horrible. Like living with a stranger. And then one day I looked at her and thought, 'Will I let this be the thing that breaks us?' I said no."

"You never know what's going to break you," I said.

"You've lived a lot in a few short years, Sage. You never know how life is going to play out. But you still gotta see it through."

He parked the car in front of the farmhouse and then squeezed my shoulder. I got out and watched him drive away towards Alice. I wondered about them. When they slept, did he fit his body against hers? Did he trace the curve of her shoulder with his lips? Did they need words between them, or did they speak the silent language of love, learned through the years of marriage and the loss of a son?

I opened the front door and went into the living room. It was dark and quiet, and I wanted to sit outside and look up at the stars before they disappeared into morning. A startled sound escaped my throat when I saw Henry on the back porch, staring up at the sky. Even in moonlight I could see he looked desolate. Desolate and alone. The pile of my regrets kept growing.

Sitting next to him, I craned my neck and picked out Orion, my favorite constellation. It made me think of Henry's three freckles on his ankle.

Without a word, he reached into his pocket and pulled out a jewelry box. My breath hitched audibly.

"It's not what you think," he said.

I stared at it for a moment and then opened it. I peered at the necklace, wondering what I was seeing. I held it up to starlight. It was a silver charm, about half an inch in length.

"It looks like a swan," I said, looking at him for confirmation.

He shook his head. "It's a loon."

Loons. "Birds that mate for life," I said slowly.

"Everyone thinks loons mate for life," he went on. "And they do. But if one of them dies, the other finds a new mate. A new partner."

"That's nature for you. To persevere. Not romantic at all when you think about."

"And romance," he said. "What is romance? Life isn't rainbows and unicorns. It's funerals and weddings and everything in between. It's braces for kids and aging parents. It's new memories in old cities. It's mortgage payments and sleepless nights. It's going to bed with the same person and wanting to see them again first thing in the morning, forever. It's about marking changes and time and discovering new things about yourself. That's life. The mundane is life. And it's more beautiful than rainbows and unicorns."

He was impassioned in his speech, so complete in his convictions. "I used to dream about him," I said softly. "I haven't—in a long time."

"What is it you wish for, Sage?" he asked. We were sitting close to one another, his thigh warm and pressing against mine.

"I used to wish for things that could never be. I never thought to wish for you."

"And now?"

"If I hadn't lost him, I never would've found you. If I hadn't lost my mother, I never would've found Kai. Don't you see? Life takes from me and gives it back in another way. But I can't lose you, too. I thought when Kai died, that was it—I barely had enough strength to live for Gigi."

"If, if, if. Doesn't that make you crazy, thinking about the *ifs*?"

"More than you realize, Henry."

———

"How are you feeling?" I asked.

George grimaced. "Like I just had major heart surgery."

"Sense of humor is still intact, I see."

He chuckled softly and leaned his head back against the hospital bed. "Was it my imagination or did you visit me last night?"

I nodded. "I snuck in past visiting hours. Had to slip the nurse on duty a twenty."

He raised an eyebrow. "Really?"

I snorted. "No. I knocked her unconscious and stuck her in the broom closet."

We laughed and it felt good. Nothing else did. I had slept alone, without the warmth and assurance of Henry next to me.

"I was wrong," he said quietly.

"About?"

"You want me to go down the list?"

I shook my head. "I think it's unnecessary at this point."

"I was scared," he admitted.

"Of what?"

"If you make a life with Henry, what does that mean for me? For Claire?"

"You mean as Gigi's grandparents?" I frowned. "You'll always be a part of her life."

"I know that. I was talking about you. I gained a daughter when Kai married you. I was worried I'd lose you, too."

"Oh," I said, tears flooding my eyes. "I thought this was about Kai."

"It was—in part. But mostly, it was about you. You're special, Sage. I'd like to think we have a... unique bond, independent of Kai."

Before I knew it, I was out of the chair and embracing my father-in-law. "I wish you knew how much I love you—Dad."

George choked on his own tears as we hugged each other. And

like two people who share a familial bond, though ours came from marriage, we let the past fall away. We reconciled and we were left with a new beginning.

I pulled back and wiped the tears from my eyes and gave him a shaky smile. "And on that note, I think it's time I lecture you about taking better care of yourself. You want to see Gigi walk down the aisle, then you'd better get your shit together."

George beamed from ear to ear. "Yes, ma'am." He leaned his head back against the pillow. "It seems I'm a grandfather again."

"What?" I demanded. "What are you talking about?"

"They didn't tell you? Lucy went into labor early. She had the baby."

My face slackened in shock. "Boy or girl?"

"Girl. Elaina Marie. They're calling her Lainey. Get Claire to show you the picture on her phone." George's eyes began to close, signaling he needed to rest.

I pressed a kiss to his whiskered cheek and went to the cafeteria to find Claire. When I saw her, I hugged her to me and asked, "How are you holding up?"

"Okay."

"I'm not sure I believe you."

She smiled, but it looked pained. "How are *you*?"

I should've been there for her. She shouldn't have had to endure George's surgery without me. There had been others, but it wasn't the same. "I'm sorry I left. I just—I'm sorry."

"Thank you," she said quietly. We sat at a table and I brought her a cup of coffee and tea for myself.

"George and I have made amends," I said.

She sighed in relief. "Good. He can't have any more stress."

"I didn't mean to cause—"

"You didn't cause this," she interrupted. "It's been a long time coming. Things are going to be different now. They have to be."

I placed my hand over hers and she gave mine a squeeze. We sat in companionable silence while we adjusted to a new reality.

"I don't know what I'd do if he'd died," she admitted.

"Good thing you don't have to think about that. Losing a Ferris man is the hardest thing I've ever had to overcome, and I wouldn't wish it on anyone."

She sighed. "Want to see the newest addition to the Ferris clan?" She pulled out her phone and showed me a photo of Lainey.

"Life goes on, huh?"

"It sure does, Sage. It sure does."

———

"I need to drink," Luc said, holding up the bottle of bourbon. I waved him inside and closed the door.

"I don't think that's a good idea," I said, Gigi on my hip.

"Come on," he pleaded.

I set Gigi in her playpen and said, "Fine, I'll have a drink with you."

He pouted. "I'll take it. It's never fun to drink alone."

"No, it's not. Sit on the couch, I'll get you a glass."

"I don't need a glass," he said, unscrewing the bourbon and taking a drink.

"What brought this on?" I demanded.

"Jules sent back her engagement ring."

"Oh, Luc—"

"Spare me your pity. Let's just drink."

It turned out he didn't really want me to drink with him—he wanted me to watch him drink himself into oblivion.

"Love stinks," he slurred.

"Not always."

"I forgot, I'm talking to a woman who found it twice. I can't even find it once. Why doesn't she love me?"

"What do you want me to say?"

"I don't know. Why are you hurting Henry?"

"I don't want to talk about Henry. You can talk about Jules all you want, but I don't want to talk about Henry." I hadn't seen or spoken to him since the night he gave me the loon necklace.

"Fine."

Around drink four or five, Luc began to pace around the living room, muttering incoherently. I didn't even try and decipher it, I just let him drink and talk, knowing sometimes having another person there made all the difference. And sometimes it didn't.

It was becoming routine for Luc to pass out on my couch. He was snoring softly as I took Gigi upstairs. She didn't even stir as I lay her in the crib.

Watching Luc field his misery only reminded me that my own heart was heavy. I couldn't turn off my thoughts and I refused to lie awake in my big empty bed.

I went to the turret and began to write, scribbling as I cried. Tears fell from my face, falling to the page below me and mingling with ink to create a blotted mess. I wondered about my inability to let myself be happy. I wondered if it was too late for me.

Words were all I had.

They were poor companions.

Chapter 22

"What are you doing?" Alice asked.

"Packing," I answered.

"Yes, I see that. Where are you going?"

"I'm taking Gigi to Paris for a few days."

"Sage, stop." Alice put a hand on mine to still me from folding clothes. "You can't run away."

"Watch me." I sighed. "I'm not running away, I just need some time away from—" I gestured to my bedroom and Henry's belongings, "—all this."

"Do you think it will make you feel better?"

"I don't know, but I can't think here. It's just too much." I blew out a puff of air. "I let Henry go. It's better, for all of us, especially him."

"You really believe that, don't you?" Alice asked in amazement. "He loves you. You love him."

"Love isn't enough."

"Sometimes it is."

I looked at her. "You think that? After all you've endured?"

"Honey, why do you think I'm still here? Keith—stubborn man that he is—wouldn't let me drown in grief."

"I'm still going to Paris."

"Don't you want to wait? George is getting released from the hospital tomorrow."

"I know. I talked to Claire. She told me to go to Paris. They're staying in *Tours* for the next six weeks so George can recover. They'll be here when I get back."

"Okay," she tried again, "but we never got to celebrate Gigi's birthday. And you have two cakes. They'll go bad."

"You have keys," I said, getting back to packing. "Eat them."

"I can't talk you out of this?"

I shook my head.

"I can't talk you into going after Henry?"

I shook my head again. "Will you watch *Chat* while I'm gone?"

She sighed. "Sure, Sage. Whatever you want."

———

I took a bite of apple, taking in the scene. A group of young men tossed a Frisbee back and forth. Gorgeous Parisian women strolled by, distracting them. They all looked so light, free, unencumbered. Maybe it was their youth. Maybe they didn't know any better.

The Frisbee got away from one of them and landed near me. He jogged over to me, his cheeks rosy with exercise and excitement. I picked up the disk and flung it at him. He caught it, and with a smile of thanks went back to his friends.

I offered a handful of cereal to Gigi. "Well, what do you think?" I asked her, gesturing to the structure behind me. She didn't pay attention to me at all, much more interested in her food.

We sat on the grass on the *Champs de Mars* until the sun set and I had a spectacular view of the golden rays lingering behind the iron monstrosity. Paris was the city of lovers. But it had never been that place for me.

Gigi turned into a tired crab, so I quickly packed up our picnic and put her in her stroller. I pushed her along a dirt path until it became a road. I wandered back to the hotel, a quaint little establishment with one working elevator. By the time I got us to our room, Gigi was asleep. I put her in pajamas and set her in her Pack-N-Play.

Though I'd had an active day walking along the Seine, shopping on the *Champs-Élysées*, I wasn't tired. My thoughts drifted to Henry. I wondered if he missed me as much as I missed him. I wondered if he'd come back for his things at the farmhouse. I wondered if his bed felt as empty as mine.

———

I watched the man pluck another orange from the tree. I closed my eyes, inhaling the smell of citrus. It sent a wave of longing through my stomach. Even the teasing scent of Versailles oranges made me think of Henry.

The man handed me a cup of freshly squeezed orange juice.

I wandered around the Versailles gardens, pushing Gigi's stroller. I'd been in Paris for four days, and so far, nothing had helped clear my head. It was full of Henry.

I was in agony.

My phone vibrated in my pocket and I pulled it out, stunned by the name flashing across the screen.

"Is it you?" I asked.

"It is."

I sighed. "God, I miss you so much."

"I know. I miss you, too."

"Jules, where are you?"

There was a pause and then, "London."

"London? What are you doing in London?"

"Drinking."

"Are you okay?"

"Not really. I sent the engagement ring back to Luc."

"I know. Luc and I had bourbon the other night."

"Shit, he drank bourbon?" she whispered. "It was bad, wasn't it?"

"Yeah."

She sighed. "How are you doing? I'm sorry it's taken me so long to—"

"Don't apologize. I get it."

"You would." Another pause. "So how are you?"

I told her about Henry.

"Yikes. We really know how to destroy good things, don't we?"

"Yep." And then I filled her in on George's condition. "He's recovering. They're staying at their house in *Tours*."

"I've missed a lot of things, haven't I?"

"Including Gigi's birthday. I'm sure she forgives you though."

"I'll send a really good present."

"She'd rather just have you."

"I'm not ready to come back."

"Yeah. Okay. What are you really doing in London?"

"I don't want to say anything. Not until—not until I know for sure."

"Know for sure what?" I demanded.

"Sage."

"Fine."

"Will you do me a favor?" she asked.

"Anything."

"Will you promise not to tell them you've heard from me?"

I sighed. "If that's really what you want."

"It is."

"Okay."

"Alice is right, you know. You should go after Henry."

"And say what?"

"Not 'say', do."

"I haven't the slightest idea of what to do."

"You love him."

"Yes." My voice came out hushed.

"Then why won't you fight for him?"

"I pushed him away."

"Because of fear. You thought pushing him away would push away the fear. Did it work?"

I paused. "No."

"Do you think he doesn't want you anymore?"

"I don't know. Who would sign up for this?"

"What's that love crap you keep spouting on and on about?"

"It's not crap," I defended.

"You're human. You're allowed to have moments of weakness. You went on after Kai."

"Only because I had to."

"Yes, but you still did it. You're trapped in your own head. Stop thinking with your head, think with your heart."

"What's going on with you?" I demanded. "That sounds like something I would say to you."

"You are your own worst enemy, and frankly, I'm a little ashamed of you."

"Wait just a fucking minute," I seethed.

"No! We don't get endless chances at happiness. You found it again, for Christ's sake. Go after Henry. Tell him you made a mistake."

"And tell him I was an idiot and that even though I'm afraid, I'm more afraid of a life without him? I was so sure, Jules."

"You're sure of nothing," Jules scoffed. "You think a black cloud follows you wherever you go. But George didn't die. Gigi went to the hospital and didn't die. Henry was supposed to die as a baby, but he didn't. He lived. All that stuff makes me believe in fate, and I'm not usually an idealist. Henry—a man who is an optimist—came to you in your darkest hour."

"Dramatic much?"

"Sage," she said softly.

"Go after him," I repeated.

"What would Lou Garretty do?" she asked, referencing the heroine from my book.

"Draw a mural on the wall in crayons," I said. "And be delightfully carefree and whimsical. So much so that Cole couldn't resist her."

"Weird."

"What?"

"Your heroine's name. She goes by Lou, but her first name is actually Henrietta. And you have a Henry. Just weird. What are the chances?"

Chances, indeed. "Thanks, Jules."

"I'm sorry I wasn't there when you needed me."

"You are," I insisted. "Just don't forget I can be there for you, too. If you let me."

"You don't know how much I've missed you."

"I have a fair idea," I said, hoping she heard the smile in my voice.

"Listen, if you call me, I'll pick up. Or if I'm occupied, I promise to call you back at a later time."

"You promise?"

"I promise."

"Bye, Jules."

"Bye, Sage."

We hung up and I sat for a few moments, absorbing Jules's words. I crouched in front of Gigi, letting her have the last of the orange juice. I pushed the stroller towards the exit, wondering if it was a wise idea to take a one-year-old to the Louvre. I decided against it and went to a café instead. I sat outside, ordered an espresso, and enjoyed watching people.

Despite it being August, it wasn't too hot. There was a slight breeze and it teased the hair at my temples. I closed my eyes for a brief moment, taking in the sounds and smells of a busy city. For some reason, the bustle of Paris didn't feel the same as New York. Maybe it was the sounds of French being spoken; the vibrancy of the people was different here.

I turned my head, watching a tall man stroll closer. He was wearing a gray suit and something about him tugged at my memory. As he approached, I took in his neatly combed blond hair and bright blue eyes. My mouth parted in surprise. The man stopped—and stared—his own mouth nearly dropping open. He quickly recovered and came towards me, stopping when he was just a few feet away. I slowly rose from my chair.

"Hello, Sage."

"Hello, Connor."

We stared at each other for a few more seconds, taking in the changes of each other. He was leaner, and the lines around his mouth had turned into grooves, but he still looked impeccable in a suit.

There was really no guidebook for how one was supposed to talk to an ex-fiancé. I had expected his face to reflect anger, resentment. After all, I'd broken up with him at my mother's funeral and then moved across an ocean. I'd eventually sent him a letter, but I had no way of knowing if he'd received it or even cared by that point.

"You look good," he blurted out. A light stain of color highlighted his cheeks and he tore his eyes from mine. He swallowed and I watched his Adam's apple bob.

"Thank you," I said. "So do you."

"Really? Or are you just trying to be polite?" he asked.

A hint of a smile drifted across my mouth. "Take it how you please. What are you doing in Paris?"

"Business," he said.

I nodded. "Ah."

"And you? What are you doing here?"

Gigi, who had been quiet, let out a squeal, pulling our attention. I heard Connor inhale a sharp breath. I unstrapped Gigi from her stroller and took her into my arms, holding her on my hip. Connor's face was a picture of shock and confusion.

"Do you have time for cup of coffee?" I asked, changing Gigi to my other side. "Or do you have to rush off? There are things that I —I'm sure there are things you'd like to say."

A flash of pain crossed his brow, but he nodded. "I've got time. For a quick cup at least." We took our seats at the small table. I called the waiter over and ordered another espresso for myself. Connor ordered a cappuccino. The waiter sneered.

"I'm aware that cappuccino is supposed to be a strictly morning beverage over here," Connor said. He loosened his tie. "But I don't care. They can think me a crass New Yorker all they want."

I laughed, feeling some of the tension spill out of me.

"You have a daughter," he said, shaking his head. "Jesus, things really do change at the drop of a hat, don't they?"

"Yeah, they really do."

"What's her name?"

"Georgia. We call her Gigi."

"We? You and your…" His eyes slid to my naked ring finger.

I took a deep breath. "She's named after my late husband."

"Late husband?"

"Kai. George Kai Ferris. Georgia Katherine Ferris."

"The man you met when you came to France?"

I nodded, tearing my eyes away from Connor's.

"When did he—? I mean—"

"Last spring."

"I'm sorry," he said.

Clearing my throat, I steered the conversation towards him. "What about you? What's been happening with you? How's work?"

"Busy. Exhausting, but I love it."

"Good. Glad to hear that." I bounced Gigi on my leg and she placed her hands on the glass table.

"Congratulations," he said suddenly. I looked at him in confusion, so he clarified. "Your book."

I felt my cheeks heat. "Oh, yeah. My book. I sometimes forget I wrote a book."

He laughed, and I was surprised that it sounded light. "How can you forget something like that?"

I shrugged. "I don't know, I just do."

"It was beautiful."

"You read it?"

"Of course I did. I was in a bookstore and stumbled onto it. 'Sage Harper Ferris' and your picture. I couldn't believe it."

"Yeah, it's pretty… unbelievable." I ran a hand across Gigi's hair, putting my cheek to her head. "Connor, I'm sorry."

"For?"

"For how I left." I made eye contact. "For how I handled things."

"You've already apologized. The letter, remember?"

"It doesn't feel like enough."

"Sage," he sighed, "it was a long time ago. I've—moved on."

"Yeah?"

He nodded. "I'm engaged."

"Now it's my turn to offer congratulations." I smiled and a weight I hadn't known I carried on my heart suddenly lifted. "Tell me about her."

"Miranda. We work together. We're getting married next month, actually." Connor's smile was peaceful and happy. "And how is Jules?"

"Jules is good," I said automatically, not wishing to explain the unexplainable. Gigi had leaned against me and I knew she had fallen asleep. It felt like she had suddenly gained ten extra pounds.

"She has your nose," Connor said, staring at my daughter.

"I know. I'm relieved. It means she won't be coming to me when she's sixteen asking for a nose job."

Connor laughed and then glanced as his Rolex. "Ah, I've got to go."

"Business?"

"Yeah. It was good running into you, Sage. Random, huh? I never thought I'd—we'd—well, anyway, it was nice seeing you."

"It was good seeing you, too. I'm glad you're happy."

He set down some Euros and he left with a wave. I watched him walk down the street, the sound of his four hundred dollar shoes fading into the distance.

———

I sat on the hotel bed, the iPad in front of me. "Okay, Lucy. Show off Lainey. Let me see her," I demanded. Lucy held up the swaddled pink bundle to the camera and I sighed. "God, she's stunning. And you look amazing." Post baby, Lucy still had thick, glossy hair and vibrant skin. "It's kind of unfair."

"Eighteen hours of labor," Lucy stated.

"Okay, it's well deserved, then."

Lucy settled Lainey against her body, looking exhausted but content. "I think my son is in love with your daughter. Dakota keeps asking when he gets to see Gigi."

475

"Oh, God, it's starting? Now? Dakota as a teenager is going to be trouble."

"I know. Part of me thinks he'll come home one day with a tattoo and a motorcycle."

"Well, let's pray he finds inner peace early on, then he won't be a worry to either of us."

Lucy grinned. "I really can't wait to see how things play out in the coming years."

"You're enjoying this, aren't you? The idea of Dakota and Gigi… they're kids!"

"Tristan's son and Kai's daughter… I don't know, I think it could be a pretty great story."

"The sleep deprivation has addled your brain," I said with a laugh.

"Don't I know it. So, when are you guys coming for a visit?"

"When things settle down."

"News flash, they'll never settle down."

"You're right. I don't think they do."

"Fine, I'll stop asking—at least for the time being. I found something the other day that I wanted to show you." Lucy reached off screen and then lifted a photograph to the camera. "Can you see it?"

"Yeah," I said, studying it. It was a photo of Kai, Tristan, and Reece. They were jamming together on the grass.

"Look in the corner—at the guy sitting on the bench."

"No fucking way," I murmured. "Is that—"

"Yep. It's Henry."

"Son of a bitch," I whispered.

"You thought it was weird they both went to Vanderbilt."

"It is weird," I said.

"What are the chances?" Lucy wondered.

"Lucy, I'm starting to think there's no such thing as chance."

Chapter 23

I know I'm dreaming, but this feels different than all the others.

We look out over the mountains, raised peaks carved from the earth. Rocky, epic, gorgeous—like our love.

We are silent for a long time, listening to the flap of bird wings and watching the subtle changes of sunlight on grass. Time is passing, even here. Even in the in-between.

"I miss you." I choke on the words. They hurt, like knife blades in skin.

"I know."

"We didn't have enough time."

"No, we didn't," Kai agrees. "But we got what we got, and we should be glad we found each other at all. You should take a chance—not everyone you love will leave you. Henry's not the leaving kind."

I take a deep breath. "You know about him?"

He smiles and I expect it to be sad, but it's not. It's... something else, something uniquely Kai. "Who do you think sent him?"

I give a watery smile. "You're playing matchmaker?"

"I want someone to take care of you, someone to love you. Someone to love our daughter."

"I love him," I say. I make the confession, yet I don't want to.

"I'm glad. Life is meant to be shared."

"*I'm afraid.*"

"*That's okay, but you can't let it drive you. You'll end up regretting decisions you make out of fear.*"

I swallow a sob, and he hugs me to his chest and says into my hair, "*If I'd lived, we would've had a beautiful story. But it wasn't meant to be.*"

Turning my head, I kiss his jaw, dark with stubble. I close my eyes and let it scratch me. "*It would be so easy to stay here. I can't ruin things here.*"

"*Here isn't real. And this is goodbye.*"

I suck in a breath.

"*You know it has to be goodbye for us—so you can really live.*"

I cry into his chest and he brushes the hair off my face and kisses my tear-stained cheeks. "*Don't cry, darlin'. I never could stand to see you cry.*"

"*I love you. I'll always love you.*"

"*I know.*" *He kisses my lips in a tender gesture of farewell.* "*You have to choose life, Sage.*"

"*What if he… what if Henry doesn't want me anymore?*"

His smile is gentle. "*Not possible. Go after what you want. Go after him if that's what will make you happy.*"

"*Gigi will know you,*" *I promise. It's a hopeful vow.* "*She'll know everything there is to know about you.*"

Kai pulls back and stands. He stares down at me, a soft smile playing on his lips. "*Be happy. Please, it's the only thing that will give me any sort of peace. I need you to be happy.*"

I can barely make out his form through my tears. As Kai walks away, I watch his retreating form. With one last look at me, he brings his fingers to his lips, kissing me goodbye from afar.

I close my eyes, knowing that when I open them, Kai will be gone—he will be gone, and I'll look towards the future. I'll look towards Henry.

My heart's wings flutter in my chest, ready to take flight.

Because I am alive.

I am alive.

———

I walked into the farmhouse, Gigi on my hip. I set down my travel bag in the foyer and *Chat* ran towards me, snaking his body around my leg. Gigi let out a squeal and reached for him.

The dryer beeped and I heard someone moving around in the kitchen. "Alice? Keith?" I called. They'd been staying at the house while I was in Paris, taking care of *Chat*. I set Gigi in her playpen and went to the kitchen.

I wasn't prepared to find Henry at the kitchen table, a massive number of open history books spread out in front of him, his glasses on his nose.

"What are you doing here?" I blurted out in surprise.

He stood up and removed his glasses, placing them on the table. "I live here."

"But I—and we— you're here!"

"I never left," he said softly.

"Oh," I breathed. "*Oh.*"

"I wouldn't let Alice tell you I was here."

"Why not?"

"Not for her to share," he explained. "Did you really think you'd get rid of me that easily?"

"I didn't know what to think."

"Have a little faith, Sage."

"That's not second nature to me."

"Not everyone will leave you."

"It feels that way sometimes," I said.

"Are you done trying to leave me?"

I nodded.

"Good, because from now on, we figure things out together."

"Promise?"

"Promise." He reached out to touch my cheek. "You haven't kissed me hello."

I wrapped myself around him, a surge of joy sweeping through me. I tilted my head back, his lips covering mine.

"Shouldn't we talk about things?" I muttered against his mouth even as he continued kissing me.

"Things like?"

"The future."

"The future can wait. I can't."

———

Gigi was down for a nap and Henry and I were in bed, curled around each other. I traced the lines of him, needing to touch him, so I knew he was real.

"Thank you," I stated. "I don't know if I say that enough to you. These last few weeks, I've been… confused, afraid, happy…"

"You name it, you've felt it?" he suggested.

"Something like that. I let my mind get the best of me. I forgot what was at the core of us, and I'm sorry for that. Thank you. For being here to come home to. Thank you for being… you."

"I really love you, Sage." His arms tightened around me and I pressed my face to his chest. "No more looking back, okay?"

"Okay," I whispered. The heat of him made me drowsy, content. "Should I sell the house?"

"The farmhouse?"

I nodded.

"Why would you want to do that?"

"So we can look to *our* future. I don't want you to feel like you're living in the remains of a future I would've had with Kai."

"You'd really give up this house? For me?"

I paused. "Yeah, I would." I looked at him, his face full of emotion.

"I can't believe you'd offer me something like that."

"Does that mean you want me—"

"No," he said fiercely. "We'll keep it and make it our own. It's home to me, Sage. I'm home."

———

"Bed rest was designed to make people go crazy," George grumbled. "I'm going insane."

I shuffled the deck of cards again and dealt. "Bed rest gives you an excuse to have people wait on you. Besides, I've been here every afternoon for the last week entertaining you."

He rolled his eyes and picked up his cards, fanning them in his hand. "How does Henry feel about that?"

I smiled. "Henry is doing research for his book. Henry barely notices when I'm gone."

"Doubt that."

He adjusted himself in the dark wood bed. The shutters of the window were open, letting in sunlight. The walls were painted a soft yellow, the color of a baby chick. Claire had a real talent for interior design and their French home was beautiful, inside and out. Softer, warmer, than their Monteagle home.

I drew a card and discarded one from my hand. "Gigi is getting ready to walk."

"Yeah?"

"Yeah. She's been pulling herself up onto things and she makes this face, like she's thinking about walking. She lifts one foot and then plops down onto her bottom, looking very surprised and confused."

"She grew so fast, didn't she?"

I nodded, reaching for another card. "Ah! Gin!"

George grimaced. "I don't know why we bother playing. You win every hand."

"Maybe I should try my luck at poker," I said. "Forget about writing, I want to be a professional gambler."

"Did Kai ever tell you about the time he and Tristan got into some trouble at a high stakes poker game?"

My eyes bugged out. "What? No, he didn't."

"They were nineteen and Tristan found a game underground at the University of Tennessee campus. Kai was visiting Tristan and Lucy for the weekend. Anyway, they sat in on a few hands and managed to lose about five thousand dollars between the two of them."

"Oh my god! What happened?" I leaned in, wanting to hear the rest of the story.

"They had two days to get the money together or else… The next night, they went back to the game—"

"What?"

"Hold on, let me finish." George grinned. "Lucy sauntered into the room, won back their money, and more."

"Lucy? No way! How did you know about this?" It wasn't a story Kai would've shared with his father.

"Lucy told me," he admitted quietly. "In the days after Kai's funeral. She was trying to get me out of bed, or at least to laugh. She got me to laugh." George leaned his head back against the pillows, his eyes closing.

He tired quickly and it would take him a while to regain his stamina. I got up and left the room, leaving George alone to snore. "He's asleep," I said to Claire who was sitting on the couch, flicking through the television.

She turned it off and shook her head. "No idea what they're saying. Thanks, Sage. Your visits cheer him up. He's a bit sick of me."

"I highly doubt that. I'll be back tomorrow. I'll bring Gigi if you think he's up for a toddler."

Claire smiled. "Five minutes with her wouldn't hurt."

When I got home, Henry was in the kitchen, deeply engrossed in research. He needed his own office—a place where he could work undisturbed. Besides, we needed our kitchen table back if we ever wanted to have people over for a meal.

"Hi," he said, setting down his pen.

I put a hand to his shoulder and leaned down to press a kiss to his lips. "Hello. God, those glasses really are sexy on you."

He grinned. "How's George?"

"Grumbling about being bedridden."

"That's good. It means he'll be ready to get up and start moving around soon."

"Hope so. I'll take Gigi with me tomorrow. That might entice him out of bed and give you the house to yourself."

"She hasn't made a peep this whole time," he said. "She's spoiling us for all future children. You know that, right?"

"I do. Is she napping now?"

"Yep."

"I'll let you get back to researching," I said, kissing him again.

"Wait. Can you sit for a minute? There's something I need to talk to you about. Something good," he said quickly.

I let out a huff of air. "Way to scare a girl." I took a seat next to him and waited for him to talk. He removed his glasses and set them aside, before his eyes found mine.

"I've been offered a temporary teaching position at Oxford."

I blinked. "Oxford? As in England?"

He nodded. "They want me there the first of the year."

"Oxford. Oh, wow," I said. "That's incredible."

"It is."

"What did you tell them?" I asked.

"I told them I had to discuss it with you first. What do you say, Sage?"

———

We lay on our backs on a blanket, staring up at the dark sky. Stars scattered across the inky blackness and I inhaled a breath. The warm air of summer would soon give way to brisk autumn. Gigi, warm and snuggled against my chest, slept soundly, hopefully dreaming sweet dreams.

"What's your favorite season?" I asked.

"Winter."

"You're a Midwesterner," I marveled. "And you like winter best?"

"Snow," he said, inching closer to me so that our arms touched. "Everything is quiet. I love fireplaces and sweaters. I love building snowmen."

"I only like winter because spring comes next," I said. "When everything is all new and fresh and young. I feel young again. Reborn. I love the feel of the sun on my skin—feeling warm for the first time in months."

"Okay, I'd like to change my answer," he said. "Spring sounds pretty amazing."

I laughed softly, not wanting to wake Gigi. "I think I'll like any season, as long as I'm with you."

"Even in dreary old England?"

"It's 'merry old England'," I corrected. "Besides, I like the rain. It gives me an excuse to stay inside and write."

"Like you ever need an excuse to stay inside and write."

"Valid point."

His hand sought mine and our fingers became entwined. "There's Orion," Henry said, pointing out the constellation of the hunter.

"It's beautiful," I said. "But I don't know why."

"It's beautiful because we're seeing light that's already millions of years old. So many of the stars we see have already died. They don't even exist anymore except that we can still see their light."

I gave his hand a squeeze. "Like people."

Epilogue

It is the end of the harvest. All the vines have been pruned, the grapes plucked, the bottles filled. The leaves are awash of autumn colors. The Germains, along with those staying at the bed and breakfast and the workers who've been hired, toast the close of the season. The cool wine hits my lips, heightening my thirst for other things. Tonight we'll light torches, dine *alfresco*, and dance under the stars.

I touch the loon necklace at my throat. It is warm from where it rests against my skin; its weight a solid comfort near my heart.

Henry's gaze catches mine from across the party. He shoves his hands in his pockets and cocks his head to one side as he stares at me. It's like we're meeting for the first time. His smile lingers, and I wonder how I ever lived without knowing the warmth of it.

Gigi struggles out of my arms, so I set her down. She takes a hesitant step towards him. She toddles in his direction, going slow, not wanting to fall.

Henry's eyes soften. He opens his arms wide as he rushes forward and scoops her into his embrace. He covers her face in rapid-fire kisses. She places her hands on his cheeks and makes sounds of delight. His attention turns to me—my pulse drums in my ears.

I hold my breath as I wait, but he doesn't make me wait long. Henry's lips find my mine and I'm filled with warmth, happiness, and the promise of a new beginning.

Wrapping one arm around Henry, I bring him close, needing to breathe him in. I stroke my hand across Gigi's hair and her laughter rings in my ears and settles in my heart.

I will remember my past, but no longer dwell in it.

I will embrace the present, but plan for the future.

I will revel, celebrate, and cry.

I will feel.

I will live.

Additional Works

Writing as Samantha Garman

The Sibby Series:
Queen of Klutz (Book 1)
Sibby Slicker (Book 2)

Writing as Emma Slate

SINS Series:
Sins of a King (Book 1)
Birth of a Queen (Book 2)
Rise of a Dynasty (Book 3)
Dawn of an Empire (Book 4)

Ember Series (SINS Series Spinoff):
Ember (Book 1)
Burn (Book 2)
Ashes (Book 3)

Additional Works

Web Series:
Web of Innocence (Book 1)
Web of Deception (Book 2)

Made in the USA
Columbia, SC
27 December 2018